VALKYRIE RISING

Book Five in the Viking Blood and Blade Saga

Peter Gibbons

ISBN: 9798373738583

Cover design by: Erelis Design
Library of Congress Control Number: 2018675309
Printed in the United States of America

A PASSAGE FROM "THE BATTLE OF MALDON", A 10TH CENTURY ANGLO SAXON POEM

Swa stemnetton   stiðhicgende
hysas aet hilde,   hogodon georne
hwa paer mid orde   aerost mihte
on faegean men   feorh gewinnan
wigan mid waepnum   wael feol eorðan

So they prevailed, sternly determined
the men in battle, they directed their thoughts
eagerly
as to who first at weapon point
would win a life from fated warriors
men at arms; the dead fell to the earth.

Valkyrie Rising
By Peter Gibbons

ONE

878AD

The enemy made their shield wall – each man overlapped the left side of his shield with that of the warrior next to him. The linden wood boards banged as they came together, and their iron rims clanked. The sound drifted through the damp fog which lay upon the field like dragon's breath, and the bright colours daubed upon their leather shield coverings moved and danced through the thick of it. Ravens, bears and snarling beasts spread across the war-fence, outnumbering Hundr and his own line of fighters.

"Looks like they are getting ready to charge," said Einar the Brawler on Hundr's left. He was Jarl Einar of Vanylven, and Hundr's friend.

Hundr sighed and bent to pick up his own shield, which rested against his leg. He slipped his left forearm through the leather strip and then curled his fingers around the timber grip which spanned the hollow bowl of the iron shield boss. Hundr hefted the shield and rolled his shoulders. He was stiff from sleeping cold in the open, covered only by his cloak. It had been an uncomfortable night, tossing and turning under the stars, awaiting the fight to come. Knowing that the horrors of the shield wall were close, where spears, axes, and swords came for a man's throat, face, eyes and belly, and where skilled warriors came to rend each other's flesh to soak the ground with blood in search of victory, glory, and reputation. Hundr wore a brynjar coat of chainmail which protected him from collarbones to belly. It was a heavy thing of tiny, interlocked iron rings and the mark of the finest warriors and lords, for a brynjar was expensive – almost as expensive as a sword. A man must either inherit one, have enough silver to have one made, or take one from a fallen foe. To keep such precious armour, a man must then have the war skill to stop another axe-wielding warrior from carving him open and stripping the thing from his corpse. Such was the life of a warrior. Hundr carried two swords, Fenristooth in a fleece-lined scabbard on the left side of his belt and Battle Fang strapped to his back. He had a broken-back bladed seax in a sheath at the small of his back, a spear in his right hand, and he wore a shining helmet. He was a warrior, a warlord, a sea Jarl, and a killer.

"They must have woke in the dead of night to swill enough ale to summon up the balls to attack this early in the morning," Bush remarked over Hundr's shoulder in the second rank of shields.

"I don't think they need ale to give them bravery," said Hundr. "They have hate for that."

Shouts rang out from across the battlefield, a sloping pasture of grass chewed short by sheep, knots of weed, and briar patches. The enemy warriors called to one another, encouraging themselves to keep shields tight, to strike without fear, and to kill the bastards across from them.

"Let's get this over with," snarled Ragnhild on Hundr's left. She fished a hand into a leather pouch at her belt and found a rolled bow string. Ragnhild wrapped a leg around one end of her recurved bow stave, fashioned in the way of the East from horn and supple wood, and bent the other end across her hip. She let out the bowstring and hooked one end to the lower tip of the bow and then the other to a horn nook at the top. A fresh, dry string to send shafts of death towards the enemy.

"Shield wall," Hundr barked. The surrounding warriors gave a clipped roar and shuffled into position. Leather creaked, shields banged, and iron clanked as they all gathered close to overlap their shields and make the solid wall of wood and iron. "Hold the line. We hold them here." Ragnhild slipped between the shields to take her place on the flanks with her fellow Valkyrie archers. Sigrid would be there, and Hundr hated that he could not see her and would not know her fate until the fighting was over. The shields along Hundr's battle line were in perfect formation, overlapped, level, and strong.

A roar erupted from the enemy line, and they marched forward, every second step accompanied by a rhythmic slam of spears upon iron shield rims. Their shield wall was longer than Hundr's by five shields on each side, and they were three ranks of warriors, spears bristling and waving above the front line like the prickly back of a giant monster coming for Hundr through the fog.

"Let's finish this today, lads," called Einar the Brawler. "These men are the last of the resistance, the last of the men who oppose King Harald. Kill the bastards, and we can all go home."

The warriors around Hundr let out a roar of their own. The clash of their weapons became a din ringing in Hundr's ears. He gripped his shield tightly and levelled his spear. Hundr was at the centre of the shield wall, where all leaders should be, where the fighting would be hardest. The centre was where the lovers of battle fought, the men who found joy in the clash of arms, where a man balances on the edge of life and death and risks everything for the glory of killing a man who comes to kill you first. The enemy warriors were ten paces away, their eyes peering out of the darkness between their shields and helmets, the whites of their teeth showing in snarls of hatred. These were the last men to oppose King Harald Fairhair's rule over all of Norway. They were the sons of jarls killed by Harald, dispossessed and hungry for vengeance. Hundr fought for the king, and he sighed as his eyes met the man opposite him. He was young, almost a boy, with bright blue eyes and golden hair. The young warrior's shield locked tight against that of an enormous man, Herjolf Blackbear, son of a northern Jarl and the leader of the freedom fighters. His prodigious size and strength, and the raven black of his hair and beard, had made his naming easy.

"Hold the line!" Hundr bellowed as the enemy shield wall responded to a guttural shout from Herjolf, a deep, rumbling, animalistic sound which set his men to the charge. They came on, cursing and snarling, with spears ready to strike. Hundr's heart quickened, and his belly squirmed. He had fought in the shield wall many times, and the feelings were always the same because he knew what it meant to stand and fight where the warriors came together to rend and kill. Hundr tensed his body and braced the top of his shield against his left shoulder and the lower rim against his left knee. An enemy shield crashed into him with bone-shaking force. The blow forced Hundr backwards, but Bush drove his shield into Hundr's spine, and he shoved back against the enemy wall. The sound of the opposing lines colliding was like the clap of a thunderbolt thrown by Thor himself. Hundr grimaced at the smell of stale ale and acrid sweat from the enemy, so close now that only the width of their shields separated his body from the man in front. Blue Eyes grunted and snarled. He spat at Hundr from across the shield wall and pushed with all his might. Herjolf glowered down at Hundr with gritted teeth, a full head taller than him. A spear blade flashed past Hundr's face, and he recoiled. It came on his blind side – the side of his dead eye.

Hundr thrust his own spear forwards, the shaft scraping over the rim of his shield. It pushed past Blue Eyes' head and into the second enemy rank, yet Hundr felt no resistance. He whipped it back but twisted his wrist so that the returning blade sliced across Blue Eyes' ear and neck below his helmet, spurting blood over the warrior next to him in the enemy line. Hundr brought the spear back, and as Blue Eyes opened his mouth to let out a grunt at the pain, Hundr slammed his spear into the man's maw, smashing through teeth and slicing through lips and tongue. Those blue eyes opened wide with shock, and his body quivered as Hundr pushed his spear on through the back of his skull. Hundr ripped the weapon free, but Blue Eyes just hung there, thick, dark blood washing down his chin and onto his leather breastplate. The men around and behind him in the press of the shield wall kept him upright, but his shield slipped away, and Hundr drove his shoulder into his own shield to drive forward.

Herjolf Blackbear roared his defiance and hate across the clash of linden wood. A bearded axe blade snaked over the huge warrior's shoulder and hooked over the shield next to Hundr. Hundr shouted to warn Hjalmar, the man behind that shield, of what would happen next. But it was too late; the axe yanked the top half of Hjalmar's shield down, exposing his face and neck, and Herjolf laughed as he smashed his spear through the pale skin of Hjalmar's throat with so much force that Hjalmar's head snapped back, almost torn from his shoulders. Bush pulled on Hjalmar's shield, took his place in the front rank on Hundr's right, and hefted his shield to block another of Herjolf's monstrous spear strikes.

A shield pushed against Hundr's again, and Blue Eyes' corpse had gone, replaced by a broad-shouldered, grizzled warrior with a stringy, grey, mottled beard. He bellowed at Hundr, and the smell of his breath carried over the shields, fetid from his mouth of rotting brown teeth. The two lines heaved and shoved against one another, all along the shield wall clash. The enemy warriors were shouting, calling for space as they crammed together, and the overlap of their shields pushed the line of men close, cramping men's arms and making it impossible to swing a weapon. Hundr felt the warmth in his belly replacing the fear. It was the kindling of battle joy because although these men were hard fighters and fought with the power born of pure hatred, Hundr and his warriors were a different breed. He had fought in more shield wall battles and killed more men than he could remember. Hundr had fought across Saxon England, in Ireland, fighting on the walls of Dublin City, in Frankia, against great lords. He had fought men of legend, like Ivar the Boneless, and his reputation as a warrior gleamed as bright as the sharpest blade.

Without needing to see, Hundr knew that Ragnhild and her archers had played their part. On the flanks of the shield wall, Ragnhild would pour shaft after shaft of deadly goose-feathered arrows into the warriors on each flank of the enemy line. The men there would shuffle away from the deadly iron-tipped arrows, pushing the warriors beside them in on their own line and crowding the shield wall.

"Back, three steps!" Hundr bellowed. Men repeated the order down the line, and his men sounded a clipped roar of recognition. "Now!" Hundr shouted, and as one, his entire shield wall took three steps backwards away from the enemy. The two ranks moved in unison, a manoeuvre they practiced daily as they did the strokes of sword, axe, and spear. The enemy shield wall stumbled forwards as the pressure upon the shields gave way, and they tripped in the ditch that traversed the field. It was a thin, ragged thing of foul water only as deep as a man's shins, but it was enough to cause mayhem amongst men off balance and equipped with heavy shields and weapons. Hundr's heart leapt, and his muscles bunched, for this was the joy of war. He had made his shield wall in front of the ditch, waiting for this very moment, and the enemy had marched onto the field hungry for his death, confident in their greater numbers. The joy came in that moment when Hundr knew he would rain death and pain down upon men who had come to kill him. He would slaughter warriors who came to the battlefield to rip his life away and kill his friends.

"Kill, kill, kill!" Hundr snarled. He threw his spear overhand, and it slammed into the grizzled man's shield. He was on one knee and struggling to rise to his feet, having tripped in the ditch. Hundr ripped Fenristooth from the scabbard at his belt, let go of his shield and reached over his shoulder to draw Battle Fang in his left hand. He lunged quickly and hammered Fenristooth onto the upper rim of the grizzled man's shield and tipped the man forward. Then, in one swift motion, he swept Battle Fang overhand, and its blade smashed into the falling warrior's helmet, splitting the iron and driving a wall of blood from its lower edge to spill down his face. Hundr darted to his left, cutting and slashing with his two swords, moving fast between the fallen enemy and ruining their battle line. Einar Rosti, the Brawler, swung an axe into the face of a man scrambling to his feet and the weapon chopped into his skull with a wet slap.

Ragnhild let out an undulating scream, a paean to Odin, and she was amongst the enemy warriors, carving into them with her axe and a war fury sent by the All-Father himself. The rear rankers in the enemy shield wall stepped backwards, and Hundr danced between the front ranks, struggling to keep any sort of order after their fall into the ditch. He dragged the edge of his sword across one man's throat and plunged the tip of his other sword into a warrior's eye. Hundr then raised Battle Fang and Fenristooth to roar at the enemy rear rankers, and they turned on their heels and ran from his blood-soaked rage. Gore dripped from his blades; the rear rankers had seen their best and bravest reduced to a swirling mass of screaming pain and death.

The war lovers, the hard men, fought at the front line. There are few men of that ilk – most prefer to fight in the second or third rank. They will still stab a spear and add their weight to the shield wall, but they do not want to be where the blades are thickest and where death is but a heartbeat away. Yet, that is where reputations are made and where a man can catch the eye of the gods and earn for himself a place in Odin's great hall of the afterlife, Valhalla. Reserved for the greatest warriors who die in battle, where heroes fight all day, drink and swive all night, and do so for eternity, until the day of Ragnarök, where they fight at Odin's side against the monstrous forces of Loki. The rear rankers saw death coming for them. They saw a man whose reputation they knew. Hundr, the Man with the Dog's Name, sea Jarl, some said the Champion of the North, warrior, killer. Viking. They saw him, and behind them, an open field, and they ran for their lives.

Hundr launched himself back into the fray. The enemy had recovered, but the shield wall had disintegrated into a mass of individual skirmishes, man against man, across the line of battle. Einar Rosti ducked underneath a wide spear sweep and came up to sink his axe into the spearman's belly. Sigrid and Hildr stayed beyond the battle line, choosing targets carefully and emptying their quivers of arrows. Herjolf Blackbear strode amongst the struggle, roaring, his face and raven-black beard soaked and glistening with blood. He slammed his axe into the shoulder of a man belonging to Hundr's crew, and there was an audible crack as the axe broke through the bones in the warrior's shoulder and chest.

"Herjolf," Hundr called to him. The big man locked eyes with Hundr. He was feral and lost in blood madness. Hundr beckoned him on and took four long steps away from the melee to give him room to fight and visibility so that Herjolf's men would see their leader fight.

"Bastard," Herjolf growled, hefting an axe in one hand and a seax in the other. "You are a slave to Fairhair. Are you his lover? Come and die." Herjolf swung his axe with a speed that belied his monstrous frame, and Hundr leapt backwards, narrowly avoiding the blade taking his head. Hundr spun and swung Fenristooth low at Herjolf's ankles, but the big man skipped away, so Hundr lunged with Battle Fang. Herjolf parried the blow with his seax and then brought his axe down with a blood-curdling scream. The strike came fast, whistling through the air, and Hundr had to let go of his sword, or the axe would have taken his hand off at the wrist.

Hundr gasped and fell back, and Herjolf grinned as he kicked Hundr in the chest, sending him sprawling in the mud churned up by the battle, trodden to slop mixed with the blood and piss of the dying. He surged to his feet and swung his sword at Herjolf, and the enormous man raised his axe to stop the blow with arm-jarring force. Hundr grabbed Herjolf's left arm as the giant went to stab low underneath Hundr's brynjar to tear open his groin. He grunted with the strain of wrestling with Herjolf's thick wrist. It was like holding onto a tiller in a wild seastorm. Hundr leaned in and headbutted Herjolf, and the big man reeled away as the gristle of his nose crunched against Hundr's helmet.

A spear came at Hundr from his blind side and hit his shoulder, spinning him, but the links of his brynjar held against the impact. Hundr kept moving with the momentum of the strike and came around to slash his sword across the knees of the spearman and then hammered the pommel of his sword into the attacker's face. A terrible war scream tore through the battle-din – it was Ragnhild fighting with Herjolf, her axe twirling and striking in a blur of iron. Her assault pushed Herjolf backwards, but then he blocked her onslaught with his seax and hammered the axe from her hand with his own. With alarming speed, Herjolf dropped his seax and reached out to grab Ragnhild by the throat. She struggled and thrashed in his grip, but the giant hammered the haft of his axe into her face. Hundr raced towards them. He held his breath as Herjolf raised his axe for the killing blow. Ragnhild's face was mashed into a bloody pulp by the axe haft. She was a Valkyrie warrior, a peerless fighter, and had fought at Hundr's side for many years. He loved her like a sister, and as Herjolf's axe came down, Hundr leapt, and with his arm at full stretch, he plunged his sword into the meat of Herjolf's thigh.

Herjolf bellowed and dropped his axe. He let go of Ragnhild's throat and glowered down at Hundr, his teeth bared in a rictus of hate and pain. Hundr whipped the seax from its small scabbard at his back and stabbed it five times in rapid succession into Herjolf's groin. Blood flowed beneath Herjolf's brynjar, and he grasped at Hundr's chest, where he lay sprawled in the battle mud. But the giant's strength leaked out of him with his lifeblood, and as he fell to his knees, Hundr drove the tip of his seax underneath Herjolf's chin and up through his skull.

Hundr scrambled over the twitching Herjolf and frantically grabbed Ragnhild. Her one good eye rolled in her scarred face, and she stared at Hundr. A tear rolled down her grime-smeared face, and she swallowed hard.

"I thought that was my time," Ragnhild whispered. "What have I done with my life?"

Hundr shook his head and smiled at her.

"It's over," Einar announced, standing over Hundr and shaking his head. "That big bastard was the last of them. All the rebels are dead. We can go home."

TWO

Fjord water lapped at Einar's toes, the shale beneath his bare feet rough against his skin, the water cool and clear. The journey south following the fight with Herjolf Blackbear had taken only a few days, with favourable winds and calm seas, sailing past the inlets, cliffs and coves of western Norway. The fjord stretching out before Einar was a calm, rippling mirror, its surface a shifting reflection of the clouds above. He bent over to scoop up some water and paused as he caught his own face peering back at him through the gentle ripples. Einar sighed and stroked a hand down his grey beard. He pressed his fingers against the crow's feet at his eyes and the deep, vertical ridge on each wind-burned cheek. His forehead was furrowed like a spring field, and Einar thanked Odin that he had kept his hair, even though it, too, had turned the iron grey of a ship's rivet. He dipped his hands in the chill water, splashed its freshness onto his face, and washed his calloused palms.

Across the bay was Vanylven, his town, his home granted to him by King Harald. Einar was a Jarl, Earl of Vanylven and the country in its environs. Gulls cawed, and Einar listened to the bustle of the place across the water; fishermen yelled as they unloaded their catch, merchants on the dockside sold their wares, and people busied themselves with daily life. Timber buildings trailed away into the valley basin, curving and snaking around the town's lanes. He couldn't see it from the beach, but his hall was within that tangle of buildings, high raftered and long. It was a good hall, a mead hall fit for a Jarl. The port and its jetties were thick with ships, beautifully sleek, long-hulled drakkars and snekker. Warships. Five of the shallow-drafted vessels belonged to Hundr, and three were Einar's own. Einar wiped the water from his moustache and beard and smiled. Out on the fjord itself, two sturdy pontoon floating bridges stretched across the water from the coast on either side of the bay. The bridges were broad, with timber walls sturdy enough to hold a fighting platform. There was a gap between the floating bridges, big enough for a ship to sail through, but a thick twist of hemp rope as wide around as Einar's thigh secured it. They would remove the rope upon the approach of a friendly ship, and it would stop any unfriendly vessels from entering the bay. Vanylven was a fine place, secure and thriving.

Laughter danced on the breeze, and Einar turned to see Finn running along the beach towards him, long strides pounding along the tiny stones, and Hildr chased him. Finn stopped and kicked a splash of water at her, and Hildr squealed with laughter, covering her face with her hands. She picked up a handful of shale and threw it at Finn, who skipped away gleefully.

"Is it time to practice, Einar?" Finn called, waving, his shoulder-length hair shaking around his head.

"It is; the gear is over there," Einar said, pointing a thumb over his shoulder towards the rocks behind him where he had left the wooden swords, spears, blunted axes, and shields for weapons training. A wide smile cracked Finn's face, and he sprinted over to the pile of weapons.

"It's good to be home," Hildr sighed as she reached Einar, slipping her petite hand into his and standing on her tiptoes to kiss his cheek. Einar put his arm around the small of her back and held her to him. She was beautiful, golden-haired and as fierce as a wolf. "He missed you." She cocked her chin to Finn, who rummaged amongst the weapons pile, picking up a practice sword, then changing his mind for a spear before dropping it to choose a different weapon.

"I think he got taller whilst we were away," which was true. Finn was fifteen summers old, Einar guessed.

"He looks ever more like his father."

"He has Ivar's handsomeness, that's for sure."

"It's difficult for him, being the son of such a legend. Ivar the Boneless, who himself was the son of Ragnar Lothbrok. They are big boots to fill."

"You have raised him well. Even though he is not our son, you have loved him like a mother."

"Valbrandr and Bush caught a deer out in the woods," she said, fussing at Einar's jerkin and turning down the fur collar. "So, there will be a good crowd in the hall this evening."

"Good, we don't get to use it as much as we should. Let's open a couple of barrels and celebrate being back."

"We don't use the hall because we aren't in it. Harald keeps dragging us off to fight his battles, which we thought were over four years ago after the battle at Hafrsfjord."

Einar stepped out of the water and sighed. "He is the King, and I am his Jarl. He calls, and we fight. That's how it works. We have been through this dozens of times. Look at what we have here,

Hildr. A home of our own, we are the lords of this place. We have more silver than we know what to do with. The price of that is my oath to Harald. Are you not happy?"

"I am," she said and gave a wan smile as she wrung her hands. "Let's enjoy the feast tonight." She put a hand on his cheek and looked deep into his eyes. "I am happy. Go to Finn; he is waiting." Hildr glanced over his shoulder and shook her head. "I must go to Ragnhild."

"What is up with her? She isn't the most cheerful of people at the best of times, but she's got a face like a slapped arse at the moment."

"Einar!" Hildr chided and punched him in the stomach. "Something happened to her when she fought Herjolf. She won't stop talking about our order, the Valkyrie at Upsala."

"She has fought and killed a hundred men; I don't see how that big bastard differs from any of the others. She will be alright in a few days."

"Einar, come on!" Finn shouted, and Einar shrugged at Hildr. She kissed him again and left to go to Ragnhild. Her boots crunched on the shale, and Ragnhild waited at the end of the beach, staring across the fjord water.

"Have you done your shield raises today?" asked Einar, striding towards Finn and rubbing his hands together.

"Yes," said Finn, and he tossed a practice sword to Einar. "Can we do sword today?"

"Are you lying to me, boy?" Einar caught the sword and flexed his fingers around the smooth wooden grip. Einar had commissioned Vanylven's blacksmith to sink a length of iron into the blades of a few wooden practice swords to make the weight closer to the real thing.

Finn smirked, his cheekbones standing prominently in his face of hard angles. "I'll do it afterwards, I promise."

"Very well. But don't shirk that, boy. Lifting the shield until your shoulders burn will strengthen you. Being stronger will help your weapon skill." Einar raised his sword in front of him and beckoned Finn on. The lad was only a head shorter than Einar, and Einar was taller than most men. He was narrow-hipped with broad but skinny shoulders. Finn held a practice sword in each hand, then twirled them in front of him.

"Two swords again?" asked Einar, shaking his head.

"Yes, Hundr fights with two. And Bush tells me my father fought with two."

"He did. But Hundr and Ivar are the two best swordsmen I have ever seen. I don't fight with a sword, lad. I use an axe, practice more with the axe, it…." Einar raised his sword to parry a lightning-fast overhand strike, and Finn laughed at the surprise on Einar's face.

"I think you are getting old." Finn came on again, lunging low and then slashing his other sword at Einar's face. Einar parried the blows, but Finn forced him to take a backward step. Finn was fast, maybe even as fast as Hundr, and sweat sprang out on Einar's brow as he worked to stop the practice sword from getting through his guard.

Finn feinted as though he would strike at Einar's face but then turned that blow into a low cut at Einar's belly. Einar grabbed his wrist with his free hand and stepped in towards Finn, barging him backwards with his chest.

"That's not fair," said Finn as he stumbled back.

"Fighting isn't about fairness. It's about stopping the bastard in front of you from killing you. Your weapons aren't your only way of hurting your enemy. I'll talk to Valbrandr and Hekkr about giving you some wrestling lessons."

"Wrestling?"

"Yes, so you can learn how to battle without weapons and some tricks of close fighting. Headbutts, a knee to the groin, a bite to a nose or an ear. The finer points of warcraft."

"Do you think Valbrandr will teach me?"

"He will, he might look frightening, but he is a good man." Valbrandr was once a warrior of King Harald's hearth troop but had stayed with Einar after the battle at Hafrsfjord.

"What shall we practice now? Spears?"

"You do your shield raises, then we will work on the spear."

"But…"

"Shield raises."

Finn tutted, threw his practice swords down, and marched off towards his shield, mumbling as he went. Einar walked up the beach towards where Hildr stood close to Ragnhild, both women staring towards the gap in the fjord wall across the water.

"You two look like you want to get back out to sea," Einar said as he approached. Hildr gave him a look with an upside-down smile. The corners of her mouth turned down towards her chin. "We have only just got home?"

"I must return to Upsala," whispered Ragnhild after an uncomfortable silence.

"There is nothing there for you now, Ragnhild; it has been years since you and Hildr left."

"It has been years. Years since I forsook my oath to Odin and to our sacred order of Valkyries." Ragnhild turned to Einar, and a frown like a thunderstorm creased her scarred face, her one good eye trembling. "Odin came to me when I was under Herjolf's axe. The All-Father told me I must return to Upsala and fulfil my oath to him, to serve him. I must go, Einar. Do you understand?"

"I understand," said Einar, and he raised his hands to calm her. He didn't understand. Ragnhild was as fierce as any warrior Einar had ever fought alongside, and she was not usually one for talking of the gods. But Ragnhild and Hildr both came from a sacred order of warrior women, sworn to the service of Odin, to feed Valhalla with the corpses of the brave men they slew in battle. Einar had met them both in England years earlier, and the two Valkyries had stayed with Einar ever since, never returning to the home of their order at Upsala in the land of the Svear, to the great temple of Odin, the father of the gods.

"So, we shall go?" Ragnhild asked, her eye flitting from Hildr to Einar and her hand rising to grab the Odin spear amulet at her neck.

"My place is here, Ragnhild. But Hundr will take you."

THREE

Laughter undulated across Vanylven's mead hall. Red-faced people ate and drank, crammed into the feasting benches which ran across its length. Chatter rumbled amongst the laughter, mead flowed freely in frothing tankards and horns, and freshly baked loaves filled the tables along with boiled vegetables, luxuriously churned butter, roast beef and pork. An ancient man with a long white beard turned a spit over the hall's central fire. He turned it slowly and carefully, watching the deer carcass roast patiently and evenly as though he were a master craftsman at work. The smoke from the fire drifted up through the smoke hole at the centre of the thatch above the time-darkened rafters.

Hundr sat with Sigrid, Bush, Valbrandr, Ragnhild, and other warriors of the Seaworm crew. He drained the dregs of the silky mead in his ale horn, and as soon as he had placed it back on the timber tabletop, they refilled it to overflow with golden froth.

"It is still early in the summer," said Valbrandr, tearing into a lump of pork with his teeth. "Shall we take to the Whale Road again?" Valbrandr Kjartansson had a neck as thick as a man's thigh, muscled and tapered beneath his wide, angular head. He was a warrior of reputation. Though not as tall as Hundr, he was twice as broad. His face was brutal, with a jutting forehead and flat, black eyes like a beast from the depths of Jotunheim.

"We are only just returned from fighting Blackbear," snapped Bush, slamming his ale down on the table and shaking his head. "Have a rest, enjoy the food, find a woman. We don't always have to be freezing our stones off out at sea." Bush was a short but sturdy man, with a heavy paunch hanging over his belt and bald save for a ring of long hair that ran around below the bottom of his skull but went no higher than his ears.

"We are Vikings. We should be out raiding. There are months left in the fighting season. We could get to the Saxons and back, or Frankia, before the weather changes." Valbrandr searched the other faces at the table for support before coming to rest on Hundr's one eye.

"We might…let's see," said Hundr, and Sigrid squeezed his leg under the table so hard he almost choked on his ale.

"Valbrandr is right. We should set out again. I spent too long cooped up in my father's hall on Orkney. It's good to be at sea with the wind in our hair and at our backs, knowing adventure is out in front," she enthused.

"Adventure?" Bush laughed through a mouthful of bread, rubbing a hand beneath the leather helmet liner he always wore to cover his bald head. "When you get to my age, lass, adventure becomes a danger. It means sailing into some sort of bloody trouble for silver and plunder and risking my neck. We have plenty of silver coming our way from King Harald. Big Herjolf was the last of the rebels. There is no one to dispute Harald's rule now, and he promised us silver once it was so."

"The silver will be here soon," agreed Hundr. "Maybe we will go to sea again, or perhaps we can summer here. Get fat and work on the ships. Put some fresh caulking into the timbers."

"Caulking?" said Sigrid, wagging a long finger at Hundr. "That is winter work. No, we should raid, fight, sail our ships – be Vikings. Building our reputations. That is what we do."

"I must go to Upsala," Ragnhild interjected. She spoke in a flat, almost bored tone. She stared at the table at her untouched plate of food and full horn of ale. "You said you would take me." She raised her head, and her one eye met Hundr's. They both shared the Odin wound, each having lost an eye. Ragnhild had lost hers in battle many years ago, and an enemy had cut Hundr's from him with a red-hot knife. Odin sacrificed his eye at Mimir's well beneath the roots of the world tree Yggdrasil in return for the gift of wisdom, but Hundr and Ragnhild's were wounds of pain.

"I made that vow, Ragnhild; I have not forgotten it. I will take you there whenever you want to go." Ragnhild had often spoken of returning to her order of the Valkyrie at Upsala but had never actually made the journey. Hundr owed her a great deal. She had risked her life sailing under his command many times and had never asked for anything in return.

"I want to go now. I must go now."

"Very well, Ragnhild. We will go in the Seaworm once we can provision the ship and get her ready to sail."

"Why now, Ragnhild, after all these years?" asked Bush. Hundr frowned at him, but Bush shrugged, raising an eyebrow at Ragnhild and shaking his head.

"Because I broke my oath to Odin, and he spoke to me when I faced death beneath Herjolf's axe.

His voice was clear, ringing like a blacksmith's hammer – I must return to my order. I will not be welcome in Valhalla unless I do," she answered in the same flat, lifeless voice. Her shoulders slumped, her one eye fixed on the table.

"There cannot be many Vikings who have sent so many brave souls to Valhalla and Thruthvangar," said Hundr, speaking of Odin's and Thor's halls of the afterlife, reserved for only the bravest and most formidable of warriors. "You would be welcome there with open arms, with pride of place under the roof of shields and within the walls made of spears."

"Exactly," Bush nodded in agreement and raised his drinking horn. "Enough of talk. We are here to celebrate a victory. Drink, Ragnhild. Eat."

"What talk?" she said and raised her scarred face to glower at Bush. "You think I jest? Or speak on a whim? I speak of my eternal soul, of breaking a sacred oath to Odin All-Father, and you say that is silly?"

For a moment, Hundr thought she would fly across the table and throttle Bush, but she stayed still. Ragnhild's shoulders shook with rage, and her knuckles were white where her hands curled into fists on the tabletop.

"Enough. Ragnhild is right, and we will sail for Upsala as soon as we can," said Hundr to break the tension. "Valbrandr and Sigrid want to go to sea anyway, and I owe Ragnhild my life many times over. So, we shall take only one ship, the Seaworm, and the others shall remain at Vanylven with Einar." Sigrid beamed and squeezed his leg again, and Valbrandr tucked into his food, happy at the prospect of returning to sea. Bush grumbled into his ale, and Ragnhild nodded at Hundr, her hand clutching her Odin spear amulet. She was distant and troubled. Ragnhild was the veteran of a hundred fights and countless shield walls, and it was an odd wyrd that her encounter with Herjolf had left her so shaken. Hundr would take Ragnhild to Upsala, but he worried she would not make the return voyage, that she would return to her order of warrior priestesses, and that he would lose one of his closest friends, a woman he loved like a sister.

Two days later, the Seaworm sat filled with barrels of salted meat, oatcakes, water, and ale. They had repaired her lines where required, and the beast-headed prow snarled out towards Vanylven's open fjord. The quayside was busy as usual with the hustle and bustle of a fresh summer morning; the fishermen returned with catch, and people haggled over the price of fish on the dock.

Hundr tossed his pack, including his sleeping blanket and spare clothes, onto the deck, where the crew clambered across rowing benches and rigging to prepare the ship for sea. He turned to reach for his shield, its leather cover freshly painted with the open-eye sigil that was Hundr's banner, and he saw Finn Ivarsson leaning against a post, staring at him. The boy had a bundle of cloth at his feet. Hundr smiled at him, then called to Bush on deck and held up his shield. Bush opened his arms, and Hundr tossed it to him for securing onto the sheer strake next to the crew's shields.

"I don't have a shield," said Finn, brushing away his tousled chestnut hair from his face.

"I thought Einar had given you a practice one to use?" said Hundr.

"He did, but I need a real one. Like one of those." Finn pointed to the line of painted shields running across the side.

"I am sure Einar can arrange that for you." Hundr smiled again, a forced smile, and turned away.

"Wait, I meant to say...."

Hundr sighed and turned back, pausing so the lad could spit out whatever words were on the tip of his tongue.

"I would like to come with you. I can..."

"No," Hundr said bluntly, and he waved a hand to dismiss the suggestion and turned to walk away.

"Wait, please…" Finn pleaded, and he sprang forwards to stand before Hundr. Hundr took a slight step back. *Finn had grown and looked more like his father every day.* "I can help, I can bail the bilge, I can…."

"We don't have room for passengers; we are only taking warriors. You are too young. Maybe in a few years you'll be ready to join the crews. But not yet."

"I can fight just as well as any of these sea dogs," said Finn, crossing his arms over his chest. "I can fight with two swords, just like you, just like my father."

And there it is. Just like his father, Ivar the Boneless. Who I killed.

"I am sure you can, but you don't own a sword or a spear or a shield. You are too young to sail with us, and my answer is no."

"You never talk to me. You don't like me," Finn uttered, his brows knitting together and his arms falling to his side with balled fists. "What have I ever done to you?"

Nothing. But I loved your mother and hated your father. Your uncle took my eye, and I killed him and your father years ago. "It's got nothing to do with like. You just aren't old enough. Now go; I must finish preparing the ship."

Finn glared at Hundr, some of Ivar's

malevolence playing within the shine of his eyes and the angles of his face. The boy snatched up his pack and stormed down the quay. He barged into a warrior who sent a curse after him, but Finn strode on, not looking back.

"He just wants your approval," said Sigrid, slipping her arm around Hundr's as he watched Finn's back disappear amongst the crowds. "He looks up to you. You shouldn't be so harsh on him."

"Harsh? You want me to let him sail with us to Upsala? To become his nursemaid?"

"He is almost a man now; he doesn't need a nursemaid. How old were you when you left your home with dreams of reputation and the life of a Viking?"

"Old enough to lift sword and axe and ready to use them."

"You are the Man with the Dog's name, the Champion of the North. He admires you; he wants to be like you. Show him kindness."

"I never asked for those names," Hundr grumbled. But he remembered himself at Finn's age, and Sigrid was right. All he had wanted then was to become a Viking warrior, just like the heroes in his mother's stories.

"He is as a son to Einar and Hildr. You should make more of an effort with the boy."

"One day, he will hate me, and he'll want revenge for his father."

"How can you know that? He never even met his father."

"He is his father's son; I can see it in him."

"That's nonsense. Show him some of the kindness you wished someone had shown to you as a boy. You don't have to bring Finn on the voyage, but help him with his weapons or give him some advice. Otherwise, he might end up hating you. But it doesn't have to be that way." Sigrid stood on her tiptoes and kissed his cheek. Hundr frowned at her as she leapt nimbly on board the Seaworm.

"We won't have any of that at sea," Bush tutted as she stood next to Hundr, testing the strength of the halyard rope. "No kissing and cuddling when all we poor men have is our stinking bench mate for company."

Sigrid laughed and gave Bush a kiss on the cheek, which shut him up. His face went as red as a summer apple, and he took off his stained leather helmet liner to scratch his egg-white head. Einar Rosti stepped off the Seaworm and onto the jetty. He tucked his hands into his belt and gnawed at his beard.

"Take care of her, lad," said Einar, rubbing a hand along the ship's beautifully carved timbers.

"You call me lad as though I were still the stripling who first boarded your ship all those years ago," Hundr replied. A smile split Einar's granite slab-like face.

"Fair enough. But look after her all the same." The Seaworm had been Einar's ship before he had given her to Hundr and was a beautiful drakkar warship. Her long sleek lines and shallow draught made the Seaworm fast and lithe, and she was more precious than any trove of gold or silver.

"I will, but you should come with us to Upsala. Maybe Hildr would like to see her old order, as well as Ragnhild?"

"My place is here. You go. Take Ragnhild back to the Odin priestesses if that is what she wants. My Hildr is done with all that now. She doesn't see it as an oath broken. Even though she and Ragnhild were girls together in Upsala and shared the same beliefs and swore the same oath. Hildr fulfilled her oath and fought as a Valkyrie, but now she is at peace. She might not come back. You know that?" Einar jutted his chin to where Ragnhild sat on the steerboard. She stared out towards the water, fingering the spear amulet hung around her neck.

"I know. She needs this, though. She must make peace with Odin. I owe her that."

Einar nodded and stroked his beard. "Something

broke in her head when that big bastard was about to kill her. Fix her and bring her home. Don't leave her there with those bloody Odin fanatics."

Hundr reached out and clasped Einar's forearm. "I'll do my best."

The Seaworm eased out of Vanylven towards the great Odin temple at Upsala, where the warrior priestesses would either welcome Ragnhild as a returning sister or curse her as an oath-breaker and damn her for eternity.

FOUR

The Seaworm made the journey south, passing the endless fjords, islands and inlets that formed Norway's west coast. She flew on a fierce sea wind which whipped the sail taut, proudly displaying Hundr's sigil of the single eye emblazoned in black upon the heavy grey wool. The Seaworm cut through the white-tipped swell like a blade. Her dragon head prow rose and fell with the surge of the sea, and Hundr left his hair unbound to enjoy the thrill of the warship's speed and the spume's fresh chill upon his face as waves crashed to ruin on the hull. Bush leaned on the tiller at the steerboard and whooped with joy as the ship sped beneath them.

As night drew in on the end of the first day, they dropped the stone anchor in the shelter of a narrow bay carved into the high, sheer sides of an island of rock whose sole occupants were sea birds. The crew put together a meal of ale, salted pork and biscuits and gathered on the deck to tell stories of past adventures and remember friends long gone. Ragnhild sat apart from the crew, huddled on a rowing bench and staring out at the clear, star-filled sky. Hundr wrapped his cloak around her shoulders to keep the cold out, and she looked up at him with a sorrowful eye. Her mouth was a thin-lipped slit of tension. It was a silent look that said thank you but also that she needed to be alone. So, Hundr left her to her contemplation of the afterlife and what her place might be within it, knowing that only the Odin priests and priestesses could give her any peace concerning her fate in eternity.

The water beneath the ship was calm, and the crew laughed and sang as they talked of the battles at Hafrsfjord, the bloodshed in Dublin, and some even remembered fighting in England with the great Ragnarsson army. Hundr left them to it, even though he had fought in each of those encounters, and it had been with the sons of Ragnar that Hundr had first built his reputation. He ducked between the rigging and made for the steerboard. Beneath the platform, his brynjar lay wrapped in an oily fleece to keep out the worst of the seawater, which would rust the precious iron rings, along with his other belongings. Hundr grunted as he kneeled on the deck; an old wound to his thigh made bending the leg sore, and he stretched out to grab his spare cloak.

Hundr recoiled as his hand brushed something that moved, and the thing flinched at his touch. At first, he thought it was a rat, but he swiftly realised that a rat would be far too quick and cautious for his fumbling hand to touch in the darkness beneath the raised platform. Decidedly, Hundr reached in further. He grabbed a bony ankle and hauled out the wriggling, writhing figure of a young man who rolled and flipped on the deck like a landed fish, all tousled hair and flailing limbs.

"What have you caught there?" called Valbrandr as the crew broke off their stories to see what the commotion was.

"It's the biggest fish I have ever seen," quipped Trygve. "It will keep us fed for a week." The crew laughed, and the flailing boy sprang to his feet, his hands bunched into fists and a defiant look on his face.

"Finn Ivarsson, you sneaky little bastard," said Bush, making his way across the deck and wagging a thick finger at the lad. "Einar will tan your scrawny hide for this."

"All I want is to sail with you," blurted Finn, his gaze flitting between each crew member and his hands held out in supplication. "I can help. I can do anything you need."

PETER GIBBONS

"At first light, we come about and return to Vanylven," Hundr intoned.

"But please..." gasped Finn.

"I told you no, and you snuck aboard like a thief. To be a warrior means more than using an axe and spear. Your word is your bond, and honour is everything. It will be a hard lesson well learned for you."

"You've got some stones on you, lad, I'll give you that," said Bush chuckling to himself. "There aren't many men in Midgard who would defy the Man with the Dog's Name." The crew laughed heartily at that and returned to their yarns and ale.

Ragnhild appeared next to Hundr, her scarred face sombre. "We can't go back. It would cost us two days. We must press on for Upsala," she said, her one eye boring into Hundr's own.

"Einar and Hildr will be worried sick about him, and this is a warship. It's no place for a child."

"I am not a child!" Finn roared, and every head on board the Seaworm whipped around to gawp at him. Hundr took a step closer to Finn, glaring down at him through his good eye.

"You will talk to me with respect. And if you ever raise your voice to me again, it will be the last thing you ever do." Finn held his stare, his

41

jaw jutting and eyes blazing.

"We can't go back," Ragnhild whispered. Hundr turned to her, surprised at the openness on her face. Ragnhild was a fierce fighter, a woman who had fought on the edge of life and death her whole life. Hundr only knew her as a brave and stoic warrior, unshaken by fear no matter the odds they had faced together. But now she looked frightened and vulnerable, and Hundr could not deny his friend, no matter how angry he was with Finn.

"Very well, we go on," Hundr nodded, and he jabbed a finger into Finn's chest. "You are a stowaway on this ship and not one of the crew. You will earn your keep by bailing the bilge, just as I did when Einar let me aboard the Seaworm. Bush, you are responsible for him. So get him to work bailing."

The crew cheered and laughed together because bailing was the bane of all drakkar crews. Like all Viking warships, the Seaworm sat shallow in the water and flexed with the power of the sea because of her clinker-built planks and the wide spacing of her rivets. They filled the tiny spaces between each plank with horsehair and tar caulking, which the crew replaced during the winter, but she still let in water, so the job of bailing the bilge was constant. The men hated it and shared the task, grumbling at their grazed knuckles and freezing hands, so it delighted them that the sole responsibility for that back-breaking task now fell to Finn Ivarsson.

"I will get you to Upsala as fast as I can," said Hundr, squeezing Ragnhild's shoulder. "I hope you can find there whatever it is you seek."

She smiled and nodded. "I seek the forgiveness of Odin Biflindi, the spear shaker. The mighty All-Father and lover of battle."

"What if you do not find that at the temple?"

"Then I am lost and will surely be denied a place in Valhalla. I will be a nithing, wandering Niflheim with the others who have not died in battle or lived a warrior's life."

"You have led the life of ten warriors, Ragnhild. No matter what they say at Upsala."

"I swore an oath. An oath to a god. It matters." She shuffled away and huddled next to the steerboard, still wrapped in Hundr's dark wool cloak.

The next morning, they rowed south in search of a favourable wind, which they found off the coast of Fensfjorden and sped southeast around the southern coast of Norway and towards the land of the Svear. King Bjorn Ironside ruled in Sweden, a man Hundr knew well, and Bush wanted to visit the old warrior king who was famous for his feasting and the welcome he extended to his friends. Hundr refused. Ragnhild grew paler with each day at sea. She ate and drank sparingly and kept to herself, still and quiet, staring at the surge of the Whale Road, dwelling on her eternal fate. Upsala lay on the east coast of Bjorn's kingdom, which they could reach quicker by traversing the lands of the Svears on foot or by buying horses. But that would all take time, and Hundr did not want to risk falling foul of a local Svear Jarl who fancied testing his warriors' mettle against theirs once he clapped eyes on their brynjars and weapons. So, Hundr led the Seaworm south, running along Jutland and around Sjaelland. Bush knew the way, and as shipmaster, he kept the Seaworm at a safe distance from the coast, spending nights in secluded bays and rarely going ashore. More than once, curious drakkar or snekke ships followed them like wolves sniffing out prey. The single ship would seem like easy pickings for the Danish Jarls of the mainland and the islands around Sjaelland, but the Seaworm ran fast, and Bush kept them away from the sea wolves.

The waters around the great trading port at Birka were thick with fat-bellied knarr trading ships, yet the Seaworm headed north for Upsala, and all the while, Finn bailed the bilge without complaint. Each day he knelt in the hull between the thwarts with his bucket, scooping out the seawater and tossing it over the side, doing so downwind for fear of soaking the rest of the crew. Hundr noticed the red raw skin of the boy's hands, the cuts and scrapes on his knuckles and fingers. He took to his back-breaking work as though it was his life's calling, and after a few days of it, the crew warmed to him. Famed warriors like Sigvarth Trollhands and Torsten took their turns with the bucket to give the boy a break. Hundr leaned against the tiller on a rain-spat morning and watched with surprise as Bush and Thorgrim showed Finn how to take a turn at the oar, and the crew laughed as the lad struggled to keep time with the rest of the oarsmen, which they made look easy but was, in fact, a difficult skill to master.

The temple of Upsala loomed large as the Seaworm rowed up the Sala river, the golden wood of the temple's structures reaching above the treetops like a glorious crown. Hundr shivered as he remembered the tales of the great tree at Upsala, where the sacrificed corpses of men and animals hung from sacred boughs in honour of Odin and the Aesir. Bush tied the ship off and ordered five men to stay with her whilst the rest came ashore. Ragnhild was in a state of constant prayer, and as her boots touched the riverbank, she clutched her spear amulet, chanting rhythmically under her breath, and Hundr hoped his friend and sword sister would find peace in this ancient place of death and worship.

FIVE

Hundr marched through the dense forest surrounding the temple. The Seaworm crew trailed behind him in a long line along a forest path which snaked through the tall trees, stretching overhead like fingers on a dark hand, close and oppressive. The golden timbers of the Odin temple rose through the high tree canopy in the distance. A peak like the gable of a feasting hall towered above the tops of oak, fir, birch, aspen, and alder. Hundr's boots crunched on fallen pines and leaves along the dark mulch trail that laced the forest's deep darkness. Birds chirped, the wood groaned and creaked, and unseen animals chittered, hidden in the depths of the woodland.

"There is a darkness in this place. I can feel the gods," Sigrid hissed over Hundr's shoulder. He nodded, though he was unsure whether the oppressive closeness he felt was the damp weight of the ancient forest itself or the looming presence of Odin All-Father, Thor, Frey, and Njorth.

"Let's hope they give Ragnhild what she needs," he said, his hand rising to grasp the hammer amulet at his neck. Like most Vikings, Hundr feared the gods and prayed to Odin and Thor for their help and favour. He lived his life in pursuit of the reputation and glory that would pave his way to Valhalla, but he was not an ardent worshipper of the gods, and he did not make sacrifices, doubting that the slaying of a good horse or any other animal would bring him the battle-luck he needed. Yet being in the woodland around Upsala, he suddenly felt guilty for that, as though the gods judged him and could sense him as he drew close to their holy place.

"Does she want their forgiveness or for them to welcome her back with open arms?"

"Let's find out." Hundr pushed his shoulders back and raised his chin. Ahead of him, in the forest's gloom, a high gate of darkened timbers rose between two thick pine trees. Before that gate stood two figures in long robes and hoods the colour of dark blood. They stood still with bowed heads, and beyond them, behind the gate, the temple itself reared up in the forest's darkness. It was as though giants from

Jotunheim had laid huge feasting halls on top of one another, each smaller than the one before, as they reached up towards the highest boughs. Most of the thick timbers of its construction were the golden colour of freshly cut wood, shining as though coated with precious gold. They had painted other timbers red, black, and blue in swirling images of dragons, horses, and boars.

Hundr approached the two hooded figures, and his boot crunched on a fallen twig. Both hoods snapped up to reveal bone-white faces with deep-sunken eyes, like the dark pits of a well. Hundr stopped in his tracks, and the line of warriors behind him also halted, with the clank of iron weapons and collective gasps as each warrior saw the strange, deathly faces before the gates of Upsala.

The two figures were tall, and their faces were thin, with prominent bones. The thickness of their jaws told that they were men. Hundr waited for them to speak, to offer him a welcome or challenge him for his name or the purpose of his visit, but they remained silent and staring. Hundr looked closer and realised that their paleness came from a chalk paint daubed onto their faces, flakes of it visible on their cheeks. The darkness around their eyes was a paste or powder smudged at the corners. They looked like the dead, risen from the afterlife, like the fetches of long-dead priests, but Hundr reminded himself that they were just men.

"I am Jarl Hundr, here to speak with High Priest Vattnar," he announced, stopping and resting his hand on the Fenristooth's ivory hilt in its scabbard at his belt. He had met Vattnar amongst the army of Ivar the Boneless in Northumbria many years ago when he commanded Ragnhild's Valkyrie force.

The taller of the white-faced figures cocked his head to one side and smiled to reveal a set of yellow teeth, the staining made worse by the pearly coating on his face.

"Lord Vattnar made the journey to Valhalla years ago," he said, his voice cracked and throaty.

"So, I would see the new High Priest, then."

"Helgi is the High Priestess of Upsala and the messenger of Odin in Midgard."

Hundr stared flatly into the black-painted eyes, refusing to repeat his request. Moments passed, the sounds of the forest echoing around them.

"Have you come to make an offering? Are you a pilgrim? What is your business with the gods?" hissed the taller white-faced man.

"I am Ragnhild, a sister of the Valkyrie," barked Ragnhild, pushing through the line of warriors to stand next to Hundr.

Taller-White-Face licked his lips and glanced at his colleague, who stared impassively ahead. "I do not know you, Ragnhild."

"Helgi was my sword sister many years ago. Let her know I am here."

Taller-White-Face looked Ragnhild up and down, and his gaze stopped at her Odin spear pendant. He inclined his head and pushed open a small door carved into the larger gate behind him. Then, just before he disappeared into the temple grounds beyond, he poked his luminous head back through the doorway. "Wait here," he scowled.

"That's a fine welcome from the gods," said Bush, tutting and sitting on a fallen log covered in lichen off the pathway. "I hope these priests and priestesses aren't as miserable as that skull-faced bastard." Chuckles pealed out along the line of men, and they all found a place to rest whilst they awaited the return of the gatekeeper.

"What awaits us inside?" asked Hundr.

"The temple of Odin," replied Ragnhild, peering up at the vast, golden-timbered structure towering beyond the gate. "The forests of sacrifice and judgement."

"They raised you here, Ragnhild?" Sigrid inquired, clearing her throat and trying to release the tension.

"Aye, and Hildr. I was my father's third daughter when he had prayed for a son, and there wasn't enough dowry to stretch to three. So, he sent me here to serve the gods, as an offering to please Odin and the Aesir, to bring my father good fortune in his hopes for a son. I was but a child then, raised to axe and spear in these forests and within that gate. This was my home."

"Is it true that they make sacrifices? Human sacrifices?" asked Sigrid.

"Of course, it's true. Every spring at the Baldr Festival, the corpses of the sacrificed hang in the sacred grove. It is a festival to celebrate death and re-birth, to honour Odin and his son Baldr, and to ensure the well-being of Midgard itself," said Ragnhild, her voice low, almost chanting the words.

The door creaked open, and Taller-White-Face emerged solemn and grim-faced.

"High Priestess Helgi will see you now, Ragnhild," he proclaimed and pushed open the door. Hundr strode through the entrance, following Ragnhild's lead. Sigrid came on his heels, followed by the rest of the crew. Through the gate, the temple rose before them on a hill, its height towering over Hundr, and the grounds surrounding it were a weave of gravel pathways. The paths meandered like a river, and their whorling nature reminded Hundr of the swirling beasts carved on ships or on the door lintels of feasting halls. On small, grassy hills between the pathways were smooth stones carved with strings of runes or snarling god faces. Some were daubed with bright colours, whereas others were coated with what looked like dried, flaking blood. A rhythmic chanting permeated the grounds, a low hum of song pulsing from the temple itself.

Their white-faced guide led them through the labyrinth of pathways, and Hundr's eye was drawn to the ancient snarl of tangled trees to his right. The boughs of the trees there twisted and clawed amongst one another, trunks in half shadow gnarled and misshapen, and Hundr's breath caught in his throat as he realised that some of those trunks bore terrible carved faces, some screaming in pain, others grimacing, or glowering like battle-hardened warriors. From the larger boughs hung corpses. The dangling corpses of men, women, horses, dogs and other animals, each in different states of decomposition, littered the sacred grove. *The gods are here. I can feel them.*

"Wait here," barked Taller-White-Face, and he marched towards the temple entrance's stained oak doors, which lay set back on a long wooden porch painted red and carved with flowing lines. Ragnhild stood with Hundr and Bush, and Sigrid was just behind them. The Seaworm crew wandered around the pathways, whispering to one another the horrors of the sacred grove and the power of the carved standing stones.

New white-faced acolytes pushed open the oak doors, creaking and groaning on monstrous iron hinges. From the darkness beyond strode a short, thickset woman in a pure white robe. An ivory-coloured cloak billowed behind her and swirled the musty-scented smoke which poured from the doorway in her wake as though it came from the depths of Niflheim itself. The woman had iron-grey hair, which she wore in a long plait resting over her left shoulder, and a thunderous frown creased her round face. She came to a halt at the end of the temple's porch with her hands on her hips, and her lip curled as her eyes came to rest upon Ragnhild.

"Sister, you return after so long. We had thought you were dead, killed in Wessex or Northumbria with your warband," the woman uttered, a sneer in her voice.

"High Priestess Helgi," said Ragnhild, and she clapped a fist to her chest and bowed her head in salute. "I have been fighting all these long years, sending souls to Valhalla and keeping raven bellies filled with the flesh of the men I have slain."

"You have been a'viking, it seems and not taking care of your oath as a war-sister of the

Valkyrie order. And this is the famous one-eyed Jarl Hundr, the Man with the Dog's Name. Is he your lover? Have you broken your vow of chastity and your vow to the All-Father?" Helgi shouted the last two words, and a line of Valkyrie warriors armed in brynjars and bristling with axes and spears bustled from the temple to stand behind their High Priestess.

"I am returned now to fulfil my duties to Odin," said Ragnhild, but her confidence slipped from her like melting ice. Her eyes fell to the pathway, and her shoulders slumped. In Frankia, years ago, Ragnhild had fallen in love with a brave warrior who had also been like a brother to Hundr, and she had broken her vow of chastity. Ragnhild and Kolo had been very much in love, and he had died in a desperate, blood-soaked battle on the walls of Dublin. Their love was so deep and joyous that it could not have been a sin, even in the eyes of the hard, cruel Aesir, but Ragnhild had thought it sinful then, and now it weighed her down as though the Seaworm's anchor stone were around her neck.

"You are not welcome here, Ragnhild Oathbreaker. By rights, I should bleed you out, give your blood to the Odin totem inside our temple and hang your corpse in the sacred grove to placate the All-Father's displeasure with you. But that might let you slip into Valhalla to sully the benches of the brave with your filthy soul and unworthy spirit. Better to let you live as the nithing you are until you die peacefully in your bed and your soul goes screaming to Niflheim."

Ragnhild closed her one eye tight and shook visibly at the High Priestess' decision. Then, unexpectedly, she spun on her heel, pushed her way past Hundr and Sigrid, barged through Bush and Thorgrim, and almost knocked Sigvarth on his arse. Ragnhild picked up speed until she broke into a run, and if Hundr didn't know her better, he would have believed she was sobbing. But then she stopped, her boots skidding on the gravel pathway. She paused, shoulders heaving and head bowed, before turning and striding back towards the temple.

"I am Ragnhild, sister of the Valkyrie," Ragnhild bellowed as though she were shouting curses across the shield wall battle lines. "I have filled Valhalla with the warriors I have slain, and I do not sit within a temple like a raven starver, pronouncing judgement with soft hands, the callouses of axe and spear long since healed."

"Begone, I command it…." roared Helgi.

"Challenge!" Ragnhild screamed, cutting off the High Priestess before she could spit more hate. "I invoke the right of challenge. I demand to fight your champion. A Holmgang against the champion of the Valkyrie, and if I win, no warrior can call me an oathbreaker, for I will return to this order and take my place as a warrior priestess of Odin."

Helgi laughed. "You look too old to fight. Your hair is as grey as mine. I should let you fight one of our novices. However, you have invoked the right of challenge, and you may fight our champion. First cut wins. If you win, you can return to our order. But you will not be victorious, and when you lose, you shall begone and never return. Oathbreaker. Make the sacred square!"

An enormous woman stepped forward to join the High Priestess. She was broad at hip and shoulder with a shaven head, bestrewn with tattoos. She drew a wickedly bearded axe in each hand and grinned down at Ragnhild, her face an unholy mess of white scar tissue around a broken nose pressed close to her face. Ragnhild spat towards Helgi's champion, ready to fight for her honour and her immortal soul.

SIX

"Where is that boy?" muttered Hundr, pacing back and forth across a knoll covered in short grass.

"He's on his way, don't worry. He's a good lad," said Bush as he peered down the pathway towards Upsala's gate and slipped off his stained leather helmet liner to rub a hand over his bald head.

"We should have sent one of the men."
Bush had sent Finn Ivarsson scampering back to the Seaworm to collect Ragnhild's mail and weapons. She had insisted on approaching the temple in a simple jerkin as some sort of show of penitence, but now that she had challenged the Valkyrie champion to a Holmgang, Ragnhild needed her war gear. She sat where the knoll sloped down in a soft bank to a lake of still water, dotted here and there with reeds. Ragnhild

was calm, her knees were tucked up and arms wrapped around them, staring out towards a small eyot at the centre of the lake. It sat low above the waterline, ringed with grey rock, and two small, gnarled alder trees stood on each end of the island.

"So, this will be a proper Holmgang then," Valbrandr remarked, nodding and staring out at the eyot. "The old way."

"Looks like it," said Hundr. The fighting of a Holmgang, or duel, was a lawful way to settle an argument. It was traditionally supposed to take place on an island within a lake or river, such as this one, or within a square of hazel branches. Each fighter had a second, and the number of replacement shields to be made available to each fighter was to be agreed upon beforehand. "There might not be a fight if the boy isn't here soon. Ragnhild might have to wear your brynjar or mine."

Valbrandr cocked an eyebrow and shook his head. No man willingly shared his precious coat of mail. It was an absurd suggestion, anyway. Valbrandr was so broad in the shoulder that it would slide off Ragnhild as though she were a child.

"I can smell those corpses," Sigrid murmured, curling her nose. "I can feel the gods' power here." She put her hand on the back of her neck and stared at the grim forest. The bodies were more visible this close, rotting and dangling from the boughs. The vast temple and ancient wood made the place oppressive and close.

"Here he is, at last," said Hundr. The gate banged open, and Finn scampered through it with a sack slung over his back which clanked at each of his footsteps. He scrambled up the gravel pathways and across to the bank, where he dropped his sack onto the grass. His normally tousled hair was wet and slick to his forehead, and his face was the red of raw meat.

"I came as fast as I could," he panted.

"You took your bloody time. We almost missed the fight," Hundr said and fished his hand into the sack. Therein were the shining rings of Ragnhild's brynjar, cool to the touch, and her belt, axe and seax.

"I rubbed her mail down with a handful of sand from the river," Finn chimed, and he smiled at Hundr. Hundr stood and held up the brynjar; it gleamed like the stars on a cloudless summer night.

"Good thinking, lad," said Bush. "You aren't as stupid as you look."

Thorgrim ruffled Finn's hair, and a smile split his handsome youthful face. Hundr picked up the sack and helped Ragnhild slide the mail coat over her arms and shoulders, and she shook herself so that it slithered down her torso like the skin of a serpent. She fastened on her belt, passed the axe haft through the loop on the belt's side and sheathed her seax in a scabbard which hung from the back of the belt by two leather thongs.

From across the lake came the beat of a drum and more low rhythmic chanting. Two lines of Valkyrie warriors marched from the temple to the water's edge, both lines wearing long white robes, with the High Priestess at their head. Between the lines strode their champion, rolling her shoulders and glowering across at Ragnhild.

"Two shields. Axes and spears. And we shall decide the Holmgang by the first cut," called Helgi, her voice carrying across the water. They had tied two small rowboats to the bank on the Valkyrie side of the lake, and a white-faced acolyte sat in each boat. One of them eased away from the bank and rowed towards Ragnhild, the oars disturbing the glass-still water. The Valkyrie champion clambered into the second boat along with a tall woman who carried the champion's shield.

"Will you be my second?" said Ragnhild, not making eye contact and keeping her gaze fixed firmly on the woman she was about to fight.

"I would be honoured," Hundr replied. As her second, he would hold Ragnhild's spare shield, which she could take up under the ancient rules of the Holmgang if her first shield was destroyed before the fight was over. "Will you stay with them if you win?"

"Yes, I must. Odin calls to me. I must honour my vows." Her hand went to her spear amulet, and she glanced at the sky as though she felt Odin's eye upon her.

Bush brought a spear and two shields and handed them to Hundr. Bush paused, wanting to say something, to pass on some encouragement to Ragnhild, but thought better of it when he saw the strained look on her scarred face and went to stand with Finn, Sigrid, and the men.

"Well then, I hope you win. Even though I will lose a sister," said Hundr. "So you can be at peace with yourself and the gods."

Ragnhild whipped up her head to look at him, and she smiled. It was a twisted wan smile, but he saw warmth and sadness in her eyes. They had shared so much together, bled together, and lost friends. Indeed, the bond between warriors of the shield wall went beyond the ties of friendship or love. Warriors who had danced together in that finest of lines between life and death, protecting each other with shields, killing others who came to kill them, shared a bond that Hundr could not put into words. In Ragnhild's eyes, he saw she knew that, too.

The rowboat reached the bank, and Ragnhild climbed in, followed by Hundr with the shields and spear. Drums across the water continued to beat, and the Valkyrie chanting thrummed. The white-faced acolyte rowed Ragnhild and Hundr to the eyot, and they made their way up its bank. The small island was only fifteen paces along its length, and its two trees took up more than half of that distance. It was a tight space to fight in, and to step into the water was to lose the fight. The Valkyrie champion stood at the centre of the eyot, spear in one hand and shield in the other, while her second remained beneath the far tree with the spare shield. She had a fierce face covered in dark tattoos, muscled arms beneath a sleeveless brynjar, and her mouth was turned down in a permanent look of disdain.

"Odin, hear me," Ragnhild whispered, bringing her spear amulet to her lips. "I fight to reclaim my place in Valhalla, to one day join the Einherjar, your warriors, to fight the Loki brood at the last battle, Ragnarök. Grant me speed and strength. Ask your raven Munin to remember my deeds, the warriors I have killed. Send me battle luck." Ragnhild hefted her shield and spear and went to fight a champion.

The drum beat and chanting from the shore quickened its pace. Hundr's own heart quickened along with it, and he glanced at Ragnhild's spear and axe. His palm grew sweaty where it gripped Fenristooth's ivory hilt, the uncertainty of what was to come eating away at him. He trusted in Ragnhild's weapon skill, but any fight with blades carried the danger of death. Even though Helgi had been clear that the first cut would decide the fight, that first cut could be a killing blow. He wanted Ragnhild to win for her own sake, but whoever won the fight, Hundr would lose Ragnhild to Odin.

Ragnhild raised her shield, brought the spear up to rest its shaft upon the upper iron rim of her shield, and circled the Valkyrie champion. Ragnhild was short and stocky, but the champion was twice as broad, and she grinned at Ragnhild over the rim of her shield.

"Fight for the gods, fight for the All-Father!" screamed Helgi, and the cloaked Valkyrie sisters around the lake raised their hands to the sky and screamed a terrible war cry that shuddered Hundr's bones. The champion echoed that war cry and rapidly lunged her bright spear point at Ragnhild's face. Ragnhild raised her shield, deflecting the blow easily, and the two women sprang apart and circled again. Ragnhild feinted a spear lunge and turned that feint into a sweep towards the champion's legs, but she leapt away from it. The champion wasn't only wide at the shoulder but also wide at the waist, her brynjar stretched tight over a bulging stomach. Ragnhild was a ball of muscle. Her hair might have been greying, and her face gouged by wrinkles, but she was all taut muscle and lean power.

The champion came at Ragnhild again, but this time she unleashed a flurry of powerful strikes, mashing into Ragnhild's shield like hammer blows, forcing her backwards under the onslaught. The champion struck high and low, trying to tip Ragnhild's shields for a follow-up strike at the exposed neck or leg, but Ragnhild held her shield firm.

"Watch the edge!" Hundr shouted. As she shuffled backwards, Ragnhild drew close to the narrow eyot's edge, and one heel in the water would send ripples across the lake's still surface, and the fight would be over. Ragnhild bunched her shoulder behind her shield, and the next strike from the champion rang off the iron boss like a bell. The champion wheeled away, and she was breathing hard, sweat glistening on her scowling face. Ragnhild came on, crouched behind her shield, and her spear levelled. Then, as fast as a hawk, Ragnhild dropped to one knee and brought her spear around in a wide sweep at the champion's ankles. She gasped and slammed her shield into the grass, trapping Ragnhild's spear behind its rim. Ragnhild let go of her spear and shield and launched herself at the champion, springing with the coiled power of a charging bull. She leapt over the champion's shield, crashed her knee into her opponent's face, fell to roll on the grass, and came up snarling to whip her axe free from its belt loop.

The Valkyrie champion roared and spat a gobbet of blood onto her shield before rising to draw her own axe. Her chest heaved with the exertion, and she charged at Ragnhild, labouring across the eyot and bringing her axe over her head in a wild swing that would carve Ragnhild in two. But it was an obvious elementary swing – a child could have seen it coming. It was an attack borne of exhaustion and desperation. Ragnhild stepped into it, coming within the champion's reach. She grabbed the wrist below the hand holding the axe and turned into her attacker's body, throwing the heavy woman over her hip.

The Valkyrie champion howled with rage as she flopped her back and tried to surge to her feet, but Ragnhild fell upon her chest and sliced the sharp blade of her axe on the fallen woman's cheek. It was a shallow, almost gentle cut, but blood flowed.

Ragnhild stood and held her axe aloft, blood showing bright on its shining blade. She raised the weapon high and screamed at the sky, bellowing to Odin to see her and allow her the chance to join his Einherjar.

"First cut!" Hundr shouted triumphantly and ran across the eyot to slap Ragnhild on the back. The defeated Valkyrie champion's second strode across the eyot and spat at Ragnhild's feet.

"Oathbreaking nithing," she hissed and helped her bested ally to her feet.

The fallen Valkyrie cuffed the smear of blood from her cheek and glowered at Ragnhild.

"You are a cheat and an oathbreaker. You disrespected the rules of the Holmgang," she said.

"I won," Ragnhild replied, and the two Valkyrie stormed away from her.

The Holmgang was over, and Ragnhild had won, but Hundr's stomach twisted as he joined Ragnhild and the acolyte in the rowboat. For although Ragnhild's victorious face flushed with colour for the first time since she had fought Herjolf, Hundr feared he was about to lose a friend.

They reached the lake's far shore, where Helgi waited, surrounded by her Valkyrie. The High Priestess stood with her feet planted shoulder-width apart and her hands on her hips. They were quickly joined by the other rowboat, and the champion bowled over the hull, stepping into the water, so keen was she to make the first landfall. She righted herself and scrambled up the shore, stumbling in her haste so that she had to brace herself with her two hands in the mud between the lake and shore.

"It was not a fair fight; she dropped her shield!" she cried out as she came upright, her face splashed with mud, and her brynjar and arms sullied with the brown filth.

"I made the first cut," Ragnhild said, leaping from the prow to land lithely on the grass-covered bank.

"There are sacred rules to a Holmgang, as you well know. There are countless years of tradition in single combat. It honours the gods and should be treated with respect."

"What has become of my order that the fierce Valkyries prize tradition over fierceness?" snarled Ragnhild.

"Your order?" said the tall woman who had been the champion's second. "Who do you think you are, you feral bitch?"

Ragnhild turned her head slowly to glower at the woman. "I have fought in countless battles across the Whale Road. I have sent more warriors howling to Valhalla than there are Valkyrie in this temple. And when I fight, I do so as though it were in battle. Full force, no quarter asked or given."

"You won the fight, but you did not follow the sacred rules," Helgi intoned, raising a hand to calm the combatants.

"She won the duel. She met your demands. So, she is a Valkyrie once more," said Hundr tersely. "Her oath is whole, and she is beloved by Odin once more."

"She is not until I say she is," the High Priestess shouted, and she took a step towards Hundr. His hand fell to the ivory hilt of Fenristooth. The lakeside suddenly exploded into a shouting melee of weapons hissing from scabbards and belt loops, spears being levelled, and curses being spat.

The Seaworm crew were calling to Hundr, and the clank and bang of their shields and weapons were behind him as they came to the aid of their Jarl. "I warn you, High Priestess, do not start something you cannot finish. This place can be awash with blood in moments."

"You warn *me*? The instrument of Odin in Midgard? Who do you think you are, barking like a puppy before a bear?" sneered Helgi, her nose high in the air.

"I am the Man with the Dog's Name. I killed Ivar the Boneless and Eystein Longaxe. I have killed Frankish lords and won a kingdom for Harald Fairhair. Do not take me for one of your acolytes. Ragnhild challenged your champion and won, and by that right, she is a Valkyrie once more. It seems to me your warriors here have seen little of battle these last years if your champion cannot fight for more than a few axe strokes without running short of breath. You need an experienced warrior like Ragnhild."

Helgi frowned and raised her eyes to the heavens. "She has defeated our champion, so Ragnhild has proved herself a warrior worthy of Odin's service. But these are dark times, and it is no easy feat to return to the service and glory of Odin." The High Priestess then looked directly at Ragnhild. "You must find redemption for the breaking of your oath. You have been away from our sisterhood for many years. It is not so simple to defy the All-Father and then stroll back into his service by winning a Holmgang."

"I won the fight," Ragnhild growled. "You said that if I won the Holmgang, I would be returned to the order."

"There is a task I must ask you to complete, sister Ragnhild, before we welcome you back into our sisterhood."

"What task?" asked Ragnhild.

"Odin's Gungnir spear was stolen from us. It must be returned."

SEVEN

"What do you mean he's gone missing?" said Einar, rising from his chair with a start. A press of people huddled in Vanylven's great Jarl hall. Farmers, merchants, warriors, potters, and fishermen. It was the one day per week where Einar would hear their disputes and complaints, and as Jarl, he would provide decisions and justice for those who believed themselves wronged in disputes over land borders, trading agreements, and even marriage disputes. Being away fighting at sea for so long meant that this was the first day of judgement held at Vanylven for months, and so men pushed and shoved to be heard by their leader. Everything from squabbles over hedgerows and damaged fishing boats to the more serious issues of murder and vendetta would all be brought before Einar for his judgement.

"Finn is gone, he isn't in his bed, and no one has seen him since yesterday," said Hildr. She had shouldered through the throng and stood before Einar's raised platform, atop which was a chair draped in white bear fur. Two farmers stared, gawping at Hildr. They were in the middle of an argument levelled against one by the other that he had moved a line of hedgerow which bordered their lands and had therefore stolen farmland.

"That boy is as prone to going missing as my bloody silver. Where is he?"

"If we knew that, he wouldn't be missing. Can you send the men out to look for him?"

"Has he gone riding? Taken out a boat to go fishing?"

"Einar, I don't know. That is why I am here. We need to look for him. What if someone has taken him again?" She wrung her hands, and Einar sighed.

"Amundr, Hekkr," he said, and two warriors who stood between Einar and the folk of Vanylven turned to him.

"Yes, my lord?" Hekkr answered. He was a short, wiry man who had lost more than half of his right ear and was the finest wrestler amongst Einar and Hundr's crews.

"Send our riders looking for Finn and get the Sea-Stallion out into the fjord. Nobody could have sailed past the barrier, but the little turd might be off fishing somewhere, worrying us all to death."

"Lord Einar," came a woman's voice from somewhere in the press of red-faced folk. People turned, mumbling and grumbling, and Einar peered into the mass of people but could not see who spoke.

"And Hekkr," Einar said. "Take a tracker. If someone has tried to snatch Finn again, they must have come in through the wall gate, which means a rider. If there are tracks, I want to know." Hekkr nodded and barked an order at the warriors to get horses ready.

"Lord Einar, it's about the boy. The Prince," came the woman's voice again; it was high-pitched and sounded desperate.

"Who is that?" Einar barked. The word 'prince' made him uneasy. Finn was the son of Ivar the Boneless and the Queen of Dublin; therefore, he was a prince, which was why men wanted to capture him. He was a living treasure, a human barrel of silver. His uncle, Halvdan Ragnarsson, had taken the throne in Dublin from the Queen and made no secret that he wanted Finn, the legitimate heir to the throne, dead. "Make way for whoever speaks."

Nobody moved, and Einar sighed, kneading his forehead with his hand. "Amundr, make them move."

Amundr grunted. He was as tall as Einar yet broader at the shoulder. Amundr's heavy boots banged on the hall's hard-packed earthen floor, and his mail shimmered as he moved. He towered over the commoners, and they shrank back from his red beard and grim face. His forehead overhanging his eyes made him look like a beast, a golem or a troll. Amundr shoved a brown-faced fisherman out of the way and reached into the press to grab the shoulder of a petite woman. He pulled her through and pushed a belligerent-looking merchant swathed in furs back with his enormous left hand. Amundr ushered the woman towards Einar, and she was tiny, the top of her head not even reaching as high as Amundr's chest

"Very well, little mouse, what is it you have to say?" Einar asked.

"I am sorry, my lord," she said, looking up at him with wide, brown eyes. Her face was elven-like, with a pointed chin and sharp ears poking through a mess of auburn hair. "But I saw the Prince yesterday."

"Don't call him that."

"Who, my lord?"

"Finn, don't call him that."

"Prince, my lord?"

Einar chewed the beard below his bottom lip and closed his eyes, wrestling with his own anger.

"Please," said Hildr putting her arm around the woman and smiling at her. "Tell us what you saw."

The woman swallowed and shot Einar a fearful look. "Well, my lady, I saw the Prin... Finn Ivarsson climbing aboard Jarl Hundr's ship yesterday whilst everyone was busy loading her up."

"You saw Finn go aboard the Seaworm? Are you sure?" Hildr asked.

"Yes, my lady. I am sure. He's a handsome little fellow, and I watched him sneak over the side and then disappear into the darkness below the steerboard."

"So, he's a stowaway with Hundr, then. Thanks be to Thor that he's safe," said Einar.

"Safe?" Hildr exclaimed, crossing her arms in frustration. "He has sailed off on the Seaworm to the Odin temple at Upsala with Hundr."

"Sounds safe to me. Who is going to attack Hundr?"

"Have the gods replaced the insides of your thought cage with turnips?" said Hildr, and there was a rumble of laughter around the hall. "When have you ever known Hundr to be out of trouble?

It follows him like flies on shit."

Einar frowned, not because of what Hildr said, which was true, but because she had mocked him in front of the petitioners. "That's all for today. Clear out now. I will hear all grievances next week," he announced. The hall erupted into groans and complaints, which Einar waved away. Hekkr and Amundr eased them out, telling the more vociferous crowd members to be quiet or risk a slap around the skull.

"But, Jarl Einar, the hedge on Five Crow field?" asked one of the supplicant farmers.

Einar grumbled to himself. "Kari says you moved the hedge ten years ago whilst he was at sea, and you both have witnesses. So, the hedge stays where it is, but Kari, you will give this man two sheep before the moon is full. Ten years is a long time, almost enough for ownership of that field to change just by right of possession," Einar said. The men both shot him thunderous frowns and stormed from the hall. Neither was happy; therefore, Einar believed he had made the right decision. "Now, everyone out. Wait, not you," he said, looking at the tiny woman. She stayed where she was, staring at Einar with her large eyes. "What was your business here today?"

"My lord, I came about my father's fishing boat."

"What about it?"

"My father died, my lord. And our neighbours took his boat. It's our only way of making a living, my brothers and I."

"Who took it?"

"Bjarni, my lord, and his son, both fishermen," she said, pointing a trembling finger towards two squat figures in woollen jerkins who were clutching wide-brimmed hats in their fingers. They had sun-darkened faces, made darker by the dirt engrained into the creases and corners around their eyes and noses.

"You there, Bjarni," Einar called after the two fishermen, and all the folk bustling to leave the hall stopped to stare, so loud was Einar's voice. Immediately the elder of the two men turned and offered Einar a crooked, toothless smile and bowed his head.

"Come here," Einar ordered. Bjarni licked his lips and shuffled toward Einar, turning his hat as he came, his son trailing behind him.

"Yes, Jarl Einar?" said Bjarni, his eyes flitting to the small woman and back to Einar, the words lisping and mangled by his gums.

"Did you take this woman's boat? The boat that was her father's?"

"No, my lord, I...."

"Don't lie to me," Einar growled and stepped close to the fisherman. Einar wore his mail and a fur cloak. He was a big man anyway, whereas Bjarni was only a hand taller than the tiny woman, so Einar towered over him, dwarfing Bjarni in both height and breadth.

"Well, I found a ship, my lord, and well...."

"Return it. Today. Or I will come to your village myself and take it. And if I come, then I bring my axe and my warriors."

The fisherman's eyes scrunched closed, and he grimaced. "Yes, Lord Einar."

"And another thing....." Einar said as the old blackguard tried to scuttle away. Bjarni's shoulders shuddered, and he turned back to Einar. "This woman is under my protection. If any harm comes to her, I will hold you responsible."

The fisherman bowed and scraped and hurried from the hall, jostling his way through the crowd at the door, and the woman bowed to Einar, then grabbed his gnarled hand and kissed his busted knuckles.

"That's enough of that now. Come to me if he doesn't return the boat," said Einar and returned to his seat, scowling at Hildr. "You shouldn't chide me like that." He sat down heavily. Making judgements made Einar weary and gave him headaches. He had always thought becoming a Jarl would bring land, wealth, freedom, and the fulfilment of his dreams. But it made him tired.

"Like what?" said Hildr.

"Head full of turnips?"

"Yes... that was a bit strong. I am sorry, my love." Hildr came to him, kissed Einar's forehead, and lifted his hand to caress her soft face. "What are we going to do about Finn?"

"He is at sea now with Hundr...which has its dangers. You are right about that. But he is not a child anymore. I was his age when I first went to sea and not much older than when I first served his father, Ivar. He is not lost or taken; he just wants to be a warrior and a Viking. It's in his blood."

"I know, but he is still so young."

"He is, but he is strong and quick. We can't keep him here swaddled in furs forever. There is much of his father in him."

Hildr smiled at Einar and smoothed his beard. "You look tired."

"I feel it. I thought this would be easier."

"You have what you have always wanted; you are a Jarl with land of your own. Vanylven is beautiful."

"It is. But there is always something to attend to, someone who wants something. There is no peace. Sometimes I miss the sea, miss being a Viking."

"You will always be that Einar the Brawler."

At that moment, their conversation was abruptly brought to a halt.

"Jarl Einar, you have a visitor," a man announced from across the hall.

"See?" Einar sighed, and Hildr kissed him again. "Who is it?" Einar called, but before the warrior could answer, a lean figure strode into the hall wearing a broad smile and a cloak of fine blue wool.

"Jarl Einar, Vanylven looks almost as beautiful as your wife," enounced the visitor.

"Lord Rognvald," said Einar, rising to greet Rognvald the Ulfheðnar, who was the right-hand man of King Harald Fairhair and always came like a storm crow from the King with a new task or command. Einar's stomach turned sour, but he forced a smile onto his broad face.

"What can he want?" whispered Hildr. Rognvald approached, and three of his warriors slinked into the hall. They were slim men, not hulking or formidable looking, but they were Ulfheðnar like Rognvald and, in the heat of battle, would turn into raging wolf warriors, fighting with supreme strength, akin to the deranged and reckless of death or injury. "Herjolf was the last of the rebels. That was supposed to be the final time Harald would call for our service."

Rognvald drew close, and Einar shook his head slightly at Hildr. She was right, and Herjolf was supposed to be the last, but he needed her to be respectful to Rognvald. There was no cunning in angering the King of all Norway, or his First Lord, his advisor and the most powerful man in the kingdom after the King himself.

"Is Hundr not with you at Vanylven?" asked Rognvald. He stood straight-backed before Einar's raised platform and searched the hall with his quick eyes. Einar beckoned to a serving boy to fetch Rognvald and his men some ale, and as the boy shuffled quickly across the floor rushes to bring a mug to Rognvald and each of his men, Einar stepped down from the high chair's platform to stand on equal footing with the King's man.

"He is at sea with the Seaworm."

"Will he be gone long?"

Einar shrugged. "He has taken Ragnhild to Upsala, to the temple of her order."

Rognvald nodded knowingly and took a sip of his ale. Rognvald had fought alongside Einar and Hundr many times during Harald Fairhair's war to become King. They had stormed Vanylven itself together when Ragnhild had scaled the fjord barrier to open the way for Rognvald's ships. The old Jarl had died following that battle, and the King had passed its rule to Einar.

"So, Herjolf is dead. Harald is pleased."

"That's the last of the bastards. Nobody left for the King to fight now," Einar forced another smile and studied Rognvald's face for any sign that might give away the reason for his visit. He feared that there would be another demand to fight, another order to risk his life in servitude to the King. Rognvald was a young man, younger than Hundr, and had seen less than thirty summers. His blonde hair was long and braided, and he had a smooth face with a sparse beard. He was not a tall man, nor was he broad in the shoulder. He wore a shining brynjar and had a fine sword belted at his waist in a fleece-lined scabbard. His arms were thick with rings, and he wore a thick silver chain doubled about his neck.

"Just so," said Rognvald. "But a king always has enemies, Jarl Einar."

"Well, thanks be to the gods, the rebels are dead, and we have fought hard these last four years to secure Harald's throne. Time for a rest now; I am getting old, Rognvald. We will fetch food for you and your men, and you can tell me why we are so honoured by your visit."

"You have fought hard, Jarl Einar. And I thank you for the offer of food, but we will take only a quick meal and re-stock our ship if you don't mind. Unfortunately, I must be away."

"Of course, I will have my men see to your ship

right away."

"My thanks. What you say is true – Herjolf was the last of the rebels from before the war. The last of the survivors from the battle at Hafrsfjord. The last but one."

"Rollo?"

"Just so. King Harald let him live, as you know, and he has gone on to become a powerful lord in Frankia. He has lands and ships and men, and he allied with the King of the Franks."

"He was a bastard then, and he is a bastard now."

Rognvald chuckled. "He has never openly challenged the King nor fought against him. Yet, there have been raids on islands, ships taken, and men killed – attacks on the King, not by rebels or by Rollo himself. But we have a description from a man who survived one such attack. He spoke of a warrior with flame-red hair, whose face was burned and fire twisted. A man like that serves Rollo, or so men say."

"Sounds like Rollo is sending his man to attack the King then. He hated Harald, fought against him with fury, right until the moment he saw his chance to live in the ashes of defeat, and left Hafrsfjord with four ships and his cause and comrades in bloody ruin."

Rognvald drained his cup and held it out

for the serving boy to collect. He wiped his moustache on the back of his hand. "Thank you for the ale. The King wants you to find this burned man and send him screaming to Niflheim." Rognvald spoke plainly and in an even tone. He adjusted his belt and met Einar's gaze with unflinching eyes.

"He wants me to kill this man?"

"Just so. Find him and kill him. Men cannot raid Norway and live. Not whilst Harald is King."

"But the rebels are dead," said Einar, trying not to frown or raise his voice. "I have served the King well; is there no other who can perform this task? My place is here, in Vanylven. I am not an assassin."

Rognvald laughed and clapped Einar on the shoulder. "You are a warrior and a killer, Einar Rosti. You will kill this man for the King. Sail to Frankia, find him and send him screaming to Niflheim, and then the King will grant you peace."

"I thought he would grant me peace after Herjolf."

"You are Jarl of Vanylven, and you swore an oath to serve Harald as Jarl. You own and rule these lands, but you swore to fight for the King whenever he calls. He is calling."

Einar sighed and nodded. There could be

no argument; indeed, he had sworn the oath. Deflated, he glanced at Hildr. She shook her head slightly, and her lips turned in on themselves. Her head hardly moved at all, but enough for Einar to understand her meaning. They had only just returned to Vanylven, and they often spoke of how they planned to spend time together, walking in the hills surrounding the fjord and riding out to visit the lands within Einar's jarldom. Einar wanted that too, he wanted to spend time with Hildr, and he had wanted to be a powerful Jarl his whole life; that had been his life's ambition and the reason he told himself that he fought and risked his life. But he was also a Viking; he loved the sea. And, like all warriors, there was the thing unspoken, the thing a man bragged about when he was young and feigned weariness of when he grew old. He loved to fight.

"I am no assassin, Rognvald," Einar repeated, Hildr's eyes boring into him like hot coals dropped on fresh snow. "And we are not long returned from the battle with Herjolf. But, if I do this thing for King Harald, if I find and kill this burned man, can you give me your word that I won't be called upon for one year? Give me that much."

Rognvald smiled, his gleaming pearl-white teeth highlighting his handsome face. "Anything for a warrior and Jarl of your stature and reputation, Einar Rosti. Find this man, punish him for attacking the King, and you will have your year of peace. I swear it in the name of King Harald."

Einar clasped forearms with Rognvald but dared not meet Hildr's eye. He must take to the Whale Road again in service of the King and pick up his axe once more. Finn was at sea with Hundr, and Einar was as worried as Hildr about the lad, despite his efforts to reassure her. Einar loved Hildr, but their dream of warm fires and long walks would have to wait because, once again, their world would be filled with drakkars, axes, brynjars and blood.

EIGHT

"She lied," Ragnhild seethed through clenched teeth. Beneath a crisp sky filled with small hurrying clouds, they marched up a winding path, around a standing stone carved with a cruel god face, and towards the high temple itself.

"She did, but she is the High Priestess, and she makes the rules. She speaks with Odin's voice in Midgard, and she is the only person who can let you back into the order," said Hundr. Helgi strode before them, her robes billowing behind her; she walked briskly, flanked by her Valkyrie guards, who marched silently.

"She is punishing me. Taking petty revenge for when we were girls here. She was of a similar age as Hildr and me, and they taught us axe and spear together."

"Why would she want to punish you?"

"As girls, they put us in troops of six, and I was the leader of our troop. I was hard on her because she was the weakest."

"Then she has done well to rise so high."

"It is easy to rise when all the warriors are at sea, dying in battle or away fighting all the time. She rarely left Upsala, rising through the ranks here, sacrificing, praying, and learning lore – gaining power and influence through her piety and devotion to Odin rather than with a blade in her hand. Or so it was when I was a sister, anyway. The revenge she wreaks upon me now is a small thing for her, but it jeopardises my place in the afterlife." Ragnhild swallowed, her fingers toying with the spear amulet around her neck, and for the first time in all their years together, Hundr thought he saw fear in her one eye.

Valkyrie sisters heaved open the monstrous doors which formed the high curving gateway to the temple, and Helgi strode into the darkness beyond. Hundr followed, and a shiver ran down his neck as he entered the gloom. The air was thick with fragrant smoke that reeked of fungus and dried plants. He coughed, and his ears rang with the chanting which had not ceased since they had entered Upsala. Inside the temple, that chanting was loud and rhythmic. Hundr's head swam with the noise of it. There was a foulness to the air when he breathed it in, the smoke seeping through his lungs and making his mind float. He felt like vomiting and fought to keep his senses against the assault of the Odin chamber.

Helgi stopped suddenly and raised her pale arms. Hundr took a step back as he noticed the rearing malevolence of a carved and brightly painted totem behind her. It was higher than two halls standing on top of one another, made from one huge, thick tree trunk. Carved runes, ravens and axes in twisting pictures curled around the trunk. It rose into a hideous, bearded, one-eyed face. It loomed above Hundr, eyeing and judging him fiercely and cruelly. He couldn't tell if the wicked slash of its mouth grinned or grimaced at him.

"Odin," he whispered, and he heard the murmurs of his men behind him as they entered the sacred temple.

Other totem statues flanked great Odin, smaller but just as formidable. There were bearded faces, soft faces of female gods, more ravens, boars and axes. Through the smoke, Hundr could make out the Mjolnir hammer of Thor beneath a bearded visage; he saw the fierce face of Njorth above writhing sea monsters and Frigg weeping for the death of her son Baldr in her wetland hall at Fensalir with sprigs of mistletoe winding around her carved hands.

"Traitors have defiled this sacred temple," Helgi boomed, her arms still raised and her face twisting into a rictus of rage in the swirling smoke. "They have stolen Odin's spear, Gungnir, the silver spear of the All-Father, destined to slay the monster wolf, Fenris, on the day of Ragnarök."

"Who stole it?" said Ragnhild, striding forwards and looking up and down the length of the Odin totem. "How did they get in here?"

"One of our own sisters stole it. Sigdriffa, now known as the Defiler. She and sisters loyal to her stole the sacred spear and left Upsala. We must return it. We must return the spear to Odin, or all Midgard is at peril. If Ragnarök descends upon us and we do not have the spear, then the great serpent Jormungandr will devour the world, and Fenris will ravage our souls. How can the All-Father stop the Loki brood without his sacred spear?" Helgi sobbed those last words and then collapsed on her knees. The surrounding Valkyrie wailed, clawing at the carved faces, and Hundr was breathing hard. He wanted to run from the place; the foul smoke and totems were smothering him. This was the closest a man could come to the Aesir themselves. They felt so close he could almost reach out and touch the gods.

"Why would Sigdriffa steal Odin's spear?" asked Ragnhild, but Helgi and her Valkyrie sisters were rocking and wailing, mad with despair.

"Grab one of them, one you know, and bring her outside," said Hundr. There could be no sense spoken in that place, where the Bifrost bridge itself could appear at any moment. That rainbow bridge linked the world of men in Midgard to the realm of the Aesir gods, Asgard. Sweat seeped from Hundr's brow, and he cuffed it from his eyes. His heart pounded, and he had to get out of the place if he wanted his head to be capable of any clear thinking. Hundr turned and dashed from the temple. His men followed, and they burst from the doors into the pathways, each one resting his hands on his knees, bent double, coughing. They were wide-eyed, not speaking a word, each struck with the same feeling of the presence of the gods and all fearing Helgi's cries as she spoke of the end of the world.

Ragnhild came last from the doors, and she had a Valkyrie warrior priestess by the arm, dragging her out into the sunlight. The priestess fell to her knees between Hundr and Ragnhild, her shoulders shaking and her hands over her face.

"Jari," Ragnhild said, but the Valkyrie couldn't hear her, so deep was she within her pit of despair. Ragnhild shook the kneeling Valkyrie. "Jari, why did Sigdriffa steal the spear?"

Jari continued to rock and wail, so Ragnhild slapped her across the face – so hard that Jari fell backwards onto the pathway, sprawling in the gravel. She snapped out of her despair, glowering at Ragnhild with a hand held to her reddening cheek.

"Why did Sigdriffa steal Gungnir?" demanded Ragnhild. Jari scrambled to her feet, looking from the temple and back to Ragnhild.

"She fell into a dispute with High Priestess Helgi and stole the spear to make a new order of the Valkyrie elsewhere. She departed with a crew of our finest warriors and left us here with our grief, fearful of the wrath of the All-Father. What will become of us if Ragnarök falls upon us and Odin cannot find his spear with which to slay Fenris?"

Ragnhild held onto Jari's hands to calm her. She was a young Valkyrie warrior with dark hair twisted into braids and tied atop her head in a bun. She had blue eyes and a face unscarred by childhood disease or battle.

"What did this Sigdriffa and Helgi argue about?" asked Hundr.

"Sigdriffa thought we had grown weak, that we were not riding or sailing out to fight as much as we had when Vattnar was High Priest. She believed our duty is to fight and kill, and to be slain ourselves in glorious battle, all in the service of Odin All-Father."

"Is that not the nature of your order?" Hundr pressed.

"Yes," shrugged Jari.

"So, what was there to disagree with?"

"Helgi believes we should pray more, be more worshipful in our actions and be more devoted to the Aesir. Rather than fighting, we should pray and offer greater sacrifices to Odin, Thor, Frigg, Njorth, Heimdall, and the rest of the Aesir."

"She doesn't want to fight?" Ragnhild intoned. Jari cast her eyes to the ground to avoid the question, and Ragnhild shook her head in disgust. "It was ever the case. So, Sigdriffa took the spear to start the order anew elsewhere."

"Yes," said Jari.

"And she took the best of you, the fighters. Which is why your champion was so easy to defeat?"

"Yes."

"Tell me more of this spear. Is it truly Odin's spear, or just one made to look like Gungnir?" said Hundr. If the spear was what the Valkyrie believed it to be, then its theft put the very existence of Midgard in peril. Indeed, they certainly believed, given the scenes of utter despair inside the temple.

"The spear taken from this temple has rested here longer than anyone can remember," said Jari. "It was here before the temple and before the figures of the Aesir you saw within. It is said that Odin left it here for safekeeping, outside of Asgard and beyond Loki's reach. Dwarves fashioned it back in the days when Midgard was young. The Sons of Ivaldi hammered its silver head under the guidance of the famed dwarven blacksmith Dvalin. Loki stole the spear from the dwarves and presented the weapon to Odin to atone for cutting Sif's golden hair. It is the perfect spear, so finely balanced that no matter who throws it, it would still strike its target with deathly precision."

Hundr turned and walked to his men, leaving Ragnhild with Jari. *Could it really be the spear of Odin? Or merely a copy forged by a skilled smith?*

"These women are bloody mad," grumbled Bush. He and the rest of the crew stood silent, pale-faced and shocked at what they had seen inside the temple.

"They believe the fate of the very world is at peril. The High Priestess wants us to go after this spear," said Hundr, and he looked for the reaction of his men. His head told him that the spear could not be real; it couldn't possibly be Odin's famed silver spear itself. But his heart and the reactions of the Valkyrie made him wary and fearful of the gods. What if Loki could bring Ragnarök down upon them, unleash his children, the monsters like Fenris, Jormungandr and other giant beasts, to tear the world asunder? Hundr hardly thought it possible, but he'd led his life with the purpose of being brave and pleasing Odin, of forging enough of a reputation to earn his place in Valhalla and join the ranks of the Einherjar. The very purpose of the Einherjar was to fight for Odin on the day of Ragnarök, which, without the spear, was a battle that could not be won. If Odin failed to slay the great wolf, then Fenris would maul the Einherjar with his mighty jaws and cast Midgard under the dominion of Loki.

"Can it be so?" asked Thorgrim. He clutched his Mjolnir pendant, the hammer of Thor. Each of the men held their own talismans, spears for Odin, boars for Frey, and ships for Njorth.

"If the only way for Ragnhild to get back into the Valkyrie order is to get the spear, and by retrieving it, we perform a service for Odin, then we should sail," said Finn Ivarsson, and all eyes turned to him. He alone amongst them was grinning, no sign of fear or apprehension on his handsome face. Finn stared at each man and then at Hundr. "Imagine the songs of it, the reputation in it. The men who rescued Gungnir from the hands of Loki's own warriors and saved the world?"

The men cheered at that. There were nods and

the shifting of boots. Finn had stirred them, and the lad smiled at Hundr, hunger in his eyes.

High Priestess Helgi strode from the temple doors. She had regained her composure and glared down at Hundr and his crew.

"Well?" she said. "Ragnhild, will you do this thing? Will you recover Odin's sacred spear?"

"If we do it," Hundr interjected, grasping the cool ivory sword hilt at his belt, "you swear you will restore Ragnhild to the Valkyrie order. No more quibbles or quests. We bring the spear back, and you, as Odin's representative in Midgard, make Ragnhild a Valkyrie. With no questions of oaths broken, and you will pray to Odin to pave the path for her to Valhalla?"

"If you return the spear, it will be so. But you must take a troop of our sisters with you. Six Valkyries will join your crew and ensure Gungnir's safe return."

"No," said Hundr. "We have enough warriors to crew the Seaworm. We cannot take passengers."

"I insist on it," Helgi retorted, crossing her arms. "This is a task in service of the gods, and it must be the Valkyrie who return it. We cannot have your... warriors... pawing at a weapon belonging to the Aesir." She looked his men up and down, disdain pulling at the corners of her mouth. The Seaworm crew bristled.

"There is no finer crew on the Whale Road," said Hundr. "We have seen today the quality of your fighters. If the best of them have gone with this Sigdriffa, then what need have we of the dregs?"

It was the Valkyries' turn to stiffen, spears levelled, and hands fell to axe hafts.

Ragnhild glanced at Hundr, her face hard and her one eye blazing. Ragnhild would lay her life down for him in an instant. She had risked it countless times and had lost lovers and friends fighting under his orders. Hundr nodded. He could not deny her this task and would not deny her the chance to find contentment and purpose with her order. Nor could he resist the task because Finn was right. There was reputation in it, a fight for Odin, a saga for the ages.

"Very well, we will take your Valkyrie," he said. "We sail today." *For Ragnhild, and for Valhalla.*

NINE

The Seaworm took to the Whale Road, running south on the wind through the Gotland strait and around the islands and peninsulas of the Danes. Waves crashed upon the hull, spume jetting into the wind, spraying the deck and their faces with ice-cold salt water. Bush kept to safe bays and coves at night, and they waited for two days at an inlet south of Sjaelland for a favourable wind. Once the sail billowed and the one-eye sigil stretched tautly, Bush sped north past Kattegat. It was sea-Jarl country. Every island, beach head and cove was inhabited by war Danes and sea wolves. The crew whooped with delight as they sped across the surging sea, away from any beast head prows who might see them as easy pickings. After that, the ship came about south and followed the coast. Hundr would stand at the prow and glory in the salty spray on his face and the wind in his hair, and the high speeds combined with the thrill of the rolling waves distracted them all from the souring presence of the Valkyrie.

The six warrior priestesses huddled close to the steerboard, much to Bush's disgust. They kept to themselves, hooded and grumbling. They took their rations of ale and food but did not take a turn at an oar, and their only interactions with the crew were sneers of contempt or mumbled curses. One of the six was the champion Ragnhild had bested at Upsala, and with her, her tall, whip-faced second.

"Do they even talk to you?" Hundr asked Ragnhild on a fresh morning as the Seaworm clipped along the white-tipped waves off the small island of Heligoland.

"Only to say that they heard some of Sigdriffa's warriors talking of sailing for Frankia to take land there and make a new Upsala," said Ragnhild. She sat on a rowing bench, checking the feathered fletchings of her arrows. "You know this; that is why we make for Frankia. Other than that, they say little."

"They make the crew uneasy. Talk to them, Ragnhild. If it comes to a fight, we need to know if we can trust them or not. What do you know of Sigdriffa?"

"Little. I don't remember her from my time at

the temple. So, she is young and fierce. She wants to fight, make her reputation."

"Sounds like you."

"And you. She sounds like any Viking hungry for the shield wall. But she should not have taken the spear...she has dishonoured Odin and broken her oath."

"So, talk to the Valkyrie, find out what you can. Sigrid will do the same."

"Very well," Ragnhild nodded, and she placed the arrows back into their quiver, covering the top with a fleece to protect the missiles from the corrosive seawater. "If Sigdriffa has gone to Frankia, you know where she will be?"

"I know. Rollo. It can't be Haesten, even though he was once the most powerful Viking in Frankia. I heard from a merchant in Vanylven that the Franks threw him out of his island stronghold last year, and so Haesten is now in the Saxon lands, fighting King Alfred. Without question, it must be Rollo."

"We have heard the rumours that Rollo has forged a place for himself there – he grew rich and powerful."

"So they say." The last time Hundr had seen Rollo had been during the aftermath of the battle of Hafrsfjord when the tall warrior had cut the throat of his lord, Kjotve the Rich, to save his own skin and sailed away with ships and warriors. His betrayal brought about the end of a war, making him a powerful Jarl.

"We should have killed the bastard on Orkney, where we found him chained and emptying Ketil Flatnose's shit pail. Rollo hates you."

"He does, and he hates King Harald for taking his father's land. Rollo stole one of my ships and led us on a merry dance, and it seems we must face him again. He is arrogant as well as ambitious, and if a crew of Valkyrie warrior priestesses turns up at his door with the spear of Odin asking to set up a new temple to worship Odin, his pride won't let him refuse."

"He fancies himself a great Jarl," Ragnhild said, and she spat over the side. "Yet he is a betrayer, a turncloak and an assassin."

"He fancies himself a King."

The weather turned still and warm as the Seaworm reached the low-lying islands off northern Frisia, and the crew rowed in search of wind. Hundr took a turn, stretching his back muscles and keeping time with the rest of the crew. Finn Ivarsson also took his turn at a bench, and the crew laughed with him the following day when his back and arm muscles burned like irons in a brazier. He welcomed the break from bailing the bilge and took to the oar eagerly. The day after, Finn retook his turn, and Hundr noted the nods of respect amongst the seasoned warriors, hard men like Thorgrim and Sigvarth. Some of the Seaworm men had served Finn's father many years ago, and like Hundr, they could see something of the Boneless in the boy who was rapidly becoming a man. It surprised Hundr how the crew had warmed to him. He had thought Finn a stubborn, prideful boy who had stowed away on the Seaworm because Einar wouldn't let him have his own way. But he had bailed the bilge without complaint, and now he rowed with the men, and they had taken to him. In the evenings, they would invite Finn to eat with them, to listen to their tales of the gods, old battles, and stories of bravery. He learned their songs and sang with them as they heaved back on their oars against the power of the sea. Hundr even found himself clapping Finn on the back and nodding approvingly as he hauled on the halyard as though he had been at sea his whole life.

Sigrid and Ragnhild spent an increasing amount of time with the Valkyrie, and after a few days, the women took their meals together, and some of the hostility seemed to vanish. During such a time, under a midday sun, and as the men sang a rowing shanty about the fair maidens of Kattegat, Hundr approached the women. They were at the steerboard, leaning over the side and talking in bright voices. Laughter pealed out occasionally as Sigrid told them a tale of her father, Ketil Flatnose. Hundr waited, holding on to the rigging, listening as Sigrid spoke of Ketil being chased by her mother with a broom around his great hall, and the Valkyrie laughed again. Bush stood above them, one hand on the tiller and the other tucked into his belt beside his paunch. He frowned at the Valkyrie and raised his eyes to the clouds when he noticed Hundr watching him.

"Sounds like a bawdy tale," piped Hundr, shouting to be heard over the snorts of amusement.

"Sigrid tells a good story," said one of the Valkyrie, a short woman with tattoos writhing across her cheek.

"That she does. Hopefully, she hasn't told you any about me."

"She told us one about old Bush up there," chimed the big champion from Upsala, who Hundr now knew to be Skögul. "She says he earned his nickname when he was shot by an arrow whilst taking a shit behind a bush. Can it be true?"

The Valkyrie women sniggered, and when Bush harrumphed and grumbled under his breath, they laughed hard, some having to rest their hands on their knees as they did so.

"It's true," smiled Hundr. "But there isn't a finer shipmaster in all Midgard." He took a step forward, nearing closer to Skögul. "We will reach Frankia today or tomorrow," Hundr said, still smiling. "What can you tell me of this Sigdriffa? I hate to spoil your fun, but anything you can tell me might be useful if it comes to a fight." Skögul walked away from her sisters and left them to their joking. Sigrid was in the thick of them, recounting another story to keep their good humour up. It was certainly a change from their previous surliness, which had plagued the voyage from Upsala to Frisia.

"Sigdriffa is the best of us," said Skögul. "She was the Valkyrie champion before she left."

"She is prideful and an oathbreaker," a brusque voice interjected. It was Gunnr, the tall, hawk-faced warrior who had seconded Skögul at the Holmgang, and leader of the Valkyrie troop aboard the Seaworm. "She fights like a Loki demon, fast and ruthless, and she is clever."

"Would she fight fellow Valkyrie?" asked Hundr.

"She believes she is right, that what she is doing serves Odin. So, yes, she would kill us without a second thought."

"If it comes to a fight, you and your warriors will join our shield wall. I give the orders, and you follow." Hundr fixed Gunnr with his one eye. Her face twisted in anger, but she measured him for a heartbeat. She saw a Viking warrior of reputation. He wore a patch over his dead eye, but his face and arms were crisscrossed with battle scars. She knew of his reputation, and those thoughts played out on her face as anger turned to recognition of simple logic. "It must be so. We must fight as one."

"The spear is sacred to us," said Gunnr. "When we retrieve it, one of our sisterhood must hold it. That is why we are here; it cannot fall into the hands of the impure. The fate of the world rests upon us."

Hundr leaned on the sheer strake, the sun warming his face. "Sigdriffa believes she is serving Odin by taking the spear to find a new temple and return the Valkyrie order to what she believes it should be. You and Helgi want it back because you believe you have the right to it in Upsala. I wonder what Odin thinks, who he wants as the protector of his spear? We will find these renegade Valkyrie, and if we must, we will put them to the sword. I don't do it for Helgi or you or because I think your cause is nobler than Sigdriffa's. I do this for Ragnhild, and so do these men. We will fight, kill, and risk our lives for her, just as she would for us. That is what we believe in."

Hundr did not look to Gunnr for a response. He just wanted her to be clear on the way of things. The coastline shimmered, hazed by the sun's warmth across the sea, and Hundr saw an object moving through the faint landward greens and browns of what could be Frisia or Frankia, depending on how far south they had sailed. He leaned and squinted to pick out the object and recognised the rise and fall of oar blades.

"Ship!" Hundr called, pointing at the distant vessel. Warriors not at their oars stopped their idle talk and raced to the side.

"It's coming this way," said Valbrandr. "Can you make out a flag or sigil?"

"Not at this distance," Hundr replied.

"Young Finn, you have good eyes," said Bush. "What can you see?"

Finn leapt nimbly between rowing benches, weaving around rigging to join Bush on the steerboard platform.

"It's a ship," said Finn.

"We bloody know that." Bush clipped Finn lightly around the ear. "Is it a drakkar, a snekke, or a karve?" Finn stared at him with an open mouth, and Bush took off his stained leather helmet liner and wrung it between his fists. The crew sniggered at his frustration. "Is it a fat-bellied waddling karve, a merchant's ship, or long and sharp like a knife blade? If it is long and sleek, is it bigger or smaller than the Seaworm? If it's smaller, it's a snekke, and we outnumber the bastards. Same size or bigger means it's a drakkar and crewed with as many fighters as we have."

Finn nodded and peered over the side. "It's a drakkar," he confirmed. "Hard to say, but around the same size as the Seaworm. She travels under oars and flies a banner. I think it's a wolf's head or a mouse."

"Why would a warship fly a mouse banner?" Bush made to clip Finn's ear again, but the boy ducked away from the blow.

"I am just telling you what I can see. Maybe it's a wolf?"

"Don't try to outrun her," said Hundr. "It's only one ship. She won't attack us if our numbers are even, so let's try to talk to them. See if they have seen the Valkyrie or know where we can find the Vikings in Frankia."

Bush brought the Seaworm about, one bank of oars rising to drip glistening beads of water into the swell as the warship turned, her hull slicing through the waves, sending salty spume to whip Hundr's face. They beat towards the oncoming ship, and she was indeed a drakkar with a wolf banner flapping on her mast, proud and snarling.

"What if they're as blood mad as you are?" asked Bush as they neared closer to the wolf vessel. "You have attacked ships of equal size before."

"Make weapons ready, just in case," Hundr barked. Bush was right. Vikings were unpredictable, war-hungry and craving battle and reputation. The captain or Jarl on that ship could be a pup looking to make a name for himself. Many on the Whale Road knew the single-eye banner meant the Man with the Dog's Name. "Anyone not rowing, gather spears and blades in the bilge and be ready. Valkyrie, ready your bows."

Ragnhild and Sigrid were already bending their eastern recurved bows across the backs of their legs and around their hips to loop dry strings over the horn nooks at their bowstaves' tips. Gunnr and Skögul followed them, as did the remaining four Valkyrie.

Bush ordered oars raised as they came within two ships' lengths of the approaching vessel, and the crew brought them to standing, resting the base of their oars on the deck between their legs so that the oar blades pointed straight up towards the sky. They would be ready to spring into action if the parlay with the wolf ship turned sour, either to slap their oars back into the water and power the Seaworm to safety or to pole away the wolf ship should her warriors try to get close enough to board. Hundr's heart quickened, men gathered at the wolf ship's prow, and for a thrilling moment, he contemplated boarding her. Drawing his swords and leaping onto her deck to cut and slash at her crew, taking everything from them, their lives, their silver and their ship. That was the Viking way, the Odin way. He glanced at Valbrandr, muscled shoulders rippling beneath his jerkin, and at Sigvarth, whose cheek muscles worked beneath his beard. They were thinking the same thing because the Seaworm crew were fighters, killers, and Vikings. Hundr let out a long breath. He was not here for plunder or glory; he was only here for Ragnhild.

Hundr leaned over the side and raised a hand in greeting at the men in the wolf ship's prow, thoughts of battle and victory quashed. A warrior there returned the gesture. The ships drew close.

"I am Jarl Hundr. Well met, friends," he called across the bows.

"I am Kvasir Randversson," came the reply from a man wearing a black hood with his hand raised in greeting.

"Anybody know that name?" Hundr said to his crew in a hushed voice. Shoulders shrugged, and men shook their heads. "Are you a Dane?" Hundr called, suspecting he was by his accent, but the man's voice was strangely muffled or slurred.

"I am a Norseman," Kvasir called back. The wolf ship came alongside, and bearded faces stared across her sheer strake above a line of shields, all painted with the snarling wolf symbol. Men with hard eyes and wind-burned faces. Seamen, Vikings. "So, you are the famous Jarl Hundr," said Kvasir. The two ships were only an oars' length apart, and men on each ship slipped oars into the water to keep them as steady as possible. "I have heard of you."

"We are looking for a ship sailed from Upsala. Maybe it came this way?" said Hundr.

"We see many ships passing this way. This is Frankia. Are you coming here for trouble?"

Kvasir spoke like he patrolled the coastline, which meant he either served the lord of this stretch of land or he himself was the lord. Spear points bristled behind the bearded faces on Kvasir's ship, and Hundr sensed his own men tensing around him, the scrapes and clangs of iron where his men readied weapons between rowing benches, out of sight.

"Women crewed the ship, warriors all. Have you seen them?"

"We don't exchange pleasantries like this with every ship that sails this strait. Your ship is a warship, and you have a reputation. Are you here for war?" Kvasir's muffled voice became stern and clipped. His dark hood covered his face, and it flickered in the breeze. The two crews were silent, glaring at each other as both ships bobbed on the tide. Eyes connected across the sheer strakes, each judging the man opposite them, wondering how skilled or savage he was. Was he a killer, or would he fall back from the flashing blades if it came to a fight?

"I said we are looking for a ship of warrior women. We are not here for trouble. Are you a Jarl to talk to me this way?"

Kvasir stiffened. "I am not. My Jarl rules these lands, and I watch these seas for pirates and raiders. Such men are not welcome here, men with reputations for murder."

"Who is your Jarl?"

"Jarl Rollo Ganger, you two are old friends, I believe," said Kvasir, and a murmur rumbled through his crew like a rock rolling down a mountain. A gust of wind rushed across the sea, and the wolf ship dipped in the swell. Kvasir's hood blew back to reveal a thick rope of red hair on the top of his skull braided down his back. The side of his head was wrinkled and raw, kissed by fire so that the skin from his nose to that rope of bright hair was patched and stretched, one blue eye staring from the raw-red flesh. His ear had been burned away, and there was a hole where his lobe should be. The healing skin had twisted his mouth on the burned side, curling upwards to reveal his back teeth as though that side of his face smirked. Kvasir raised his hands quickly and fumbled for his hood but then mastered himself, realising he looked weak, trying to cover his disfigurement when the Seaworm crew had already seen it. Kvasir placed his hands calmly on the sheer strake and locked eyes with Hundr again. Blue eyes, cold and pale.

"Have the warrior women come this way, or not?" Hundr pressed, adding a hard edge to his own voice this time.

Kvasir chuckled and raised a hand in peace. "They have. They were here, and they met with Jarl Rollo. You should come ashore, up yonder river. Rollo will be happy to see his friend Jarl Hundr."

"I don't trust this ugly bastard or that turd Rollo," Bush hissed in Hundr's ear.

"Very well, we'll follow you in," said Hundr, and Kvasir smiled his twisted grin. The wolf ship backed oars, and Hundr's belly curdled. He trusted Rollo even less than Bush did. He was as slippery as a fen eel and a cold, vicious killer. But, if the Valkyrie were here with Gungnir, then Hundr needed to know. Even if he had to sail into a viper's nest to find out.

TEN

Rollo strode down a long pier of dark timbers, the planking rattled beneath his heavy boots, and he walked with his shoulders back, and his head held high. He was a full head taller than any of the other men clamouring on the wharf to watch the ship glide into port. His eyes searched the Seaworm deck, and when they found Hundr, a smile split Rollo's face, and he stopped to stand with his hands on his hips. A thick, luxurious bear fur cloak was draped across his broad shoulders, even though the sun shone. He wore a golden torc at his throat, twisted ropes of shining gold coming together at each end in snarling dragon heads. The Seaworm crew threw lines at men waiting on the jetty, and they pulled the warship close.

"Watch him," growled Bush. "Leave me here with some of the lads in case we need to get out of this place sharpish."

"All I want to know is if Sigdriffa and her lot were here, are here, or where they have gone. I don't enjoy being here any more than you do," said Hundr. He had pulled on his brynjar as they had rowed up the wide river towards Rollo's fortress. It was a stout wooden palisade of high timbers cut to spikes, and all sat upon a raised bank above a deep ditch. Gulls circled the wharf, and the smells of cooking fish wafted from the walls on the river's breeze. "I'll take Ragnhild, Sigvarth, and Thorgrim with me. You keep the rest, including Sigrid. I'll also take the boy."

"Finn? Would he not be safer on the Seaworm?"

"They might attack you first," said Hundr, and Bush's mouth fell open. "The lad might be better off with Ragnhild and me. So, once we've gone inside, get the lads in their mail or whatever armour they've got. Get them armed and keep a keen eye. Like as not, there will be some sort of feast so Rollo can show us how successful he has become, which means we'll be here for the night. Light torches and keep a watch all night."

"I wouldn't put anything past that streak of piss," Bush spat over the side and cast a withering look in Rollo's direction.

Hundr nodded and went to find Sigrid to tell her she would stay behind with Bush aboard the

Seaworm.

"What do you mean I can't come with you?" she exclaimed, her brows knitted together as though lightning would spit from her eyes, and her lips pursed tight like she had bitten an onion.

"I need you here, with the Valkyrie and your bows. If Rollo's men attack the ship, you can fend them off from a distance and give us a chance to fight our way back to the river to join you."

She clicked her tongue at him and strode away. Hundr ignored her anger and turned to follow Thorgrim off the ship when another furious face appeared to block his path.

"I won't stay here whilst you go inside. Sigdriffa might be in there with Gungnir," said Gunnr, her hawk-face fouler than a weasel who had licked a nettle.

"If she is, then what are we to do? We can't storm a fortress with one crew in broad daylight. I must talk to Rollo. It seems most likely to me that Sigdriffa was here but has since left. Kvasir said she *was* here, not that she *is*. And besides, if she was, Rollo would flaunt her here like his cloak and torc. I will try to discover where she has gone. You stay here with your archers and protect the ship."

"I demand…"

Hundr held up a hand and closed his eye. "I am

the Jarl of this ship. Whilst you are on it, you do as I say. You will stay here."

Gunnr spluttered and marched away across the deck, following Sigrid. Bush laughed, and Hundr scowled.

"You've got your work cut out for you on this voyage," snorted Bush, holding his bulging belly with laughter.

Hundr stepped over the side on the jetty where Rollo reared up before him, his vast frame almost blocking out the sun.

"The Man with the Dog's Name, slayer of Ivar the Boneless and hero of Hafrsfjord... welcome to Frankia," said Rollo with a broad grin. He stretched out his hand, and Hundr grabbed his wrist in the warrior's grip. Rollo maintained his smile, but there was a curl to his lip, something feral, hate or malice hiding behind his grin, and his eyes bore into Hundr's one eye with such intensity that it was hard to hold his gaze.

"Rollo, you have done well for yourself," said Hundr.

"The years since that battle at Hafrsfjord have been good ones. Come, take your rest in my hall, and we will eat together tonight." Then, before Hundr could ask Rollo about Sigdriffa, he strode away, barking orders at his men to make Hundr welcome and to break open an ale barrel. Hundr watched Rollo's broad back moving through the crowd and caught sight of the hooded figure of burned Kvasir weaving between the warriors to fall in next to Rollo, the two in deep conversation as they strode towards the palisade's gateway.

"A salty-looking lot," remarked Ragnhild at Hundr's shoulder. The men who had crowded at the quayside to watch Hundr's and Kvasir's warships drift into port melted away. They were all clad in baked leather or bits of torn chainmail fastened to breastplates or sewn over shoulders. Those shoulders were broad, their arms thick, and their faces were lean and scarred. All grizzle bearded men walking with straight backs and their heads held high. They were proud men; they were warriors.

"No farmers or millers here," said Hundr, and they made their way towards Rollo's fortress. As they came closer to the walls, the welcoming smell of freshly chopped timbers cut through the stench of fish, and a blacksmith's hammer rang over the din of men's voices. Hundr turned and beckoned to Finn, and the lad scampered forward to walk with Hundr. He wore a simple jerkin but had a seax belted to his waist. "Where did you get that?" asked Hundr.

"Bush gave it to me," said Finn, clutching its bone hilt as though it were a precious thing forged by dwarves beneath the mountains.

"Keep it in its sheath," Hundr scowled. "And

keep your head down. This is a hive of growlers and killers. We go in, eat, and get out. So keep yourself to yourself."

"Yes, lord," said Finn, nodding vigorously. Hundr reached out and ruffled his tousled hair. The lad had grown on him during the voyage. He was hardworking and had become a popular figure amongst the crew, which was no simple thing when that crew were Viking warriors. Thorgrim and Sigvarth strode behind Hundr, both clad in brynjars and bristling with axes, knives and seaxes. They were both thick-necked men, rowers and fighters and looked every bit as fearsome as any in Rollo's force.

They spent the afternoon waiting in Rollo's newly constructed hall. Men brought them ale, fresh water, food and bowls to wash the sea from themselves. Hundr spent most of the time pacing the hall, watching the goings-on of the fortress out of the open shutters. Patrols of warriors marched in and out of the river gate and a larger gate on the landward-facing side. Rollo had built his walls in a circle, split by two intersecting pathways and with buildings filling each of the four segments created by the crossing paths. There was a forge, a granary, and extensive buildings like barns, which Hundr thought were likely barracks or quarters for the large number of warriors in the place. Rollo had close to three hundred men, as far as Hundr could guess, but as the afternoon wore on and servants prepared the hall for the feast, he saw no women warriors and no Valkyrie.

The sun still shone as warriors jovially entered the hall, talking and laughing and taking their places on eating benches. The floors were covered with freshly cut rushes, and servants lit candles around the hall to brighten the dark corners. There was a hearth, of course, and a smoke hole above it cut into the thatch, but no fire was required on such a balmy summer day. When all was ready, serving women and boys brought in wooden platters of loaves, fish, and wonderfully steaming meat and tankards of ale clanked and brimmed with froth.

Kvasir appeared before Hundr with his hood up over his face, even in the humidity of the hall's warmth. "Come, Rollo bids you join him," he said, his head held low so that his hood shadowed his face. Hundr, Ragnhild, Finn, Thorgrim and Sigvarth followed Kvasir to Rollo's table. "Apologies, the invitation is for you alone. Your men and woman can sit here." Kvasir gestured to a table at the rear of the hall, in the thick of where Rollo's growlers were already supping ale like men who hadn't drunk a drop of anything for days.

Ragnhild frowned at Hundr, and she shook her head slightly. Leaving them there didn't feel right to Hundr either, but he'd come to talk to

Rollo, and that had to happen if they were ever to pick up Sigdriffa's trail. So, he followed Kvasir and left the others to take their seats amongst the growing crowd, which was becoming louder and more raucous.

"Ah, Jarl Hundr. Here, do me the honour of sitting beside me," said Rollo, rising from his seat and gesturing to a space next to him. Warriors in brynjars filled the rest of the double-sided bench, arms thick with warrior rings and necks draped in gold and silver. Hundr sat down next to a grey-haired man with a bulbous purple nose above a bushy black beard. He eyed Hundr whilst chewing noisily on a crust of bread and then turned back to his meal without saying a word.

"Thank you for your hospitality," said Hundr, and he raised a horn of ale to Rollo, who clanked his own against it so that ale slopped onto the table.

"Nonsense. You set me free from Ketil Flatnose's chains. The least I can do is welcome you to my home."

"Don't the Franks mind you being here?"

Purple-nose laughed so hard he almost choked on his bread and thumped the table with his fist. "Mind, he says!" The warriors at Rollo's table all laughed along with the joke, which to Hundr seemed about as funny as a turd in the ale barrel. "He's a Duke, as well as a Jarl. Duke of Frankia,"

Purple-nose mimicked a Frankish accent and bowed to Rollo.

This is new. Rollo, a Viking, aligned to the power of the Frankish throne. New and dangerous. "My congratulations," said Hundr, raising his horn again. "How did that happen?"

"Sometimes the Franks pay us Vikings to go away when we attack, like the famous Jarl Haesten, who grew rich and powerful on such payments. Instead, I asked for land."

Clever bastard. "So, you protect their rivers with your ships and warriors and take tithes from their farmers and tenants on your lands."

Rollo raised his horn and winked at Hundr. Hundr forced himself to smile.

"Who is your man, the hooded warrior with the burned face?" Although the folds of the hood hid the warrior's face, there was a malevolence about the man, which made Hundr wary. A sure-footed warrior who walked on the balls of his feet, Kvasir made Hundr prickle, and he couldn't put his finger on exactly why. At first, he had thought it was the scarring, but he had met scarred men before, and he himself carried the Odin wound upon his face.

"Kvasir?" said Rollo, and he smiled and frowned at the same time. "He is a veteran of the war, one of Jarl Kjotve's men."

"So, he fought at Hafrsfjord, then?"

"No," Rollo chuckled. "He was recovering. However, he hates you, Jarl Hundr, and the only man he hates more than you is Einar Rosti."

"Why?"

"Because you burned him when you burned Jarl Kjotve's hall at Agder. At the same time as I fought Einar the Brawler in the flames of that burning building, Kvasir lay trapped underneath a fallen timber. It burned him terribly. Such pain." Rollo tutted and shook his head, and Hundr understood the weft of Kvasir's hatred.

"If you hadn't stolen King Harald's sword, we wouldn't have had to burn the hall to get it back." Rollo's eyes blazed at that truth, and he shot Hundr an iron look, but he mastered himself, and his easy smirk returned.

"Come now, you didn't sail all the way here to reminisce about old times. So? Why are you here?"

"Have you seen a crew of Valkyrie warriors pass this way?" asked Hundr, trying his best to make the question seem unimportant. He reached for a slice of hot pork and tore a strip from the greasy, gloriously roasted meat as he spoke.

"Is that why you are here?"

"No, we are simply on the Whale Road plying

our trade, looking for good raiding. Ragnhild knows these Valkyrie. You remember Ragnhild?"

"Who could forget how she stormed the sea wall at Vanylven?"

"Have you seen them?"

Rollo took a long draw of his ale and ate an apple slowly. Each crunch made Hundr's dead eye pulse, and he pressed a finger against the empty socket beneath its patch. "Did Fairhair send you?" asked Rollo. The chatter at the table stopped dead at the mention of King Harald's name, and all eyes fell on Hundr. "You are still his man. No? You still do his bidding. You come running when he barks?"

"Like a pup," laughed the purple-nosed lackey.

Hundr took a deep breath. In his mind's eye, he sprang from his seat, whipped his seax free from its sheath at the back of his belt and stabbed it into the purple-nosed lackey's face a dozen times, ripping him to bits and washing the table in his blood. But instead, Hundr just smiled and took a sip of his ale.

"I am not here for King Harald."

"But you are his dog? That is to say, he is your master, and you are his servant?" said Rollo.

Just like when I found you chained to Ketil Flatnose's chair, emptying his shit pail and living off the scraps of his table.

"I jest, Jarl Hundr. Forgive me. Yes, your Valkyrie were here weeks ago. They babbled on about founding a new temple of Upsala here in Frankia, on my land. But I told them to piss off. I can't have Odin-mad priestesses taking up valuable farmland and driving the peasants mad with sacrifices and the demands of the Aesir. So they left, sailing for the Saxon lands, if I am not mistaken. They went to seek Jarl Guthrum." Rollo quizzically raised his eyebrow, momentarily distracted. "What is going on over there?" He rested his elbow on the table and pointed lazily towards the back of the hall, searching for a scrap of food between his teeth with his tongue.

Hundr heard the commotion before he saw it. At the rear of Rollo's hall, men sprang up from their tables, shouting. There was pushing and shoving, and one man flew across a table as another punched him square in the face. Blades flashed in the candlelight, and Hundr's heart sank because young Finn had drawn his seax and was bellowing his defiance at a group of snarling warriors around the punched man.

ELEVEN

"Oh dear, this will need to be settled," grinned Rollo, looking like a man appreciating a magnificent horse or a hunting falcon. Hundr leapt up from the table and forced his way through the throng, elbowing past warriors who rubbed their hands at the prospect of a fight for the evening's entertainment.

"They provoked the lad," said Sigvarth when he saw Hundr burst through the crowd. Sigvarth was red-faced and glowering, his hands bunched into fists. "They were calling him names, throwing food and splashing ale at him. If Finn hadn't attacked the bastards, I was about to."

"Thor's balls, but we could be out of this place. Sigdriffa was here, but she sailed west to the Saxons. Now we must sort this mess out before we can get away," said Hundr. "Rollo planned this. He wants to hurt us, and we stumbled into it like a drunk into a dung pile."

"Their hate for Harald runs deeper than a cut from a war axe," said Thorgrim.

"Like as not, half the bastards in this shit hole fought at Hafrsfjord against Harald. We probably crossed axes with many of them ourselves," said Ragnhild.

"This pup insulted one of my warriors and struck another. I demand satisfaction," shouted a huge, bellied man in a bright green tunic. He was tall and broad, and his arms were thick with rings.

"We are leaving, and we apologise for our young friend. Too much ale, I fear," said Hundr and reached his hand out to the man, who slapped it away and spat at Hundr's feet.

"Are you afraid to fight? There has been a provocation!" bellowed the big-bellied brute.

"I'll fight you now then, you fat bastard," said Hundr, and he drew his seax. Men shuffled backwards to make room, and Hundr felt the war-rage slip over him like a welcome blanket on a winter evening. He had a reputation earned in blood, and he'd fought too hard to be insulted by this pig, even if Hundr knew Rollo had laid the trap for the Seaworm crew.

Big-belly spluttered, and he waved his arms. The jowls beneath his neck wobbled, and his face turned red as men pushed away to create space for the fight.

"Seems to me the fight is not with you, Jarl Hundr," sneered a voice, lisping over the words. The hooded figure of Kvasir ambled into the space, the lip of his hood pulled low so that it shrouded his disfigured face.

"The fight is with the pup, not with him," agreed the big-bellied man, pointing between Finn and Hundr.

"Any man who challenges my crew fights me first," said Hundr, and he prowled across the floor rushes, seax at his side, feeling the jaws of the deep cunning trap set by Rollo and Kvasir closing in around him.

"Your man cannot fight for himself, then? Is he a coward, a nithing?" Kvasir taunted, and the men packed into Rollo's hall laughed. Hundr closed his eye, and his heart sank again.

"I am no nithing, and I can fight my own battles," spat Finn, and he shouldered past Hundr with his own seax drawn. He shot Hundr a murderous look. His eyes were glassy, and his mouth set. Kvasir was humiliating him, and if Finn did not fight now, he would have to live with the stain of a man who had shirked a fight. Big-belly easily weighed twice as much as Finn, and the lad was still a youth. He had grown wide at the shoulder, but it was all lean bone and long muscle, and the challenger would be a killer, a veteran of countless fights.

"Very well then," said Kvasir. "Let them fight to submission or death." The crowd roared their approval, and Hundr glanced over at the head table. Rollo grinned at him and raised his horn of ale in salute.

Hundr grabbed Finn's arm and pulled him close, fixing him with his good eye. "They want this fight, lad. They have goaded you into it."

"What of it? I am not afraid," said Finn. But his eyes were wider than a wolf moon.

"They mean to kill you, Finn. To hurt me. They hate us because we fight for King Harald...."

"I am not afraid," Finn repeated, interrupting Hundr and twisting his arm from Hundr's grip, wide eyes flitting to the man he must fight.

"You should be; I would be. You are not a man yet. Listen to me!" Hundr shouted the last three words and jerked Finn around to look at him. "I was just like you at your age, full of bravery and hungry for reputation. But this man means to kill you. He will let you attack him, reckless in your pride, and he will use his strength to bully you. When you take a wild swing at him, he will open your belly like a trout and spill your guts on the floor. Be calm." Finn stared at Hundr and nodded his understanding. Finn's tongue snaked out to lick at dry lips. "You are a lad, and this bastard already has reputation. Look at his rings; he has earned those with his blade, he has killed bearded, snarling drengr all his life, and he thinks killing you will be as easy as wiping his nose. Wait for him to make a mistake. If you can frustrate him – make the fight draw on, the fat pig will not only be out of breath, he will lose face. The longer it goes on, the more angered he will become. Then, when he makes a wild lunge or sweep, that is when you strike. Take off your boots to make you quicker; use your speed to dance around him."

"Thank you," said Finn. His adam's apple bobbed up and down as he swallowed hard. Then, the lad knelt and pulled off his boots.

"And Finn," said Hundr, clapping him on the shoulder, "kill the bastard."

Finn smiled wolfishly and turned to face his enemy. Big-belly was laughing smugly and striding before his crew mates. They howled at Finn and shouted encouragement at their own man. Kvasir stood at the centre of the space between the baying warriors. Rollo's men were shouting and whooping at the entertainment to come. Ale flowed, and their faces were crimson and sweating, mouths leering, and fists raised to the rafters.

"If he dies here, Einar will kill us both," said Ragnhild as Hundr stepped back away from the fighters. Which was true. Einar and Hildr loved Finn as though he were their own child, and Einar would wreak bloody ruin on any man who harmed his fostered son.

Big-belly raised his seax in salute, and the men inside the hall roared their support. Kvasir stepped back into the ring of warriors. Even though Hundr could not see his fire-scorched face beneath the hood, he could sense the smirk there, the delight at a chance to harm Hundr. He was an enemy, just as Rollo was, and a man to be wary of. Finn sidled forwards, leading with his right foot and his seax held in front of him. They had left swords and axes outside the hall, as was the custom amongst Northmen, to avoid lethal violence when ale flowed. Hundr had thought it strange when Rollo's men had allowed Hundr and his warriors to keep their seaxes, and now the deep cunning of it showed itself as a trap well baited.

"Calm, Finn," Hundr called. "Keep loose; use your speed."

Finn reached the centre of the space between the throng, and his seax wavered before him, trembling. Hundr held his breath, his heart itself pausing. Big-belly advanced on Finn, grinning, laughing and confident.

"The lad's scared," Sigvarth whispered in Hundr's ear. "That fat bastard will carve him up like a yuletide hog."

Big-belly came on. He jerked his blade at Finn, and the lad sprang backwards. The crowd laughed, and the brute barked like a dog. The raucous cheers of the crowd echoed around the thatch, and Hundr clenched his teeth, fearing that not only would Finn die, but he would die with dishonour.

"My name is Hvitserk Snorrisson, and you cannot be the son of Ivar the Boneless, you spineless whelp." Big-belly strode forward to slay the son of a legend. He took long strides and lunged his seax forwards towards Finn's chest, but Finn skipped away with light feet. Hvitserk spun, whipping his blade around in a powerful strike aimed at slicing Finn's throat open. Finn leant back so that the blade sang past his face, and he smiled at Hvitserk and punched him in the nose.

Hvitserk roared and stumbled. He put a finger to his nose and snorted out a burst of blood and snot. "You little turd," he snarled. He came at Finn in a whip-fast series of cuts and lunges, crowding Finn with his bulk and driving him towards the crowd. Finn dodged and weaved and twisted away from the attacks, and before Hvitserk could drive into the heaving swell of bodies behind him, Finn ducked under an overhand lunge and walked casually back to the centre of the fighting space.

"He's toying with him," smiled Ragnhild. "He's fast. Reminds me of you."

"Finn is going to kill him," Hundr said, leaning in to speak into her ear. The crowd's mood had shifted. Their eager anticipation of seeing Hvitserk butcher a crewman of those they had fought and lost to at Hafrsfjord changed to anger as they felt the tide turn against their fighter. Hvitserk's red face gleamed, and sweat soaked his jerkin through at the chest and beneath his arms. He lunged desperately at Finn, and the young fighter sprang aside again. This time he kicked Hvitserk up the arse, sending him sprawling, and the crowd surged forwards, seething with anger.

"He had better do it quickly and stop taunting the bastard, or we will hang from these rafters like cured hams," piped Ragnhild, having to shout to be heard above the baying warriors.

"Take Thorgrim and go outside. Get the weapons from the door guards. When we come out, we will come fast. We make for the river and the Seaworm."

Ragnhild ducked out of the crowd and dragged Thorgrim with her.

"Stop baiting him," Hundr called to Finn as he circled in front of him, dancing on the balls of his feet and looking as fresh as though he was taking a seaside stroll. "Just get it done."

Hvitserk lumbered towards Finn, slashing with his seax, and for the first time in the fight, Finn brought his weapon to bear. He came inside with a wide lunge and dragged his blade across Hvitserk's ribs, opening jerkin and flesh in a line of bright blood. Hvitserk bawled an animal cry of both pain and rage. He swiped his seax in a desperate attack, sweat flying from his soaked hair, and his teeth bared in a tortured grimace. Finn blocked the blow with a raised elbow and came up inside Hvitserk's reach. He drove his seax upwards, leaning into the blow so that the point of his blade sliced into the soft flesh beneath Hvitserk's chin, and the wicked broken-backed weapon, as long as a man's forearm, passed through Hvitserk's mouth, slicing off his tongue and rammed into his skull. The big man quivered on the end of the seax like a caught fish, and the top of his severed tongue flopped onto the floor rushes as a wash of dark blood slopped from his mouth and down his sweat-soaked jerkin. Finn ripped the blade free, and Hvitserk toppled face-first onto the hard-packed earthen floor.

The crowd went silent and still, flinty eyes all staring at their fallen fighter and then at Finn, who stood triumphant with his hands on his hips, one arm soaked in his enemy's blood. Finn grinned at Hundr, and Hundr leapt forward to grab the lad by the arm and drag him from the hall.

"We need to go. Now!" Hundr hissed in his ear as he pulled him from the fighting space, Finn dipping to snatch up his boots as they went.

"Where in Thor's name do you think you're going?" a beady-eyed warrior snarled in Hundr's face and stood in his path. Hundr kicked the man in the groin and elbowed his way through the stunned warriors, pushing towards the open doors at the hall's rear.

"I won," said Finn. "Shouldn't I claim his warrior rings and his weapons?"

"You should," Hundr replied over his shoulder. "But if we don't get out of here quick, we are both dead men."

"Stop those bastards!" a voice boomed from deep in the hall. Hundr ran and dragged Finn with him. A hand grabbed at his shoulder, but Hundr shook it off. Another warrior tried to block his path, and Hundr punched him in the throat. Strong hands yanked Finn from Hundr's grip, and Hundr spun around just in time to see warriors grasping at the young fighter, pulling him towards them. Hundr whipped his seax free from its sheath at the back of his belt and sliced two fingers from a meaty hand in a spray of blood. Finn sprang free as the injured man roared in pain, and they dashed for the doorway.

"Don't look back! Just run!" Hundr shouted to Finn as they burst into the evening, the air cool on his face after the sweltering humidity of Rollo's hall. They ran along muddy pathways and past gawping warriors, twisting through a tangle of lanes and running for their lives towards the river. Ragnhild and Thorgrim ran ahead of them. Ragnhild dropped Hundr's swords and belt into the mud and kept on running, and Hundr swept them up, fumbling with the clasp as he belted Fenristooth to his waist and slung Battle Fang across his back. Hundr's ears rang with the rabid shouting and roaring from the warriors he knew were streaming out from the hall behind him. Finn kept pace, running at his shoulder as they raced through the snarl of muddy side streets at the heart of Rollo's fortress. Hundr swerved around a smith's forge, where smoke billowed from the rooftop and out onto one of the four wide paths which cut through the fortress. He could see the gateway ahead, and there he spotted Ragnhild and Thorgrim fighting with two guards between the open doors.

Hundr risked a look over his shoulder, warriors still streaming after them, spears and axes waving, and faces snarling. Hundr and Finn darted past the corpses of the two guards dispatched by Ragnhild and Thorgrim and then sprinted along the quay. Ragnhild leapt onto the Seaworm's deck, and Thorgrim hacked at a mooring line with his axe. The Seaworm sprang into life, and as Hundr's feet thundered on the timbers of the jetty, arrows whipped past him, loosed from the Seaworm's deck and into the pursuing warriors. The Seaworm was alive with ropes, men, and oars, but they could not get the ship moving fast enough.

"Get on board," Hundr said to Finn, gasping for breath, lungs bursting from the race through the fortress. Hundr drew Fenristooth from its fleece-lined scabbard and strode up the jetty, its narrow planking only wide enough at this far section for two men to walk abreast. Further along on the quayside, the timbers gave way to a wider area where cargo could be loaded, but the Seaworm's mooring stretched out into the river itself, and Hundr strode towards his pursuers with his blade held low.

"What are you doing?" Finn called after him. But Hundr ignored the lad and the shouts from his crew. He had to buy them time to get the ship underway. Otherwise, Rollo's men would pour over her side and overwhelm the crew with their sheer numbers. Rollo's men came on, the two warriors at the head armed with axes and as blown from the race through the town as Hundr. He took deep breaths to calm himself and held his sword with two hands, its ivory grip cool and welcoming. The men did not slow themselves in the face of Hundr's blade, the warriors behind them cursing, shouting and spitting hatred over their shoulders.

"We have you now, Harald's dog," grinned the leading warrior on the right, a clean-shaven man with a thick brow covering his eyes in one continuous line of hair.

"No," snarled Hundr. "I am the Man with the Dog's Name, and it is I who have you." He leapt forward to meet their charge and lunged long and low with Fenristooth's blade like a perfect extension of his arm as it snaked forward so that its tip pierced the clean-shaven man's groin, and Hundr whipped it back and across the calf of the warrior next to him in one smooth movement. The clean-shaven warrior stumbled forward with his mouth hanging open, slack and surprised that his lifeblood splashed between the jetty's dark timbers. The second warrior toppled to his knees as his wounded leg gave way, and the warriors behind were too close to their fallen comrade, so they fell over him in a sprawling mess of shouted curses and sprawling limbs.

Hundr danced backwards, sliced open a warrior's throat, then whipped his other sword over his shoulder and cracked her point into the forehead of an attacker who clenched his teeth so hard as he saw the blade coming for him that his front teeth shattered. His face broke apart under the blow and sagged to ruin under his smashed skull. Blood splattered Rollo's jetty, and the warriors paused their attack, wary now of the one-eyed swordsman before them who had killed three of their number and wounded two others.

"Come now, brave men. Warriors who fled Hafrsfjord like broken curs. Come and fight with the Champion of the North." Hundr was shouting, goading them. Boasting of his hard-earned name and legend. Though he spoke pridefully, he spoke to men who came to kill him, and Hundr wanted them to know who they fought. He was aware of the Seaworm crew calling to him over his right shoulder, but the red fury was upon him, and he wanted to fight. He wanted Rollo or Kvasir the Burned to face him, and he wanted to drench his swords in their blood. An arrow sang past him to thump into a black-bearded warrior's shoulder, and another warrior cursed as a shaft sank into the meat of his thigh.

"Hundr, come now before it's too late!" That was a woman's voice, with a lover's desperation shrieking in it as though his life depended on it. It was Sigrid. Hundr turned on his heel and ran down the jetty, just in time to see the Seaworm had poled away from the riverbank with her oars. Panic made his strides longer, pumping his arms as he ran, swords dripping blood. Hundr thought he wouldn't make the leap and that Rollo's men would capture him and subject him to untold tortures in revenge for the lands their fathers had lost to Harald and for the lives he had taken on the jetty. He leapt, holding his breath. Water passed beneath him, stirred to wide ripples by the Seaworm's hull. He stretched out his swords and landed heavily on the sheer strake, pain flaring in his ribs and his feet splashing in the ice-cold river water. Floki, a flaxen-haired crewman, reached over and grabbed his arms.

"I've got you, my lord. Let's get out of this shit hole," said Floki, and he hauled Hundr over the side as Sigrid, Ragnhild, and the other Valkyrie gathered at the stern to pour their vicious arrows into the baying mass of Rollo's warriors huddled on the jetty. Hundr fell hard onto the Seaworm's deck and came up panting. He reached out to clap Floki on the shoulder and thank him for pulling him aboard, but Floki was flung backwards, a spear protruding from his chest and quivering. More spears clattered into the hull and splashed into the river. Hundr dashed to Floki, staring at his wide blue eyes. The dying man coughed up a gout of dark blood, and Hundr pressed Fenristooth's hilt into his clammy palm.

"Go to Valhalla, brave warrior, veteran of the shield wall. You saved my life. Take your seat in Odin's hall and save a place for me," he said, leaning to speak into Floki's ear. Floki coughed again, and his body rattled violently. Life fled from him as though a Valkyrie from Valhalla tore his soul away to make the journey to the afterlife, and Hundr rested his forehead against Floki's own. *Another good man lost on the Whale Road, another soul for the Einherjar. We will meet again, friend.*

TWELVE

The Seaworm arrived at the shores of what had once been the country of Mercia to find the Saxon kingdom of Wessex overrun with Norsemen. A great army of Danes, led by Jarl Guthrum, had pushed Alfred, the King of Wessex, into the west of the country. The rumours at the town where Hundr brought the Seaworm to port were that Alfred would be dead before the summer was out and that the Danes would rule in Wessex. Danes already ruled the entire east and north of the country, with Viking lords now settled on the thrones of what had once been the kingdoms of Northumbria, Mercia, and East Anglia.

The Seaworm had sailed from Frankia across a brown sea spattered with squalls. It had been a short journey, and the wind had filled her sails, driving the ship across the narrow channel. The coastline of East Anglia was familiar to Bush, and the shipmaster had guided the Seaworm along white-walled cliffs thick with gulls, racing past golden beaches hazing under a sun which had poked through churning clouds, blown by the wind's strength.

Finn had been quiet since the fight in Frankia, and Sigrid spoke to Hundr of the lad being unable to sleep with nightmares of dead Hvitserk's fetch haunting him. Finn still bailed the bilge, and he took his turn at an oar, but under the sailcloth at night, when the crew asked for the tale of his fight, Finn had shaken his head. The dead warrior lay heavy on him like a millstone. The boy was fast, just like his father, and he had fought with calmness and skill. Einar had taught him well, and Hundr knew Finn would grow into a fine warrior. But, of course, it is difficult to kill a man, particularly at first. Northmen are raised to it, urged to it by the gods and by skalds at winter firesides. Indeed, a sharp blade will stab or cut a man open easily enough, and with enough skill and battle luck, a blade will strike the death blow. But a man clings to life and fights for it with all his strength and savagery. To rip that life from another is a terrible thing. Hundr remembered those feelings himself, of when he had first taken a life before he was a warrior or Jarl. The heart-pounding battle fury brings joy at the death of one's enemy, at the victory over one who would rip the life from you, who wanted to tear and rend your flesh with sharp iron. But later, when the shouts and the glory have gone, and you are alone in the dark, the dead man's fetch comes to you. His eyes appear in your mind, and the twist of pain on his face eats at your heart. You wonder if he had a wife, a son or a daughter, a mother and a father. You remember how it felt to lose a loved one of your own. Hundr's mother's death had been like the dawn of Ragnarök, world-ending and life-changing. All those things came after the first kill and then became less. Until killing became nothing at all, simply a warrior at his work, like a smith at the anvil, killing men who took to the Whale Road knowing and accepting its risks in the hunt for wealth and reputation. On the journey from Frankia, Hundr had wanted to tell Finn of these things, to tell him that the pain would get easier. But he had stayed away from the lad. He was the son of Ivar the Boneless, a man who had once been Hundr's greatest enemy, and that history built a wall between him and Finn – hard to be a friend to a man whose father you have killed.

Bush had carefully guided the Seaworm through the dangerously tidal waters of a wide estuary with dark sand banks sprawling along ridges thick with briar and brush. Bush had hailed merchants in fat-bellied knarrs at the mouth of the estuary, and they were good west

Norsemen waiting for the wind to change. This was the land of the Vikings now, they proclaimed with proud voices, their ships heavy in the water, laden with goods. They brought tin, fleeces, and silver traded for furs and amber, and Hundr's heart warmed when a trader with drooping moustaches spoke of a great Jarl along the river Chelmer who had taken over a fortress at a ford in the river. Haesten, an old friend and a Viking Jarl famous wherever Northmen sail. After the fight with Rollo, a friendly face seemed as good a place to start as any in the search for Sigdriffa and the Gungnir spear.

The port at Chelmer's Fort was busy with traders and fisherfolk. The river cut deep into the Saxon countryside, green and lush and a reminder to the Seaworm crew of why Northmen craved this land with a hunger so deep that they risked their lives to take it. A reeve demanded coin for the berth, and Hundr paid it gladly, so eager was he to see Haesten. This time, Hundr brought Gunnr and Skögul ashore, along with Bush, Ragnhild, and Finn. The rest he left with the Seaworm, with orders to keep watch on the ship and ask around the busy port for news of Valkyrie warriors.

Hundr strode through the fort's gates, which were wide open and unguarded. Folk came and went with carts of fish, apples, loaves and other wares for trade. Hundr stole an apple from a passing cart, and the juices from its crunch ran into his beard. It tasted like summer in England, and he remembered it well, for it had been on these shores where he had first made his name in the world of warriors.

"A fine place," remarked Gunnr, striding in shining mail with an axe at her belt.

"They don't seem worried about the Saxons wanting their town back," Ragnhild noted.

"There are as many Saxons here as Northmen," said Hundr. Several accents melded together in the rumble of chatter. Hundr recognised the different burr or intonations of Danes, Norsemen and Saxons, all talking in the Norse tongue and going about their business as though they were safe in Hedeby or on the Vik. "Maybe the Saxons are already conquered. It seems peaceful here, Saxon and Viking living and working together."

"Can we trust this Haesten?" asked Gunnr. She strode confidently, but her eyes flitted around the fort's lanes and buildings like a hungry magpie. It was a thriving town of wattle buildings and sturdy thatch, and its place at a ford across the river made a trading port rich in silver and people.

"We can trust him," Ragnhild nodded. "We fought alongside him in Frankia. He was an ally of Bjorn Ironside in those days."

"You have been busy in your time away, sister," said Skögul. She took a skin of ale from a stall along the town's principal thoroughfare and paid for it with a small coin, which she fished from a pouch beneath her armpit. "Little wonder you stayed away so long, meeting and fighting alongside warriors of fame and reputation whilst we stayed and honoured our oaths."

"I stayed away because I was fighting, filling Odin's corpse hall with the souls of the brave. Can you say the same?"

"I am not an oathbreaker, and I have served the All-Father loyally and faithfully."

Ragnhild kept her teeth together, but Hundr saw the provocation in a twitch of Ragnhild's eye, and he smirked to himself. Skögul's pride was still bruised from her Holmgang defeat, and Ragnhild so desperately wanted to be accepted back into the embrace of her former sisterhood. His amusement came because if that provocation came to blows, there would only be one winner. Hundr strolled over to a clutch of three warriors, all clad in leather breastplates and leaning on spear shafts.

"I am looking for Jarl Haesten," said Hundr.

"Everyone wants to speak to the Jarl," uttered a lanky warrior in a tired voice. "What is it? Amber drops as big as babies' heads? White bear furs? We've seen it all, friend. Sell your wares at the market like everyone else."

"I am an old friend."

"And I was friends with Ragnar Lothbrok himself. Now go on, piss off. We won't have no trouble here," the lanky warrior snapped. He yawned and turned to chortle with the man next to him.

"Just tell Haesten that Hundr is here to see him."

"What kind of a name is Hundr? It's a bloody dog's name," Lanky retorted. One of his mates stood to attention and elbowed Lanky in the ribs.

"I will let the Jarl know you are here. Please, follow me," said the second warrior. He set off at a brisk walk, and Hundr followed him. They waited outside Haesten's hall mere moments before Haesten came strolling out. He walked with the same easy confidence as always, and his blade-sharp face creased in a lop-sided grin. His hair had thinned, his gut had grown larger, and Haesten, who had once been a straight-backed, proud man, walked with hunched shoulders. Time had not been kind to the wily old Viking.

"You have become a man of reputation since last we met, Jarl Hundr," Haesten beamed. He had his thumbs tucked into a thick belt studded with silver buttons, and he stretched out a powerful hand to shake Hundr's own.

"You look well, my lord," smiled Hundr. He honoured Haesten with the title, but he was happy to do so for a warrior who had sacked the city of Paris itself and sailed a fleet of warships south to raid far Ispania.

"I look old, but it does me good to see you. Is Kolo with you?"

"Kolo died on the walls of Dublin. Fighting against Halvdan Ragnarsson and Ireland's seiðr witch Queen. He fought bravely and died well."

"He was a good man." Haesten paused and glanced up at the sky as though he said some brief silent prayer for the dead fighter who had been a friend to them both. "You will stay and feast tonight?"

"I would love nothing more, and hopefully, we can drink together upon my return, but I must be away with all haste. Are you settling here with your ships and your people?"

"Maybe," Haesten shrugged. "It is pleasant land and easily won. My warriors need to fight, and there is still war here. We stayed too long in Frankia, I fear."

"Why did you leave?"

"The Franks pushed me out of the island, and I grew tired of the place."

"What news of your wife?" The last time Hundr had seen Haesten, he had been newly married and his wife heavy with child. "She liked your Frankish fortress by the sea, or so I remember."

Haesten offered an upside-down smile, and his shoulders dropped even lower. "She died in childbirth. So, the place lost its lustre for me in the end."

"I am sorry, Lord Haesten," said Hundr, knowing the words were too simple but struggling for the right ones.

Haesten nodded, and then he raised his head, trying to snap himself out of his melancholy. "So, Jarl Hundr. What can I do for you if you won't let me feed you and get you drunk?"

"I seek a band of Valkyrie warriors, women like Ragnhild. They are here in England somewhere, perhaps with Guthrum. Have you heard of them or seen them?"

"There are no other women like Ragnhild," said Haesten, which was true enough. "I have not seen them, but I heard of a band of such women from one of my men, who took a message from me to Guthrum. They are with his army. No man can forget such a company of all women warriors."

"And where is Guthrum now?"

"He is in the West, pursuing King Alfred and his Wessex men. Guthrum, it seems, will do what

Ivar and the sons of Ragnar could not. He will take Wessex, and when he does, Northmen will rule this entire country."

"You will take a piece for yourself, my lord?"

"I don't know. I am only here to keep my warriors happy. I am tired, my friend," Haesten allowed a wan smile, and the lines on his face creased at his eyes and forehead. "We must be good lords, good ring givers. Otherwise, our warriors and ships melt away like the snow in spring."

"I must go to Guthrum with all haste. If you have horses here, I would buy some from you?"

"You may not," said Haesten haughtily, "but you can take as many as you need without payment. The price is the feast we shall enjoy together when you return." Haesten placed a warm hand on Hundr's shoulder. "Do you need men?"

"No, my lord. But thank you, the horses will be more than enough. I would also leave the Seaworm in your river here."

"Of course. Now, let's find you some nags for your journey."

They walked together in companionable silence, and Hundr felt for the old warhorse. He plainly felt the loss of his wife and child, and the sharp wit and deep cunning which had always marked Haesten out as a man apart seemed to have been torn from his shoulders by his grief.

"What kind of man is this Guthrum?" Hundr asked as they strolled past two women haggling furiously over the price of an intricately woven basket.

"He is a war Dane," Haesten shrugged. "A nephew of King Horik in Denmark. The Great Army split last summer. Lord Halvdan took half the crews north to Northumbria to fight the dreaded Picts, and Guthrum stayed here to make war on Wessex. He is a man of deep cunning, not a fighter himself, but a leader. He attacked Alfred in midwinter, and the defeated Saxon King is now on the run. Guthrum will be King here one day, maybe soon."

"How do I get to his army?"

"I will give you a couple of men to show you the way."

Hundr thanked Haesten, and the great Jarl waved him off as Hundr thundered out of Chelmer's Fort with his men mounted on fresh horses. Hundr rode a piebald mare flanked by the two warriors Haesten had provided as guides. One was tall and lean with red hair and a face covered in tattooed images of ravens and swirling dragons, and the other was stocky and scarred with a long, braided beard which bounced on his brynjar as he rode. Hundr left six men to guard the Seaworm, and Haesten promised to keep those men fed and watered. The rest, including Gunnr, Skögul and the other four Valkyrie, rode out across the hills and dales of what had once been Mercia in search of Sigdriffa and the stolen Odin spear.

They made camp that night in a copse of sycamore and elm. Sigrid and Ragnhild caught a brace of rabbits with their bows, and Bush cooked up a hot meal over the fire in an upturned helmet. Hundr found Finn sitting with his back to a tree, drinking from a waterskin, and he sat down next to him on the soft, damp leaf mulch. Finn held out the waterskin, and Hundr took a drink.

"What do you make of England?" Hundr asked. He wanted to talk to the lad, yet he still struggled with what to say, so the question came out awkwardly.

"It's very green," said Finn, keeping his eyes on the forest floor.

"That's why men want it; it's rich land, fertile. A man can be happy here and wealthy."

"My father fought here with his brothers."

"He did. I fought alongside them in those days."

Finn looked at him. His mouth moved as though words tripped on the end of his tongue, but then they disappeared back down his throat like a startled badger down its set.

"The first one is the hardest," Hundr said after a moment of uncomfortable silence. "But this is the life we choose if we want to be warriors. Do not feel guilty for killing a man who would have killed you without hesitation. You fought well. You are fast and skilled, and you fight like your father."

Finn nodded slowly, and then he raised his head to meet Hundr's eye, his own eyes glassy. "He comes to me, Hvitserk. The dead man. He keeps me awake at night, his draugr smothering me as though he has not yet passed to the afterlife."

"Are you still a Christian, or do you pray to Odin now?" When Einar had first come across Finn as a boy in England, he had been pious and under lessons from a Christ priest. His mother wanted it that way, for the Irish are fearsome Christ men.

"I do not know. It seems to me that Odin, Thor and Tyr are better gods for warriors, and I would like to spend an eternity in Valhalla rather than the Christ heaven. My father will be there...." The words trailed off – the accusation unspoken.

"He will, and so will your grandfather, Ragnar Lothbrok, feasting and fighting with the heroes until the day of Ragnarök." Hundr spoke softly, trying to be kind, which was a thing he rarely practiced.

"Is it true that the walls of Valhalla are made from spears, and the roof is made from shields?"

"Who can say for sure? For no living man has passed the Bifrost Bridge to tell the tale."

"But Jesus and God are powerful. The Romans and the Franks all worship him. They say he will subdue the Aesir in the end."

"Perhaps that will be Ragnarök itself," Hundr shrugged. He knew little of the Romans or thought much of the battles between the gods. They were things best left for priests, whether of Odin or Christ, the nailed god. "Hvitserk's fetch might be trapped between our afterlife and the Christ heaven until you decide to which you will offer your allegiance. Maybe if you decide, he can cross the Bifrost Bridge to Asgard and leave you alone. But the next man you kill in battle will be easier. If you want to become a warrior, death will be your profession. Just like a smith, farmer, or potter. I have something for you." Hundr slipped a silver warrior ring from his wrist and handed it to Finn. It was a finely carved thing with running boars, and a tusked head met a busy tail at its end.

"For me?" Finn grinned

"You earned it. Now, you are a warrior. You can pull an oar with the men, and you won't bail the bilge alone anymore. You are a drengr now and must follow the warrior code, drengskapr, if you want to join my crews."

"Thank you, my lord." Finn turned the ring over, marvelling at its carvings and shining beauty.

"When you lead men, which something tells me you will one day, you must be a good ring-giver. You must reward your warriors for their bravery; that is the way of things between a Jarl and his drengr. Here, one other gift." Hundr stood, reached for the rear of his belt, and pulled free an axe. It was his own fighting axe, with a leather-wrapped haft and a shining bearded blade, well balanced and not too heavy to fight with one-handed. "A warrior should be properly armed. Come to me in the morning, and we will practice weapons together before we ride."

Finn smiled for the first time since they had dropped the anchor stone in Frankia, and it warmed Hundr to see it. He turned to look for food and found Gunnr and Skögul waiting for him, arms crossed and frowns sour enough to curdle milk. He stopped and tucked his thumbs into his belt, fixing one and then the other with his one eye.

"We linger too long. First in Frankia, then with this Haesten. We should have found Gungnir by now. What is your plan when we find Sigdriffa?"

said Gunnr, and Skögul nodded dutifully.

"My plan?"

"We know Sigdriffa is with Guthrum and that he is a powerful lord. What if she has sworn to him and has his protection? What if Guthrum possesses the Odin spear, and it is the sacred weapon giving him power, enabling his victories?"

"What of it? We are here to get it back so that Ragnhild can be a Valkyrie once more and for her Odin oath to be intact. Whether Sigdriffa has it or Guthrum has it, I will get it back."

"I warn you...."

"You warn me?" Hundr stepped closer to Gunnr, and she bristled. Skögul dropped her hand to the axe in its loop at her belt.

"Don't touch your weapon at me," Hundr spoke as calmly as he could, despite becoming weary of the Valkyrie's constant griping and challenging of his decisions. "There will be a time to use that before this thing is done, that's for sure."

"I do not trust you, Dog's Name," uttered Gunnr, her lips twisting, the words spitting from her like a mouthful of food gone bad. "We are the servants of the All-Father himself, and we will return the spear to Upsala. You know too many marauders and desperate men for us not to fear that you will try to take Gungnir for yourself."

"If by marauder, you mean Jarl Haesten, then you are sorely mistaken. He is one whom Odin will want in his war council when the end of days comes. Can you say the same of yourself?"

Hundr strode away before the Valkyrie had time to respond. He took a bowl of hot rabbit stew from Bush and made for the far side of the camp. Haesten's men had tied a line between two trees to hobble the horses during the night.

"Get some food," he said to the two warriors as they finished securing the last horse.

"We will, with thanks," replied the red-bearded man. "Bjarki is my name, and this is Bolver."

"Good to have you with us," smiled Hundr, and he took a slurp of his stew. The rabbit was stringy, but the hot meal was welcome.

"Why do you seek these warrior women?" asked Bolver.

"They have Odin's Gungnir spear, and we are charged by the All-Father to get it back," he said, too tired to lie about it and not caring about how far-fetched a tale it was.

Bjarki reached for an amulet beneath his copper-red beard, a small spear for Odin. "Can it be true?" he whispered.

"It's true. They have it, and they are with

Guthrum, and we must get it back."

"Guthrum is at war, and we ride straight into the eye of its storm. The whole of Wessex is turned upside down. Saxon and Viking war bands roam the land, fighting for the scraps left by Alfred's defeat. I feel the gods are with us. These are strange days indeed," said Bjarki, and he kept hold of his amulet and made a sign with his left hand to ward off evil.

That was the peculiar warp and weft of it. Hundr found himself at the centre of a war, searching for a god's spear. The Valkyrie plagued him at every turn, and he was trying to make amends with the son of a man he had killed. Finally, he finished his stew and lay down alone under the stars. He fingered the cold ivory of Fenristooth's hilt and tried not to feel the gaze of Odin upon him.

THIRTEEN

"Do we have to do it this way?" said Hekkr, cursing as his boot slipped on a cow turd. The moon was just a thin sliver, sharing its mean light sparingly through shifting clouds gliding like shadows across a sky as black as a raven's wing.

"We do," grunted Einar, keeping low and moving slowly across a pasture, his legs burning from the crouch.

"Couldn't we just walk into the place and ask them if they know this man? In daylight. When it's not raining," said Amundr, massive and brooding next to Einar like a bear.

"Men here know me, and Rollo is slippier than a wet shit. I've fought him. He's a lucky bastard, and I don't want to stumble across him in his shit-stinking fortress," Einar answered. He had never liked Rollo, right from the moment they had met on Orkney, back when Hundr and Einar robbed Ketil Flatnose's treasure horde.

"There are more turds in this field than there is grass!" Hekkr swore another curse to Frey as his other boot slipped on cow droppings.

"We get in, find one of Rollo's guards, and get him to tell us where this burned bastard is. Once we know, we find him and kill him. That's it. So, keep your cheese pipe closed and let's get on with it."

"It might have been better...."

Einar halted and stood to rub his eyes. "Since when did this turn into a village elders meeting? I am Jarl, and you are my warriors. If either of you had anything but otter shit in your thought cages, you, too, would lead men. You are fighters, hard men, and we go to fight. That is it, don't think, just fight. Leave the thinking to me."

"Yes, Lord Einar," Hekkr and Amundr said simultaneously. Einar pressed on, moving cautiously and deliberately towards the looming shadow of Rollo's fortress rising beyond the field. Movements flickered and danced on the palisades fighting platform, illuminated from below by the warm yellow glow of brazier or torch fire. Sentries slowly patrolled that platform which sat behind the sharpened timber stakes from where the defenders could pour arrows, rocks and whatever else they could lay their hand upon, down onto the heads of any attacker below. Such an attacker would then need to scale the ditch and raised bank and then climb the sharpened stakes, which were twice as long as a man, and meet the defenders standing on the platform with axe and spear. Einar shuddered to think of the horror of attacking such a place. He had spent most of that afternoon watching Rollo's fortress from a distant hill, and the place was well-defended and busy with warriors.

"Remember, we make for the river wall," whispered Einar. They were now too close to the fort to risk being heard by the patrolling sentries. Amundr and Hekkr were silent, but Einar sensed their nods in the darkness, which was enough.

They paused in a crouch, listening as boots creaked and banged on the planking of the fighting platform over the wall. It sounded like a giant stomping across the fortress because the night amplified the noise. Finally, the sentry came into view. He wore a hooded cloak pulled tight around him, and a long spear rested on his shoulder, its wicked-tipped blade catching a flicker from the firelight within the fortress. The man coughed and thumped his chest with his fist before hawking a mouthful of spit over the wall. He grumbled and continued his rounds.

"Let's go," Einar hissed. The three big men scrambled through the field, keeping so low that the damp tips of the pastures' grass tickled Einar's knuckles. The deeper blackness of the ditch showed three paces ahead, and Einar went down it feet-first, skidding on his arse into the heavy, damp soil at its base. His boots squelched into the filth, and Hekkr cursed Thor's balls as he reached the bottom and pitched forward to land in the muck on his hands and knees. Einar pulled himself up to the far side of the bank using clumps of grass and rocks for handholds, his boots and knees losing purchase, but eventually, he reached the summit and sat with his back against the raised bank upon which the palisade stood. The three warriors waited there for the sound of the sentry's boots to go plodding past in the opposite direction. Einar held his breath because he was panting from the exertion of clambering out of the ditch. As soon as the sentry's boots faded into the darkness, he blew out a long breath and waited until he breathed normally. To be caught at the base of the walls was to die. There would be no way Einar could talk his way out of it. It would mean interrogation, torture, and death. What knotted Einar's guts was the terrible prospect of Rollo's leering, grinning face as his men burned Einar's flesh with hot irons or cut him with sharp blades. That was not death worthy of Valhalla, and he would not die at Rollo's hand.

Einar scuttled around the base of the walls,

moving swiftly towards the sound of the rushing river, to where the guards would not be expecting attackers without first having sailed along the wide river in ships. He paused and waited with his back against the rough whorls and knots of the wall's stakes, Hekkr and Amundr flanking him. After ten heartbeats, Einar was sure there was no sentry above him.

"Ready?" he said. Amundr knelt and cupped his hands, and Hekkr stepped into the cup. Hekkr counted to three and launched himself upwards, and Amundr's enormous frame surged with him, grunting as he launched Hekkr's leg towards the wall's spiked summit. Hekkr's boots scrambled and kicked against the stakes, and Einar winced at the noise of it. But then the legs disappeared into the gloom above and were replaced by a dangling rope. Einar grabbed it and pulled himself up, walking up the stakes as he pulled hand over hand. At the top, Hekkr took his hand, hauling Einar over, and Amundr followed. Einar slipped his seax from its sheath at his belt and tugged off his boots. He hurried along the fighting platform, his bare feet silent on the planking where his heavy boots would have woken the dead. The sentry coughed again, and Einar came up behind him like a shadow demon, slipped his left hand around the warrior's mouth, and dragged the edge of his seax blade across the sentry's throat. He pulled the blade towards him, and the cold, sharp edge sliced through flesh and gristle. Warm blood flowed as Einar tugged against the resistance there, and the sentry jerked and shuddered in his grip. Einar lowered him gently to the wooden platform and wiped his blade clean on the dead man's cloak.

"Why didn't you ask him where the burned man is?" asked Hekkr.

"You want to ask a sentry questions and give him a chance to shout the warning and raise the whole bloody fortress against us?" hissed Einar as quietly as possible. "Remember, I do the thinking, and you do the killing. Amundr, put on his cloak, take his spear, and walk the walls. We will return as soon as we can."

Amundr donned the cloak, rested the spear on his shoulders, and took up the sentry's watch. He was a head bigger than the dead man, who Hekkr tipped over the wall and into the ditch's black depths, and Einar hoped nobody would notice in the darkness.

Einar pulled his boots back on, and Hekkr dropped from the fighting platform into the fortress. Einar followed. An iron brazier crackled with three thick logs burning to cast a golden light against the palisade and the walls of the buildings within. Einar avoided the light and ran into the snarl of streets between the close-knit buildings. A dog barked somewhere, and a woman sneezed. The place was still and quiet, and Einar thanked the gods that they had evaded Rollo's men so far.

Hekkr halted and tapped Einar on the shoulder. He pointed to a pale building with three shields and spears stacked outside. Einar nodded, and they ran to the door, which was little more than three boards hinged to the wall by strips of leather. Einar dipped his head inside, and in the darkness, three warriors snored, huddled under cloaks. They lay peacefully upon cots filled with straw. Einar pointed at the closest two and then ran his finger across his throat. Hekkr nodded, and they crept forward, but a dog snarled from behind the closest man's cot, white teeth bared and shining in the room's darkness.

"Frigg's tits," Hekkr cursed. The men stirred in the cots, and Einar sprang forwards. He leapt upon the closest man and stabbed his seax once into the man's guts. His eyes burst awake, panic making his body spasm, and Einar cut his throat with a swift slice of his broken-backed blade. The dog barked and snarled again and bit Einar's ankle, its teeth unable to break through the tough boot leather. Einar shook and kicked his leg, but the dog dug in, its hind quarters low and the whites of its eyes showing. Hekkr cracked the neck of the second man, using his wiry strength and wrestling skill to grapple the head and twist it violently. The third warrior sat up in his bed and stared at the carnage, momentarily stunned from sleep and unsure if he was awake or dreaming. Hekkr landed on him, and they rolled together on the hard-packed earthen floor, and Einar kicked the dog hard in his maw. The beast whimpered, and Einar reached forward to stab it in the neck. The dog released him and squealed, and he stabbed it again, his stomach churning to kill the poor animal.

"Is there a man in this fortress with a burned face – a man who serves Rollo the Betrayer?" Einar demanded harshly. He no longer whispered, fearing that the dogs' bark and the fight had woken the whole fortress.

The warrior struggled in Hekkr's wrestler's grip, which was as strong as a shipbuilder's vice. He mumbled behind Hekkr's hand, which was clamped over his mouth.

"If you shout, we will cut off your balls and hands and leave you to live like that," Einar warned. The man clenched his eyes tightly closed and nodded to show he understood the horror of what that life would mean for a warrior. "Is there a man with a burned face here?"

The man nodded, and Hekkr slipped his hand away. The warrior licked his lips, and his face trembled. "He is Jarl Rollo's man. He has his own crew."

"Is he here?"

"No, my lord. He has gone to sea."

"Thor's balls. Nothing is ever simple," said Einar, rubbing his hand down his face. "Where has he gone?"

"He has gone to kill a man, a great warrior."

"Who?"

"The Man with the Dog's Name," answered the warrior, and Einar's breath caught in his throat. "He's one of Harald's war dogs. The bastard."

"Is Rollo here?"

"Yes, in his hall."

"What is the burned man's name, and does he fly a banner?"

"His name is Kvasir Randversson, and he flies Rollo's wolf banner."

Einar nodded at Hekkr, and recognition of what was about to happen spread across the warrior's face, but before he could shout in alarm, Hekkr snapped his spine with an audible crunch and let the corpse flop to the floor.

"What now, if the burned man isn't here?"

"We kill Rollo and get after this Kvasir before he can kill Hundr."

Hekkr nodded and shrugged, but then he

froze, raising a finger to his lips. Einar dipped his head, listening, and sure enough, he heard boots outside the door.

"Bjorn?" shouted a gruff voice, and a fist rapped on the door. "What are you doing there?"

Hekkr put his hand over his mouth and mumbled, "Piss off."

The voice laughed. "Have you got a whore in there, or are you and Hrolf keeping each other warm?"

Einar shook his head at Hekkr, wishing the wiry, muscled fighter had kept his mouth shut. At that moment, the door creaked open a sliver on its leather hinges, and Einar thought it was the man on the other side, trying to get a peek at whatever had caused the noise within. So, Einar kicked the door hard, and the man beyond yelped as it smashed into his face. Einar tore the door open and stabbed the man three times in the belly with his seax, three short quick blows, and then slammed a thumb's length of the blade into his temple. Hekkr came bursting from the door, though not quick enough to stop a second warrior from shouting at the top of his lungs.

"Help, attackers, murderers..." called the second warrior, but Hekkr's axe cut his alarm short, cracking open his face with a wet slap. The iron tang of blood was in the air, and torches moved in the night.

"Shit, let's go," said Einar, and they both ran hard for the palisade. Voices shouted behind them, but Einar sprinted, his knee aching from an old wound and his right arm wet with the blood of the men he had killed. Amundr was there waiting for them, and he leant over the fighting platform to heave them up towards him with a muscled arm for each man. Einar clambered up and fumbled along the timbers, looking for the rope. "You two first," he said. Hekkr went over and slid down the rope. Shouting erupted in the space between the platform and the wall, and Amundr grunted as he launched the sentry's spear into the crowd appearing there. A man cried out in pain, and Amundr went over the top of the wall as nimble as a dancer, belying his vast frame. Einar followed, and the three men scrambled down and up the ditch, running for their lives, back through the cow shit pasture and towards their ship, the Fjord Bear.

"Did you find the burned man? Did you kill him?" panted Amundr.

"No, but Einar killed a dog," piped Hekkr, hirpling along on his bowlegs.

"Why?"

"Just run," said Einar, shaking his head at the question as Hekkr laughed. Einar felt worse for killing the dog than he did about the men he had slain. He gasped for breath and ran in the darkness, away from Rollo's fortress in Frankia. The burned man was gone, and he was hunting Hundr. An assassin and a killer searching for his friend amidst the frontier of war-torn England.

FOURTEEN

"I thought King Alfred was finished?" said Bush, taking the stained leather helmet liner from his head to scratch his bald head.

"He looks fairly hale to me," Bjarki remarked, his mouth gaping at the vast number of Saxon warriors below. Hundr sat astride his horse at the peak of a valley which sloped along gentle hillsides steeped in the deep greens and browns of an ancient forest. The trees seemed to move, shifting and pulsing, and where shafts of light penetrated the canopy, there were glints of steel. Within the forest, a tremendous force of men marched. Fallen leaves rustled, and branches crunched under the tread of masses of unseen boots, all combining in a constant rumble like the sigh of the sea.

There were thousands of Saxon warriors in the forest, all descending to meet on fields in the valley basin, where an army of fighters gathered to rally around their king – a man whom they said was beaten. The warriors seemed to have sprung from the very land itself, like an army of legend, crawled from the depths of the English soil to aid its king in his last fight for survival and to throw off the invaders from across the sea.

"You said Alfred was living in a marsh like a toad, eating flies and eels," said Gunnr, frowning at Bjarki. "I have never seen such a force."

"You have never left Upsala," Ragnhild intoned, and the Valkyrie priestesses puckered on their horses like soured apples.

"The King must have rallied warriors from every corner of his kingdom," said Hundr, talking to himself rather than his crew. "When we came here with Ivar, the English were split into separate kingdoms. It was Mercia, Wessex, Northumbria and East Anglia. Maybe this is the power of Alfred's new England, all the old kingdoms united under him, rallying to his banner of Wessex." That banner whipped in the breeze, a dragon snarling proudly at the centre of the field next to a monstrous ancient rock, long and jutting from the earth as though tossed there by a giant.

"There will be a battle here," Valbrandr murmured. His eyes stared like flints at the massing fighters because this was the dream of all warriors. The shield wall. Not a one or two-crew shield wall, but the war fence of thousands. The battle line of linden wood, steel and iron, where a man made a reputation or forged a place in the Einherjar for himself. Stories of such battles were told in every Norse hall and fireside. Skalds in deep winter would keep men and boys enthralled with tales of bravery, the breaking of enemy shields, glory and legend.

"There will, and it will be the battle to decide the fate of this land," said Hundr.

"And a lot of poor bastards will bleed their guts out for it," muttered Bush.

"We are not here to fight other men's battles," Gunnr uttered tersely, and Hundr could feel her eyes boring into the back of his head. "We are here for the spear."

"Where do you think Sigdriffa and her war-hungry sisters will be?" said Hundr without turning to her, tired of her constant complaining and second-guessing of his command. "She who left your order precisely because you would not fight?"

"So, let's find Guthrum," barked Ragnhild, and she wheeled her horse around and rode away from the Saxons to search for Jarl Guthrum and his Viking army.

Of course, it is not hard to find an army. Scouts, both Saxon and Dane, patrolled the countryside, seeking each other out, searching valleys and dales for the hidden enemy and noting the lay of the land to report back to their leaders. A commander needed to know his enemy's movements or risk running into an organised force over a hill or at a river's ford whilst he marched in a column, and that would mean the annihilation of his force and himself. Then, there is the scar across the land where thousands of boots, hooves and wagons have torn up grass and bush. Not to mention the shit left by horses and men alike and the detritus so many men leave on the march. So, Hundr found Guthrum and his Vikings a half day's ride away in the walled town of Chippenham. It was a large town nestled in a wide sweep of the river Avon. The place was brimming with Viking warriors and horses, and the ring of the forge combined with the earthy smells of leather and shit which accompanied any army Hundr had ever been a part of.

Hundr and the Seaworm crew rode to the banks of the fast-flowing river but could not cross the bridge which spanned it. It was an old bridge of roman work, reinforced by timbers where time had chipped away at its pillars of neatly dressed stone. Guthrum had reserved the town for his own crews and a few of his close allies. A burly guard who barred the bridge turned them away with a bark and a wave of his hand. He bore Guthrum's raven banner upon his shield, and Hundr followed his pointing finger to where they could find shelter. The rest of the army was hard at work making camp on the grassy riverbank, thousands of warriors busy with wood, pots, and spears and making themselves as comfortable as possible. Sailcloth tents, cookfires, and groups of warriors drinking, playing at knucklebones, and supping ale covered the flatlands between the town and the river itself.

Once they had found a place to camp, Hundr charged Bush, Finn and most of the crew with erecting a shelter and starting a fire to make a meal. Hundr, Ragnhild, Bjarki and Sigrid, and then Gunnr and her Valkyrie set off in opposite directions to find Sigdriffa. The day grew long, and as the light faded, the land around Chippenham became alive with crackling campfires, song, shouting and laughter. Hundr strode around the various tents and groups of men, feeling hard eyes following him as grim warriors, bearded and scarred, sat and ate their meals, knowing that the Saxon horde was within marching distance. He caught the eye of a grizzled warrior sitting on a milking stool and surrounded by his crew. He flashed a mirthless grin at Hundr, and he nodded back. A young warrior bumped shoulders with Hundr as they walked past one another. The man turned and shoved Hundr, pride and arrogance on his beardless face as he reared up, chin up and chest out. Ragnhild's hand fell to her axe hilt, but Hundr apologised, and the pup marched away laughing with his friends, buoyed by the meaningless victory.

"Wasn't so long ago you would have killed him for that," said Ragnhild. "We'd be watching you fight a Holmgang now."

"True enough," agreed Hundr, shaking his head. "The days for strutting and fighting for no good reason are long gone."

"Were you as cocksure as that pup, really?" asked Sigrid, smiling, searching his face for the young man he had once been.

"Worse," smirked Ragnhild, and they laughed. The army Guthrum had assembled at Chippenham to destroy the last remnants of the Saxon lordship in England was vast. Hundr walked until his feet ached. Endless crews surrounded the riverbank, but there was no sign of the Valkyrie. Hundr asked around for any news of the warrior priestesses as Ragnhild bought ale and food from friendly crews, but there was no sign of them.

"We can't walk the camp all night," said Sigrid, standing on her tiptoes and gazing at the horde stretching before them into the darkness. "Sigdriffa might even be inside the town with

Guthrum's men."

"She might," agreed Hundr, scratching his beard. He set off at a brisk march back in the direction from which they had started.

"Where are you going?" asked Sigrid.

"To see Guthrum and find this cursed spear."

The bridge guard from earlier who had turned back the Seaworm crew met Hundr with similar bored disdain. "Piss off back to the camp," he said, and he yawned in Hundr's face.

"I'm going in there to see Jarl Guthrum."

"King Guthrum," the guard retorted. "And you are not going in there. Nobody is going in there unless the King says so."

"I am Jarl..." began Hundr, but he didn't have time to finish because Ragnhild dragged the guard into a savage headbutt, the sound of it like meat slapping on a chopping block, and she drove him to the edge of the bridge and shoved him into the darkness of the fast-flowing river below.

"Come on," she said and strode towards Chippenham's high gate. Haesten's man Bjarki laughed and followed, a grin splitting his tattooed face. The captured Saxon town's gate was the width of two men and was now wide open beneath a tall tower where archers could pour their arrows into any attacking force.

Hundr passed under the gate, and the inside of Chippenham was just as busy with Viking warriors as the camp outside its walls. The smell of roasting pork assaulted Hundr's senses, making his mouth water, and across from the gate was a lane which led straight into an open square where a man in a leather apron turned a pig on a spit. The square itself was crammed with warriors, drinking, shouting and laughing. Hundr weaved through the throng of men, the stink of their sweat and their foul ale breath thick in the air.

"There," said Sigrid. She pointed to a group of men at the far side of Chippenham's square. Five men, all wearing bright brynjars and with arms and necks heavy with gold and silver. A loose ring of warriors surrounded the group, each man bearing shields with Guthrum's raven painted on leather covers.

"That's Guthrum, the one with the big belly and the rings in his beard," said Bjarki, pointing at a stocky man at the group's centre. "The rest are Danish Jarls. The army is not what it was. Half the force went north last year to secure Northumbria and fight the Picts."

"Why did the army break up?" asked Hundr. Chippenham was overflowing with warriors, and he marvelled at the size of the force Guthrum would have led had the Great Army remained intact.

Bjarki shrugged. "Men came here because the Saxons have fallen. There is land here for us all, for any Viking with a crew and the courage to take it. The powerful Jarls split from Guthrum to make themselves Kings and Lords in the north rather than make Guthrum King here. If he doesn't defeat Alfred now, men will think Guthrum has lost his luck."

Hundr nodded at that truth. Luck can flee from a man like an old cloak in the same way it can make a man wealthy and powerful. "That's why Haesten is here, then? To take a slice of England for himself."

Bjarki grinned and wiped a hand down his tattooed face. "Haesten will be a Lord here, and there is silver for us all. So, you think Guthrum will have your Valkyrie with him here in the town?"

"They are here," said Sigrid, as though she felt it in her very bones. "How are we going to get close enough to talk to him?"

"We don't need to," Ragnhild spoke up, her one eye blazing. Next to Guthrum was a tall woman with muscled, bare arms and long legs in a fish-scale brynjar. She had long golden hair, and a sword slung across her back. "That's Sigdriffa."

"So, the rest of her warriors must be in this place somewhere with the spear," Sigrid nodded.

Across the square, Sigdriffa bowed her head

to Guthrum and clapped a fist to her breast. He nodded to her, and she strode out of the square and waited with her hands on her hips. Moments later, a line of horses came trotting from a side street from behind a line of timber buildings topped with greying thatch. The riders were Valkyrie, their bows and quivers bouncing on their saddles as they rode past Sigdriffa, and in a fluid motion, she leapt upon the back of a bay mare, and the line of horses burst into a gallop. They rode up the main street and thundered out of the gate.

Hundr, Ragnhild, and Sigrid ran after them but stopped as they reached the bridge because the Valkyrie riders sped off towards the forest, black and shadowed in the moonlight.

"We will never find them now," exclaimed Ragnhild, slamming her hand onto the bridge rail.

"They must be off scouting or harrying the enemy," said Hundr. "But if what we have heard about Sigdriffa is true, she will be on the field when Guthrum fights Alfred. And that is where we will find her."

"So, we will fight in the great shield wall?" asked Sigrid, her eyes wide at the prospect of witnessing and taking part in such a mammoth battle. Hundr smiled at her. This was her dream, her burning desire. Sigrid sailed with Hundr because she had fled her father, Ketil Flatnose, and from an arranged marriage she did not want. She had left in search of glory and reputation, and there was plenty of that to be found sailing with the Seaworm.

"We march to the battle, and if we have to, we fight," said Hundr. "But we are here for the spear and for Ragnhild. If we stand in this shield wall, which is surely the last stand of the Saxons, men will die. Alfred fights for his life and the freedom of his people. If he loses that fight, all the old Saxon kingdoms will fall under Viking rule. So, the Saxons will fight like demons." He shuddered, recalling the horrors of the battle at Jorvik many years ago when he had scaled the walls with his old friend Sten and had fought inside the Roman city back-to-back with Ivar the Boneless.

Hundr left Chippenham's town, where Guthrum drank and ate with his leaders and his men, on the cusp of becoming what all Vikings dreamed of, a King by his own hand and by the blade of his axe. Eventually, he reached the camp where the men had scrounged together an evening meal, and Bush cooked over a campfire. He smiled when he saw Hundr and brought him a piece of flatbread.

"We found Sigdriffa," Hundr said, tearing a strip of the bread with his teeth.

"Thor's luck is upon us then," smiled Bush. "Did you see the spear?"

"No," said Hundr, chasing small stones from the bread around his mouth with the tip of his tongue. "She left with her warriors on horseback, riding into the night. There will be a battle here, Bush, and like as not, we must fight in it."

Bush grimaced. "Can we not ride out after them, get the bloody spear back before the battle, and get out of here before the shield wall?"

"We'd never track them. It's dark, and there will be scouts riding all over these hills, both Viking and Saxon. By the time we could go after them in the morning, they would be long gone. There will be on the battlefield, though, and that will be our best chance."

"It will be a grim day. You saw the number of Saxon bastards in that valley."

"This battle is a sign from Odin," Gunnr interrupted. She had appeared next to Bush, clutching the Odin spear amulet at her neck. "We can retrieve Gungnir in the fire of the shield wall as corpses fly to Odin's mighty hall sent there by our blades. I can feel the hand of the gods in it." Her sisters nodded and shot nervous glances at each other, flanking their leader to face Hundr.

"It's a sign that many will die," said Hundr, rubbing the tiredness from his eyes. "How many of you have fought in a proper battle before?

There will be thousands of warriors on each side tomorrow, and the shield wall line will stretch beyond sight. It will be a day of blades, strength, blood and death. The fight will ebb and flow around us, and we won't know the warp and weft of it as we fight for our lives. Our line could collapse, and foes could surround us, and we won't know anything about it until the blades become too many for our shields to repel. Or, we could have won the battle and will still kill for hours or be killed ourselves before we realise it. You will not be the same after it, so prepare yourselves. What is the name of this place?"

"Ethandun, I believe, Lord Hundr," said Sigvarth. "I heard it from a man who sold me that bread."

"Tomorrow, we fight in the battle of Ethandun, so sharpen your blades and ready your shields."

FIFTEEN

Guthrum's messengers woke Hundr and the Seaworm crew before dawn. Their gruff voices barked the army awake, poking heads in tents and nudging warriors out of their slumber. Hundr rose from beneath his cloak and took a swig of ale and a bite of some hard flatbread which he had kept from the night before to break his fast. Sigrid stirred next to him, and he passed half of his bread to her.

"Is it time?" she murmured, her voice thick from sleep.

"It's time." He reached over and stroked the softness of her face and pushed her loose, golden hair behind her ear. She was beautiful, too beautiful to be sleeping wet-arsed on a Saxon riverbank. She would grace any hall in Midgard. Tall, elegant and proud.

"I could not sleep," she said, sitting up to eat

her bread. She yawned and cuffed the sleep from her eyes.

"Most of the men in this army are the same unless they do not understand what they will face today. Few will have spent a restful night. You know, you saw some of what awaits us today at Hafrsfjord. But that was a sea battle, where we fought on the decks of ships. The battle today will be a different thing. A shoving match of shields where blades come unseen for groin and neck. Stay close to me today, my love."

She smiled at that word, for he said it rarely, even though he loved her more than he had ever thought possible. He rose and pulled on his brynjar, its metal rings cold and heavy. Hundr raised his arms and shrugged it on, and the chainmail slithered down his torso like the skin of a dragon. He buckled on his two swords, Fenristooth and Battle Fang, and nodded greetings to Valbrandr, Sigvarth and Thorgrim. They checked the boards of their shields and the edges of their blades one last time. They were good men and brave, and Hundr hoped they were still with him at the end of the day.

Gunnr, Skögul and the Valkyrie stood in a circle and prayed together, a sonorous chant to Odin, and Ragnhild stood with them. Hundr smiled at that because that sliver of Valkyrie acceptance would make Ragnhild happy, and she deserved that. Sigrid whispered along with them as she stood and pulled on her own war gear. The sun rose beyond the distant forest, casting a red hue across a sea-grey sky. A cockerel crowed from behind Chippenham's walls, amongst the wisps of morning cookfires, the clank of iron, and the whinnying of horses. A dog's bark drowned it out, first one and then a pack howling at the new day. *Those hounds might have new masters before the day's end, or Guthrum would be King of Wessex and, therefore, England.*

"Time to go, lads," shouted a rider, a grey-bearded warrior on a white horse. He gripped a spear from which Guthrum's raven banner hung limp in the still morning. "Follow me. Today is the day." He clicked his tongue and allowed his horse to pick its way lazily amongst the tents and burned-out campfires. He repeated the same message, and men roused themselves to trail after him. Coughs and grumbles resounded from the army as men filed after the rider, spears banging on shields and orders called from unseen captains.

Finn sat upon a log, running a whetstone along the blade of his spear, his seax resting against his leg. He looked young, fresh-faced and innocent. He glanced up and smiled at Hundr.

"Find a shield and stay out of the front rank," Hundr said. "Keep your shield up. Just as Einar taught you and as you have practiced. This will be your first shield wall. Men fear it, for it is a place of death. You will never be closer to your doom than in battle. And do not die, or else Einar will skin me alive."

Finn nodded and swallowed hard. Hundr understood the fear gripping the lad's guts. The shield wall was a thing all young men craved, desperate to emulate the stories of heroes, hungry to make their reputations as warriors. But Hundr knew better. He knew it for what it was, a place where enemies pushed together across the linden wood wall, as close as lovers, where blades came to rend and tear at a man's flesh from above and below. Axes, spears and swords looming to kill or cause the grievous wound that will rot a man green and deny him his place in Valhalla.

Bush kicked a few still-sleeping Seaworm men up the arse to wake them, and then the crew followed the army towards the field at Ethandun.

The Saxons lined up at the bed of a gentle valley with patches of forest dotted on intersecting hillocks. Hundr's breath caught in his chest as he crested the peak of that valley, looking down at the vast length of the Saxon shield wall. There were thousands of enemy warriors, helmets and spear points glinting in the morning sun, and they roared their defiance as the Viking lines massed above them. The Saxons were so many that their rear lines disappeared into the woodland at their rear. A few sheep and cattle grazed, uncaring of the bloodletting to follow, between the battle lines on the soft slopes of Ethandun's pastures. Those animals, sheep and cows, had shorn the grass below Hundr's feet short, and the crews around him spread out to form a jagged line. Men jostled and clumped into bands, keeping back and in groups, reluctant to be found at the front line where the killers fought – the brutal men, the lovers of battle.

"Come on," Hundr said, and he pushed forward, holding his shield, which bore his one-eyed sigil, high against his chest as he wove through the massed warriors. "Find Sigdriffa." Ragnhild flanked him on one side, and Gunnr pushed her way to his right. She curled her lip at him, and Hundr shook his head.

They moved over the ridge at the valley's peak and started downhill towards where the front rankers massed. They shared around ale skins as men looked for courage in the drink. A band of bare-chested berserkers slapped each other's faces and roared spittle at one another as they worked up their war frenzy. Hundr turned and stared back up the hill, looking for any sign of the Valkyrie amongst the horde.

"I hate berserkers, bloody mad bastards," grumbled Bush. Hundr chuckled. They had fought such men before, and they were indeed madmen, as likely to lose you a battle with their recklessness than win you one with their ferocity.

"I see them," said Skögul, and she pointed west across the army to the flank, and sure enough, Hundr saw the Valkyrie stood with their hair unbound, not a helmet between them and bows ready.

"Archers on the flanks, let's get closer," Hundr nodded. It was a sound plan from Guthrum to pack the sides of his army with bows. Arrows won't win a battle, but they would cause the Saxons to huddle together, avoiding the wicked barbs, most of which would sink into shields or be deflected by helmets or iron and leather armour. More of the missiles would sail over the battle line harmlessly. But some would hit faces and necks or feet and shoulders. So, the enemy would shuffle away from the arrows, and their army would bunch the centre of their line, fouling spear arms and axe swings.

"That is a lot of Saxons," said Torsten to Hundr's left.

"There are more of them than us," agreed Thorgrim.

"How many are fighters, though?" Ragnhild intoned. "Many of the men the Saxons bring to fight are farmers and bakers – they have called out their simple folk to fight us."

The fyrd. Hundr remembered the word from

when he had fought in England before, and Ragnhild was right. Every man in Guthrum's army was a warrior who'd sailed to these shores on warships, searching for blood and silver. Each Viking was armed with an axe or spear and swords if they could afford one, and all had been trained to fight from the time they could stand. The farmers and gentle folk stayed in the north, on their farms in Kattegat and the Vik, and the hungry men, the adventurers, took to the Whale Road. So, the Saxons had more men but not necessarily more warriors.

Hundr kept moving, weaving between bearded growlers with burning eyes staring at the Saxons below.

"Easy lads," said a big man with a bushy beard poking from the underside of his helmet, who Hundr barged past. "There're enough Saxons for us all to kill. Stand here and fight next to us."

Hundr ignored him and kept moving towards the Valkyrie. A horn blared, loud and resonant, as though it piped from Asgard itself. The army immediately stirred and surged, spaces tightening, so the surrounding crews held Hundr in place. Another blare of the horn and riders came around the Viking ranks flying the raven banner. Guthrum sat astride a huge, black warhorse. He rode grim-faced before his army and raised a shining sword in salute. The rings in his beard glinted, and his arms and neck were thick with silver and gold. The warriors erupted in cheers, and Guthrum and Odin's names were bellowed, rumbling like a shifting mountain across the valley. Hundr couldn't move; he was two ranks from the front but still twenty men away from Sigdriffa and the flank.

"What is he saying?" asked Valbrandr. A man shouted at him to be quiet, and Valbrandr shot him a murderous look. Guthrum was at the centre of the front rank, waving his sword around his head and making a battle speech to the army, but all Hundr could see was the sword waving and his mouth moving.

"He says kill the Saxon bastards," piped Bush, and all the nearby warriors laughed.

"I wonder how many he is going to kill?" came a voice three ranks back, to more laughter but also some curses from men loyal to Guthrum.

A roar went up from the Saxon warriors below in the valley, and it rippled along their line like an ocean wave. They roared again, and when Hundr looked up to see where Guthrum was, the Viking leader was riding back along the front line and towards the opposite flank. Away from the front line. The raven banner was still there, and it wavered as its wielder took up a position at the centre of the army.

"Advance! Advance!" a rough voice called from the front, and the lines shuffled forwards. Hundr took small steps so as not to collide with the man in front, and Thorgrim apologised as his spear shaft banged on Ragnhild's head.

"In it up to our bloody necks," said Bush, and he cursed as the warriors behind jostled him. The Viking army moved down the pale green hillside. On the opposite flank, the warriors flowed around a small wood, and drums struck up behind the lines. The sound was deep and rhythmic, war music. It pulsed in Hundr's heart, and his breathing quickened.

"Bush," Hundr spoke up, glancing over his shoulder. "Keep Finn with you. Don't let him out of the line." Hundr feared that the bellicose youth would dart forward to strike at the Saxons when the shield walls came together and would be rewarded with a Saxon spear in his throat.

"How are we going to get Gungnir amid this battle?" said Gunnr, still on Hundr's left. Her sharp face had turned pale, and she licked at her dry lips.

"This is your first battle, Valkyrie?" asked Hundr. She nodded. "Keep your shield overlapped with mine. Do not let it drop. We are not at the front line, but our time will come. When it does, keep your shield up and don't leave a gap, or we will both die."

"How are we supposed to get the spear if we are dead?" her voice was strained. They grew closer to the enemy, whose lines broiled and surged at the bottom of the hill, weapons shining and war songs roaring.

Boom, boom, boom, boom, boom, ba boom went the sound of Guthrum's war drums, over and over again. Hundr took a spear passed to him by one of the Seaworm rear rankers and clashed it on the iron rim of his shield.

"When the lines break, and they will," he said, "either they will break our wall or we theirs, but when it happens, we push across the battlefield towards Sigdriffa. No one will notice what we must do amongst the chaos." He continued to bang his spear, and others around him took up the rhythm. Ahead of him, the front rankers were shouting and roaring, helmeted heads rolling and shaking, working themselves up into the killing fury. "Stay close to me; keep your shield up," he said to Sigrid, and she nodded, eyes wide and beautiful.

The hill's slope softened, and Hundr marched on level ground. Orders came from the front for archers, and the thrum of their bows on the flanks was like a thousand birds taking flight simultaneously. The air was thick with arrows which sailed high, seeming to travel slowly on the way up towards the sky and then picking up speed on their downward arc to rain pain and death on the Saxon ranks. The roars of defiance across the battlefield were now joined by cries of agony, and the Saxon lines compressed, bunching together to avoid the murderous arrows pelting their flanks.

Shafts came in response from the Saxon army, but they aimed at the Viking centre, and whilst Hundr heard the tonk of arrows on steel and the cries of injured warriors, the shafts did not threaten the Seaworm crew.

A long, wailing horn sounded from across the field, and the Saxons let out a roar to shake the heavens, chilling Hundr's heart. This was their last stand. The warriors from across King Alfred's lands gathered here to fight for their homes, their wives and children, for their very existence. The front rankers in the Viking line halted suddenly, and Hundr's shield crashed into the warrior in front of him, as the warrior's shield behind thumped into Hundr's back.

"Bastards are charging," said Bush. "Hold fast, lads."

"Odin, Odin, Odin," Valbrandr chanted in his deep voice. A man vomited along the line from Hundr, and somewhere a warrior wept.

Boom, boom, boom, boom, boom, ba boom continued the drums, and Hundr felt the war hunger upon him. He felt young again, just like when he had scaled the walls at Jorvik to fight alongside Ivar the Boneless, the hero who had become his enemy. Hundr felt like a stag, strong, chest heaving and ready to charge. Then the clash came, the Saxon shield wall thundered into the Viking line, and the sound of it was like a forest collapsing, crunching and tearing at wooden shields, flesh, bone, steel and earth. Hundr braced his shoulder behind his shield and thrust forward as the lines in front pressed against him. His boots slid back in on the grass before he found purchase and heaved forward. Hundr saw blades thrusting, iron grey and tipped with dark crimson, through the gaps of helmeted heads in front of him. He saw snarling faces, bared teeth and twisting limbs as men cut, stabbed and slashed at other. The roar of the battle was deafening, and it filled Hundr's head like a violent storm upon the Whale Road.

The snarling faces came closer, and they forced Hundr to shuffle backwards as the great monster of the army shifted, pushed back by the ferocious Saxon onslaught. Ahead, he saw a thick-necked Saxon striking at the Viking front line with a short seax, and men fell away from him like summer wheat under a scythe. Next to Hundr, Gunnr was keening a high-pitched wail, and her bottom lip quivered. Blood flew and slopped across Hundr's chest and onto Gunnr's face, and she shouted at the warm horror of it. Hundr wriggled his shoulders to give himself room and raised his spear high overhand so that its point rested on the rim of his spear.

"Shield up," he growled at Gunnr, and she raised it to keep the boards tight to Hundr's own. The Saxon was closer, and Hundr could see his brown eyes shining with death fury as another Viking fell to his murderous blade. Hundr judged the distance and waited until the lethal warrior barged his shield into the Viking shield wall again, only two ranks in front of Hundr now, and he thrust his spear forwards, but it went wide of the Saxon's cheek. He saw Hundr then, that Wessex front ranker, and he surged towards him, slashing at the Viking before him and cutting off a man's ear as he went. Hundr thrust again, and just as the Saxon opened his maw to bellow at Hundr, the spear burst through his teeth and into his mouth. Blood was on the spear blade, and Hundr ripped it free. The warriors in front of him roared and shoved their shields back at the Saxons. And so it went, Hundr pushing his shield into the backs of the men in front of him, Gunnr and Sigrid's shield's tight on either side of him, and when chances came, Hundr struck with his leaf-shaped spear blade. Along the line, men grunted, shouted, killed and died. The drums beat, horns wailed, and what had been a lush green field was now a brown, torn, muddy bog churned by boots, blood, and the shit and piss of the dying.

Gunnr pressed into Hundr's shield arm, and he sensed the swing of the Viking line from that side. It was impossible to see what happened along the centre and left flank of Guthrum's army, and as in any battle, Hundr could only deal with the enemy in front of him, but a surge of emotion swept across the Viking shield wall, like an unseen wind. Doom. Hundr felt it, and his chest tightened. Men craned their necks to look left.

"There's a swing out there on the flank," said Ragnhild, shouldering behind her shield as a Saxon spearpoint jabbed at its top edge, too far away to punch through and injure her and too jammed between the push of the shield wall to move anywhere else.

"Can anybody see whose flank has collapsed?" Hundr shouted. If it was the Saxon line, the press of the shield wall would break, and the shoving and stabbing would cease. Then the fight would become an open battle as the collapsing lines fled, and the victors moved among the defeated to pick off the pockets of resolute fighters and pursue the runners.

"Can't see anything," shouted Bush.

"If we are losing, we make for Sigdriffa and get out of here alive. We don't die here for Guthrum," Hundr called, and he was rewarded with scathing looks from the press of warriors around him.

The Saxons hacked furiously into the Viking

lines. Men died or fell, and Hundr found himself in the second rank. Front rankers who had survived the onslaught pushed back into the rear lines to rest their exhausted arms, weary of fighting, their faces drawn and pale from the battle's terror. Shields parted, the ranks enveloped them, and the men next in line came forward to stand toe to toe with the Saxon enemy. A warrior in front of Ragnhild screamed in agony as a Saxon axe chopped into his shoulder, cleaving him open so that bright red tissue and white bone showed vividly in the wound. The Saxon axeman dragged the dying man forward into his own shield wall, and Ragnhild filled the space with her axe. She sliced the sharp edge of its bearded blade across the Saxon's throat, and his angry face turned to wide-eyed shock as his life pulsed out of the red gash at his neck, washing his brynjar in blood. Hundr surged into the space with Ragnhild and smashed his spear into the neck of one Saxon, leaving the weapon there. He shoved with his shield, and Valbrandr came alongside him, slashing and cutting with a seax as long as a man's forearm.

There was room around him, and Hundr reached over his shoulder to drag Battle Fang free of her scabbard. He brought her blade down overhand to crash into the helmet of a bearded Saxon, and the iron caved in to crush the skull beneath. The opposing war fences were broken, and the lines had deteriorated into smaller skirmishes.

"They have turned our flank," Sigvarth yelled in Hundr's ear. "Guthrum's left has collapsed. The Saxons are amongst us."

Hundr took an axe blow on his shield, which jarred up his arm, and he punched its boss into the face of the attacker. A knife blade jabbed underneath his shield and scraped up his thigh, scoring his flesh like fire through his trews before catching on the hem of his brynjar.

"Make for the Valkyrie; push right," Hundr shouted to his crew. "Ragnhild, line up with Gunnr and lead her warriors with us. We go for the spear." The battle was over; all that remained would succumb to the slaughter. Alfred's larger, desperate Saxon force had defeated Guthrum's army. The King, who all had thought finished, who had lived like a toad in the marshes, had won a glorious victory over the Viking invaders of his land. The Saxons were vengeful. They would show no mercy for the enemy who had ravaged villages, towns and cities.

Hundr stepped back from the snarling, spitting Saxons. They came on recklessly, shields abandoned and hacking their blades two-handed into the retreating Vikings. A short man came at Hundr, spittle in his beard and teeth bared. He drove a spear with venom, but it was all fury in the blow. Hundr batted it aside with his shield and stabbed Battle Fang's point into the Saxon's chest, piercing his leather breastplate and the bone beyond. The Viking lines withdrew like the tide from a beach. What had been roars and bellows of war now became shrieks and panic for survival. As warriors turned their backs on the enemy, Saxon weapons cut at necks and shoulder blades, soaking the land with the blood of the invaders. Hundr was relieved to see that none of his crew had fallen, and his heart warmed to find Finn's youthful face grinning at him from behind his shield, kept safe next to Bush and his experience.

Ragnhild had formed the Valkyrie into a wedge formation, with her at the tip. The rear rank faced towards the right flank, and they moved in that direction, with the Seaworm crew following them in good order. The Saxons avoided their organised shields, with easier prey for their thirsty axes and spears fleeing across the field of battle. Hundr deflected the wild blows of Saxons who surged past him, but none stopped to engage. A giant Saxon warrior with hair as blonde as a Norseman, wielding a shining sword, strode through the fleeing Vikings, cutting and slashing with his right hand and clutching a wicked-looking seax in his left. He surged towards the Seaworm crew and cut down an oarsman named Arne with a brutal stab to the chest. Haesten's man Bolver struck at the big Saxon with his axe, but the warrior parried it with his short blade and gutted Bolver with a sweep of his sword. Bolver fell to his knees, and the Saxon punched the tip of his seax into Bolver's eye, taking his life with frightening speed.

Hundr leapt at the Saxon, and their swords came together in a clang which shook Hundr's bones like thunder. The Saxon swung at him, and Hundr ducked beneath the strike. The warrior was young, fierce and huge, and his seax banged into the shoulder of Hundr's brynjar, but the mail held. Sigrid attacked the man and forced him back with her screaming fury, but he kicked her savagely in the gut, and Hundr lunged at the man, driving him back with a flurry of blows. He cursed at Hundr in Norse, which was surprising coming from a Saxon, and turned instead to slay a big, bearded Dane.

Hundr kept moving, pushing towards the flank, searching for his prey. He stumbled on a corpse of a gut-stabbed Viking, his entrails purple and pink against the brown mud of the battlefield. What had once been a shield wall battle had turned into a butcher's block of torn flesh, leaking blood and the suffering of the wounded. Hundr wiped blood and sweat from his eye with the back of his hand and tried not to hear the screams of the injured.

"I see Sigdriffa," called Skögul, and the Valkyrie in Hundr's crew let out an undulating war cry because Gungnir was finally within their grasp.

SIXTEEN

Sigdriffa fought at the front of her Valkyrie warriors. They moved in a circle formation, efficient and organised, up the hill stretching away from Ethandun's blood-churned battlefield in retreat. Her spear snaked out from behind her circular shield wall like the forked tongue of a Loki monster. Hundr followed the trail, which left dead Saxons in its wake like a trail of breadcrumbs. There were also corpses of Sigdriffa's own Valkyrie littering the field, torn to ragged shreds in the crushing defeat to King Alfred's warriors.

The Seaworm Valkyrie wailed as they marched past their dead sisters, kneeling to snatch up spear amulets from their necks or spare white feathered arrows from the dead women's quivers. The pursuit was grim amongst the marauding, victorious Saxons who hacked at Guthrum's forces mercilessly as they retreated towards the safety of Chippenham's walls and its surrounding river. Ragnhild burst from her wedge formation as they reached the summit of the hill above Ethandun. She ran forward with her axe and shield outstretched, screaming Sigdriffa's name. The renegade Valkyrie paused, and she, too, emerged from her defensive formation to face Ragnhild.

Sigdriffa was tall, lean and fair, and Ragnhild was short, muscular and scarred. They faced each other, crouched like animals ready to pounce, both viciously skilled warriors whose blades had already drank the blood of their enemies that day.

"I come from Upsala for the spear," Ragnhild said, letting her weapons rest at her side.

"I remember you, Ragnhild," Sigdriffa replied, raising her spear in salute, its tip soaked in gore. "We thought you were dead, but here you are, unlooked for."

"The fallen will glut the halls of the gods," Ragnhild said and cast her eye over the carnage which spread down the hilltop. Corpses lay in ragged clumps or alone and slashed to bloody ruin. Wounded men crawled away from the slaughter, wincing and wailing at their injuries.

"Why are you surrounded by those nithings?" Sigdriffa pointed her spear at Gunnr, Skögul and the Seaworm Valkyrie. "I am surprised to see raven starvers such as they on such a glorious battlefield. I feel Odin's hand on my shoulder today, Ragnhild. Do you feel it? He is here. He watches and takes only the most glorious for his Einherjar."

"I feel it."

Sigdriffa smiled. A wide, mirthless grim thing of white teeth and madness beneath a face slathered in blood and battle filth. "Many of our sisters have fallen today. I envy them, for they will feast tonight with heroes in Valhalla."

A pack of Saxons came over the hill's crest, took one look at the two groups of Vikings, and marched the other way. The pursuit of the Vikings had continued over the hills towards Chippenham in a ragged fashion. The easy prey was dead, and now the Saxons would regroup. Alfred had taken the field and routed Guthrum, but he would need to get them out of Chippenham and turn his battle victory into a war victory if he wanted his kingdom back.

"Give us the spear," said Ragnhild evenly, no anger in her voice. "It belongs at Upsala, where Odin can find it when the time comes."

"Upsala?" Sigdriffa spat, her mouth twisting in derision. "It has fallen, sister. What was once a hall of the mighty, a place of warriors in Odin's service, is now a den of nithings and cowards. The temple is rife with battle-shirkers like those who march with you. The spear does not belong there. I go to build a new temple for Odin. He calls to me, Ragnhild. He bids me to build Upsala anew, filled with warriors such as we, sisters who can do him honour and fill his corpse hall with warriors worthy of Ragnarök. Join us; we take the All-Father's path. The righteous path."

"I have come for the spear," Ragnhild replied, and the warriors behind Sigdriffa bristled, wails and growls erupting from their shield wall. "Where is it?"

"Safe, sister."

"Hand it over, oathbreaker," demanded Gunnr, striding past Ragnhild with her spear held before her, levelling the weapon. But faster than Hundr thought possible, Sigdriffa's hand shot out like the head of a striking serpent and grasped its shaft just below the iron point. She hauled Gunnr forwards, tipping her off balance and punched her hard in the face with the haft of her axe. Gunnr dropped to one knee with a gasp. Her nose had twisted brutally against her cheek, and blood flowed freely down her chin. Sigdriffa had the blade of her axe at Gunnr's throat. The Seaworm Valkyrie took a forward step but halted when they saw their leader's predicament.

"You are not worthy of Gungnir," sneered Sigdriffa. "For such as you to hold it, sullies its blade, soaks away its power. How can Odin fight the Loki horde? How can he kill Fenris with a blade touched by you?"

Shouting at the rear of the Seaworm crew snapped Hundr's head around. A group of Saxons marched at them, a large band of warriors bristling with spears and blades.

"Shield wall!" shouted Bush, and the Seaworm crew turned away from Sigdriffa's Valkyrie to face the new threat. Sigdriffa pushed Gunnr to the grass, curling her lip at her, before turning and loping off with her warriors towards Chippenham. Hundr cursed. Ragnhild stared after them, fingers twitching on her axe. She watched her dream disappear into the forest and turned to stare at Hundr with a haunted look in her eyes. The destiny of her eternal soul lay with that spear. Only by returning it to Upsala could she rejoin the Valkyrie, restore her oath, and secure her place in Valhalla.

"Saxon bastards," she said, and turned on her heel to join the Seaworm shield wall. Hundr would have followed her had she charged after

Sigdriffa, and he would have fought and died to get that spear at Ragnhild's side. But she had chosen her crew and her friends over her dream, and that was why Hundr loved her like a sister. He let his shield drop and pulled Fenristooth from the scabbard at his belt so that he held a sword in each hand. The Saxons were twenty strong and beat upon the Seaworm shield wall with their blades, still drunk with victory and without shields of their own, their sheer hatred for the invader filling their arms with strength and viciousness. Hundr ran around the left flank of his warriors, who outnumbered the enemy by ten men. He passed the Valkyrie who huddled around Gunnr, helping her rise to her feet, and he came around in a wide arc to strike at the flank of the Saxon attackers.

Hundr cut Battle Fang across the knee of the rightmost Saxon and slashed Fenristooth across the face of the second. He struck with speed and fluidity, the strikes launching so quickly that before those two men fell away screaming from their attack, he had one sword in the belly of the next man and another piercing the throat of the fourth. Ragnhild burst through the Seaworm shield wall, her shrill Odin cry piercing the clash of weapons like a raven's call whipped by a storm. She hacked her short, hafted war-axe into the chest of a burly Saxon and ripped it free to parry a spear thrust and slash at the next man.

"Bows, now!" Sigrid shouted at Skögul, Gunnr, and the Valkyrie. She unslung her bow from her shoulder and fired two arrows at the Saxons in as many heartbeats. Skögul joined her, and the Saxons reeled away from their attack, running down the hill towards the scarred battlefield in the valley below.

"Back to Chippenham," said Hundr, wiping the blood off his swords on the jerkin of a fallen Saxon. "We must get inside the walls before the Saxons surround the place." Valbrandr cut the throats of the injured Saxons, and the crew quickly checked the bodies of the fallen for coins and anything of value. Bush ruffled Finn's hair, and Thorgrim clapped him on the back. Hundr had not seen it, but Finn's spear blade was darkened with Saxon blood. The lad had survived his first shield wall and struck at the enemy, which was no small thing. Finn had retrieved a sword from the battlefield, its blade stuffed into his belt, the hilt resting across his stomach, and there was a gleam in his eye. It was familiar, and Hundr's shoulders shivered at the memory of Finn's father, Ivar the Boneless, his viciousness and unnatural speed coming back to Hundr from distant battlefields.

They loped off towards the treeline, shields, spears and axes banging with the rhythm of their strides. The hills teemed with Saxons, who had broken off their pursuit of the fleeing to begin their plunder of the dead and dying. Hundr jogged past injured Vikings who looked at him with pleading eyes and outstretched arms. They groaned, wept, and rolled in the grass. A big man with a braided, golden beard cried like an infant as he held in his guts with two bloody hands. A young warrior, not much older than Finn, clutched the stump of a severed hand as the wound pumped dark liquid over his leather breastplate.

"Saxon turds," Thorgrim growled as they reached the treeline and ran past a Viking with tears on his cheeks as a group of five Saxons prodded him with spears and laughed at his misery. The branches and leaves whipped at Hundr's face, and he breathed in time with each stride, knowing that they must reach Chippenham or face a fighting retreat across the countryside to get back to Haesten and the Seaworm.

It was mid-afternoon when Hundr reached the River Avon's banks, and the walls of Chippenham loomed up against a clear sky. The journey had been fast, and the crew had encountered no further Saxon attacks. Hundr called the halt, and the crew dropped to their knees or stood with hands on hips, gasping for air in burning lungs. To run in a brynjar, or leather armour, along with the weight of shield and weapons, was more arduous than the fighting itself. He did not want the Seaworm crew barrelling into Chippenham, winded like men who had fled the battle in fear. There would already be enough of those inside the walls, and Hundr did not want his reputation tarnished as one who ran. Once the men could stand, they marched across the bridge over the wide bend in the river and under Chippenham's gate. Warriors massed in that entranceway, big men with blood-spattered mail and pale faces, men who had faced the Saxon shield wall and experienced defeat. They shouted at the Viking crews who streamed over the bridge to hurry, for soon they would destroy that bridge and close the gate.

"Why does this Alfred not press his advantage?" asked Finn as Hundr looked amongst the desperation for Sigdriffa. The square where Hundr had seen Guthrum for the first time was now the place to bring the injured and dying. The ground moved and writhed with their torn bodies, and the ferrous smell of blood was thick in the air.

"Alfred should be here by now, lad," said Bush. "This place will fall."

"And we won't stay," Hundr intoned. "Find Sigdriffa, and then we leave with the spear."

Ragnhild found one of Sigdriffa's warriors sitting against a timber post forming part of an awning before a tavern facing the square. The warrior had a topknot of brown hair, and the sides of her head were shaved to the skull. Blood pooled in her lap, it dripped from her mouth, and her breastplate was slashed open at the chest. Ragnhild kneeled next to her and slipped the axe from the loop at the wounded Valkyrie's belt to place it in the woman's hand. The Valkyrie glanced at Ragnhild and smiled, but then a cough racked her body, and thick black blood spilt from her mouth onto her chin.

"What is your name?" Ragnhild whispered.

"Her name is Gefn, and she is a traitor, an oath...." Gunnr began, but Hundr turned on her, and the fury in his eyes caused the Valkyrie leader to take a step back.

"Now is not the time. The woman is about to cross the Bifrost Bridge, do not deny her place in Valhalla with your poison," said Hundr sharply. Gunnr's lip quivered as though she would say something, but the defiance in her melted away, and she raised her hand to her smashed nose and walked away.

"What is your name? I am a sister, just like you," said Ragnhild, and she wiped loose strands of hair away from the wounded warrior's face. "I remember you from when you were a child learning your weapons at Upsala. You were taught the bow by Hrist, if I am not mistaken?"

The injured Valkyrie coughed again but smiled at Ragnhild through bloody teeth. "Hrist, yes," she said with a wheeze. "Gefn. My name is Gefn. I do not think I am long for Midgard."

"You are badly hurt. But if you die, you died in battle with your axe in your hand."

Gefn's eyes blazed, and she nodded fervently at Ragnhild. "As it should be, we are warriors."

"We are. Where is Sigdriffa taking the spear?"

"To find a new temple, one which follows the...." Gefn coughed again and winced with pain. Her voice became little more than a sigh, strained and hissing with air. "... follows the old ways."

"Where is she going?"

"The pain, sister. The pain is terrible." Gefn rolled her head and gritted her teeth.

"I can ease your passing, send you on your way

to Valhalla. Tell me where Sigdriffa is going, and I will end it for you now."

"Water," Gefn said with difficulty. Ragnhild held out her hand, and Sigvarth handed over a skin of ale. Ragnhild poured the liquid across Gefn's cracked, dry lips, but she coughed it straight back up, mixed with stringy crimson. "East, she goes to Novgorod. To the Vikings there. East to build a new shrine to the All-Father."

Ragnhild gently patted her cheek and then drove her seax across Gefn's throat. The Valkyrie bled out, her boots shaking on the square's stone ground. Ragnhild leant into her and rested her head on Gefn's cheek. She croaked an incantation to Odin, low and guttural, and the Seaworm Valkyrie joined her, including Gunnr.

"She's gone then?" said Bush.

"And we go after her. East," Hundr replied. East. Back to his home, then. He ground his teeth at the thought of it, the muscles in his cheeks working beneath his beard.

"If we can get out of this place of death and doom," said Torsten. "Sounds like Alfred is here."

Horns blared, and Chippenham fell to silence, men dashing for the wall to see what sort of force Alfred had brought to finish Guthrum, whose luck had run out like milk from a leaking churn.

SEVENTEEN

The Seaworm crew left Chippenham two days after King Alfred and Guthrum made peace. They rode from a back gate on a balmy morning under a pale blue sky the colour of Sigrid's eyes. The crew had spent most of their remaining silver, along with what they had looted from the dead at Ethandun, on fresh horses, and Hundr was glad to be rid of the place and of the defeated army, fearing that Guthrum's ill luck would spread like a plague. Each day he had remained trapped in Chippenham, Hundr had felt it creeping towards him, a hungry sprawling thing seeking to suck all luck from the surviving army and himself.

"Maybe their god is winning," said Ragnhild, riding next to Hundr on a roan stallion. "The nailed god has come to the aid of his people at last."

"Their god is for the weak," he tutted. "They pray too much, and his priests are greedy little weasels."

"Guthrum, a great Viking Jarl and leader of an army, will now turn Christian. He turns his back on Odin and the Aesir to follow the nailed god." Ragnhild shook her head and turned to stare back at Chippenham over the rump of her horse as though hoping it might have been a dream or that the town was a thing of seiðr that would disappear, and the world would right itself.

"What was that awful bloody Saxon name he will take?" asked Bush behind them.

"Aethelstan," said Hundr.

"What kind of name is that?" Bush despaired, removing his leather helmet liner and scratching at his bald, egg-white scalp.

"It's a good name," chimed Finn, his youthful voice as bright as pipe music amongst the sullen faces and bowed heads of the Seaworm crew. "Guthrum will be baptised, become a Christian, and will be a king in England. Not a terrible result, considering he lost the battle. Guthrum bargained well, I think."

Hundr looked at Finn with a raised eyebrow. "You cut through to the deep cunning of it, lad," he nodded. "Guthrum lost a battle but gained a kingdom, and all he must do is let Alfred's priests wash his head and change his name. He could have saved the lives of his warriors and poor Bolver and done it this way weeks ago."

"That lot's even more miserable than before," said Bush, jerking his thumb over his shoulder at Gunnr and her Valkyrie.

"They aren't much help in this thing," Sigrid added. "Ragnhild led them on the field at Ethandun, and all they do is complain and spit venom. Maybe this Sigdriffa has the right of it. Gungnir might be better off in her hands than theirs. Sorry to say it, Ragnhild."

Ragnhild grumbled under her breath and stroked her horse's mane, chewing over that hard truth.

"So, back to the Seaworm?" Bush asked.

"Back to the Seaworm and back to sea. We follow the spear East. It is not over, Ragnhild," said Hundr. She offered him a wan smile, and he thought better of asking her what troubled her thought cage. The defeat at Ethandun weighed heavily on them all, and the subsequent time spent within Chippenham had been low and hungry, listening to the wails and cries of the injured and dying. The lucky ones died within days of the battle, the rest when their wounds turned green and stinking. Hundr was glad to have fresh air in his nose and the wind in his hair. He led his horse through a field of high golden crops and followed the flow of a stream back towards Haesten.

The Seaworm lay safe and well in the
river beside Haesten's town. The war between
Guthrum and Alfred had not reached this far
east, and this part of England was very much
under the control of Viking Lords. They had
marched past fortified halls where Jarls ruled
over their Saxon churls in peace, and Hundr
supposed that to a farming man with a family,
it mattered little whether he paid his tithe to
a Saxon or a Dane so long as his children
were safe under the protection of that man's
sword. Haesten laughed when Hundr told him
the news of Guthrum's peace and the carnage of
Ethandun's hill.

"I think if you asked him," Haesten said over a
meal of pork, cheese, and fresh bread, "Guthrum
would have made that peace with Alfred before
the battle. The dream of defeating Wessex died
when the army split. When the Jarls rode north,
they did not leave Guthrum with enough men to
overrun the whole of the southeast."

"So why did he fight?" Hundr had asked,
having seen the slaughter for himself and bitter
at the seemingly needless loss of life.

"How can a man lead Vikings if he refuses
to fight another hiding in the marshes? He had
to fight, but he did not expect Alfred to rally
so many warriors to his banner. People think

Guthrum is unlucky because he failed to take Wessex, but he is a King now, and all he had to change is his name and let Alfred wash his hair."

Hundr smiled at that truth. Guthrum had achieved the dream of all Northmen who take to the Whale Road. He had set sail as a Jarl with ships full of hungry warriors and carved for himself a kingdom and a reputation as one of the great Viking Lords. "Thank you for allowing Bjarki and Bolver to ride with us. I am sorry that only one of them returned."

"Bolver was a good man," Haesten raised his horn of ale and slopped some of it on the ground as an offering to his dead man. "But I am happy that he died a good death. He waits for us in Valhalla."

They ate and drank that night, and Ragnhild, Gunnr and the Valkyrie sat together, sullen and quiet. Ragnhild had grown closer to her former sisters since the battle, and they looked to her as a leader, and Hundr was glad to see it. Although concerned with the fate of the spear, the Valkyrie were accepting of Ragnhild now. There was no more talk of oathbreaking, and it warmed Hundr to see Ragnhild returned to the fold of her sisterhood. Later, Hundr spent a warm night with Sigrid beneath a covered alcove of Haesten's warm hall. They held each other close, and she spoke of the horror of the shield wall and how the memories of the injured and fallen haunted her dreams. So Hundr kissed her and stroked her golden hair, caressing her soft face until she slept, and he could listen to the gentle sigh of her breath. They had survived the battle but were no closer to Gungnir, and if Sigdriffa had taken Odin's spear to the East, then its path would lead him to the land of his birth.

Haesten provided provisions for the voyage, and the Seaworm departed full of dried fish, pork, hard-baked biscuits and freshly brewed ale. Hundr embraced his old friend and wished him luck, hoping that Haesten could find peace in his new lands following the death of his wife and child. Bjarki stayed with his lord, and Hundr stood in the Seaworm's stern and waved to them both as his crew rowed the drakkar towards the Whale Road. Haesten had changed since Hundr first met him in Frankia, in what felt like a different life. Hundr had been desperate then, pursued by Ivar the Boneless and fighting for his life. Haesten had seemed impossibly powerful and successful. He had achieved the reputation and battle fame Hundr craved, and he had been in awe of the clever, hatchet-hard-faced Jarl. But since then, Haesten had lost some of his lustre. Hundr and Haesten commanded the same number of crews now, and Haesten was old and still fighting. Hundr watched Haesten and Bjarki disappear behind a meandering turn in the river, and as an overhanging willow tree blocked them from sight, Hundr wondered at his own future. King Harald had offered him Vanylven after the victory at the battle of Hafrsfjord, but Hundr had happily passed that honour on to Einar, who had always dreamed of becoming a landed Jarl. Hundr wondered at Haesten and if that was his own destiny – to fight and hold land for his crews wherever possible, moving from country to country with the tides of war, seeking battle and silver for his men.

"You look very serious," said Sigrid, joining him at the stern to watch the river rippling in their wake.

"Thinking about the future," he sighed, putting his arm around her shoulder, "and what fate the Norns are weaving for me."

"Hopefully a future with a silver spear in it," she smiled.

"We must sail to the East for Novgorod. Which is where I was born."

"Does that make you sad?" She frowned at him, examining his good eye as though deep within it, she could read his thoughts.

"I remember how I felt when I left the place and the things I vowed to accomplish."

"You have risen to be a wealthy Lord, a man of fearsome reputation."

"I return as a thief, and my half-brothers are

princes."

"Ship!" came a cry from the prow, ending the conversation. Hundr picked his way across, moving hand-to-hand along the rigging and stepping carefully around benches, chests, and supplies. When he reached the prow, he hooked his arm around the snarling beast head to peer along the river and its widening estuary leading out onto the sea itself. A ship beat oars towards them.

"Drakkar?" he asked.

"Aye," said Bush frowning. "Can't make out any banner or sigil yet."

"Not Saxon, though?"

Bush snorted. "If it were, we would row around her like a rock, but that's a sea wolf, just like us."

"The estuary is wide. Just sweep across to the starboard side of it," said Hundr. He kept his eye on the sleek ship as Bush barked the orders. Then, rapidly, Bush went up to stand on the steering platform and had Finn lean over the side, ready with a stone tied to a length of rope to test the depths as they approached the dark sands which edged the tidal estuary. This was unfamiliar water, and if they ran aground, the Seaworm would become stranded and open to attack, never mind the damage it would do to her hull.

The ship banked towards them, following the Seaworm's change in direction, and Hundr felt heat in his belly, the nervousness that comes before a fight, and he knew the sea wolves were coming for the Seaworm. "She's going to attack," he shouted down the deck. "Get the weapons and armour out, now!"

Hundr fished out his own brynjar from beneath the platform at the stern and unrolled it from its oiled fleece. The fleece would protect the precious iron rings from the worst of the seawater's corrosive spite, and no wise man wore his heavy mail at sea unless he was fighting. Hundr slipped it over his head and wriggled into its familiar tight embrace. Ragnhild ordered the Valkyrie to assemble on the port wide with their recurved bows at the ready, and they obeyed, even if Gunnr did so with a sour look on her heavily bruised face; her nose was still purple and swollen.

"She flies a wolf," called Trygve, who had shinned up the mast post to get a better look at the triangle of cloth which flew from the attacking ship, snapping in the sea breeze.

"Rollo," spat Hundr, using the word as a curse. The ship beat oars towards them, racing through the wide river. Helmets and blades glinted in the morning sun, and bearded killers crammed her deck. Rollo hated Hundr for fighting alongside King Harald in his battles to become King of all

Norway, but he had never expected his enemy to follow him to Saxon shores. The ship's snarling beast head showed teeth painted white as she raced prow on, straight at the Seaworm's belly.

"He means to ram us," Bush bellowed from the steerboard.

"He'll turn at the last moment and use his speed to come alongside," Hundr said. "He will try to cant us so we are off-balance before he boards us."

"Can we outrow him?" Sigrid asked, nocking an arrow to her bow.

"Charge him," Hundr said through gritted teeth.

"Have you lost your bloody mind?" spluttered Bush, throwing his arms up into the air.

"Bank now and charge that ship. We have enough time if we row hard."

Bush gave the order as the oars on the starboard side came up dripping glistening pearls of water onto the deck, and Hundr joined an oar bench to add his weight to the desperate manoeuvre. They hauled on their oars, and the Seaworm came round. She tilted as the oars bit into the murky brown river water, and Bush barked another order as the two beast-headed prows faced each other. The starboard oars lowered again, and the Seaworm lurched forwards. She would not have as much power in her hull as Rollo's ship, but they were head-on now, which spoiled the wolf ship's plan of attack.

"Shield wall on the port side, Valkyrie make ready," Hundr roared and leapt up from the oar bench to grab a shield from the bilge.

"You want us to pull them close, my lord?" asked Valbrandr, hefting his axe and rolling his mighty shoulders.

"No, we won't board them. We have seen enough killing on these shores. Hurt them, throw them back and then we get away from this cursed island. Bush, get oars ready to pole away on my command. When we break free, we pull like Thor himself was at our benches. Make for the sea and get the sail up in whatever direction the wind blows." He needed to go east, but first, Hundr had to get his crew away from Rollo.

The enemy ship surged through the river, water rising on her hull white and foaming. Hundr's heart tightened in his chest, and he braced himself for the impact. The Seaworm's oars came up, and his warriors overlapped their shields on the sheer strake. He joined that wall in its centre and readied a spear against the iron rim of his shield. The enemy vessel raised her oars, and the two hulls impacted, timbers grinding and the ships canting under the blow. Hundr grabbed onto the side to stop himself from being thrown across the deck, and his warriors did the same. Across the bows were snarling enemy faces and bright weapons.

"Loose!" Ragnhild roared, and the Valkyrie poured white feathered shafts into the enemy ship. A warrior fell screaming with an arrow in his eye, but most shafts thudded into the enemy shield wall. Between the shields, men appeared with hooks, and they were the men to kill, the ones who would try to lash the two ships together and turn the fight into a pitched battle on the water.

"Kill the hook men," Hundr called to his crew, and he hurled his spear at one such man, a tall warrior with a golden beard. The spear took him in the shoulder, and the warrior disappeared onto the enemy ship's deck. Then, from the corner of his good eye, Hundr saw a flash of iron, and he raised his shield just in time to catch a throwing axe on his shield's timbers. The thud of it rattled his teeth. It had come from his blind side, and Hundr saw a snarling, spitting face amongst the enemy shields. A red face, twisted and scarred, with bright blue eyes. It was Kvasir, the burned man, Rollo's hound, who had tried to kill him in Frankia, and the stretched features of his face twisted into a rictus of hate. The ships drifted, moving alongside one another as warriors hacked at shields and launched missiles across the decks. Kvasir skipped over two of his men, keeping up with Hundr as the Seaworm carried him along the wolf ship's keel. Kvasir raised his arm, and another throwing axe whipped across the deck. It turned head over haft in the air and hurtled past Hundr's head to bury itself with a crack into the face of the warrior next to him. That man's name was Halbard, and Kvasir's thrown axe crushed his face like rotten timber. The axe head carved off half of Halbard's jaw, and Hundr's face was wet and warm with his crewman's blood. Halbard's body pitched forward, quivering, and fell into the black river water between the battling ships. Burned Kvasir had come for his vengeance.

EIGHTEEN

Missiles flew across the decks, and Hundr's shield shuddered under the massive impact of a viciously thrown hand axe. Valkyrie bows thrummed, their arrows whistled across the bows, and Hundr's men urged each other to keep the enemy from getting their hooks into the Seaworm deck to draw them close enough to board. With Halbard's blood still wet on his face, Hundr's heart ached for him to fight, and his dead eye pulsed under the ferocity of the enemy assault. That part of him wanted to let Kvasir draw the ships in close, to embrace the fight and send his enemy screaming to the bottom of the silted Saxon river. But his head won that internal struggle. The open sea was before them, and their fate drove them east towards Sigdriffa and Odin's spear.

A hook drove into the Seaworm's timbers with

a thud, and a Seaworm man tried to wrestle it free, but an enemy snaked out and lopped his hand off at the wrist, sending the man reeling back into the Seaworm's thwarts, screaming in pain, with the stump of his hand spraying blood. Hundr drew Battle Fang over his shoulder. He lunged forward beneath the bottom rim of his shield and stabbed the tip of his sword into the axeman's armpit as his arms raised to swing his axe again. Hundr withdrew the blade, its tip now red with the blood of his enemies, and he hacked at the rope behind the hook until it sprang away. The ships were still in the water, unmoving, floating beside one another as the warriors slashed at each other with blades across the water.

"Pole them off," Hundr shouted, and Bush responded in a storm of barked orders and rushing men. On the wolf ship, Kvasir stood in the front rank, one foot on his sheer strake so that he could strike at the Seaworm men.

"Meet your fate, Harald's thralls, nithings, turds of Loki!" Kvasir roared, his twisted face furious. His eyes bulged, and spittle flew from his lips in his bloodthirsty hunger for revenge.

Wanting to face his enemy, Hundr tried to push his way towards him, itching to tear the burned bastard's life from him in payment for his own dead and wounded crewmen. The warriors were thick at the centre, and Trygve and Kvasir exchanged blows, axes striking at one another's shields, probing each other across the treacherous gap between the two warships. Kvasir went low, and Trygve bought the feint so that Kvasir's axe sliced open his belly with a shout of triumph. Thorgrim hauled Trygve back onto the deck before Kvasir could strike again or before the injured Seaworm man tumbled into the dark river's depths. Kvasir locked eyes with Hundr and roared his defiance, urging his men on to death or glory. A man tried to jump across to the Seaworm deck, but Sigvarth simply barged him with his shield so that the warrior slid into the river to be dragged down into Njorth's icy embrace. Another warrior made the leap, but two Valkyrie shafts thudded into his chest, and he, too, fell into the river to drown.

Bush slid an oar against the wolf ship's stern, and Hundr ordered his men back from the sheer strake in good order. They kept their shields raised as the Seaworm moved away from the enemy bows. One of their warriors stabbed his spear forwards, reaching to strike, and Hundr grabbed the weapon below the tip, dragging the warrior off balance to fall with a splash into the widening gap. Kvasir bellowed at his men to attack, to drag the ships back together, but Bush brought more oars to bear, and as the distance widened, oars bit into the river, and the Seaworm drove forwards, away from the wolf ship and Kvasir's red-faced fury.

"Now!" roared Bush as soon as there was clear water between the two drakkars, and Finn scampered about the deck, unfurling the mast and hauling its beam up the mast post. The one-eyed sigil showed in a whip of spray as the wind caught in the woollen sail, and the ship surged forwards. It wasn't a wind to make a man's heart leap from the thrill of it, but it was enough to drag them away from the enemy, and the Seaworm charged northeast, out of the Saxon estuary and towards the Whale Road. Hundr looked back at the wolf ship, her deck like a kicked bees nest as her warriors scampered to bring her about and get their own sail up.

"She will be after us," Thorgrim spoke up, baring his teeth and gasping for breath.

"We ran this time, but we won't again," Hundr said, clapping Thorgrim on the shoulder. He regretted withdrawing from the fight. He had lost good men anyway, and his only aim had been to avoid more bloodshed. "Is Trygve hurt badly?"

"Bad enough," answered Thorgrim, and they

turned to look at Trygve writhing in the bilge. He was being held down by Ragnhild and Sigrid whilst Gunnr carefully pulled the shattered rings of his brynjar from the red lips of his wound. Kvasir's axe had cut through the chainmail to open his belly, but the burst rings were hooked into the wound, and before the Valkyrie could use their healing skills, they had to make the wound safe.

"If anyone can save him, it is they," said Hundr. Valkyries were taught to heal as well as they fought, and Ragnhild's skills had saved Hundr's life more than once. The warrior who had lost his hand in the fight sat with his back against the mast, his face as white as a fetch and shivering as Skögul bound the wound tight with cloth wraps. The bilge was red with blood, and Hundr had an enemy behind him with Gungnir somewhere in front. His crew stowed weapons and worked at the rigging, driving the Seaworm out into the white-tipped waves and away from Kvasir and England.

"He came for you, for us," said Bush, shaking his head at the injured warriors.

"Kvasir hates me because we burned his Lord's hall at Agder during Harald's war. He was in the hall, and his body now bears the scars of the fire. He hates us for his Lord's death and for his own pain," replied Hundr, watching the wolf ship struggling to turn in the river.

"So, he will come again."

"He will, but next time we fight him to the death. We should have just fought him here today. Should have got it over with."

"There has been enough blood. This spear might be cursed, or so the men are saying."

"Could be, losing his spear has enraged the All-Father." Hundr glanced up at the dark clouds forming ahead of them, swirling and malevolent. "Rollo has a hand in this burned man's fury. He provided the ships and the warriors."

"So, we run on the wind and turn east when we can?"

Hundr nodded. He sighed and leant upon the sheer strake, its timbers showing gold beneath the older, darker wood where weapons had hacked at it during the battle. Hundr was a Jarl, and his decisions lay heavy upon his shoulders, as weighty as an extra brynjar on his back. It was Hundr who had decided to fight for King Harald. During that war, they had won fame and the land at Vanylven, but it had cost good men's lives. It had also been his decision to help Ragnhild, his friend, on her quest to retrieve Gungnir and find peace in returning to her sisterhood of the Valkyrie. Because of that, more men had died, and he scrunched his good eye closed against the moans and groans of the injured. The Valkyrie worked on them, sewing and binding wounds. Trygve, a stout and brave fighter, clutched at his stomach wound. It seeped dark blood onto the deck. Trygve wept as the Valkyrie prised his hands away so Ragnhild could pass her bone needle and thread through the lips of the cut, free now of the torn chainmail links. Men suffered because of Hundr's decisions, but so it had to be. He was a Viking Jarl, a leader of warriors, and they all knew the risks when they took to the Whale Road. Trygve roared with pain, and it bit deep into Hundr's chest. Knowing what he was and how it must be did not make the suffering of his men, his friends, any easier.

Waves broke white on the Seaworm's bows, and wind filled the heavy wool sail. The one-eye sigil blazed as the wind pulled it taut, and the ship ran northwards away from the estuary where the wolf ship floundered on the sandbanks. By the time the ship was free of the channel, rain squalls already hid the Seaworm. The rain came from the West, whipped and sharp, and the gusts pounded on the ship as they passed.

Hundr could feel the wolf ship behind them, even though he could not see it. The squalls continued to shroud the Seaworm whenever they came, and under the force of a larger rainfall, Bush ordered the sail to be lowered and leaned into the tiller so that the Seaworm banked northeast. The crew took to the oars, and Hundr himself took a turn. His back muscles stretched and screamed, which was a welcome distraction from the weight of leadership. The Seaworm escaped before the churning grey of the horizon, the bow smashing into the wind and the rolling sea and every stroke burned Hundr's muscles until he thought he would fall to the deck with exhaustion. Each warrior took their turn, Finn and Valkyrie taking an oar when men could pull no more. Finally, the moon rose from her slumber, ending the back-breaking oar work. Hundr nodded at Bush's request, and the shipmaster gave the order to ship oars and plug the oar holes with their circular stoppers on lengths of rope. The crew dropped to the deck, gasping for breath, clutching at burning chests, and Bush let the ship heave and wallow in the black surge of the sea.

Dawn found the Seaworm alone and drifting. The men took a meal of flatbread and ale, and wind and rain lashed the ship, but their luck had changed, for this wind would blow them east towards the Skagerrak. Bush and Finn hoisted the sail, and Hundr looked aft, but there was no sign of the wolf ship. The warrior who had lost his hand in the fight had lost his life in the night. He died in his sleep clutching his stump and was found as white as a gull's wing in the morning, as though a Loki monster had climbed aboard in the darkness to drain the remaining lifeblood from his corpse. The Valkyrie chanted words to Odin and Njorth, and they tipped his body over the side. Trygve was still alive, but sweat sheeted his face, and he grimaced and groaned while the sound of it kept the rest of the crew silent and sullen.

The Seaworm sailed through the clouds and rough waves of the Skagerrak and down through the Kattegat straits, where seabirds cawed and floated on the bitter wind. Bush drove her east and then north, back towards Upsala and then east again, following Sigdriffa and Gungnir to the place of Hundr's birth.

NINETEEN

Einar lost sight of the wolf ship in a sea fog off the coast southeast of Sjaelland. The drakkar flew a dark sail painted with a snarling wolf's head, and Einar had followed the ship all the way from Saxon England through the Skagerrak and around dangerous islands thick with Viking Danes. The wolf ship was sleek and fast, cutting through the Whale Road like a seax, and the Fjord Bear raced along after her through storms and fair seas alike, rowing hard when Njorth turned the wind against them. She ran under sail now. The morning fog lifted, shadowing the coast and heading northeast, towards colder seas and towards the lands of the Svear where Bjorn Ironside was King.

"We should put in for a day or two," said Hekkr, turning a scrap of dried pork over in his hand as though someone had dropped it in a sheep turd. "Take on fresh food."

"And ale," piped Amundr. The big man ducked underneath the halyard rope and grimaced at the meat in Hekkr's fist.

"We have chased this bastard halfway around Midgard. We won't break off now so you can fill your bellies," Einar said. He squinted across the Fjord Bear's prow, searching the white tips of the waves for signs of the enemy sail. "Get someone with good eyes up here. The burned bastard can't be far away. We only lost him for a quarter turn of the sun."

"Galti, get up on the prow there and look for the wolf's head," Hekkr called to a whip-thin youth. Galti scampered over rowing benches and between rigging to climb into the snarling bear's maw at the Fjord Bear's prow. His lean arms were like knotted rope, and he wrapped them around the prow beast, fixing his eyes on the horizon. His head moved slowly from west to east.

"A couple of fishing boats, nothing more," Galti called, his voice somewhere between that of a high-pitched boy and the deeper voice of a man.

"Keep looking," said Einar. He took the meat out of Hekkr's hand and tossed it over the side. "It's for eating, not staring. Your screwed-up face staring at it was making my thought cage hurt."

Hekkr shook his head but thought better of

protesting when he saw the thunder in Einar's frown. "We know where this Kvasir is going. We had it from Haesten himself," he said. "If we keep on course for Novgorod, we will come upon him."

"We know Rollo set his dog Kvasir off his chain to kill Hundr, and we know Hundr makes for Novgorod looking for the Valkyrie renegade and her spear. We also know that Kvasir and Hundr fought at the mouth of a river downstream from Haesten's town. Haesten had reports of that. If we wait until we reach Novgorod to find Kvasir, who is to say that he won't have already found Hundr and killed him?"

"You are the man for the cunning work, Einar, and no mistake," said Amundr, scratching his head at the warp and weft of it, gnawing at his red beard.

"We must find and put this Kvasir in the dirt before he finds Hundr, Ragnhild, and Finn. I don't want to find the corpses of those we love floating in the sea like flotsam. And I need a burned-faced man's head so I can get home and get King Harald off my back."

"We just need to take on some supplies; that's all I was saying," grumbled Hekkr, and he went back to the barrels to fish out some dried fish to fill his belly.

"Why do you think Jarl Hundr ran from Kvasir?" asked Amundr. "We heard the tale from

Haesten, but it's hard to believe."

Einar chewed on the beard at his bottom lip. "It's not like him to run from a fight, two evenly matched crews like that. But they had just fought at the great shield wall between Alfred and Guthrum, and Haesten said they were fair banged up after that. So, maybe Hundr wanted to avoid more bloodshed if he could. He will know now, though, that Kvasir hunts him, and Hundr is not an easy man to kill."

"Guthrum," Amundr said, curling his lip and spitting over the side. His hand rose to the Thor's hammer amulet at his neck, and he stroked its silver carving. "Turning his back on the gods, taking a bloody Saxon name. What was it again?"

"Aethelstan."

"Bloody Aethelstan. What kind of name is that for a drengr? I am surprised that the All-Father hasn't struck him down already for turning his back on the Aesir."

"Guthrum is a King now, and he's sent many souls to Valhalla. Just because a man says to the Saxons that he now worships the Christ god and lets some black crow priests wash his hair doesn't mean he has forsaken Odin. Let the Saxons believe what they want. It's a small price to pay to become King. Besides, in his own hall, Guthrum can worship whoever he wants. He's the only man I ever heard of who lost a war and won a kingdom."

Amundr nodded and rumbled in his throat at the hard truth in that – of how defeat had turned to victory and how Guthrum had forged for himself a crown in the lands of the Saxons.

"Sail," croaked Galti in his breaking voice and pointed northwest. "Two sails."

Einar leapt to the sheer strake and peered over the side, but he could see nothing beyond the swell of the dark sea. "Can you see anything?" he said, squinting into the distance.

"No, my eyes are almost as bad as yours, my lord," replied Amundr, his nose wrinkled and his cliff-like brows furrowed as he stared at where the lad pointed.

"The wolf?" asked Einar.

"Can't tell yet, my lord," answered Galti. "One ship looks to be anchored, though, close to land, and the other rows towards it from the south. Drakkars, I think."

"We have wind," said Einar. "Let the sail out; get the lads in place. Full speed."

Amundr nodded and shouted orders at the men. Rigging creaked, and the men flowed around the ropes and knots, letting out the sail and taking their positions on deck so that the Fjord Bear was balanced for speed. Her prow lifted, and she raced into the swell.

"It's the wolf," Galti shouted, the wind whipping his word along the deck like a jerkin thrown high into its pull. "I think it's the Seaworm at anchor, my lord."

Einar's knuckles turned white, his fists gripping the sheer strake, and his stomach souring. Finn was on that ship, along with Hundr and Ragnhild. People he loved, people he would die for. The wind roared off the starboard quarter, and the crew let out her seal hide ropes so that the sail lifted and bowed under the force. The prow rose, slicing through the waves, and Einar clenched his teeth, staring at the wolf ship beating its oars towards the Seaworm. He could make out both ships now and the rise and fall of his enemy's oars, beating like the wings of a great serpent driving her warriors towards his friends and the lad he loved like a son. Icy spray whipped Einar's slab-like flat face from where the swell crashed against the prow, and his flinty eyes fixed on the burned man and his crew.

"Get my brynjar," Einar barked at Galti, and the boy whooped for joy at the speed of the Fjord Bear, flying faster than a falcon through the sea. Galti slipped down from the prow and scuttled along the deck to fetch Einar's armour and weapons. He shrugged on his heavy brynjar and fastened his axe. The crew strapped on leather breastplates and found their own weapons, careful not to shift far or all at once from their benches or risk spoiling the balance of the drakkar in her race along the wind towards the burned man.

"We won't make it," huffed Amundr, appearing alongside Einar, his brynjar rings gleaming, and a helmet pushed down over his red hair, its nasal protector shaped like a boar's head.

"We'll make it," said Einar. The Fjord Bear's rigging groaned, and seawater burst onto the deck as she broke through the swell like an axe smashing the boards of a shield. Galti and another lad squatted in the bilge amongst the ballast stones and set to bailing, throwing buckets of freezing cold seawater over the side, frantically trying to maintain speed. There was movement on the deck of the Seaworm, bodies moving like ants in their nest. They must have pulled up their anchor stone because oars appeared like ribs and dipped into the glistening wave tips. Hundr had spotted the wolf ship and was desperately trying to get his ship underway.

"If Kvasir rams her, she's done for," said Amundr.

Einar nodded because the wolf ship charged the Seaworm prow to bow, and if she struck her, then the Seaworm would cant over and could capsize. It would throw her crew and rigging into turmoil, and the wolf ship's warriors could board her and bring their weapons to bear without resistance. So, Einar gripped the Fjord Bear's timbers and said a prayer to Njorth. He prayed for the wind to hurl them forwards and get to Kvasir before he could destroy the Seaworm, and then he asked Odin for blood; he begged the All-Father to get him close enough to the wolf ship to board her so that he, Einar Rosti, could bring his axe to bear and send his enemies souls to Niflheim.

The wolf ship's oars rose and fell in quick time. Her oarsmen's shoulders and back muscles would scream from the pain and effort it took to haul their warship across the grey-green sea. Einar ducked beneath the halyard and picked his way to the steerboard, taking the tiller. The power of the sea surged through the timber, juddering Einar's bones as he fought with it to keep the Fjord Bear angling towards the gap between the wolf ship and the Seaworm. It would be close, and Einar felt his stomach clench with fear as the ships drew closer. The Fjord Bear's sail was high and taut, her lines whirring under the wind and sea spray. Einar could make out the colours painted on the wolf ship's shields lined up along her sheer strake, reds, browns and yellows. He could hear her shipmaster bellowing at the oarsmen to pull, urging them on to blood and glory. Einar watched them and fought with the tiller and realised suddenly that the wolf ship focused entirely on her prey, the Seaworm. Einar was racing the Fjord Bear along from her rear, and they had not seen him.

The enemy warriors pulled, their ship surged forward, and the Seaworm was also underway, her oar blades biting into the dark waters. Arrows launched from the Seaworm's deck in a high arc, flying across the fast-moving cloud before diving to slam into the wolf ship. Einar ducked and leaned to his right, nudging the tiller to perfect his aim. The ships came closer, and for a horrifying moment, Einar thought he was too late. Yet just as he clenched his teeth against the sound of crushing timbers as the wolf ship crashed into the Seaworm's bows, his own crew whooped for joy. They cried out in delight because the Fjord Bear crunched instead into the wolf ship's oars, slamming the handles back into the ribs and chests of the enemy oarsmen with horrifying force. Einar flew forwards and landed heavily on the deck, thrown there by the impact of the Fjord Bear's prow scraping on the side of the wolf ship and stopping her dead in the water. Einar scrambled to his feet, as did the surrounding warriors, clutching at each other and the rigging to their feet. The Fjord Bear's sail caught the wind, but she had turned under the impact, and it dragged the ship about, veering as the sail billowed and then emptied to loosely hang like a wet rag.

Amundr bellowed at the men to see to the

rigging and right the ship, and Einar picked up a loose spear from the bilge and leapt aft, searching for the enemy. The wolf ship rocked in the water, her men as scrambling and desperate as Einar's own. Einar searched the deck, raising his spear above his shoulder, searching for his target. The ships drifted away from each other, and arrow shafts slammed into the wolf ship's deck as her crew shouted orders to one another, desperate to recover from the surprise of the impact. A man toppled into the sea with an arrow in his back, and another hauled on a rope with an arrow stuck in his shoulder. Then he was there, the burned man pushing his men, his red face snarling and twisted amongst the frantic ship work. Einar grunted as he threw the spear. It flew across the waves, low and hard. Einar held his breath. His aim was true, and the bright point flew towards its target, and when it struck, Kvasir would be dead, and this cursed quest for his head would be over. But a grizzled warrior with a long beard leaned back as he hauled on rigging rope, and the spear took him beneath his shoulder blades, throwing him across the wolf ship's deck.

Kvasir roared with fury, staring down at his crewman felled by Einar's spear. He bent low, disappearing beneath the tumult of men, weaving in and out of each other like bees on summer flowers. Kvasir appeared again, but this time at the stern of his ship with the same spear held aloft, ripped from the body of his crewman and dripping blood. He gazed at Einar, cursing because the ships had drifted too far for him to reach his enemy, and launched the weapon at the closest part of the Fjord Bear. Einar followed its cast, hearing a scream of pain and then a roar of horror from his crew, but he could not see which man had been struck. Kvasir locked eyes with Einar across the bows, their two ships drifting away from each other as more men launched spears. The distance grew too great, and most splashed harmlessly into the swell. Kvasir dragged a thumb across his own throat and then pointed at Einar, his eyes like black flints in his tortured face. Einar stumbled again as the Fjord Bear's sail filled, and the ship lurched forwards, away from the wolf ship whose men found order and brought their remaining oars to bear, beating away from Einar's ship and the surprise attack. Einar turned, looking for the Seaworm and saw her veer on the port tack, coming about in a wide sweep, turning back towards the fight. They outnumbered Kvasir now with two drakkars filled with warriors, and the burned man's wolf sail rose in jerking motions on its spar before filling and carrying Kvasir and his crew away from danger, heading east.

"Do we chase them?" asked Hekkr, panting from the exertion of restoring the ship to order.

"Let them go," said Einar. "We can go after them once we are in good order." He walked the length of the keel, pleased that he couldn't see any injured men other than a few bumps and cuts from the collision, and the crew busied themselves securing lines and righting upturned barrels and sea chests. But, then, his heart clenched because young Galti sat against the inside of the prow, where its timbers rose and feathered out into the sweeping lines of the hull. As he drew closer, Einar realised Galti wasn't sitting. The force of Kvasir's spear pinned him. The weapon had pierced little Galti's stomach and travelled through his body so that its point stuck into the Fjord Bear's hull. Amundr crouched next to him, shaking his head and pulling his beard. Galti's eyes were open, and he was sweating, tears rolling down his pale cheeks. He looked down at the spear and the terrible wound in his gut and then up at Einar. Galti licked his lips, his head trembling.

"Will I go to Valhalla, Lord Einar?" he asked, his voice now that of a boy again, squeaking and desperate.

"You will go to Valhalla because you have died in battle, brave Galti," Einar said, crouching next to him.

"Please let me go to Valhalla. I am not a nithing, am I?" Galti stammered. His bottom lip shook, and blood trickled from the corner of his mouth. He coughed, and a gout of dark crimson slopped from his lips and over the spear shaft. The gathered men moaned and wrung their hands.

Einar slipped his axe from the loop at his belt and pressed it into Galti's bloody hands. "You have died in battle, a warrior of the Fjord Bear. Brave Galti Farseer, I name you for your keen eyes. Save a place for me in Odin's hall, warrior."

Galti smiled at Einar, his thin hands clutching the axe to his chest. He coughed again, and then his head lolled. The poor young lad was dead.

"I am going to kill that burned bastard. I want his head, and I want his soul," Einar whispered, the hate of it crackling in his chest like a roaring fire.

TWENTY

"Einar!" Finn shouted, and he sprinted along the white sand, his boots flicking up clods of it as he ran. Hundr trudged out of the seawater behind him, its icy waves breaking against his legs as he came ashore. The crew had rowed the Seaworm up onto the sands, and Bush had dropped the anchor stone. He barked at them, peering over the side to ensure the ship sat low enough against the beach so she would not become stranded at low tide. The shipmaster had winced as the hull grated on ridges of sand beneath the waves. None of the crew had any knowledge of the island itself, save that it was large and due east of Upsala, close to the lands of the Rus. The beach was narrow, forming the end of a spit of land at the southernmost tip of the island, like a finger pointing out into the rolling mass of grey sea beyond. Small hills rose beyond the white sands, but no higher than the height of a man, and coarse dark green bushes covered the slim length of it.

"He could come back, you know," Bush uttered, emerging from the water with Hundr and turning to stare out to sea.

"Not whilst we have two ships. Burned Kvasir will wait for a better opportunity to strike," said Hundr, striding onto the sands and smiling as Finn and Einar embraced like father and son. Einar scooped the lad up into a bear hug and lifted him from the ground. Finn laughed, and they clapped each other's backs as though they had not seen one another for a decade. Einar dropped Finn to the sand and nodded a greeting to Hundr, who raised his hand to return the gesture.

"Hildr is worried sick about you, lad," said Einar, shaking his head at Finn. His slab-like face switched from its joyous smile to a craggy frown. "You are lucky Hundr didn't toss you overboard, stowing away like that."

"Look!" Finn exclaimed, ignoring the scolding to drag the sword he had won at the slaughter of Ethandun free of its scabbard. "I fought in a battle." He held up the blade, and the anger dropped from Einar's face like a stone. He clapped Finn on the shoulder and then bade Hekkr and Amundr look at the sword and hear Finn's tales of war in Saxon England. Einar stepped around Finn and strode to Hundr, the two old friends clasping forearms in warm welcome.

"Well met Einar Rosti," said Hundr.
Einar grinned. "That's another one you owe me," Einar replied and then winked at Bush. "I am getting too old to be trawling the Whale Road, saving your worthless arses."

"How did you find us, and how did you know to come?"

"I've been hunting the burned man just as he has been hunting you. It was Odin luck that we came upon him today just as he was attacking you. I have followed him from Frankia to England and then through Sjaelland to here."

"He is Rollo's man. Sent to kill me. I met him in Rollo's hall in Frankia. Kvasir is his name, and he was there that day when we attacked Jarl Kjotve the Rich's hall at Agder. We burned him in that fire. He hates you even more than me, Einar – he blames you for the fire and for his pain. How is it you are hunting for him?"

"He's a vengeful bastard, sure enough. Rognvald came to Vanylven after you left and charged me with killing a man with a burned face, Rollo's man."

"Why does King Harald want him dead?" asked Hundr. Rognvald was the King's man, the leader of his forces and the master of his affairs. Hundr's thought cage turned over at the weft of destinies coming together in the hunt for Gungnir. He could almost hear the Norns cackling at the foot of the great tree Yggdrasil as they pulled the threads of his life in a weave with those of Kvasir, Einar, Sigdriffa, Ragnhild, Haesten, and Guthrum together in the quest that might well determine the outcome of Ragnarok.

"Bastard has been raiding in Norway, hitting the King's ships and raiding the coast. Harald wants the burned man gone. Seems his impudence is causing him embarrassment."

"So why send you? Are we to be the King's assassins now?" Hundr shook his head and turned to stare out at the sea. Sigvarth and three other men carried Trygve from the Seaworm to shore. The injured man groaned and shrieked at the wound in his guts. Each cry made Hundr flinch. Sigvarth and the men struggled with Trygve's weight in the shallows and the heavy sand. Each time they jerked or stumbled, Trygve whimpered like a child. He was a Viking warrior, a man of the shield wall and a front ranker. Kvasir had reduced him to a husk of his former self.

"I am a Jarl, and I do as the King commands. That is the price to hold Vanylven, the price to be a Jarl. What happened to him?" Einar scratched at his beard and winced to see Trygve.

PETER GIBBONS

"He and Kvasir fought across the bows. Kvasir cut his belly open with an axe. Ragnhild sewed him up, but the wound has turned rotten. He has had Valhalla stolen from him, and Trygve was surely a man for the Einherjar."

Sigvarth and the others laid Trygve down gently on the sands, and Ragnhild emerged from the rolling surf to kneel beside the injured warrior. She removed the wrap from his wound, and the men around wrinkled their noses at the smell. Ragnhild examined the stitches and gently placed her hand on Trygve's sweating brow. She looked over at Hundr, their singular eyes meeting, and she shook her head. Hundr nodded his understanding and sighed.

"We lost young Galti to a Kvasir spear. Now Trygve is done. We must kill Kvasir." Einar's eyes shone like the north star, his hard slab of a face thunderous, and Hundr hoped Kvasir felt the shiver of that fury wherever he was on the rolling sea.

Ragnhild motioned to her Valkyrie sisters, and Gunnr, Skögul and the others knelt beside her on the sand, performing a chant to Odin. They called upon the All-Father to remember Trygve's deeds and his reputation. They reminded Odin of how he struck with the spear and how he was a reaper of his enemies.

"Who are they?" asked Einar, leaning in to talk

to Hundr above the low rhythm of the Valkyrie prayer but not loud enough to interrupt the sacred rite.

"Valkyrie, from Upsala," said Hundr, and he held up a hand in understanding at Einar's raised eyebrow. "It's a long story. We should rest here for the night. I'll tell you all about Upsala and how Guthrum the Unlucky became a king with a Saxon name."

The Valkyrie chanting increased its intensity, the sisters rocking on their haunches until Ragnhild whipped a knife from her belt and cut Trygve's throat in a swift slice. The warriors on the beach bowed their heads, and Hundr saw the hate on their faces. Hate for the enemy, for the burned man who must die. Hundr, like his men, would miss Trygve, but this was the life of a Viking. They were warriors, and death was their trade.

Einar strode away from Hundr towards Finn, and the two practiced weapons, Finn wielding his new blade. There was joy on Einar's face, and he laughed as Finn danced around him like a faerie, ducking and lunging with speed and power. Finn was so like his father, and memories of Ivar the Boneless flooded Hundr's mind. He remembered Ivar's vicious speed and ferocity. If Finn learned to fight with even half of Ivar's skill and strength, he would be a formidable warrior. Hundr ordered his men to make camp and bring food and ale to the beach. The night was clear and bright, the stars glittering boldly above the sigh of the sea.

The men ate and drank, the Seaworm crew telling the men of the Fjord Bear tales of Ethandun and how Alfred had won back his kingdom when all thought him beaten and skulking in the marshes like a whipped dog. Hundr told Einar the tale of Ragnhild and Upsala, of how they must retrieve the stolen Gungnir spear from Sigdriffa, the renegade Valkyrie. Einar grumbled and complained about King Harald's demands upon him and also his task to kill Kvasir. That task had been unwelcome at first, but now Einar had a reason to hate Kvasir. Perhaps the Norns' interference had fashioned that reason, but it was there. So, the task was no longer a thing for Harald but a matter of vengeance. But there was a gleam in the old warrior's eyes. Despite his moaning, Einar was happy to be at sea. As long as Hundr had known him, Einar had loved to be aboard a ship carving his way across the Whale Road. He might be a landed Jarl now, a Lord of Norway, but he was a Viking at his core.

As the warriors tired and their snoring rumbled across the beach, Hundr lay back under his cloak with Sigrid asleep and her head resting on his chest. Her blonde hair smelled fresh like a forest in springtime, and he breathed it in, her head rising and falling with each breath he took. Hundr stared up at the stars until he found the Eyes of Thjazi. The group of twinkling stars blinked at him, and the lid of his good eye closed lazily as he remembered the tale of those eyes, as told to him by his mother at a fireside in Novgorod when he was Velmud, the bastard. His eye closed, and darkness came, and with it, his mother's smiling face and soothing voice... telling him tales of Asgard.

The fire warmed Velmud, and his mother brushed his hair back from his face. Her soft fingers traced the bruising on his cheek from where his half-brothers, the princes, had beaten him following that day's weapons training. Velmud smiled, and his mother's beautiful eyes dripped a single tear down her round cheeks.

"I will tell you a story of the stars," she said, and she hugged him close to her, wrapping him in a fur blanket. "You should sleep, my son. Learn to be clever and fast. You must outwit your brothers' cruelty if you are ever to have a life in the palace. Many years ago, Loki, Odin, and Hoenir were travelling across a mountain range. One day, they came across a herd of oxen and being hungry, they stopped to kill one and roast it in an earthen oven. His stomach grumbling, Odin opened the oven and was dismayed to discover the meat was not cooking despite the fierce heat beneath the soil. Then, the three gods heard a voice coming from a nearby oak

tree. They looked and saw a giant eagle which they knew to be Thjazi, the giant, in eagle form. Thjazi told the gods that he was using his seiðr to stop the meat from cooking. Of course, the gods were hungry from their journey, so Thjazi made a deal; he would allow the oxen to cook in the oven if Odin, Loki and Hoenir gave him a portion of the cooked meat. The gods agreed, and the oxen cooked, the smell of its roasting glorious and causing Loki's mouth to water. When it was ready, Odin took the meat from the oven, but Thjazi swooped down and ate most of it, his sharp beak tearing huge steaming chunks from the freshly cooked oxen. Loki struck Thjazi angrily with his walking staff, and Thjazi, the eagle, caught Loki in his talons and flew away with him. Loki called and pleaded with Thjazi to let him go, yet the eagle flew low so that the god's legs dragged across the tips of mountain pines, and his knees banged against the rocks and boulders of the high places. Thjazi responded to Loki, saying that he would only let him go on the condition that Loki would lure the goddess Iðunn down from Asgard with her apples of youth and that she would take Loki's place as Thjazi's prisoner."

"Loki promised to fulfil the bargain, and at the arranged time, he persuaded Iðunn to come down from Asgard and meet him in a forest, for he had found some truly magical apples which outmatched her own, and that she should bring hers to compare them. A bite of one of Iðunn's apples restored youth *to the eater, and they were prized across both Asgard and Midgard. Iðunn wandered the forest searching for Loki, but Thjazi swooped down in his eagle form and carried her off. Without Iðunn's apples, the Aesir in Asgard aged. To their dismay, beards turned grey and faces wrinkled, and all searched for the goddess Iðunn. The gods discovered Iðunn was last seen with Loki, and they raged at the trickster god with threats to kill him if he did not return her to the halls of the gods."*

"Loki transformed himself into a falcon using Freya's magical coat and flew to Thjazi's great hall in Jotunheim, finding Iðunn alone whilst Thjazi himself was off at sea. Loki turned Iðunn into an acorn and flew back to Asgard with her. When Thjazi returned to his hall, he was furious that Iðunn had escaped, and he set off in pursuit of Loki. The gods, however, were ready for Thjazi and set a great fire which burned his feathers, and he tumbled to the ground. The gods set upon the giant and killed him whilst Loki returned Iðunn safely to Asgard. Odin took Thjazi's eyes and cast them into the sky forever to shine amongst the night stars. So, you see, my son, my Velmud, the gods teach us that cunning and cleverness are weapons to be wielded, just like the swords and spears to practice with each day. Embrace that and protect yourself."

Hundr woke with a start, sweat sheeting his face. He sat up, carefully removing Sigrid's arm from around his neck without waking her.

A dark shape was huddled by the campfire remnants. The shape turned as Hundr rose from his bed, and in the glow of the orange faggots, Hundr saw Ragnhild's scarred face staring at him.

"At first light, we make for Novgorod," he said, warming his hands on the embers.

"Should we not hunt this Kvasir first and have done with him?" Ragnhild asked, taking a sip of ale from a wooden cup.

"Gungnir first, then the burned man. We have tarried too long chasing Sigdriffa. When we get to Novgorod, we find her and strike fast. We have been trying to use force to get the spear when we should have been using our heads."

"What if Sigdriffa is no longer at Novgorod or has sailed to another destination to make her new temple dedicated to Odin?"

"Her dying sister at Ethandun told us Sigdriffa made for Novgorod, and now so do we."

"Thank you," Ragnhild smiled at Hundr, which was a rare thing, for Ragnhild was ever a grim beast.

"I said I would get you back to the Valkyrie order, Ragnhild, and I will keep my word. Can you not sleep?" The night grew long, and on the distant horizon, above the gentle swell of the sea, the rising sun spread a pallid yellow smear below a grey sky.

"No. Men died on this quest for me. For the spear."

"It is Odin's spear. If its rescue is not worth dying for, I don't know what is. If we recover and return it, then there is reputation in that. That in itself will keep the crew happy. How can Odin refuse entry to Valhalla for the brave warriors who have fought for the spear with which he will slay Fenris?"

Ragnhild laughed silently and placed her hand on Hundr's forearm. They sat together in silence before the fading warmth of the fire and watched the sunrise. Then, Hundr rose the men from their slumber and set sail for Novgorod and the Gungnir spear.

TWENTY-ONE

The Seaworm and the Fjord Bear coursed on an eastward heading, their hulls slicing through the grey-green sea before a brisk wind. To the north lay the cold, wild lands of the Finns, and to the south lay the towns, cities, and vast lands of the Rus, Slavs and then, even further south, the Khazars. Bush and Einar let the ships run with the wind until they found what they searched for, the narrow mouth of a river thick with fat-bellied trading ships. Norsemen manned those ships, and shouts across the bows told Hundr that the river was the gateway south towards Novgorod, or Holmgard, as some called it. The crew groaned as the sails came down, knowing that it meant back-breaking oar work, but it had to be so. They lifted the oars from their resting hooks and lowered them into the swell to row the ships into the river mouth. The crew took turns at the oars, including Hundr, as they beat upriver, tracking the trading ships' pathways to avoid running aground in the unfamiliar waters.

Gulls and terns shrieked, diving from the skies, and Hundr stood in the prow, eyeing the traders as they rowed downriver out towards the sea. The crew filled Finn's head with the wonders held within the bilges of those ships, golden amber, soft luxurious silks, and smooth wine for the tables of kings. They maintained tracking the steering marks and withies along the river to avoid dangerous shallows and continued behind the traders to the mouth of the Neva and on into Lake Ladoga before heading further south on the Volkhov River. Throughout those days of rowing and exchanging their hacksilver with traders for small treasures in the long evenings at anchor, there was no sign of the burned man or his wolf ship, but Hundr could feel in his belly that his enemy travelled this way. Kvasir either ran before them, knowing their destination and laying a trap ahead, or followed behind to strike when least expected.

The crew rowed upriver until they came to the town of Aldeigjuborg and headed to an open berth on the riverbank. They lit cookfires and stretched the sail across the deck as an awning so the men could take a meal under shelter. Hundr and Einar met on the bank and scratched their heads at what to do with the warships and how to move towards Novgorod along the busy River Volkhov. The Norseman on the river told them it would be near impossible to row the entire way to Novgorod in the drakkars without either running aground in the summer river or attracting attention from the patrolling druzhina warriors who patrolled the waterways towards the great city of Novgorod. They decided that most of the crews would remain with the Seaworm and the Fjord Bear, and Hundr and Einar would make the remaining journey south, along with Sigvarth, Bush, Hekkr, Amundr, Sigrid, Thorgrim, and Torsten. Ragnhild, of course, made the journey, and Gunnr and her Valkyrie griped and complained at being left behind when it must be they who handled the mighty spear. Hundr, however, would brook no more of their petulance and so would take only Gunnr and Skögul. The remaining Valkyrie grumbled, and Gunnr complained, but Hundr brushed her off like a harridan on market day. Einar persuaded Hundr to allow Finn to join the company, and he relented. It was a risk to leave Finn where neither he nor Einar were close. The boy was a prize, the son of Ivar the Boneless and heir to the throne in Dublin; he had been kidnapped before, and Hundr shivered at the memory of his captor, Black Gorm the Berserker, who they had killed in the seas close to the lands of the Svear.

The travelling company found a berth on board a flat-bottomed riverboat favoured by Slav traders. In return for a handful of hacksilver, her crew poled them along the river, rowing where depth permitted, passing through dark forests of fir and pine where churls worked the land along the riverbanks with ploughs and oxen. The Volkhov meandered both wide and narrow as it twisted through the lands of the Rus, its currents at times calm and at others, swirling treacherously, which made Bush whoop with delight at the thrill of it. Further south, the farmland turned a rich, dark black like the lush soils of England, which Vikings hungered for, and Thorgrim swore he had never seen finer land for harvesting.

The riverboat tied up at an enormous wharf at Novgorod, and Hundr paid the sailors with the agreed hacksilver from his pouch, which was almost empty. The grizzle-bearded captain grumbled at its quality, running his tongue across brown stubs of teeth before grudgingly accepting payment as Einar added his own silver to the man's calloused palm. Hundr stepped off the boat onto the wooden wharf, taking in Novgorod's great walls that rose before them like the walls of Asgard itself, not the stone-built walls of Jorvik or Chester in England, but all sharpened wooden stakes, ditch and bank. Hundr felt his chest tighten with a foreboding feeling as his boots trudged along the wharf, the walls towering over him.

"Good to be home?" Einar said, marching next to Hundr. Hundr didn't reply because he did not feel like he was home. He remembered the walls well and the central fortress, the Citadel, where he had grown up. It was a formidable place, and the memories were neither warm nor welcoming. They were brutal, cold, and miserable. The druzhina guards in their conical helmets and horsehair plumes at the main gate lazed against its pillars, and the crew strode inside. The city smells of iron, foul meat, shit, and piss flooded Hundr's nose. He vividly remembered sleeping on freezing nights with the animals on the palace fringes, and of course, he remembered learning to fight. It was the only kindness his father had ever shown, allowing him to be instructed by the palace weapons master. Most of all, he remembered the heartrending sorrow of his mother's death. She had been the only person to show him kindness in those days. After that, he had fled the place, not along the river, but across the land. Stealing food and making his way north, dreaming of reputation and the life of a Viking warlord.

Inside the city was more timber. Darkened, rotting stakes mixed in with freshly cut golden rafters, spars, and turf or thatch-covered roofs. Its people strode along the wooden planked walkways, which weaved through the narrow streets, wearing sable furs and jerkins of green and brown. Rus druzhina soldiers were everywhere, clogging the lanes and paths in groups. There were far more soldiers than Hundr remembered and more than was required to keep the city safe.

"So, this was your home?" asked Sigrid as they picked their way through a busy crowd.

"This is where I was born," replied Hundr. He had never thought of the place as his home. He had been unhappy as a child. Rejected and scorned as a bastard, he was forced to live on the fringes and forever reminded of his status by his cruel half-brothers.

"Are there people here you know who could help us in the search for Sigdriffa?"

"There is nobody here I know," he uttered. Hundr remembered his weapons master and his loremaster. He had thrown himself into his training from the time his father permitted him to enter the training ring. Hundr remembered few, if any, friends from those days.

"What of your parents? You must have had friends?"

"Did you have friends on Orkney?"

"Many," Sigrid smiled, her bright eyes shining. "It was a happy place, cold but happy." Sigrid's father was Ketil Flatnose, a famous warrior and Jarl of the Orkney Islands.

"Do you miss it?"

"All the time I was there, I wanted to get away, to live this life of a warrior," Sigrid smiled sadly, the corners of her mouth turning down. "I miss my father and my brothers. But I am happy."

"Your father was a brave man," Hundr said, knowing the words were shallow and simple, but it was too awkward to talk with her about the famous old Jarl because Hundr had killed him at the battle of Hafrsfjord and Sigrid had never spoken of that heart-rending fact. Hundr's boots rattled on the walkway's planks, and a filthy urchin scuttled around his legs, racing through the crowds away from an angry merchant chasing him with a red face and a raised fist.

"This place is huge," Sigrid murmured, her eyes poring over the tall tower of the Citadel's inner fortress, rising above the wooden city to cast it in shadow. The snarl of streets and lanes twisted away out of sight, and the people who shouldered past them were a mix of Norseman, Slavs in furs babbling in their own language, and the occasional Khazar with copper hair and blue eyes, curved sabres slung from their thick belts.

"So how do we find out where Sigdriffa is?" said Gunnr, appearing at Hundr's shoulder, her face twisted into a frown.

"Same as in England," shrugged Hundr. "Even here, I think a crew of warrior women claiming to be Odin's Valkyrie would not go unnoticed. So let's find a tavern close to the inner fortress and ask around."

Bush rubbed his hands together at that, and Thorgrim clapped Amundr on the back at the prospect of tavern ale, frothing and fresh, instead of the warm barrelled ale of the Seaworm and Fjord Bear. The walls of the inner fortress rose high as the crew reached its gate, closed and guarded by four druzhina warriors in bright brynjars, black horsehair plumes, and long spears stood to attention. The planking street widened before the gates and branched out into a vast square in front of the gate itself, from which five different lanes led off to a mix of narrow streets, dark and shadowed, and then the wide central street, which led to the river.

"There, see?" said Bush, pointing towards one such lane, whose two-story buildings seemed to lean in on the walkway like trees arching over a forest path. Just inside that shadowed lane came two portly men stumbling and swaying with one arm each draped over the other's shoulder and singing a slurring song as the people of Novgorod spread around them, avoiding their drunkenness like water flowing around a boulder in a riverbed. Two druzhinas marched up the laneway behind them, and one of those warriors shoved the leftmost drunk in the back, sending him sprawling on the mud of the timber walkway. The second drunk spun around with raised fists, almost falling over as he turned, but he dropped his hands when he saw the armour and drooping moustaches of the Rus warriors. The fallen man half rose with a snarl before the same druzhina who had pushed him kicked him in the chest to send him sprawling again. People scuttled away, and the first drunk helped his friend to his feet before they both scurried off with less noise and heads bowed. The druzhina marched on, turning left at the end of the street to walk up the next of Novgorod's twisting lanes.

"Stay out of trouble," said Hundr, and was rewarded by a wink from Bush. Hundr shook his head and followed Einar towards the lane. Twenty paces along and past a butcher's shop where red meat sat on tables beneath a grimy awning buzzing with flies was a tavern whose wooden sign bore a faded image of a dog. From inside its shuttered windows pealed laughter and raised voices, and amongst the sounds of men at their ale danced the strings of a lyre. Hundr ducked underneath the door lintel and into the gloom of a sprawling room, as long and wide as a Jarl's hall, with rows of eating benches that stretched from wall to wall. At the far end of the room was a fire and, before that, a baldheaded man on a stool playing his lyre.

"I thought the place would be full from the noise pouring out of the place," said Bush. Instead, the central benches were empty, men keeping to the edges of the dark room, sitting or leaning against the walls. However, a noisy crew of Norsemen drank by the open windows facing onto the street.

"Those lads look like they've been drinking since daybreak," Hekkr remarked, glancing at the empty ale tankards stacked on their tables. One of the Norsemen toppled from his bench to land sprawling in the floor rushes, and the rest of them broke down into raucous laughter, slapping shoulders and banging the tabletop with their fists. "The rest of the place seems quiet."

"Good, we'll get our ale faster," grinned Amundr. Hundr sat on a bench next to Sigrid and Ragnhild, and Finn sat opposite him with Bush. A small man with beady eyes and a freshly shaved face came to their tables with a large tray full of tankards of frothy ale, and Hundr's men thirstily grabbed them. Bush plonked one in front of Finn, and the lad's eyes grew as wide as a wolf moon. He licked his lips and glanced at Einar, who frowned but then nodded his agreement. Finn brought the ale to his mouth and took a long pull. When he lowered the tankard, white froth covered his top lip, and he grinned at Bush, who laughed and took a swig from his own mug. Sigvarth Trollhands downed his ale in one and then drank half of Torsten's while his back was turned.

Hundr stood and fished out some more shards of his ever-dwindling hacksilver and handed them to the tavernkeeper. The small man fingered through the shards and passed two back. Hundr then pulled out a Saxon-minted coin with the head of a king he did not know the name of and pressed it into the man's hand.

"Have you seen a band of warrior women in the city? They call themselves Valkyrie and look similar to the women here," Hundr said, gesturing to Ragnhild, Gunnr, and Skögul.

The tavernkeeper sniffed and stuffed the coin into the pocket at the front of his stained tabard. "Rarely you see women such as them, armed and bristling with warrior swagger," he responded in Rus-accented Norse. "I saw them; they arrived here a week ago. Marched through the city with all the pride of you Danes and Norsemen. They went into the inner fortress, welcomed by the Prince himself."

"Prince Rurik?" Hundr asked. Speaking his father's name felt strange, falling heavily from his tongue.

"Rurik died last year. Oleg is Prince now."

"Died how?" asked Hundr. The shock of his father's death was like a slap across his face.

He had never really known the man. He had been a distant, cruel figure throughout Hundr's childhood.

"In his bed, sickness took him. He made Oleg Prince on his deathbed. That's why we are drowning in druzhina; Oleg gathers the army to march south. He wants Kiev, and he wants to make his name as a war Prince."

"What of Rurik's sons?"

"Prince Yaroslav runs the city, second only in command to Prince Oleg."

Hundr nodded his thanks to the tavernkeeper and sat heavily on the ale bench. The surrounding room spun. He glanced up at the smoke-darkened rafters, trinkets hung there, and they seemed to swell and circle in Hundr's head – a stuffed raven, the skull of a dog, a rust-darkened sabre, and a giant wagon wheel with melted candles on each spoke.

"What is it?" asked Sigrid, shaking him by the shoulder.

"My father is dead," he whispered, still reeling from the news but also mindful of her own loss.

"But you had no love for the man?"

"No," said Hundr. He lifted his tankard and drained the ale, the liquid harsh on his throat and warming his belly. *But I wanted to show him what I had become, that I wasn't just a worthless bastard.* Hundr thought of his mother. Only he had mourned her loss. She had been a concubine to Prince Rurik, and Hundr had not seen his father since her death. After that, they refused him admission to the palace, leaving him to remain in the stables with the animals, his only joy in his daily weapons practice. His other lessons had ceased immediately, lore, languages. There was only the joy of steel left and the promise that they would allow him to join the druzhina once he was old enough. But his half-brothers had ripped even that dream from him.

"Sigdriffa is here, inside the city," Hundr said, turning to Ragnhild. The change of subject refocused his senses. "The Valkyrie are inside the Citadel itself, welcomed by the Prince."

"She will have the spear with her," Ragnhild intoned. "She would not have left Odin's sacred weapon with her ship, which is probably somewhere close to our own. If she plans to make a new Upsala here, then she will keep Gungnir close."

"But how are we going to get it?" asked Sigrid.

"Well, we can't just march in there," Hundr supposed. "So, we'll need to get inside and have a look around, see where she and the spear are."

"Steal it, you mean?" said Ragnhild, raising an eyebrow above her good eye.

"If we must, yes. Get the spear and get out of

this place before they know it's gone. If Sigdriffa has the Prince's ear, then attacking her Valkyrie or taking the spear will bring down the might of the entire city upon us. We wouldn't get back to our ships alive."

"But we must get inside the gates first?" asked Sigrid.

"And then the fortress?" Ragnhild added.

"We must get inside both and then search the palace and its grounds until we find the spear. We will have to get over those monstrous walls without being seen or through the gate. Once inside, we will need to evade the druzhina whilst we search. Only a few of us can go, and if they find us, we will die. This is a task unlike any other. The risk is beyond that of the shield wall, for the death we would suffer at their hands would not be worthy of Valhalla. So, we must risk everything. I will go. I know the place, or I used to, at least."

"I will go with you," said Ragnhild.

"And I," Sigrid nodded. Hundr took another pull at his ale without agreeing. He wanted to go in alone. He could slip inside, follow the ways he knew as a child, through the servants' quarters and around the animal pens. One man could do that, but any more would attract attention. Nevertheless, he had to watch the gates first and find a way inside.

"Watch where you're going," boomed a voice across the hall in Norse. A big man with a braided beard shoved Skögul hard in the chest, throwing her backwards from where she had stood with her Valkyrie sisters.

"You barged into me," said Skögul angrily, recovering herself and striding to square up to the Norseman.

"What kind of crew lets their whores wear brynjars and carry weapons?" the big man called to his cronies beside the wall, and they all laughed and made gestures about the Valkyrie's breasts over their own chests.

"Did you call me a whore?" Skögul uttered, her voice even and cold.

"Yes, I have some Serkland coin here. I'd bring you out the back for a tupping if you weren't so ugly."

Skögul's hand fell to her axe, but before it could touch the iron, Einar placed a hand upon her forearm and eased it away. He stepped in front of the Valkyrie and grinned at the Norseman.

"This woman is part of my crew, and she is a warrior. Go back to your ale; she didn't mean to barge you," Einar said, his voice amiable.

"He barged into me!" Skögul insisted, but Einar inclined his head to quiet her.

"Are you her father, greybeard?" said the Norseman, and he turned to laugh at his shipmates, who chuckled along with him. But when he turned back, he found Einar's hard slab of a face a finger's breadth from him, flinty eyes staring furiously into his own.

"I am Einar Rosti!" Einar roared into the Norseman's face, and the big man took a step back. Einar was a hand taller than him and broader at the shoulder. The group of Norsemen snarled and reared up, and the men of the Seaworm crew leapt from their benches, whooping at the entertainment of it.

"Should we not help Einar?" asked Finn, rising from his own bench and looking at Hundr, fear for Einar in his eyes.

Hundr smiled, glad to have something to release the strange feelings swirling around his thought cage at the news of his father's death. "Don't worry about Einar. You are about to find out how he got his name."

TWENTY-TWO

The Norseman's face flushed, and he bared his teeth like a maddened dog. He let out a roar of anger and raised his hands as though to shove Einar in the chest. As the Norseman's hands came up, Einar grabbed the rope of his beard, yanked it savagely towards him, and smashed his forehead into the Norseman's nose. It was a brutal headbutt which crushed the man's nose, splitting it and spurting blood across his surprised face. The Norseman tried to pull away, clasping his hands to his ruined nose, but Einar kept hold of his beard and punched the Norseman twice in the head. Einar kicked the man in the chest, sending him sprawling on the floor rushes. Einar flexed his calloused hands, the knuckles split across both hands where he had connected with the Norseman's skull. His breathing came heavy, and the thrill of combat flooded him with strength. Einar closed his eyes for a moment, savouring the feeling of being strong again. He felt young and like he could defeat anyone, just as he had once been when men had given him the name Einar the Brawler.

The Norseman's crewmates surged from their benches at the window end of the tavern. They shouted curses at Einar and reared up in front of their fallen friend with puffed-out chests and snarling faces. There were five of them, all with combed hair and Viking beards. None wore the chainmail brynjar that marked out a wealthy warrior or a leader. They were clad in leather and wool, and each man was armed with an axe and a knife. Hands had not dropped to weapons, which was wise. Once that happened, if weapon violence erupted in the tavern, its floor would run with blood, and both sets of warriors knew that fact. So, there would be a fist fight, and even though Einar's head told him he was too old for brawling in back street taverns and that such actions were beneath a Jarl of Norway, he laughed loudly. Einar threw his head back and laughed to the heavens, thanking Odin for the fleeting chance to feel like a younger man again, like a simple warrior without the cares of leadership around his neck. Benches surrounding him scraped against the hard-packed earthen floor, and Einar sensed Hundr, Ragnhild, Bush, Hekkr, Amundr and the rest of his men surging to support him, but he waved them down, like calming a pack of baying dogs. He wanted the fight.

Two of the Norsemen jumped at Einar as he stepped forwards. He ducked under a barrel-chested man's attempt to grab him, and as Einar came up, he punched the second man twice in the guts. Einar kept moving and kicked the first attacker in the back of his knee, and as the man fell to his knees, Einar crashed his elbow into the back of that first attacker's skull with an audible crack. He turned and laughed again as the man he had punched in the stomach clutched himself and doubled over, vomiting hot, stinking ale onto the tavern floor. The three remaining Norsemen had stopped their shouting and now came on warily, eyes flitting from Einar's brynjar to those of his shipmates and understanding too late the man they faced. Einar smiled at them – he welcomed the violence; it was part of him. He darted at the central Norseman and threw a feinted punch, instead taking a wide sidestep and crashing his elbow into the right most Norseman's chest. He spun around that warrior and pushed him towards the other two, blocking them as they lunged towards him. Einar saw the flash of a blade in a Norseman's hand, and he grabbed a brawny wrist and twisted the blade. The Norseman was strong and did not lose grip of his knife, so Einar pulled him close and punched him in the throat, flinging him towards

Hekkr, who caught the knife man and threw him over his hip, locking the arm holding the knife until the Norseman squealed for mercy. Yet Hekkr was not a merciful man, and with a brutal crack and crunch, he broke the Norseman's arm.

Einar advanced on the remaining two Norsemen, and they did what they should have done when the fight started. They came at him as one, both leaping at him and grappling him between them. They came fast, and Einar could not spin away. Strong arms gripped his torso and left arm, and a fist cannoned into his cheek, sending a flash of pain through his face. Einar stamped on a man's foot and grabbed another by the throat with his free hand. At that moment, the door to the tavern burst open, and four druzhina warriors marched into the tavern, spears lowered and helmets gleaming. The little tavernkeeper scuttled between their legs, pointing at the Norsemen and babbling in a high-pitched voice.

"No fighting in the city," barked a stocky, long-moustached druzhina. "Stop it now, or I'll throw all of you stinking Norse bastards in the river."

The Norsemen peeled themselves away from Einar's body, and one pushed him in the chest for good measure. Einar smiled and winked at the man, who touched gingerly at the red finger marks around his throat.

"No trouble here, soldier," said the man, and he raised his palm in apology to the tavernkeeper and to the druzhina.

"What about you, big man?" asked the long-moustached druzhina, pointing his spear at Einar. "You want to go in the river?"

"No, I washed only two weeks ago," Einar said, smiling.

"Bloody Norsemen," grunted another of the druzhina. "Could start a fight in an empty room." The rest of the druzhina laughed, shaking their heads.

"No harm done. We'll ensure the tavernkeeper here is paid for his trouble," said Einar, putting his arm around the Norseman he had been strangling only moments earlier.

The leading druzhina sighed. "Keep out of trouble. If I have to break up any more of your Norse drunkenness, they will find your corpses downstream bloated and rotting a week from now." The soldiers marched out of the tavern as quickly as they had arrived, the horsehair plumes of their helmets swishing.

"Leave this place," Einar growled at the Norseman whose shoulder still had his arm draped around it. "If I see you in Holmgard again, I'll kill you myself."

The Norseman shook himself free of Einar's

arm, and the group of them cursed and spat, nursing their injuries, and slunk from the tavern like whipped dogs. The man whose arm Hekkr had broken moaned as they helped him up from the floor.

Finn stood in front of Einar with his hands on his hips and a grin splitting his face. "Einar the Brawler," he said and chuckled.

The tavernkeeper warmed to Einar as the day went on, and after the Valkyrie and Amundr had drank and paid for enough ale to soothe his anger, he allowed them to purchase two rooms above the tavern to stay for the night. Later, the tavern became busier, and the soldiers of Prince Oleg's mustering army were soon as thick in the place as fleas on an old dog. Einar and Hundr waited until dark fell across Novgorod and then left the tavern with their cloaks pulled about them to keep out the evening chill, leaving the rest of the company behind with orders not to get into any more trouble. The wooden walkways directly outside were bustling with the overflow of soldiers trying to get a drink of ale, and Einar weaved through, careful not to barge into any of them or upset any tankards of ale.

"Let us through," called one young soldier, trying to snake his way through the maze of armour and leather. "We march tomorrow. This might be our last chance to get a good drink before we sack Kiev." A group of soldiers cheered and ushered him towards the doorway, laughing as he grinned sheepishly.

Hundr kept his head low, and Einar did the same. They marched towards the Citadel, rising like a dark mountain against the pitch-dark sky.

"We need to find somewhere to rest up," said Hundr, "so we can watch for a while. Like I said to Ragnhild, there must be a weak point. Somewhere we can slip inside. A change of watch at the main gate or a side door where city burghers or even whores come and go without the entire square noticing."

"So, you still think we can just steal the spear?" asked Einar.

"Unless you can think of another way to get it."

Einar shrugged. Over the years, he had learned that the cunning work was better left to Hundr. Einar himself was much more comfortable helming a ship or back on his Jarl's seat at Vanylven. Even there, he supposed, Hildr did most of the deep thinking. As they tramped along the planks of Novgorod's walkway and onto the main square, Einar imagined Hildr warming herself by a fire at their hall in Vanylven. He knew the place would run just as well as it did when he was there. She could run the town with her eyes closed, but he missed her. So, any plan to get the cursed spear and get

Ragnhild back to her sisterhood was fine with him as long as he could get back to Hildr as quickly as possible.

They found a ginnel running between two houses which faced towards the Citadel's gates – the space was only wide enough for two men to walk with shoulders touching, and the two-storey wattle buildings on either side cast the narrow alleyway in darkness.

"This will do," said Hundr, and they both hunkered down to watch. Two druzhinas manned the gate facing onto the square, and every so often, other soldiers would approach and greet the guards. They would exchange a few words and occasionally a joke, and then the gate guards would bang on the timber and call an order to the men beyond. Soon after, guards from the inside would heave open one side of the two monstrous gates, each side as wide as six men, and then the soldiers could enter. At one such opening, Einar glimpsed a long thick spar held upright within the gate by a soldier, which he would slide back into the iron callipers on the inside of the door frame, barring and securing, should any attacking force wish to break the gate down.

They watched until the singing from the taverns throughout Novgorod increased in noise until it undulated across the city, where soldiers spent the dregs of their silver on ale and women before they marched off on Oleg's war against Kiev and the Khazars to the south.

"I can't see any side doors or other ways in," said Einar. "Unless you want to take a stroll around the perimeter?" He stood and groaned as the bones in his knees clicked and strained from being huddled down for so long.

"Let's take a walk then," agreed Hundr. They were about to set off when two men bustled into the opposite end of the ginnel, laughing and pushing each other in drunken jest. They darkness shadowed them. One man coughed and sighed before piss pounded the ground as though it fell from a horse. "I think I've got an idea," said Hundr quietly.

"What, inspired by a drunk's piss?" replied Einar, shaking his head.

"They look like druzhina to me. Let's just hammer them here in the dark, slip on their armour and go in through the front gate?"

"Have you lost your mind?"

"Why? We were looking for a way to sneak in like rats when we could just march through the front gate. I speak like these men. I was born here. They won't suspect a thing."

Einar's face creased into a frown. His mind ran over the dozens of ways they could be caught and killed. Then he remembered Ragnhild and the countless times he had fought next to her in the clash of arms, and that to get Gungnir, he and Hundr had to get inside the Citadel.

"We've followed worse plans, I suppose, and we're still alive," Einar said. Hundr grinned and clapped Einar on the shoulder.

"Ho there, friends," Hundr called, walking up the alleyway towards the two soldiers, who swayed as they relieved themselves in the darkness.

"What do you want?" mumbled one of the druzhina. "Can't you see I'm busy?"

"We are trying to join up with Oleg's army. Where do we...."

Hundr's words were cut short as Einar shouldered past him and punched the closest urinating warrior in the face. It was a hard blow, overhand and brutal. Einar's knuckles crunched into the man's eye, smashing bone, and the man crumpled into his own piss. The second warrior gasped, and his hand fumbled for the sabre at his belt, but Einar kicked the hand away and grabbed the man around the head. His two huge hands gripped either side of the druzhina's skull, and Einar smashed it twice against the wall. His calloused, rough hands pushed into the skin of the man's face and snapped his head, savagely twisting and breaking his neck in one powerful motion. The first warrior whimpered on his knees, clutching at his broken cheekbone. Einar whipped his axe free from the loop at his belt and buried the blade in the warrior's forehead with a crack. The man pitched backwards, dead.

"No need for words," Einar said with a shrug.

"The longer you are away from your Jarl seat, the more like your old self you become," Hundr quipped, a smile playing at one corner of his mouth. Einar frowned at that truth because since he had been away from Vanylven, he had felt more like he remembered himself to be. The joy of the sea surging beneath the Fjord Bear and his strength battling against the tiller, the thrill of battle and the heart-racing challenge of combat were more a part of Einar and more important to him than he had believed.

"We are far from the warmth of Vanylven. This one looks the biggest." Einar stripped the armour, helmet and boots from the largest druzhina and pulled them on. The mail was tight across his chest, and he stretched his arms and groaned. The trews were short at the ankles, and the boots curled the ends of his toes because they were so tight.

"I never thought I would enter this place in stolen armour, sliding in like a thief," Hundr grumbled. Nevertheless, Hundr's armour fit perfectly, and he nestled the helmet on his head.

"You look a better druzhina than that fool.

What do you care if the folk here know of your deeds?" Einar spoke the words, but he knew they were empty. All Vikings cared about their reputation. That was the reason for taking to the seas and the force behind their monstrous pride. Hundr undoubtedly imagined himself returning to his home city as a champion, a successful warrior of fair fame with a horde of bright ships and shining warriors at his back. But, instead, he returned as a thief in the darkness. For a heartbeat, Einar remembered Hundr on the day they first met at a fish-stinking trading port south of Jutland. He had been a stripling then, in travel-stained simple clothes begging for a berth when the Seaworm had been Einar's. He remembered seeing something in the lad, a glint in his eye, or maybe it was the Norns weaving the threads of their lives together, but either way, that day had changed the warp and weft of their futures forever.

"Come on," said Hundr, grimacing as he fastened the helmet's strap under his chin. "Let me do the talking."

Einar followed Hundr across the square. They casually strolled as though they had spent the evening drinking with the rest of Oleg's soldiers who thronged the city. Einar rested one hand on the pommel of the druzhina's sabre and tucked his other hand into his belt. He felt uneasy without his trusty axe. He and Hundr had rolled their weapons and brynjar coats of mail in their jerkins and stuffed them inside the damp thatch of a building that butted onto the alleyway. They could not have approached the gate armed with Hundr's two swords and Einar's bearded axe, and the thatch would keep them safe until they returned. If they returned. They left the shadow of the ginnel behind them and wove their way amongst the groups of soldiers crisscrossing the timber walkways to enter and leave the bustling streets of Novgorod. Hundr approached the darkened gates to the Citadel, and the two guards there noticed their approach and fixed them with bored, flat-eyed stares. Hundr smiled and raised a hand in greeting, and one guard hawked up a gobbet of spit and launched it onto the pathway with indifference.

"There," came a yell from one of the streets leading off from the central square. But Einar kept his eyes fixed on the guards. Men shouted, and a disturbance in the crowd caught the corner of Einar's eye. He turned to see a group of men charging across the square in his direction, and as the crowd parted before them, he recognised Norse growlers with their long hair and braided beards. Immediately, he saw the brawler from the tavern pointing straight at him, and then Einar's guts loosened because at that Norseman's shoulder grinning a smile of triumphant malevolence was Kvasir, the burned man.

TWENTY-THREE

"Take them," said Kvasir Randversson, the words spilling from his mouth slowly, rolling off his tongue like summer honey. He spoke as though he had waited his whole life for that exact moment to utter that very line. His warriors bristled with blades, axes, spears, seaxes, and the gleam of a sword. They were big men, bearded and muscled from the oar. They were Vikings, come to lay Hundr and Einar low, and the druzhina soldiers in the square, unused to violence as they were despite their uniforms, fled from the weapons like frightened fish in a disturbed river as the burned man came for vengeance.

Hundr dragged his newly gained sabre free of its flimsy scabbard and held the curved blade before him, pointing it towards Kvasir and his men. He recognised the drunks from the tavern among them. Their bruised faces and angered eyes marked them out as the Norsemen Einar had beaten to the floor rushes. Kvasir had followed Hundr and Einar to Novgorod in his hate and searched the city for their whereabouts. The Norsemen must have met Kvasir somewhere in the city during his search, had known that he was looking for a one-eyed man, and then ran to Kvasir following the tavern brawl. So, here he was with the raw, taut skin of his face stretched and twisted and his teeth flashing in a broad but vicious grin.

Kvasir's men spread out into a half circle and came on. It was surprising to see three druzhinas behind them. One of those men, his helmet trailing a white horsehair plume instead of the usual black, shouted an order to the gate guards. One lowered his spear, whilst the other knocked urgently on the gate with four quick raps of his knuckles before slipping inside, the gate creaking and slamming closed behind him. Warmth kindled in Hundr's belly, the kindling heat of fear. They were surrounded, and there was no sign of Ragnhild or the rest of his warriors, yet a man who hated Hundr enough to pursue him across Midgard had him cornered like a pig for the slaughter.

"Looks like the plan of sneaking in has gone to shit," said Einar, a wry grin flashing on the slab of his face. He held his sabre low at his side and took a wide step away from Hundr, making space to fight.

Hundr breathed deeply. He cast his eyes towards the dark, pewter sky and prayed to Odin. *See me, All-Father. See how I fight and make a space for me in the halls of your Einherjar. Many are there to welcome me who have fallen to my blade.* Hundr allowed the fear in his belly to take fire, to grow into a fire of anger and hate. It surged through his chest, and he felt strong, the power of it pulsing in his arms and chest as his heart quickened.

"Few against many, let's make a saga tale which will never be forgotten," Hundr said, flicking the tip of his sabre towards his enemies as they formed a circle. Axe blades shimmered in the torchlight cast from the Citadel's walls, spears wavered like great fangs, and Kvasir's killers came to do their work.

"I am Einar Rosti," Einar bellowed in his aged warrior's voice. "Named 'The Brawler' by the Boneless himself. Who are you to come and fight with me? It was I who burned the hall of Kjotve the Rich at Agder, and I who lit the fire that burned your master's face. What kind of Jarl sends his men to fight whilst he skulks behind them like the raven starver he is? I am drengr, warrior, come and die!" Einar beat his fist against his chest, and there was spittle in his beard. His eyes were as wide as a wolf moon, and he drew a knife so that he held a blade in both hands.

"If this is my time, then I am glad to fight and die beside you, Einar," Hundr spoke quietly, and his old friend winked at him. Einar then leapt forward with the speed and savagery of a warrior half his age and slashed his sabre across the eyes of a spearman who had ventured too close. The warrior screamed and dropped his spear to clatter on the timbers of Novgorod's timber-planked square, and as blood spurted between the fingers clutched to his face, Einar kept moving. An axeman parried a slash of Einar's sword but missed the following knife slash, which carved a gash across the belly of his leather breastplate. The circle of enemies leapt backwards, mouths agape at Einar's vicious attack. Hundr drew his knife and held it in an underhand grip so that he had a sword in his right and the knife in his left. He darted forward, and a spear shaft blocked a flick of his sabre while another axeman leapt away from the follow-up slash to his right.

The Norsemen growled and came on together, realising that to attack as lone fighters meant death. A crowd of druzhina soldiers had gathered around the edges of the square to watch the battle, and they roared and cheered for Kvasir's men. The blinded warrior fell to his knees, sobbing at the pain of his injury and the horror of his blindness. Einar edged behind the kneeling man to create an obstacle between him and the enemies before him. A short, bearded man jabbed at Hundr with his spear, and Hundr swivelled around the strike to stab the spearman in the armpit with his sabre, plunging the tip of the sword in deep and twisting the hilt to tear and rend the soft flesh. The spearman contorted away, and Hundr brandished the bloody tip of his weapon towards the ring of enemies as a warning.

"Come and fight with Einar," Einar growled, and the ring of Norsemen tested him, striking out with axe and spear so that the square rang with the clang and dunt of each parry. The crowd around the square thickened, their ale breath drifting on the wind and their shouts for blood echoing off Novgorod's walls like the crash of the sea. A flurry of blades came at Hundr. He parried two and ducked under another before a spear point punched into his ribs. Hundr grunted at the pain, but his druzhina armour took the strike. Hundr swerved as one came at his face, and he stabbed his knife into the attacker's groin in two quick jerks, hot blood spilling over his hand. A punch scuffed off Hundr's ear, and the enemy closed in around him, the foulness of their breath washing over him. Wide-eyed and grunting, they strove to drive their blades into his neck and body. His back was pressed against Einar, who moved with jerking power as he fought the foes on his side of the enemy circle. Hundr tried to bring his sabre to bear, but the Norsemen were too close, and the blow fouled as his elbow crashed into an axe haft. A blade sliced across his bicep, and Hundr could not tell if it was a spear, axe, or seax. They were all around him, hacking, kicking and punching, smothering him in a blanket of violence. Hundr dropped his druzhina sabre and grabbed the beard braid of an unseen foe, dragging his chin downwards to meet the point of his knife so that the weapon stabbed up into his mouth and through his tongue. Hundr shouldered into the gap as that man became a corpse, and he snatched up his fallen axe, turning to chop the axe head into another enemy's calf. The bearded blade sliced through muscle as though it were butter, half severing the warrior's leg. The wounded man toppled onto the wooden boardwalk, and the square before Novgorod's Citadel was a gore-splashed battlefield. Blood covered Einar's face like a mask, making his eyes and teeth stand out like those of a demon as he fought with his enemies like a warrior of legend. Hundr brought his axe up in a wide sweep, and another axe parried the blow, stopping the swing dead and jarring Hundr's arm to the shoulder. He glanced up to see snarling teeth in a twisted face, stretched skin like a melting candle and eyes burning with hateful rage. Kvasir and Hundr locked eyes, and their axes pushed against each other.

Kvasir's arm was like iron and didn't move a finger's breadth as Hundr shoved against him. The burned man whipped a broken-backed bladed seax low at Hundr's belly, who blocked the hit with his own knife. A blow thundered into Hundr's back, felling him to one knee, and for a horrifying moment, the pain between his shoulder blades made Hundr fear an axe had sunk into his body, but the blow had not been true. He withdrew his axe from Kvasir's and tried to rise from his knees, but a boot connected with the side of his head, driving him onto the blood-slicked walkway. Hundr scrambled and came up just in time to lurch away from Kvasir's axe, which sang through the night air, aimed to take his face off, and Hundr felt the wind of it as it whipped past his head. He slashed with his knife, and the blade connected with Kvasir's leg, giving Hundr time to surge to his feet. A roaring warrior with a black beard so thick that it covered his face below the eyes came at Hundr with a long-handled war axe. He raised the weapon above his head in what would be a monstrous blow that must surely carve Hundr in two, but the warrior's foot slipped on gore so that his leg shot out sideways on the walkway's timbers. The war axe blow stopped halfway through its arc as the bearded brute tried to regain his footing, and Hundr thumped his own short, hafted axe into the warrior's gut, which he followed up by slicing the blade of his knife across the wounded man's throat. He fell to the walkway, and Hundr had to brace his boot against the dying man's head to wrench his weapon free of the corpse.

The crowd had fallen silent, and Einar stood next to Hundr, drenched in the blood of his foes. Cuts slashed across his arms and face. Their enemies writhed and moaned in their own lifeblood, and Hundr sucked air into his lungs, which burned from exhaustion. Kvasir straightened and came on again, spitting at his warriors to attack. Then suddenly, Kvasir paused. His eyes fixed over Hundr's shoulder from where the sound of boots stomping filled the air, which only moments earlier had rang with the din of battle. A murmur washed around the crowd of soldiers like the tide sighing on a shale beach, and they fell back to stand well away from the fighting men.

"What is the meaning of this?" came a deep voice, outrage and anger thick in it like day-old soup. The two druzhinas who had stood behind Kvasir bowed their heads, and the crowd all did the same, banging fists to their hearts in salute. Hundr turned towards the vastness of the Citadel's open gate to see a figure striding before armed warriors. He was a man of average height, with a shaved head apart from a long braided top knot stretching from the top of his skull to rest over one armoured shoulder. Hundr's heart sank as he recognised his half-brother, Prince Yaroslav of Novgorod, flanked by Sigdriffa. Her golden hair shone in the torchlight, and her Valkyrie flanked the Prince in a boar's tusk wedge. "Who spills blood so brazenly in my city before the gates of the fortress itself? How dare you, you Norse pig…" the words died in Yaroslav's throat as he peered at Hundr, a mix of doubt and recognition rattling in his thought cage.

"My Lord Yaroslav," Kvasir said, striding towards the Rus Prince. "I caught these dogs attempting to enter your Citadel disguised as your own druzhina warriors. This is the man you have been seeking. His goal was to enter your fortress and steal the Gungnir spear. He would have killed you in your bed like the nithing assassin he is. Just as he did my own Lord Kjotve in far Norway."

A smile played at the corner of the Prince's mouth, and he tucked his thumbs into his belt as he shook his head at Hundr. "You have done well, Kvasir. For this is my bastard brother. Is it not, Velmud?" Yaroslav spoke good Norse but with a heavily accented Rus accent. The Rus were descended from Viking stock and clung to that heritage by speaking the language as a mark of honour between the high Rus lords.

"It is I, brother," said Hundr, spitting the last word as though it were rotten food in his mouth.

"Are you here to kill me, bastard?"

"If I were here to kill you, you would already be dead."

Yaroslav chuckled at that but shook his head. "You choose this night to return to our city? The night before Oleg marches his army south. Do you do this to shame me? Are you jealous that I have become Lord of the greatest city in Midgard?"

Hundr cuffed blood away from a cut on his cheek and shook his head to clear the fog from the blow he had received during the fight. The surrounding warriors took a step back now that the Prince had arrived, their chests heaving from the fight. Yaroslav sneered at the wounded, groaning men on the planking, and Kvasir's men dragged their shipmates away to suffer out of sight. Enemies surrounded Hundr. The burned man and his warriors, although they had broken off their assault, were still thick around him like trees in a forest. Facing him was his hated half-brother, the man who had made his childhood a misery, who had shattered his dreams of becoming a soldier of the druzhina and driven him from the city. Sigdriffa stared at him, her golden hair swept back from the cliff of her angled faced in tight braids; she who had led them across the Whale Road in pursuit of Gungnir. All of Hundr's enemies were in one place for the first time, and only he and Einar were there to face them. If he only had his crews, his five ships of warriors, he would cut them all down and wash the streets with their blood. But he did not have his men, not even the band of fighters he had brought to Novgorod. There was just Einar and him, outnumbered and trapped.

"I will fight you, brother," Hundr retorted, shouting the words so that all present in that wood-floored square beneath the night's darkness could hear. "I come here alone, with one companion, against the forces of your druzhina and this snake who would sell me to you like a slave." Hundr pointed his axe at Kvasir. "This man is wanted by King Harald Fairhair, King of all Norway. He is a murderer, a raider, a nithing of ignominious reputation." Hundr pushed himself straighter, shoulders back and chin up. "I am no longer the bastard you forced to sleep in the cold with the animals. I am the Man with the Dog's Name, Jarl Hundr, master of five ships and a sea Jarl feared wherever men brave the Whale Road. A drengr and follower of the old ways. I challenge you to fight a Holmgang here in front of your warriors. Just you and I."

Yaroslav ground his teeth, his jaw muscles working beneath the short hairs of his close-cropped beard. His eyes bore into Hundr through the torch-lit darkness, like those of a serpent, clever and malevolent. Those eyes flickered around the square with only the slightest movement from his royal head. He gauged the mood of his men, and Hundr knew his pride cursed the challenge because it was one Yaroslav would never expect. They had fought countless times in the training grounds of the palace, and the Prince knew his bastard brother's skill at arms, skill he could never match.

"A Prince does not roll in the filth with bastards and beggars," Yaroslav sneered and spat in Hundr's direction. "You, a beggar, come home spouting lies about jarldoms that don't exist and with only an addled grandfather for company." He looked to the druzhina. "I want him alive. Stake him inside the walls!" the prince shrieked and turned on his heel, waving a dismissive hand in Hundr's direction. The stake. Hundr had seen the punishment many times as a child. A sharpened timber stake, like the posts of the Citadel itself, was driven into a man's arse and pushed through his body until its point burst through the gap between neck and shoulder. They then fixed the stake into the ground, and the impaled soul would hang there for a day or more in agony for all to see until death mercifully took them to Niflheim, for it was surely not a death worthy of Valhalla. Hundr would not die writhing, impaled on one of his hated brother's stakes.

Just as the Prince turned his back, Hundr threw his knife underhand. A flick of his wrist sent the blade spinning through the darkness in a low, flat arc. It turned, blade over hilt across the space between Hundr and Yaroslav, and it flew true towards his brother's back. Hundr held his breath. He could die well under a hail of blades, content if he knew he had revenge upon his brother for all those years of sadness and pain. The knife was suddenly dashed from the air with a ringing clang, and Sigdriffa was there twirling her short, hafted axe, which had blocked the throw. The knife clattered to the planking at her feet. Yaroslav paused, turned his head to check the noise, and marched back through the Citadel gates flanked once more by the Valkyrie. Sigdriffa levelled her axe at Hundr and smiled haughtily before turning to accompany the Prince into the city. Hundr flexed his hand around the haft of his axe and tested his footing. He would not die impaled at his brother's pleasure under his mocking gaze. Hundr roared at the heavens and charged towards Kvasir. He slashed his axe blade across the neck of the closest warrior and then swung the blade low to smash the knee of another. The square, which had been as silent as a frosted winter morning, now erupted into shouting and pain-filled screams.

"Bastards!" Einar roared out of sight. The clang of weapons rang across Novgorod like a bell. The Norsemen converged on Hundr again, but he wove between them like a fetch, as light and fast as the air. He cut and slashed and danced amongst them, hot, thick blood splashing his face and hands as he killed and maimed, nothing left to him but an Odin death, a death worthy of a place in Valhalla. Kvasir reared up before him again, and the burned man swung his axe. But Hundr did not parry the stroke. Instead, he ducked beneath it, using his lifetime of training and war experience to anticipate the attack. Hundr came up beneath it lithely, and he was close to Kvasir, so close he could smell the acrid stink of his sweat and hear the gasp of breath as his knee thudded into Kvasir's belly. Hundr punched Kvasir in his scarred face with his left hand and chopped his axe into the burned man's shoulder with a wet thud.

Kvasir fell away, and the attacking Norsemen roared in defiance as they saw their leader fall. They charged Hundr, who had lost the grip on his axe, which remained lodged in Kvasir's shoulder. A warrior charged into Hundr's chest, knocking him off balance. He stumbled, and a huge druzhina reared up before him, all armour and horse-tailed helmet filling Hundr's vision. The druzhina snarled, his drooping moustaches twitching, and he hit Hundr hard in the face with the pommel of his sabre. The blow was thunderous, and Hundr thought his entire skull had shattered. Lights flashed where once he had seen enemies, and he crumpled to the timber walkway. Hundr scrambled, clawing to escape his enemies, but blows rained down upon him, crashing into the armour covering his torso. His vision cleared, and he stared beneath the shifting legs of his enemies as they stamped on him and cut at him. He searched for Ragnhild, Sigrid, Valbrandr, or Amundr. But none came. A blow smashed into the back of his head, and darkness swamped him like a mighty wave in a storm of pain.

TWENTY-FOUR

From the darkness came pain. It lanced through Hundr's skull like a blade, as though the insides of it were too big and would burst out to shatter his head like an overripe apple. The pain made Hundr retch in the dark, his stomach heaving, but all that came up was burning bile to sting his throat. He tried to open his good eye. His dead eye socket throbbed with swelling, aching across that whole side of his face, and his right eyelid flickered, something heavy, dry and thick in his eyelashes keeping it closed. Blood. Hundr tried to wipe it away, but something held his hands fast above him, and the clank and chafe of cold iron told him he was chained. He was resting on his knees and secured at his hands from above, a dry-stone wall cool against his bare back. Hundr turned his head to wipe his face on his shoulder, which sent another ripple of agony through his skull. Some of the crusted blood fell away, and he opened his good eye a crack. The light hurt his head, and he retched again. This time, a stab of pain across his ribs brought back the memory of boots and spear butts slamming into his back as he lay injured outside the gates. Finally, the blurred light cleared to reveal a courtyard busy with churls hurrying back and forth with buckets and carts of hay.

"You are alive then," came a mumbled voice next to him. Hundr turned through the pain to see Einar shackled beside him. They had stripped Einar to the waist, and he hung from his wrists, chained to the wall. Einar's face was a mask of swelling and blood. His eyes were puffy and bruised, and one side of his mouth was swollen, causing his words to slur.

"I'm not sure yet," said Hundr, running his tongue across two loosened teeth at the back of his mouth.

"Better we had died out there." Einar flicked his head to the left, where two men in leather aprons worked with chisels at long golden tree trunks. They had stripped away the bark and now ran their tools along the lengths of timber, making them smooth and sharpened to a point at one end. The men laughed as they worked, as though they crafted a chair or a table and not horrific stakes, which they would impale through Hundr and Einar's bodies. Two of the terrifyingly sharpened stakes rested against the walls of a wattle outbuilding, golden and fresh wood honed to a long, sharp point. "No place in Valhalla for a warrior who has died with a piece of wood up his arse."

"I can't die in this place. Not here." Hundr had fled Novgorod searching for his fortune and to make for himself a reputation with which he could return dripping in glory to show his brothers what he was truly made of. To die in that place, impaled and naked, was beyond horror. All he had done in his life, all the battles he had fought, the men he had killed, was to prove that he wasn't a useless bastard. To prove that he was something better than a beggar forced to sleep with dogs and cattle. He pulled and yanked at his shackles, but the chains were fixed to an iron ring fastened into the very mortar of the building itself. All his straining managed was to rip open his skin around the manacles, and blood flowed down his arms in slow, thick trickles. *This cannot be my fate. Please, Odin, hear me.*

The sun flickered between rolling charcoal clouds, brooding and folding into lighter, white clouds like a dark dough kneaded by the gods. Although it was summer in Novgorod, a biting wind blew over the high walls of the Citadel and chilled the bare skin of Hundr's chest and stomach. He opened his mouth wide like a yawn to stretch the bruising and swelling of his face, which screamed in pain but loosened with the movement. His dead eye socket pulsed, and the wind blew into the empty cavity. Smells of the city wafted into the fortress, damp wood burning on morning cookfires and the dank stench of urine and waste. To his right were the stables and animal pens inside the fortress, which also held the Prince's palace. Those enclosures were much the same as Hundr remembered them, built of silver birch planking and topped with decaying thatch. Horses brayed, and dogs barked. He had spent much of his life living and sleeping in those pens when he was a boy, hoping and waiting for the ever-too-brief visits when he could see his mother in the palace once a day. The training square lay within the inner building, where he would train daily with swords, axes, spears and shields. But he would rise early to train before his brothers, his father granting him the mercy of permitting his instruction in weapon craft but wanting him to learn separately from his true-born brothers once he learned of his bastard's prowess.

"You remember the place?" asked Einar, flickering a leather-dry tongue across parched lips.

"I remember all of it," Hundr replied. "It was never a happy place for me. Do you remember your own childhood?"

"I do. Mine was the same as most Norse upbringings. I was often cold, and there was never enough to eat for a growing boy. But I was loved and taught to fight. My father was a fighter and raider who served the mighty Ragnar Lothbrok. As did I, eventually. I was raised to love Odin and the axe." Einar tried to shrug but groaned at the pain in his injured shoulder, held painfully upright by his shackles. "I have no complaints."

"There is comfort in knowing your destiny, your place in the world. I often think I would have been happier to have been born a thrall, with no expectations of destiny." The pain in his head sent a scream of agony across the back of his skull, and Hundr closed his eye against the day's brightness.

"But you were a bastard son of the Prince, so you resented your brothers. That is a cruel trick of the Norns, I think. To have what could have been dangled in front of you but out of your reach forever. Yet it strengthened you. The gods work in strange ways."

Hundr laughed mirthlessly, and the shudder of it jabbed at his injured ribs and back, adding to the pain of his memories. "The gods have no plan for me, old friend. My mother was a whore thrall to my father, Prince Rurik. The only kindness my father gave to me was the gift of steel. He allowed me to train with the weapons master and the loremaster who tutored his true-born sons and the sons of other nobles."

"Why would your father let you learn weapons if he had no plan for you?"

"He told me I would serve in the druzhina when I became a man, that I would be a warrior. That was my dream, to use my skill at arms and live the life of a soldier."

"So why did you run away, then?"

"Because my mother died, and my father forgot about me. I never set foot in the palace again after that. I lived out here with the animals; my only joy was my daily practice. My brothers took that away from me in the end, so I left. I went to find a man like you, Einar, to join a Viking crew and make my name." Hundr chuckled again at his dreams, the ambitions of a child. "I vowed to return here as a famous Jarl, with ships and warriors at my back, dripping in silver and reputation. My mother told me stories of the great drengr and of drengskapr, the way of the warrior. And I wanted that life more than anything."

"And the Norns saw you where they huddle beneath the great tree Yggdrasil, and they wove your dreams into your fate. You have become what you set out to be. You are a Jarl whose name they know wherever men of the blade sail the Whale Road. Many would kill for your reputation."

"And what is it worth, all the battles we have fought, the men we have killed? Here I am, returned to my home as a prisoner. No wealth on my person but my breeks. I return as I left, a worthless bastard."

"That's enough of that talk. I won't hear it. We are Jarls, you and I. Men know and fear our names. Even if we die here today with these Thor-forsaken stakes up our arses, we have lived as men. We have lived the lives others only dream of. I do not think Odin will forsake us. We have earned our places in Valhalla."

Hundr shook his head. It had all been for nothing, his life of war. The gods had forsaken him, just as his father had many years earlier. He had failed to return as he had dreamed, to show his brothers his mettle and what he was worth. He had failed to retrieve Gungnir and deliver Ragnhild back into the fold of her Valkyrie sisterhood, and he had failed his greatest friend, Einar, who hung next to him, bloodied and beaten. The most incredible man Hundr had ever known, the fiercest fighter, the most cunning leader, and one of the few people who had ever shown Hundr any kindness in his blood-soaked life. Hundr was sure he would die here, impaled at the pleasure of his hated brother, and that he would be forgotten. Who would mourn or remember him? His greatest enemy has been Ivar the Boneless, a man he had killed but whose name lived on like a legend. Would that be the same for the Man with the Dog's Name?

"Ah, dear brother. Here you are as you were meant to be," came a familiar voice, sneering and dripping with venom. Yaroslav. "Trussed up like a disobedient slave."

The Prince wore his lamellar fish scale armour. The back and sides of his head were so freshly shaved that they gleamed in the morning light. He smiled at Hundr, a smile of victory, triumphant and sickening. In the distance, a horn brayed, dancing on the wind.

"Do you hear that? That is the sound of Prince Oleg, who marches now with our armies to bring more glory to the Rus people," said Yaroslav.

"You do not march with him?" asked Hundr, his voice croaking with thirst.

"I do not. In his wisdom, our father left the throne to Prince Oleg, his brother-in-law. Oleg will march on Kiev and that great city and its peoples to our empire."

"You are the eldest. Our father didn't trust you to rule. He saw you for what you are," Hundr laughed, ignoring the pain it sent pulsing through his head and across his ribs because he knew the barbs would cut his half-brother deeply. "He put his brother-in-law on the throne rather than you because you are a nithing turd. I wouldn't put you in charge of shovelling shit."

"I am the Prince of Novgorod!" Yaroslav shouted, raising a clenched fist, his mouth twisting with anger. The people in the square stopped to stare at his outburst. "I rule the city, and Oleg leads the army. Who are you to judge me? You are and have always been a useless bastard. And now you are mine."

"You don't march with the army because you are a coward. Where are our other brothers? With Oleg no doubt riding to glory?"

Yaroslav's face turned red, and his head twitched to one side. He turned to glare at the staring thralls, who hurried back to their duties. Hundr laughed again. *He knows I am right; they leave him here because he is a useless turd.*

"You are full of mirth this morning, bastard. Let's see how amusing you find the surprise I have for you. Is the prisoner ready?" Yaroslav spoke over his shoulder to a hooded figure who nodded and waved a hand towards the shadows cast by the high palace's inner walls. It was Kvasir, the burned man hiding the ravages of his disfigured face. His injured shoulder slumped slightly. Two Norsemen came from the darkness, dragging a third between them. The third man hung limp, and his bare feet trailed in the dust of the hard-packed ground. As they reached Kvasir and dropped the man to earth, he crumpled. Dried blood matted his hair, and his naked body was a pattern of blue and purple bruising.

"No," hissed Einar.

Hundr squinted to focus his good eye, and when he recognised the prisoner, who had curled himself into a ball, Hundr's breath caught in his throat. *Hekkr.*

"Not laughing now, are we?" Yaroslav sneered and tucked his hands into his belt, which was wide and studded with silver. "I sent Kvasir out into the city last night to search for your crew because you and the grandfather here would hardly have come to my city alone."

"We went back to the tavern where you fought yesterday," said Kvasir, lowering his hood to reveal glinting, malevolent eyes. "But your crew had gone. Shame, I hear one of them is pretty." He stared at Einar and then at Hundr, searching for a reaction. Hundr knew he referred to Sigrid but would not give him the power of that knowledge. "But we found this one lurking outside the gate, looking for his shipmates." Kvasir kicked Hekkr in the head – hard. Hekkr grunted and flopped over onto his back. Einar surged forward, snarling like a chained bear. He bucked and hauled on his iron shackles, kicking and spitting at Kvasir. "This one is your friend, then? Good."

"Sigdriffa," Yaroslav called, and the Valkyrie marched across the square flanked by her sisters. "Clear the square. We shall impale this cretin."

The Valkyrie ushered the thralls out of the square and formed a ring of warriors, spears resting on the ground and eyes in front, all in perfect order.

"Do you like my new household guard?" said Yaroslav. "They have brought me Odin's very own spear, if you can believe it. They will serve me for one year, and then I will grant them land by the river where they will found a new temple to Odin in my name. The Aesir will know *my name*, Velmud. What do you say about that? Twirling your swords and axes like a child. My name will ring across Asgard whilst yours will die with you." He leant forward and smiled as he locked his eyes on Hundr's one, searching for the pain there and relishing his victory. Once he was satisfied that he had enjoyed enough of Hundr's suffering, he beckoned to the two leather-aproned men. They downed their tools, hefted one of the prepared stakes, and came for Hekkr.

Einar twisted and bucked against his bonds once more, kicking and raging at Yaroslav, but the Prince only smiled. Kvasir stepped forward so that he was but a pace away from Einar's reach and bent to stare at the Jarl. Kvasir pushed his burnt head forward to stare at Einar, allowing his enemy to gaze upon the stretched and taut scarring of his hairless face.

"This is just the beginning of your suffering," Kvasir hissed. "The gods have cursed you, Einar Rosti, for what you did to Agder and to my people. I have sought powerful Volva in the depths of Svearland and Sami lands, where seiðr still flows across forests and lakes just as it did in the old times. I have had those witches curse you, Einar, and you, Dog's Name. There is evil seiðr upon you and your crews, and you will suffer for what you did to my Lord Kjotve, for your service to Harald, the slaughterer and usurper. I will impale your friend here so you can watch him die, and then I will come for you. Your pain will be like that of Loki, chained by the Aesir in a mighty cave, fettered with the entrails of his own son whilst a great serpent drips poison from its fangs to burn his face. But for you, there will be no Sigyn, no wife to catch the burning poison in a bowl. Instead, you will suffer and writhe in agony, and I will rejoice in your suffering as payment for the pain you have wrought upon me. Feel the seiðr, Einar." Kvasir shook with fury, his teeth bared and grinding around his words. "The gods brought us here, to this place, with the Valkyrie and this prince, where a new temple to Odin will be founded. This will be your ruin, Einar, and I will find the rest of your crew, and they shall all suffer the same fate."

Hundr sat back, resting against the cool wall to which he was chained. Einar continued to rage. The iron chains holding them were too strong, even for him. There was no use fighting, so Hundr just slumped, hanging from his manacled hands. His dead eye pulsed beneath his swollen face. Kvasir viciously spat on Einar and turned to Hekkr. He lifted the wrestler by the hair and punched him twice in his already mangled face. Hekkr's blue eyes flickered under the blows, and his gaze rested upon Hundr and Einar. A smile split the ruin of his face, showing smashed teeth laced with blood. Hundr's stomach turned to see that smile. Hekkr was a good man and a fine warrior, a trusted fighter of Einar's household troops and, above all, Einar's friend. Kvasir dragged Hekkr by his hair, and the big man stumbled and followed, his bare feet dragging and catching on the earth. They had beaten his great strength out of him, and Kvasir kicked him to the ground, where his men tied Hekkr's hands and feet with braided rope to splay his limbs wide. Kvasir winced and put a hand on his own wounded shoulder. The leather-aproned men approached with their viciously sharp stake, sharpened like the deadly point of a seax, and they knelt between Hekkr's legs, scratching their chins and conversing quietly, like shipwrights poring over a troublesome strake joint.

The two craftsmen cut away Hekkr's clothes so that he lay fully naked, and they positioned their stake to begin their deadly work. One braced the timber, and the other drew back a hammer and struck the flat end of the stake to drive into Hekkr's arse with the force a man would use to hammer a nail. Hekkr screamed, and the terrifying pitch of it made Hundr shudder. Einar gave up his raging protests and slumped to hang like Hundr, rocking against the wall, dangling like curing meat. The impalers drove the stake with care, the one holding the timber guiding it and the man with the hammer driving it. Sigdriffa looked away, and Yaroslav stared slack-jawed at Hekkr's suffering. The wrestler cried out, begging his torturers for mercy and, most heartbreaking of all, calling out for his long-dead mother in the throes of his unimaginable pain. A warrior of the shield wall, lain low by Kvasir and the Prince of Novgorod.

Hekkr fell silent as the stake burst through the flesh between his shoulder and neck. The impalers beckoned to Kvasir's Norsemen, who helped them to pull the stake upright with Hekkr now fully impaled upon it. The timber slid into a prepared hole in the ground, and the leather-aproned men secured it so that Hekkr hung upright, the pole driven expertly through his torso, and his lifeblood dripped down its length to pool on the earth.

Hundr was beyond despair. All he had sought was lost, his life destroyed, and his friend tortured beyond what Hundr thought possible. Beside him, Einar sobbed for Hekkr, and the sound of that from such a man as Einar almost drove Hundr himself to tears.

"He will live for a day or more like that," said Yaroslav in an even tone, like a man explaining how the eaves of his hall roof had been constructed. "You can watch him suffer for the rest of the day, and then we shall impale you both next to him."

TWENTY-FIVE

Hundr watched Hekkr bleed and twitch as the day waned to darkness. A drizzling rain spat across the square as the sky turned to shadow, washing the blood from Hundr's wounds in pale red rivulets down the skin of his arms and across his chest. The fine rain rinsed Hekkr's pale body white and free from blood so that he hung like a fetch of his former self, flitting between Midgard and the afterlife, tethered to this world by his pain. Einar spoke no words that day but hung from his bonds in despair, watching his friend die slowly. A renowned fighter and a good friend, Hekkr was a man to raise a laugh in the mead hall or to lead the line in battle. Hundr spoke within his own head and only to the gods. He called to Odin and Thor, begging them for a chance at vengeance, imploring them to use their power to grant him the chance to kill his enemies. He promised Odin a blót, a sacrifice, in his honour if the All-Father would grant him revenge. Hundr swore to Odin to return his spear to the temple at Upsala and waited. Hundr waited for a sign, a raven or some signal from the All-Father, or Thor to show him he heard his prayers. But nothing came, just the whimpering horror of Hekkr's tortured death and the hopeless cruelty of Hundr's brother.

Rain soaked through Hundr's hair and dripped into his empty eye socket, stinging its bruised, puckered skin. The pain of his wounds burned and ached. The sun had disappeared behind the Citadel's high walls, and in the twilight, a red hue splashed the sky, ferrous and dark. Clouds moved, darkened and formed familiar shapes, forms of faces from the past. He saw men he had killed, Ivar and his son Hakon, the man who had taken his eye with a fire-hot knife. He saw Eystein Longaxe, a monstrous fighter he had killed in a vicious fight for Dublin city. Other faces came, friendly faces. Hrist, a fallen Valkyrie, and Blink, a Seaworm man killed long ago. Sten came to Hundr, his broad face smiling in the shifting cloud, so skilled in war and yet so gentle. Sten had been like a father to Hundr. Seeing Sten's face in the sky brought Hundr closer to death, brushing against the afterlife, Hekkr's suffering making death a welcome escape from the horrors of Midgard. He wondered if the god Heimdall had opened the

Bifrost bridge for Hekkr, the rainbow bridge to the heavens. Perhaps those old faces had sneaked across that bridge, taking their chance to visit Hundr from the sky before the gates closed, and they returned to the worlds of the afterlife held upright by the great tree, Yggdrasil. Hundr laughed at himself, hanging, waiting to be impaled by his enemies. A failure. Lips cracked, body scarred, ripped, and torn by blades. Fresh wounds marked his face and body. He was tired and weary of his life. A hard life. *I am ready to go, Sten. Take me with you to Valhalla.*

"I can't take you to Valhalla, but I won't leave you here to die like this," said a voice. It was familiar, another ghost from his past. Hundr kept his eye closed, trying to place it, wondering if it was an old crewmate or perhaps another man he had killed in some distant battle. "But we must be quick. Your guards will return soon. I have brought weapons, just in case."

Hundr frowned. The familiar voice wasn't in his dreams; it was there, before him. He opened his eye, the dried blood washed away by the rain. Hundr saw an old man before him, grey-bearded and balding. Tall and lean but hunched over with thin fingers bulging at the joints. The old man set down a long bundle wrapped in a jaundiced cloth. He looked up from his bundle at Hundr and shook his head. "What has become of you, Velmud?" he said. "You don't remember me?

All those days we spent together in the practice square?"

Hundr's jaw dropped. "Weapons Master Sveneld?" he whispered.

"Aye, it's me, alright. It never sat right with me, the way they treated you. You were a good lad, Velmud. One of the best I have ever taught, such speed. I should have spoken up for you to Prince Rurik. He and I were brothers in the shield wall long ago. Maybe my words could have helped you with your brothers. But I said nothing. Now I have a chance to right some of those old wrongs." He pulled a smith's iron hammer from the waist of his trews and hammered at the pins which clasped the manacles around Hundr's wrists.

"Is this a cruel dream, or is it really you come to help me?" asked Hundr.

"It's no dream, lad. But we must hurry. If they catch us, your brother will impale me right next to you. And I don't fancy one of those cursed stakes up my arse."

He hammered again, and the pin sprang away, leaving Hundr's right hand to fall free. The blood rushed back into the limp joint, replacing the numb tingling with strength and feeling.

"What are you doing there, old one?" a shout came from the darkness. Sveneld gasped as two druzhina guards approached from the gate side of the wall.

"Time for one more fight," Sveneld said and winked at Hundr. He turned with his old, thin arms stretched wide and grinned at the guards. "I was just bringing water for the prisoners. I have ale in my sack there; let me get you some." Sveneld shuffled towards his bundle and knelt with a groan.

"Leave the ale and piss off. They are prisoners of the Prince, away with you," growled a burly guard with bandy legs.

Sveneld held up a hand in acknowledgement of the order but went back to delve into his bundle. The druzhina guard sighed and shook his head, taking a step towards the old man, but he stopped dead in his tracks because Sveneld came up slowly into a crouch, with a shining sword in each hand, moonlight playing on the blades as Sveneld twirled them expertly. The guard held up a hand and was about to speak when Sveneld lunged forward with the speed of a man half his age. He spun on his heel and brought the sword in his right hand around his body to slice open the bandy-legged warrior's throat in a movement so lithe and swift that the second guard could only stare on in amazement. Bandy-legs clutched at the gash in his neck, which now pulsed thick, black blood across his hands and down his breastplate. He fell to his knees, coughing, wide-eyed and dying. Sveneld returned to a crouch, one sword held above his head, pointing at the second guard, and the other blade held low and ready. The second man licked his lips nervously. He glanced at a long building away to his right, likely a barracks building containing more of Yaroslav's warriors, and then back to Sveneld. He lowered his spear and shuffled to his right, trying to turn the old swordsman. Sveneld moved like an animal, feline and threatening. The guard brought his spear up to parry a strike, but Sveneld went left. He darted around the guard, bringing his high sword down in a flashing arc to cut through the guard's leg at the knee with a wet chop whilst stabbing his second blade into the druzhina's armpit, finding the gap in his armour, and twisting the blade, rending flesh and tearing into the man's chest. He toppled silently to the ground, twitching and dying.

"That's done it," said Sveneld, sucking in huge mouthfuls of air and wincing as he lay down his swords to rub the small of his back. "They will be out here like flies on shit soon." He grabbed up his hammer and knocked the other pin from Hundr's left hand manacles and caught him as he fell.

"Thank you, weapons master," Hundr whispered, staring into those pale blue rheumy eyes.

"I'll get you out, then I can die in peace. No

regrets."

Sveneld shuffled to his bundle, and Hundr took up the hammer, fighting against the screaming pain of his wounds to strike the pins free of Einar's shackles. Einar hugged him, his bright eyes staring from the crag of his face.

"I thought I was dreaming. That old bastard fights like a demon," Einar murmured.

"He was my old weapons master. Sveneld taught me to fight. He was not a kind man then, but he comes now for his redemption and gives us a chance to be free." Hundr did not mention his prayers to the gods and his promise of the blót, but Hundr was in no doubt that it had been the Aesir who had sent Sveneld to set him free. And any gift from Odin, or any of the gods, came at a price. "Can you walk?"

"I'll bloody walk out of here, no matter how hurt I am," Einar said, pushing himself to his feet. "Thank you, old one."

"I am not so much older than you," Sveneld said, his face creasing into a frown. "Axe or sword?" he held another sword and an axe in the crook of his arm.

"Axe," Einar grinned, then winced at the pain in his bruised face.

"You take the two swords, Velmud," Sveneld nodded. "You were good with twin blades, if I remember rightly." Sveneld kept one for himself and shuffled towards the shadows of the walls.

"Wait," said Einar, looking up at the terrible, tortured figure of Hekkr. "I can't leave him like that. He was my friend."

Hundr nodded and handed Einar a sword.

"Hekkr, if you can hear me, the gods have seen your bravery. We will not remember you like this. We will honour your memory, and I swear I will avenge you. I swear on my place in the Einherjar that Kvasir will die at my hand." He gently touched Hekkr's foot and bowed his head. Hekkr's eyes flickered open, and his body twitched. He glanced at Einar and Hundr, and then his eyes closed. Einar reached up with the sword and stabbed it into Hekkr's throat. He placed a hand under the pommel and drove the blade home, ending Hekkr's suffering and placing his soul in the hands of the gods.

"Come on, we must go now!" Sveneld hissed, beckoning them on.

Hundr ran, taking the second sword back from Einar, and followed Sveneld into the shadows. They skirted the timber wall and ran past the gate alongside the dark shapes of the palace buildings. A dog barked in the darkness, and someone coughed, the sound of it escaping from an open window shutter.

"How will we get out if not by the gate?" asked

Hundr.

"You don't live in a place as long as I have without knowing a few secrets," Sveneld replied, showing his gums in a gap-toothed smile. Hundr and Einar followed him, keeping close to the wall, first running and then slowing to a brisk walk. Sveneld led them through an arch in the inner palace structure and then through a lane between buildings. They wove between a snarl of thin alleys, avoiding torchlight and sticking to the shadows.

"The place is empty," said Hundr, surprised that he had not heard a voice or seen any palace warriors during their escape.

"Oleg has marched with the army. He has taken all the druzhina with him, save one company left to patrol the city. Yaroslav prefers his guard of Norsemen and those arrogant women warriors with him in the Citadel. The city was full of soldiers, but all have now marched with Oleg's host for Kiev." Shouting erupted in the distance, quickly increasing into barking orders as the guards discovered the corpses. "We must be quick. It's not far now."

Sveneld led them on until they emerged into the south-facing wall, and he grinned as he pointed to a gate as high as a man and as broad as two. "The shit gate," he said. "Known only to the palace slaves. Can't have royal shit carted out the front gate now, can you?" He stepped forward towards the wall and then stopped, turning to stare at Hundr with wide eyes. Boots stamped on the earth behind them, warriors' boots accompanied by the creak of leather and clank of iron. "They've found us."

Five Norsemen stood opposite them, armed with axes and knives. Hundr recognised them as men of Kvasir's crew, those he had fought outside the walls. He swallowed and turned to face them, with no shield or brynjar, and weakened from his beating and imprisonment.

"You two go; I'll hold them here," Sveneld commanded in a low flat voice.

"Put the blades down. If you give up easy, we'll give you a quick death. No stakes up the arse," said the central warrior, a broad man with a long beard.

"We won't leave you," Einar shook his head. "We've a score to settle with these bastards."

"Get out before more of them arrive," hissed Sveneld.

Hundr's heart sank because the old weapons master was right. Only four Norsemen faced them, but he and Einar were injured and weakened from their beating and hanging in chains. More of Yaroslav's men would arrive as soon as the sounds of a fight broke out, and then there could be no escape.

"If we want to avenge Hekkr, and do what we came here for, then we must go," said Hundr. "Master, you were always good to me. Come with us."

"My time is over, and my soul is at peace." Sveneld smiled at Hundr, whose heart leapt, for that was something he would have killed to see back when he was Velmud. The weapons master had been a hard man but a wonderful teacher. The skills that Sveneld had taught him in those early mornings when most of the palace still slept and before his brothers arrived at the training ground had given Hundr the chance to become the man he now was.

"Take them," said the long-bearded foe. He hefted his axe in his right hand, and a knife flashed in his left. The other four Vikings spread out to come on in a line, fierce and armoured in iron and leather. Kvasir's killers. Longbeard opened his mouth to speak again, to threaten or warn the escaping prisoners, but the words died in his throat as Sveneld darted forward without warning or signal. He skipped and lunged with his sword, the lines of his outstretched legs and the stab of his arm perfect, like the lines of a finely built drakkar. The blade tip punched through the Norseman's gullet before he could bring his axe or knife to parry. His eyes went wide with surprise, and as Sveneld whipped his sword free to spray the three remaining men with their shipmate's blood, they stared open-mouthed, astonished at the speed and skill in the old man.

"Go!" shouted Sveneld. Hundr tore himself away, dashing for the low gate and tearing at the spar which locked it from the inside. Einar was next to him, and they dragged open the creaking timbers of the shit gate, its bottom scraping against the sodden ground of the Citadel. Einar fled into the darkness beyond the gate, and Hundr ducked under its lintel. He turned in the opening and wiped the rainwater from his brow and his good eye to catch a last glance at brave Sveneld. Two of the Norsemen ran towards the gate, but Sveneld shuffled backwards. He flicked the tip of his sword at the face of one man and then spun on his heel to slice the blade across the shins of the second. That man toppled to the ground, howling, clutching at his injured leg. The two remaining warriors charged at Sveneld, and though unarmoured, he met them in a flurry of parries and strikes, the clash of iron ringing out across the city and piercing the shadows to send the message of his glorious death to the heavens. That sound would bring more warriors, and Hundr ran. The sounds of the weapons master's last stand echoed behind them as they disappeared into the snarling tangle of Novgorod's streets and lanes. Vengeance burned in Hundr's heart like a fire, stoked by the hate and the deaths of Hekkr and Sveneld. As the pain of his wounds pulsed and stabbed at him, Hundr wondered how many of Kvasir's Norsemen had been killed by Sveneld before he died, how many of Kvasir's growlers had fallen to the skill of the old soldier and teacher. Hundr hoped that although he had not seen Sveneld fall, he would fight on forever in the front line of the Einherjar with the greatest of heroes.

TWENTY-SIX

Einar grimaced as he raised his arms whilst Skögul bound his ribs with a length of cloth. He grunted as she jerked the wrapping tight, clenching his teeth at the pain. Skögul nodded with a downward smile, appraising her treatment of his injuries. She had stitched and bound him back together with care and skill. The tattoos on her face writhed as she moved, and she itched at the stubble of her shaved head.

The image of brave Hekkr impaled, hanging there with the wooden stake through his body, would not leave Einar's thought cage. It sat behind his eyes, burned there, like a cow brand. The horror of Hekkr's cruel death made Einar's own pain fade away. The cuts on his face, arms, and body burned, but he blocked it out because it was nothing compared to his friend Hekkr's suffering.

"It has to be tight," Skögul said as she pulled

the wrappings and tested the knot. "I don't think your ribs are broken, but they are heavily bruised. That druzhina armour did its job."

Candles flickered on a stained tabletop, and gusts of wind rattled the window shutters. Ragnhild had found the crew lodgings by the river in a room above a merchant's warehouse. The owner was from Skåne and a good Norseman, and he also provided them with food and ale.

"Thank you," Einar nodded, twisting his torso and testing the wrappings. He pulled on an old spare jerkin that Amundr had brought on the journey and glanced across the faces of the warriors in the room. He and Hundr had run and stumbled through the city until they had collapsed from exhaustion. Freezing from the rain and the chill of the night, they had huddled together in a shadowed alley, waiting for the burned man and his warriors or Sigdriffa and her Valkyrie to find them, fearing their rough hands would come to drag them back to the Citadel and the impaling that awaited there. But their enemies had not come. The city streets were thankfully quiet now that the army had marched out on Rurik's war of conquest. Einar had waited a whole day, hiding like a nithing. Hekkr's death had shocked both Einar and Hundr, so they had to be sure that they would not blunder straight into their enemies as they moved through the unfamiliar city streets. Eventually, as darkness had fallen on the second night, they left their hiding place. Hundr had a vague recollection of the streets from his time growing up in the palace, and so they had started at the tavern where they had left Ragnhild and the others before their capture and travelled back towards the river in search of the crew. Reduced to skulking, injured and bedraggled, stumbling through the streets of Novgorod like beggars.

"Lucky we found you," said Gunnr, the leader of the Valkyrie group, as she passed Einar a chunk of hard bread across the table. He bit into it, and teeth at the back of his mouth that had become loosened during his ordeal stabbed pain along his jaw. "Two urchins at the quayside."

"Lucky, aye," said Einar. He had spotted Gunnr and Skögul buying food from a cart pushed by a crone along Novgorod's riverside quays. A collection of warehouses and taverns faced onto the great river road, which meandered from Aldeigjuborg to the north, through Novgorod, south down to Kiev and on to the great city of Miklagard and all the wealth of the Musselmen. Hundr had called to the Valkyrie, who had helped them stumble up to the room above the warehouse. Einar found it hard to meet Gunnr's eye. He had been in a shivering mess when the Valkyrie had found them. Such weakness and suffering was beneath a drengr. Now that he had the warmth of a fire, food and drink, that shame had passed, but Gunnr had seen Einar at his lowest ebb. All that remained now was only anger and the burning desire for vengeance against Yaroslav and Kvasir.

"They should be back soon. Do we go tonight?" asked Gunnr.

"We go tonight. They must pay the blood price. There can be no rest."

"Hekkr wanted to look for you. He insisted on it," murmured Amundr, talking to the floor and wringing his hands. "I should not have let him go alone."

"Had you gone, you would now hang dead on a spike alongside him."

"Bastards," Amundr seethed. He clenched his fists, which were like shovels, the muscles in his forearms trembling.

"How are we going to get in if the gate is the only way?" said Gunnr. Yet there was no time to answer because Hundr came through the door, grim-faced but clad in his brynjar with his two swords strapped to his belt and back. He slammed Einar's gear onto the tabletop, and the candlelight flickered at the jolt of it. Einar's axe and seax were wrapped in his brynjar, and there were strands of hay in the armour and weapons from where they had lain hidden in the building's thatch opposite the gate. Valbrandr followed Hundr, having to turn to get his hugely broad shoulders through the doorway.

"No trouble?" asked Einar.

Hundr shook his head, his face still swollen purple and blue. Sigrid came to him with food and ale, and Hundr took a drink. "No sign of Kvasir's men either. Only a small force of druzhina patrol the city."

"So how are we going to get inside, then?" repeated Gunnr. "Can we even get in?"

"We can, and we will," said Hundr. "We'll force our way in. The walls aren't properly guarded, given that most of the druzhina are marching with Oleg. Yaroslav cannot guard the entire length of the Citadel's wall."

"Do we go in the gate you escaped from?" asked Bush. "The shit gate?"

"They will expect that and will have men there."

"Shame," Bush quipped, "sounds like such a pleasant part of the city."

Finn sniggered, but otherwise, the jest fell on ears too serious for mirth.

"We go in on the east side, along the river," said Hundr.

"Doesn't the Citadel wall butt right onto the water?" asked Ragnhild.

"It does. But we can scale it from a boat."

"Climb it?" asked Gunnr, shaking her head. It was a reasonable challenge. The Citadel walls were high, fashioned from well-kept timbers, and there would be little or no hand or footholds for the climb. Einar had seen the walls close up, and builders had filled any gaps between the vast trunks with tar and hair caulking, just like the planks of a drakkar.

"We won't be able to get ropes up there," Ragnhild spoke, stroking her scarred face, her eye distant as though she imagined attempting the climb. "Too high to throw a long rope over the top with a hook or a blade to catch over the rampart."

"We'll use axes," said Einar, catching Hundr's eye, and Hundr nodded. "We'll use our axes to hack into the timber and claw our way up."

"Axes? Did your thought cage become addled inside those gates...." crowed Gunnr, but her words died in her throat once she saw the look on Einar's face.

"We claw and rend our way up those walls," Einar uttered, trying not to shout, wrestling with his fury to stop it from overcoming him and tipping him into violence. "Only a few of us need to make it to the top, then we can lower a rope for the rest. I will make the climb... for Hekkr and for Ragnhild."

"For me?" said Ragnhild.

"For Gungnir, which you must recover to find peace and return to your order. That is why we are in this cursed city. Sigdriffa is in there with Kvasir, all the rats in one nest. We kill Kvasir and get the spear." Einar turned to face Gunnr, his eyes steely, brimming with contempt. "We would not be here if you had not forced this quest upon Ragnhild. She who is the bravest of all of you," he growled, pointing at the Valkyrie leader as he spoke the last words, his teeth gritted and his finger shuddering. "You and your High Priestess could have allowed her to rejoin the Valkyrie in honour, even forged the spear anew, but you forced her here, and here we are."

"Forge a spear crafted by dwarves back in the darkness of time?" spat Gunnr.

"If you believe that, you are more of a fool than you look."

She reared up but thought better of it. Hands fell to hilts, and the air in the room was thick with the tension of it all, like rigging pulled to breaking point by a north sea wind.

"There has been enough of your complaining on this voyage," said Hundr. "We will go into the city and do it as Einar says. Kvasir will die, as will my brother, the Prince. We will recover your spear and be done with this wyrded quest. Einar, Ragnhild, and I will climb the walls. You and your Valkyrie will go now and find a rope long enough for us to drop for you. Are you with us or not?"

Gunnr glanced at Skögul, who nodded. "We are with you," she answered. Gunnr stood and met Ragnhild's stare. "We will recover the spear together, sister." Then she turned to Einar. "You should not doubt the reality of Ragnarök, Jarl Einar. Or the truth of the spear."

Einar shook his head. He was tired, wounded, and had eyes only for vengeance. He believed in the gods as much as the next man, and he prayed to the Aesir. But, like most Northmen, he was not a slave to the gods. If the spear was indeed Odin's, then why didn't the god take it back for himself? Why did he not visit Midgard in one of his many forms, as he did in the legends, and take back his spear from Sigdriffa? Or, what if it was indeed Odin's spear, but he wanted Sigdriffa to have it for her to build a newer, more warlike Upsala? Einar didn't have the strength to argue with Gunnr about it. It didn't matter. What mattered was Kvasir's death and Ragnhild's soul. She had earned peace, and if that could only be achieved by retrieving the spear, then so be it.

"We go at first light. Make ready. Get that rope and prepare yourselves, for we scale the walls of Novgorod's Citadel," said Hundr, and he fixed each one of them with his one eye, burning and fierce.

"Would it not be better to attack in darkness?" asked Gunnr.

"Enough!" Hundr roared, shaking the very room itself. "We do it this way. No more questions or challenges." He stormed through the doorway, followed by Sigrid.

Gunnr's mouth hung open, and she looked to Skögul for support, but the Valkyrie looked away.

"We must be as one. If we are going to succeed and get out of this alive, we must be as one crew. Fighting for one another, ready to die for one another. Can you do that?" Einar said, holding his arm out to Gunnr.

She clenched her teeth, swallowed her pride and took his wrist in the warrior's grip.

"As one," she agreed.

Ragnhild, Gunnr and Skögul left to source the rope they would need for the climb, and Einar remained with Amundr, Finn, Bush, Sigvarth, Torsten, Thorgrim and Valbrandr. Einar took his weapons from the table and checked the edges, noting some notches he would need to ease out with a whetstone.

"I am sorry, Einar," said Finn at Einar's elbow. "For Hekkr. He did not deserve to die like that."

Einar put his hand on Finn's shoulder. Hekkr had spent time with Finn, teaching him to wrestle and the finer points of fighting without weapons. "Nobody deserves to die like that. Sometimes in life, things happen which require a response from us as drengr. What Kvasir and Yaroslav did to Hekkr, and indeed would have done to Hundr and me, must be repaid. This is the blood feud. We swear vengeance, and we cannot rest until vengeance is ours. This is the way of the drengr."

"I want to go with you. I want to fight."

Einar frowned. Finn was young, and Einar could not bear to see the lad hurt. Still, Finn was older now than Einar had been when he first took to the Whale Road, and he'd already proved his mettle in a fight. "You can come with us," Einar nodded.

"Then we will fight together, as drengr," said Finn, standing with his shoulders back and chest high.

"Some of us will die inside that fortress, lad. There might only be a handful of druzhina, but Kvasir's crew is in there, as are Sigdriffa's Valkyrie. Those Norsemen will protect their Lord, and Kvasir will not die easily. Nor will Sigdriffa give up the spear without a fight."

"I will remember all you have taught me and all that Hekkr taught me too."

Einar placed a heavy hand on Finn's shoulder and looked him in the eye. He was a head shorter than Einar, but so were most men. He had the confident look of his father, Ivar, and a season at an oar on the Whale Road had filled him out. Einar was proud of Finn and thought of the lad like a son. He wanted to tell him that, to bring him close and hold him tight, just as he used to when Finn was small when he would cry for his lost mother and father. Finn was now a young man, however, and almost a drengr. So, Einar clapped him on the shoulder instead and offered him a curt nod to show he thought Finn was ready. It was enough, and Finn beamed.

Einar moved to the table and unrolled his brynjar. He unfurled the heavy armour shirt out flat over the whorls and knots of the wooden tabletop and ran his calloused hands over the iron links. Hundred of small, circular rings interlinked to form a hardened mail coat. That mail had saved Einar's life more than once. The iron was cool under his touch, and the links moved and slithered like the skin of a Loki monster. He sighed. The brynjar, above all else, was the sign of a drengr. Only the most successful and wealthy of warriors could afford such an expensive piece of war gear. When a warrior faced a man in a brynjar, he knew he came face to face with an opportunity to make himself rich. If he could kill that man and strip the brynjar from his corpse, he would instantly become wealthy and respected. Until his next fight, where the enemy would target him, would try to thrust sharp blades into his flesh and snatch his life away to take the mail coat from him. Such was the life of a Viking.

"You will need that," remarked Bush, sagging onto a stool on the opposite side of the table and taking a long drink of ale from a hard-worn tankard.

"Seems like I will always need it," Einar said, thumbing at a torn link on the short sleeve.

"You miss Vanylven, my lord?"

Einar looked up at Bush and raised an eyebrow at the use of his title. They had sailed together since they were young men in the service of Ragnar Lothbrok and then Ivar, and they knew one another like brothers. "I miss Hildr, and I miss my hall."

"And you miss battle."

"That too," Einar allowed, admitting that he had felt like a younger man on this voyage, the clash of arms, testing himself against other men in the fight for his life, in mortal combat.

"We are getting too old to be climbing fortress walls and searching for dwarven forged weapons."

"When have you sought a dwarven forged weapon before?"

Bush laughed, and Einar grinned at him. Bush slid the stained leather helmet liner from his head to run a hand over his egg-white bald pate. He was old, Einar thought. Older than Einar by a few years, as far as he could remember. Light brown spots dotted Bush's scalp, and the hair around the base of his skull was thin and wispy. The life of the Whale Road had sun-darkened Bush's face and left it heavily lined. His eyes were small and flinty, set inside a furrowed brow, and deep crow's feet pinched the corners near his temples. He had thin, wiry arms which belied his strength earned at the tiller forcing warships to his will across distant raging seas. He was a good man and a good friend. "Maybe this should be our last journey. I remember our first, with Ragnar down to Frankia, where you earned your name."

"Don't drag that up again."

Einar chuckled. "You went for a shit in the bushes when we knew the enemy were close and came back running with your breeches down and an arrow in your arse."

"I had to go. My stomach was in knots!"

"Even the old boar Ragnar himself laughed."

"Ragnar. We won't see his like again."

"Fierce, daring, cunning. He was good to us, though."

"He was. You think this will be your last sailing?"

Einar shrugged. "My place is at Vanylven now, with Hildr. When I was at sea, all I dreamed of was to be a landed Jarl, to own some land where I could settle with a good woman and a warm fire. I have that now, even if I am beholden to King Harald. But when I am there, when the nights grow long, and I stare into the fire with a belly full of ale, all I want is to be back at sea."

"Aye, well. You want both, seems to me. We can't pull rigging forever. I always thought I would die in battle or at sea, a good death worthy of Valhalla. I never thought I would get to the age where I had to get up to piss three times each night. What will become of me when I am too old to helm a ship?"

"You will sit by the fire with me, and we shall tell each other stories of the old days."

Bush grinned at Einar, warmth in his eyes. "Might be better to die here at the end of a good sword rather than having to listen to you prattling on about how good a fighter you were when you were young."

Sigrid came through the door, her golden hair tied back from her face, and she searched out Einar amongst the group.

"We have found a boat we can use to approach the walls, fat-bellied but steady," she said.

Einar nodded and lifted his brynjar. He pushed his hands into its cool folds and lifted the heavy mail above his head. He grimaced at the pain in his ribs and face and shrugged the mail down over his jerkin until it fell into place like the skin of a serpent. Einar buckled on his thick leather belt, slid his axe into its loop at his left hip and fixed his seax into its sheath, which hung from two thongs at the small of his back. The seax was a cruel weapon, as long as his forearm, with a broken-backed blade coming to a wicked point. Perfect for close-quarter fighting, for ripping and tearing at a man's guts and innards. For that was what lay ahead as they stormed Novgorod's Citadel. Bloody war. Einar wanted revenge for Hekkr, and he welcomed the fight, hungering for the blood of his enemies.

TWENTY-SEVEN

Hundr huddled in the bows of the riverboat. It was flat-bottomed, like the ship on which he had made the journey south from Aldeigjuborg. Her mast had been removed, and oars stowed on crutches. The boat was wide and used for transporting goods up and down the river, linking the north and south of Midgard. He and Sigrid had bargained with the same merchant who had rented them the room above his warehouse, and because he was a Northman, he didn't ask questions but charged a high enough price for his silence. It was morning, clear and fresh, with a cool summer breeze on the river which kissed the hairs at the back of Hundr's neck. The river was vast, flowing past Novgorod. It swept around a wide bend thick with dark green forest to where Novgorod's Citadel stood on a gently sloping hill. The main gate to the fortress lay on the opposite side of the city, facing away from the river and towards the wooden-planked streets of the town beyond. The wharf where Hundr waited was to the north of the city, and there was no gate into the high wooden walls from the river-facing side.

He waited for Valbrandr, Amundr and Einar, who had gone into the city, and Hundr would not approach the Citadel without them. He glanced at the walls, darkened by the glare of the bright morning sun. The wall timbers were sharpened to points all around the fortress walls, with higher squared turrets every hundred paces. Hundr remembered those walls from his childhood. A walkway was on the other side, running along the top edge and wide enough for two men to walk shoulder to shoulder, with stairways between each turret. The fortress was well built and would be simple enough to defend from an attacking army if the defenders packed the Citadel with the Prince's druzhina. Only it was not under attack from an army, nor was it filled with druzhina warriors. The ruling Prince, Oleg, had marched south with the army, leaving Yaroslav's household guard to protect the walls. Hundr had watched the walls for most of the previous afternoon and on into the night, during which time spear points had sauntered along the summit only twice. He assumed they were the remaining men of the druzhina who split their watch between patrolling the walls and the outer city. From that shadowed, hidden position, Hundr had watched Kvasir's men searching for him and Einar through the city, and he'd resisted the urge to attack them, consoling himself with the grander ambition of killing his brother and the burned man if his plan to get inside the Citadel worked.

"Shouldn't they be back by now?" asked Sigrid. She huddled next to Hundr, peering across the wharf, staring at the town. She licked at dry lips and fidgeted at her belt and knife's hilt. The warriors in the riverboat were all silent, ensuring knives, axes, and other blades were secure, sharp and ready. Hundr had the same hollow feeling in his guts, the same fear gnawing at him, telling him to run away, to forget the attempt to scale the walls and kill his enemies, to flee Novgorod and leave danger and death for another day.

"Yes," he replied, squeezing her hand gently. "You have fought many times before. You fought in the battle of Hafrsfjord, which men will speak of until the end of time. Your father was Ketil Flatnose. Let the fear strengthen you. What is bravery, if not the overcoming of fear? We will hear of Einar before we see him."

"I am not afraid," Sigrid lied, smiling at Hundr. She was beautiful, and for a moment, Hundr wondered what he was doing by allowing her to accompany him into what was almost certain death either on or inside the walls. But then he caught himself. He did not *allow* her to do anything. She had run from her father and her familial duty to marry for her father's benefit to instead live the life of a Viking. She was a warrior, a drengr, and would do as she wished.

"What's that?" hissed Bush, craning his neck to hear the sound of shouting and screaming from deep within the city.

"Einar," Hundr grinned. Within twenty heartbeats, Einar came loping onto the wharf, flanked by Amundr, Thorgrim, Sigvarth and Valbrandr. "Is the rope ready?"

"Ready," said Ragnhild.

"Remember, we will leave axes in the walls. The last one up the rope brings the axes with them. We will need them once we are inside."

"I will go last," Skögul volunteered. "I won't forget the weapons."

"It's done," said Einar, stopping before the riverboat, hands on his knees, sucking in gulps of air.

"Four of Kvasir's bastards are dead," growled Valbrandr, "and we made a mess of them. More of his men have come out of the gate to see what happened."

"Which takes their attention from the walls," said Hundr. "Now we go."

Einar clambered into the boat, followed by

Valbrandr and Amundr. The ship rocked under their considerable weight, and Hundr grabbed the side to steady himself. Bush lifted oars from their crutches and passed them out. Hundr took one, as did Finn, Sigvarth, Torsten, and Bush himself. The oar blades dipped into the river's shining green surface, and they hauled the ship away. Einar moved to the prow to guide them now that Hundr faced away from their direction of travel. He hauled on the oar, and the muscles in his back stretched. The boat lurched forward, and Hundr gritted his teeth, listening to the early morning commotion inside the town, hoping that it would distract Kvasir's warriors and draw them out of the Citadel.

"Where did you leave the corpses?" he asked over his shoulder.

"Deep in the town, near the tavern where we drank and Einar fought," Amundr answered. His voice rumbled from his broad chest. "We took their heads and left those somewhere else for bastards to find. I want them to fear us, to know we are coming for them. For Hekkr."

"Good," Hundr nodded. He pulled again at his oar. He had tasked the five warriors with finding and killing Kvasir's men wherever they sought Hundr and Einar. To hurt them badly enough to anger Kvasir and his crew, to draw them out to see the horror of their shipmates' deaths. They had done well.

"Three more pulls," Einar called from the prow. Hundr looked to his right, where deep green grass rose into the hill atop which the Citadel sat, and then the walls themselves appeared, as high as five men, each huge timber pointing to the sky like a spear. Hundr made the three pulls, and Einar moved along the hull to dip an oar into the water behind the boat and guide into the shore. She glided and nudged into the riverbank amongst reeds and high grasses. Finn leapt nimbly onto the bank, and Skögul tossed him the coiled length of rope. Amundr slid over the side so that his boots squelched into the riverbank mud, and he pulled the boat close to the rise of the bank where it rose into the Citadel's hill. He held it there whilst the crew, including Hundr, stepped ashore. Once everyone was safely on land, Amundr took lurching steps through the river to the bow and fished out a mooring rope to tie the boat off around the base of a briar.

"We might need her after," shrugged Amundr.

They marched to the walls, and Hundr ran a hand across the rough wall timbers. He took an axe from Sigrid and reached up to slam the bearded axe into the wood. He hauled on it, and the blade took his weight. Hundr turned and stared at Sigrid. She smiled at him and handed him two axes from her belt.

"May Thor guide you and watch over you," she

whispered.

The crew handed all the axes they had gathered to Hundr, Einar and Ragnhild, who each tucked as many as they could into their belts. Hundr had five, and he looked up at the towering wall, which seemed twice as high now that he was standing at its base.

"Ready?" asked Ragnhild, a bearded axe blade in each hand. Hundr nodded. He grabbed the haft above him, which he had already sunk into the walls, and hauled himself up, leaping to slam a second axe blade into the timber above the first. Hundr walked his legs up the wall and ripped the first axe head free so that he still gripped the second haft with his feet braced against the wall to help dislodge the axe. He then hauled himself up and slammed the first axe in again, an arm's length above him. The thud of axe blades on his blind side, where his dead eye could not see, told Hundr that Ragnhild had begun her climb. On his left, Einar grunted as he began the ascent, cursing to himself with the effort.

Hundr released his grip on a haft and reached down to his belt to grasp a spare axe. He would leave one axe here for the others, even though they would have the rope to climb. An axe to grip would help them ascend with speed. Hundr thought of Sigrid making the climb, then of the risk of her falling to break her back on the riverbank below or plunging into the deep

Volkhov wearing her armour, dragged to its murky depths to drown without even drawing her blade. He stretched up and struck his new axe into the timbers to hoist himself up again, the strain now pulling at his forearms and shoulders. Hundr glanced upwards, seeing the pale sky above him, but thankfully no enemy spears. He quickened his pace. Hundr hoped that the distraction of the dead Norsemen outside the Citadel and the noise of their discovery masked the sound of the axes hammering into the wall timbers. Otherwise, bearded faces would soon appear above him, and it would be an easy matter for Kvasir's men or Sigdriffa's Valkyrie to pick them off with spears from above the battlements. Hundr's stomach clenched, and he hauled himself up again. Two more pulls, and he could see the sharpened stakes of the summit.

His breath came laboured from the effort, and beads of sweat trickled down Hundr's back beneath his brynjar and jerkin. It ran from his forehead to sting his dead eye socket and blur his good eye. Hundr's hands were aching from the grip. He hauled again and reached up to drive another axe into the wall, and just as the bearded blade sunk in, his left hand slipped. Sweat-slicked, it slid from the smooth haft to send Hundr reeling. Hundr swung to the side, legs scrambling against the timbers, and his heart was in his mouth as he glimpsed the dark waters of the Volkhov below, waiting to welcome him into its icy grip and deny him his vengeance. He scrambled at his belt, dragging free his final axe and sunk it into the wall. He hauled and moved upwards again, his boots finding purchase so that he pulled himself higher, ripping an axe head free, leaving the one he had slipped from in the wall, and thrust himself upwards to keep climbing.

"I'm too bloody old for this. Thor's balls, I miss my fire," Einar growled. But the old Jarl was moving slowly and inexorably upwards. He made short reaches with each axe, but his climb was steady and unyielding. There was a steely determination in the crag of Einar's face, for he had seen what Yaroslav and Kvasir had done to Hekkr, and revenge motivates a man like nothing else. Hundr was within an arm's length of the summit when Ragnhild scrambled over the top, the rope tied to her belt dangling behind her like an enormous writhing snake. She reached down, red-faced from the exertion and offered a hand to Hundr. He gripped her outstretched palm, and she hauled him up. The pain in his back and ribs from his beating at the hands of Kvasir's men screamed at him, and the bruising on his face pulsed to match the burning of his shoulder muscles from the climb. But Hundr forced away the pain, swallowing it, using it to make him angry. He slumped onto the walkway behind the wall and searched left and right, but no guards were on the walls.

"Einar," Ragnhild said, and Hundr forced himself to his feet to reach over the helm to help pull Einar over. At the top, the wooden wall stakes were not sharp. They had been when they were first cut, but now they were aged and dull, so they were merely something to hold on to as he hauled Einar over, and there was no barrier to the climb at all. Ragnhild tied the long rope, made for a halyard or some other ship rigging, and tossed the end down to the waiting warriors below.

"That was a bastard of a climb," panted Einar, sliding down the wall to sit on the walkway, his face red and pumping with sweat. Einar dragged a hand down his face and blew out his cheeks. "Give me a shield wall any day rather than do that again."

"Keep watch," said Hundr, clapping Einar on the shoulder. He turned to lean over the edge, where Valbrandr hoisted himself up the rope, using the axes left in the wall by Ragnhild, Einar and Hundr for purchase.

"I am sorry," Ragnhild uttered, staring down at Valbrandr and waiting with Hundr to haul the warrior up once he came within reach. "I'm sorry that we had to come to this place. And for Hekkr."

"You would have done the same for any of us,

Ragnhild. How many times has your axe saved my life over the years?" said Hundr. She turned to meet his gaze. Both had suffered the Odin wound, and each had only one eye. Hers blazed and quivered with intense ferocity.

"I feared my soul was to be denied Valhalla, that I was an oathbreaker. I thought the sisterhood would let me back in. If I had known that we would have to sail in search of the spear... Ethandun, Novgorod. All my fault."

"The Valkyrie are a sisterhood, but we are also bound together, Ragnhild. You, me, Einar, Bush and the rest. We are brothers and sisters of the Whale Road. I do not think Odin looks on your Valkyrie with more favour than he does our crews. Look at the things we have done, Ragnhild. How many skilled warriors have we sent to Odin's hall? More than most, I would wager. I would die for you, Ragnhild, and we don't need a temple or a dwarven spear to prove it."

"And I you." Ragnhild wrapped her arms around him, holding him tight. Hundr did not know how to react. The gesture was unexpected; Ragnhild rarely showed emotion. She held him there for three heartbeats and let him go, pushing him away. "Help me drag this lump over," she growled, her voice cracking slightly.

They each grabbed one of Valbrandr's meaty

arms and pulled him over. Next came Sigrid carrying both hers and Ragnhild's bows and quivers on her back. Then Finn and so on until all had made the climb, save Skögul. As she climbed, Skögul ripped the axes left in the timbers free and tucked them into her belt whilst Valbrandr and Amundr hauled on the rope to help her climb. Ragnhild and Sigrid watched the Citadel, bright in the morning sunlight, with bows ready to shoot at any sign of the enemy. Hundr leant over the edge, and Skögul was close to the top. She smiled at him, creasing the tattoos on her face, and let go of the rope with one hand to reach up to him. Hundr stretched down to grasp her hand, but suddenly her smile turned to panic. Her right hand slipped on the rope, and Hundr reached for her, brushing the tips of her fingers with his own, but it was too late. She tumbled backwards, eyes fixed on his one, screaming and waving her arms in terror. She splashed into the murky Volkhov, her mail and weapons dragging her below the surface instantly. Hundr stared open-mouthed and slammed his fist onto the wooden wall.

"Skögul," whispered Gunnr. "Gone to Ran or Njorth, and hopefully to the afterlife with honour."

Which was wishful thinking. Skögul had not died in battle, and those lost to the sea gods would not feast or fight in the halls of Odin,

Thor, or Freya. Those gods would select the honoured dead to take a seat in Valhalla or Thruthvangar or by Freya in her golden meadow at Folkvangr. Hundr hoped Skögul would find her way to a place of honour, but the underwater kingdom of Ran was her likely destination. Suddenly, shouts of alarm interrupted Hundr's concern for Skögul's soul.

"Druzhina," barked Ragnhild. Hundr turned to see ten of the Rus warriors emerge from inside the Citadel's network of buildings. They were armoured, and each man wore his horse-plumed helmet, along with a round shield, a spear and a curved sword at his waist.

"Kill them," Hundr ordered, and no sooner had the words left his lips than Ragnhild's powerfully recurved eastern bow thrummed, and a white feathered arrow flew swift and straight from the battlements to slam into a druzhina's chest, knocking him to the earth. Sigrid also loosed her shaft, punching through the torso of another enemy warrior, and the man howled in pain. That was it. The defenders would know now that something was awry. The guards must have heard Skögul's scream or finally heard the hammering of their axes during the climb. It was time to fight, time for blades and blood work.

Hundr pulled Fenristooth free of her scabbard, the ivory hilt was cool and welcoming in his grip, and he pulled Battle Fang across his shoulder. Then, armed with his two blades, he ran for the nearest stairway, and the pounding of his shipmate's boots banged on the fighting platform behind as Valbrandr, Einar, Amundr, and Finn all charged towards their enemies. A thrown spear clattered off the stairway at Hundr's feet, and he leapt down the last four steps to come up in a crouch. He ducked as another spear flew over his head to stick in the wall behind him, the force of it quivering the shaft.

"We have no shields," shouted Einar, running past Hundr, axe in one hand and seax in the other. "Charge the bastards!"

Hundr followed him, sprinting towards the druzhina who made a shield wall in the open space between a long building and the Citadel walls. One of them peeled away to run back into the snarl of the palace to bring more blades to the fight. An arrow, shot by Ragnhild or Sigrid, hit the running warrior in the shoulder, and he fell but rolled to his feet and kept moving. Spears bristled above the druzhina's black shields, but Einar did not break his stride. Instead, he roared a mighty war cry, loud enough to shake the halls of Valhalla itself. He threw himself at the shields, his size and weight smashing through two of them as his axe blade tore a plumed helmet from a druzhina warrior. The fear in Hundr's belly was gone. In its place, that fear had blossomed into battle fury, and Hundr welcomed it. The calmness fell upon him; the noise faded, and his senses became heightened. This was his world – battle. What he'd trained his whole life to do. And he was a killer, just as Sveneld had taught him to be.

He darted into the gap that Einar had smashed into the makeshift shield wall, driving Battle Fang into the belly of one druzhina and slicing Fenristooth across the throat of another. He ducked and turned, twisting Fenristooth free of the druzhina's guts to splash blood red and bright in the morning. The warrior with the cut throat fell to his knees, clutching at the terrible wound, just as Amundr's axe crashed into his skull to spray the dying man's brains and teeth over the next druzhina in line. A spearman thrust his weapon at Valbrandr, but the broad-shouldered warrior grabbed the shaft contemptuously and pulled the enemy into a vicious headbutt before chopping his axe into the spearman's face with a wet slap. The druzhina crumbled under the attack, which was swift and bloody. The town guards were no match for Hundr's hardened fighters, whose skills had been forged in the furnace of countless battles.

"Norsemen!" shouted Sigrid as she and Ragnhild ran from the wall with their bows. Gunnr came with them, her cheeks streaked with tears for her drowned sister, keening a high-pitched battle cry and armed with a long knife. Too many axes had fallen with Skögul, so the three women had only bows and seaxes to bring to the fight.

As the druzhina died, Thorgrim kneeled to cut the throat of a screaming warrior who clutched at his ruined face. A line of Norsemen armed with axes, shields and swords came from the Citadel's innards, marching slowly and purposefully in unison. They were the professional warriors of Kvasir Randversson, the burned man. Rollo's men, killers and Vikings, just like Hundr and his crew. They came on with grim faces, braided beards, and shining helmets to make their shield wall across the space between the Citadel and the lane which ran into the palace complex. Kvasir himself pushed his way out of the line to stand before his men, hooded to hide his burned face. Malevolence and hate pulsed from him in waves, and Hundr felt the heat of it as Kvasir's Norsemen made a shield wall behind him. Their shields overlapped in proper order, the linden wood boards banging into place, and they clashed their axe heads three times on the iron shield bosses to show they were ready to fight and to die.

"I have you now," Kvasir purred. He raised his axe and pointed it first at Einar and then at Hundr. "You should have escaped when you had the chance. Your deaths will be slow and painful. You should see what we did to the old man. So much pain. So much suffering." Kvasir's tongue flicked across his scar-tightened lips. "On me!" Kvasir's warriors responded with a clipped shout of recognition of his order. They shuffled forwards as one to remake their shield wall around Kvasir, with the burned man at their centre. Hard faces set and stern, ready for battle.

"We have no shields," Gunnr hissed in Hundr's ear. Hundr and his warriors faced two dozen Norsemen who stood in three ranks. Their shield wall was a solid mass of linden wood and iron, bristling with the gleam of sharpened blades. "We cannot fight that." She had the right of it, and Hundr swallowed with frustration.

"If we fight that, we die," said Bush.

At that moment, a flash of movement to Hundr's right caught his good eye, and he turned just in time to see Finn dash down a shadow-darkened laneway.

"Finn!" Einar called.

"Where in Thor's balls is he going?" Hundr said.

"Your men are running already, Dog's Name," Kvasir shouted from the midst of his Norse growlers.

"Did you find the men I killed in the town?"

Einar said, stepping forward with his weapons held low. He smiled at Kvasir, a feral, fearsome grin on his broad face. "I killed them, and they did not die well. I cut off their heads and left them for you. They were nithings who died screaming." The enemy line bobbed as their collective heads turned to Kvasir. The anger flowed from them like seiðr. "I burned you, Kvasir. I killed your people at Agder, and I burned you like a suckling pig. You lost the war with King Harald, and I enjoyed your defeat. We laughed at you, at your dead, whilst we drank your ale and whored your women."

Kvasir let out a terrible roar, lifting his face to the heavens like a wolf. Einar turned and winked at Hundr. "Now he's angry. So let's level the tafl board a little," Einar smirked.

"Kill them all!" Kvasir called to his men, and they came on. Each boot stomped as one, the iron of their weapons clanking as they came to kill Hundr and his warriors.

Hundr hefted his two blades and glanced at his line of fighters. They stood no chance without shields against three times their number. "Spread out; use the space," Hundr said. "Don't give them a line to fight."

Valbrandr ran at them. He shouted his defiance, calling out to Odin All-Father, and, holding his axe above his head, he crashed into the shield wall like a maddened bull. But the line of shields held firm, and they threw Valbrandr back as though his muscled frame was that of a small boy. He reeled away, grunting, scrambling to keep his feet and darting from the spear thrusts which came for his chest and back. Finally, Valbrandr scuttled away, and Hundr and his warriors took a step back.

"Why don't you come out of your war fence and fight?" Einar called. "Do you fear me, Kvasir Randversson?"

Kvasir snarled and surged forward, but his men held him in line. The burned man's hood fell back from his white face to reveal a wide-eyed fury. The big men on either side of Kvasir had him boxed in with their shoulders, knowing well that their advantage lay in their numbers and shields. Sigrid loosed an arrow, and it slammed harmlessly into the rightmost warrior's shield. Then Ragnhild shot at the left side to force the Norsemen to bunch together.

"Ragnhild," said Hundr. "Go for the spear. Take Gunnr, Sigrid, and Amundr with you."

She flashed him an angry look, an arrow nocked, and the string pulled back to her ear.

"Get the spear and get out," he hissed. "There's no sense in us all dying here. Go."

Ragnhild lowered her bow, and the three women darted away from the fight towards a laneway spanning the distance between two of the Citadel's buildings. Amundr followed them, grumbling and shouting curses over his shoulder. Hundr set his feet and made ready to fight a three-deep shield wall with only four men. It was suicide, but running from battle was not drengskapr.

"Looks like this is it, then," said Bush. He stood between Hundr and Einar, armed with an axe. Valbrandr took up a place on Hundr's right. "Let's give Odin a death worth remembering."

Hundr gritted his teeth. The enemy was so close now that he could smell the leather of their clothing and armour and hear the blow of their breath as they neared in for the kill.

"Lothbrok!" came a shout, long and loud. Hundr searched the Citadel's walls and timber buildings but could not see where the cry came from. Then, suddenly, Finn Ivarsson leapt from a golden thatched rooftop with his blade held high, bellowing the name of his legendary grandfather as his war cry. Finn landed feet first in the centre of Kvasir's shield wall, sending the Norsemen sprawling, and he came up slashing and cutting. Hundr sprang forward without hesitation, the front line of Kvasir's shield wall broken apart, and where Hundr had felt the shadow of certain death upon him, now he saw the chance to slay his enemies on a bright summer morning.

Hundr barrelled into a gap, not even cutting at Kvasir's men, just shoving to get amongst them and get to Finn. Valbrandr did the same, and on Hundr's dead eye side came shouts of panic where Einar and Bush made an attack of their own. The shield wall broke apart like smashed driftwood. A leather-helmeted Norseman tried to headbutt Hundr, but the blow fouled on his shoulder. Blades pressed against his arms and chest, but the crush of men was too close for the weapons to be effective. Hundr's own swords were tight at his sides, and he bucked and wriggled to get free. Behind the lines, Finn fought with a stocky Norseman, trading blows with his sword against his foe's spear. The enemy who had tried to butt Hundr snapped his teeth at him, brown, filthy pegs aiming to bite at his nose, so Hundr leant back to escape the foul maw. That enemy's head flew backwards and then came forward with a white feathered arrow in his eye, a thick stream of blood oozing from the wound. Hundr glanced over his shoulder and saw Sigrid disappear down the laneway after Ragnhild. The foul-toothed Norseman went limp, and Hundr was free. He powered his legs forward and burst from the press of bodies just in time to see Finn bury his axe in the spearman's chest. Hundr spun on his heel and sliced Fenristooth across the back of an enemy's skull, feeling the bone crunch beneath the sword's edge. He drove the point of Battle Fang into the back of another Norseman's knee, sending him roaring to the ground and then sliced his throat open in a gout of dark blood. Finn hacked into Kvasir's men, and all was blood and chaos.

TWENTY-EIGHT

Einar hooked the edge of his axe over the rim of a Norseman's shield and hauled it down to reveal dark eyes hidden amongst a bushy beard. The enemy brought his own axe up to strike at Einar, but he was too slow. Einar's seax was already buried in the man's groin, and Einar ripped and twisted in until his hand was covered in warm, pulsing blood. Kvasir's shield wall was scattered. Finn had broken them with his daring leap from the rooftops, and Einar sheathed his seax and tore the shield from the dying man's hands. He took a spear thrust on that shield and drove into the blow so that the iron shield boss punched into the spearman's face to mangle his nose and thrust him backwards. Einar shouted to Odin and chopped his axe into the spearman's neck. This was red war, and Einar soared in its ferocity like an eagle.

Valbrandr strode over a twitching corpse, and

he, too, had taken up a fallen man's shield. Kvasir had lost eight men to death or terrible injury in the space of a few heartbeats. That was what it meant to fight Seaworm men, to fight against Einar Rosti and the Man with the Dog's Name. The enemy Norsemen fell backwards, reeling from the horror and brutality of the attack. Sigvarth, Thorgrim and Torsten used their experience to wield their weapons with deadly efficiency, cutting and slashing, taking up falling shields. Valbrandr took a heavy blow on his shield from an axeman, and Einar sliced his own axe across the attacker's calf to drop him to one knee and then brought the iron-rimmed edge of his shield down on the man's head, crushing his skull.

"Einar!" came a cry, and Einar raised his shield just in time to take a thunderous strike from a bearded axe. A shield slammed into him, bullying him backwards, and Einar tripped over an injured warrior. His heart leapt into his mouth as he expected a blade to pierce his flesh, but he righted himself and came up snarling behind the cover of his shield. No blow came, and there, staring at him with his stretched, scarred face, was Kvasir. Einar stood to his full height and beckoned his enemy on with his axe. The ring of iron on iron filled the Citadel and lingered in the air with the ferrous tang of spilt blood. Einar glanced to where Valbrandr struggled under an assault from four of Kvasir's warriors, and the burned man himself turned to hack at the broad-shouldered warrior. Einar couldn't see Finn or Hundr but could hear the fighting, furious and desperate. Valbrandr swerved away from a stabbing sword and smashed his war axe into the face of his attacker before ripping the blade free to fend off another foe.

"Einar!" Valbrandr roared and threw his short, hafted axe overhand so that the blade flashed through the air. It flew straight towards Einar, and for a blood-curdling moment, he thought Valbrandr had launched the axe at him, but the blade turned head over haft and spun past Einar's face. A man gurgled behind Einar, and he turned to see a Norseman with Valbrandr's axe stuck into his chest like a wood axe in a chopping block. The dying warrior had been about to strike Einar down with a spear thrust, and Valbrandr's throw had saved his life. Einar turned on his heel to dash to Valbrandr's aid, but he moved just in time to see Kvasir plunge his sword into Valbrandr's stomach and rip the blade free with a savage twist. Valbrandr groaned in pain, and Einar's mouth fell open at the wyrd of it. Valbrandr had saved his life but had lost his own to do so.

"Kvasir Randversson, you mangled-faced son of a whore," Einar roared, and Kvasir and his warriors left the injured Valbrandr to face him.

"Let's fight now, you and I. This is what you want, isn't it? Why you pursued us? Why you had Hekkr impaled? Here I am, you ugly bastard." Einar held his shield and axe wide, inviting the attack. Kvasir snarled, dropping his blood-slathered sword and taking up an axe. He rolled his injured shoulder and roared at Einar before lunging at him. The burned man was fast, his hatred driving him on, and his axe licked out like a bolt of lightning hurled by Thor himself.

Einar had to duck to let the blow pass over his head, and Kvasir's shield slammed into his own, forcing him backwards. Einar brought his axe around in a wide sweep, but Kvasir blocked it with his shield, juddering Einar's arm to the shoulder. He couldn't see Finn and panicked for the lad. Einar needed to get past Kvasir and get to Finn's side. If Finn died, Einar would never forgive himself. He tried to stomp on Kvasir's foot, but the burned man danced away and, in the same movement, brought his axe down to catch on the inside rim of Einar's shield. He yanked the shield wide, and his knee smashed into Einar's ribs with such force that Einar yelped as the pain of it rattled his body as if a horse had kicked him.

Einar fell to one knee, and Kvasir roared his hate and pounded at Einar's shield with his axe. The assault was relentless. Spittle flew from his scarred mouth as the axe hammered into Einar's shield. It was all he could do to keep it raised and fend off the blows as they rained down. Kvasir was shouting incoherently, and the boards of Einar's shield split and shattered, a sliver of linden wood cut across Einar's cheek. The axe head smashed through the shield boards and came to a stop a finger's breadth from Einar's eye. Einar held his breath, staring at the notched blade, waiting for it to carve into his face. But the killing blow did not come. The shield remnants held firm, and Einar thanked Odin for his battle luck. He surged to his feet and twisted his shield so that it ripped Kvasir's axe from his hand. Einar tossed his shield away and set his jaw. He had to get to Finn and kill Kvasir. Einar shouted in anger as he chopped his axe blade into Kvasir's shield arm, and he almost laughed with the glory of it as Kvasir's eyes went wide with panic. He had thought Einar was finished, that he would bury his axe into Einar's face and send him screaming to Valhalla. But that was the joy of battle, to kill a man who had done his all to kill you, to survive the clash of arms and drive your enemy into the dirt. Einar crashed his axe across Kvasir's knee, and the joint burst open to splay his leg at a terrible angle.

Kvasir Randversson fell to his knees, unarmed and beyond fighting. He closed his eyes, waiting for the death blow, and Einar gave it to him. He stepped forward, sliced his axe blade across

Kvasir's throat, then pushed off his helmet with his free hand and grabbed the dying man by his hair, which grew only in patches on his fire-scorched head.

"Kvasir is dead!" Einar bellowed, shaking Kvasir by his hair so that the blood spurted from his open throat. "Throw down your weapons. Your Lord is dead."

The Norsemen stared at Einar, openmouthed, unable to believe that a handful of unshielded fighters had destroyed their shield wall. But so it was. Hundr and Finn backed away from the battle, and Einar rejoiced at seeing Finn alive. He was slicked with the gore of his enemies, but he was standing. The warriors who had fought with Valbrandr stood back, and Valbrandr staggered towards Einar. He dropped his shield and clutched his left hand at the wound in his guts.

"We don't surrender," growled a big man in a bright brynjar. He hefted his shield and axe, but before he could rouse his shipmates to continue the fight, the big man toppled onto his face, crashing onto the ground, dead. An axe was buried in the back of his skull, and Einar looked up to see that Finn had made the throw.

"I am Finn Ivarsson, son of Ivar the Boneless," Finn said, striding amongst them with his arms raised in peace. "Defeat to us is no shame, for this is the Man with the Dog's Name and Einar the Brawler, Viking drengr of fair fame. Swear to us, become our men. Your Lord is dead, and you need a new Lord."

It was cleverly done, and Einar nodded at Finn, who kept his eyes on the enemy. He had dazzled Kvasir's men with their famous reputations, adding his father's legendary name to sharpen that shine. The Norsemen exchanged twitchy glances at one another, and the fight fell from them as Kvasir died shuddering in Einar's grip, their reason to risk their lives leaking away with their Lord's lifeblood.

"So be it," said Hundr before they had a chance to think. "You will swear to Finn, he is young, but he is a Lothbrok. You now serve the heir to Ragnar and Ivar's legend, so kneel to him, and the fighting is over."

Finn swallowed, and Einar's heart swelled with pride. The survivors of Kvasir's crew dropped to their knees and swore an oath to serve Finn Ivarsson. Hundr had made Finn a leader of men, and the lad deserved it, for without his breaking of the shield wall, they would all be corpses. At that moment, a sudden high-pitched scream erupted from deep within the Citadel, and Hundr's face paled.

"Sigrid," he mouthed.

"Go," said Einar. Hundr sped off armed with his two swords, leaving Einar, Finn, Bush,

Sigvarth, Thorgrim, Torsten and Valbrandr with Finn's new oathmen and the bloody aftermath of the battle with the burned man. Many of the Vanylven men were injured, with cuts and gashes on their forearms and legs. But they were drengr, stoic against the pain.

"I thought we were done for," sighed Bush, wiping sweat from his brow with the palm of his hand.

"Aye, well. We live to fight another day, and all thanks to Finn," said Einar. Finn walked amongst the kneeling growlers who, moments earlier, had done their utmost to carve him open like a yuletide hog. Finn went to each man, accepting an offered hand and holding it between his own. He raised them up, asked each their name and bade them pick up their weapons. "He knows how to lead. It's in his blood." Finn had started the voyage as a stowaway on the Seaworm, and now he had killed men in the shield wall. He was a leader of men and a drengr. Einar was proud of him.

"Risky though, what's to stop one of those big bastards sticking a knife in his back right here amongst the blood of their fallen shipmates?"

"They won't. These men are drengr. Look at their weapons, their brynjars and helmets. All cared for, all battle-ready. These are not backstabbers."

Valbrandr groaned and stumbled to his knees, still clutching at the wound he had taken to the belly. He coughed, and blood spilt from his mouth to catch in his beard. Einar went to him and crouched beside him, offering a hand for the broad-shouldered warrior to take. Valbrandr smiled, his teeth stained red, and his face turned as white as morning ashes.

"That was a rare fight," he uttered and winced at his pain. "One for the skalds."

"It was, and you fought like a warrior from the finest tale," said Einar. He put his arm around Valbrandr's muscled shoulder and leaned into it, scrunching his eyes closed at the pain. Einar eased Valbrandr's hand away from his stomach and sighed as he saw the bright purple of his insides poking through the torn mail like snakes in an iron pit. Einar pushed the hand back over the wound, and Valbrandr pushed his own innards back with shaking fingers.

"I saved your life, Einar," he coughed, and blood spluttered from his lips to stain his chin. "I told you I would repay you." He grinned and laughed.

"So, you did, and I will make sure that throw is spoken of in the hall at Vanylven as long as I am Jarl."

"I need a blade, my lord. For the last journey, for the Bifrost."

Einar pressed his axe into Valbrandr's hand. "Here, take mine. And save a place for me in Valhalla, for we will surely meet again under the ceiling of shields and wall of spears." Valbrandr smiled again and then went still.

Bush knelt beside Einar and passed his hand over Valbrandr's face to close his eyes, and Einar lay the dead warrior down carefully onto the gore-strewn earth.

"What now?" Bush asked, taking off his helmet liner and using it to wipe the sweat from his face.

"Now we go for Odin's spear," said Einar, and he stared into the tangle of the Citadel's buildings and lanes, where Hundr, Ragnhild and the others searched for Gungnir, Sigdriffa, and the Prince of Novgorod.

TWENTY-NINE

Hundr ran towards the scream. He pounded down a path flanked by shaped, well-tended trees, one of four straight pathways of hard-packed earth which quartered the Citadel. The smaller lanes and paths of the walled fortress wove in and out of the barracks, living quarters, and stables of the palace itself and fed off the main four thoroughfares. The sprawling trees on either side of him were as familiar as the smell of boiling vegetables and the stink of animal hay in this part of the Citadel, for it was where Hundr had spent most of his childhood. He ran, ignoring the pain of his injuries and the burn in his shoulder muscles from the climb and the desperate fight inside the walls. The scream had come from deep within the palace, and Hundr feared for Sigrid, so he dashed towards it.

He rounded a sharp corner, sprinting across an open square covered with cobblestones, and his memory flooded with the clip-clop sound of his father's beautiful white horse, which he had ridden like an emperor, tall, straight-backed and proud. The place was empty now, and Hundr ran across the smooth square stones towards the high palace building, crested by a fine gable decorated with writhing beasts and painted bright so that it shone in the morning sun. He ducked under a door lintel and came up in a hallway, one end of which led into the feasting hall and the other to the training square and royal stables. He paused, listening, craning his head for a sound or a clue as to which direction he should go to find Ragnhild and Sigrid. There was silence for a moment, no noise save for Hundr's panting breath, but then it was there. The unmistakable clash of iron and Hundr sped towards it, towards the training square, Sigrid, and Gungnir.

Hundr ran along the corridor and out into a garden of small trees and bright flowers. The memories there were so thick he almost had to bat them away with his arms. His mother sat singing softly, picking flowers, and he, a small boy climbing the trees. Through the garden was an archway, and Hundr ran across another courtyard of timber planks, feet thundering across the dark stained wood until he came out onto the royal stables, where Hundr stopped and stood still, as though rooted to the spot by seiðr.

Only it was not magic which halted him. It was horror. A crimson smear across the cobbles led to a pale corpse. It was a man... torn, ripped, and bloodied. Hunting hounds lazed around it with bloodied muzzles, and Hundr bent double to vomit onto the pewter-coloured stone. It was Sveneld, the weapons master who had first taught Hundr to fight all those years ago and had now saved Hundr's life at the cost of his own. Kvasir, or Yaroslav, had subjected Sveneld to terrible torture. The welts and cuts on his naked body spoke of that ordeal. Then, as an ultimate act of dishonour, they had denied the old man a decent burial and thrown his naked corpse away like leavings, unwanted fodder for dogs. Hundr roared at the sky, bellowing so loud that his voice would carry along the boughs of Yggdrasil and to the halls of the Aesir. He cursed his own Odin luck for surviving and Loki for the cruel twist of Sveneld's fate. Hundr knew then that his survival and quest for vengeance had come at a price, and he regretted the blót, the sacrifice he had promised to Odin in return for his escape from the impaling stake. For Odin had heard him, and the Norns had cackled in their dark corner below the great tree. They had changed the thread of his life and intertwined it with that of Sveneld, with such terrible consequences.

Hundr strode across the stable forecourt and through a gateway, where he found his half-brother Yaroslav and six Valkyrie warrior priestesses.

"You found old Sveneld then?" Yaroslav quipped, smirking. He leant on a spear with a broad leaf-shaped blade. The Valkyrie bristled behind him, axes drawn and brynjar gleaming. "Bastard was a traitor. So, we put him to torture, and then I fed him to my hounds. He wept like an old woman in the end, begged me to stop like a nithing. Your whore is in the palace. Sigdriffa hunts her and the scarred old bitch. I have sent for the rest of the druzhina who will return from the town. You will die today, Velmud. And I think I will impale you, then before you die, I will give your whore to my men, and then I will feed you to my hounds. Let's see how you weep, see if you cry like you did when your whore mother died. She was pretty, though. I should have asked my father for a tup of her, but I have never been overly fond of the palace trollops, the playthings of the druzhina."

Hundr shivered with hate, his neck and shoulders trembling. He had never experienced a feeling like it, white-hot and visceral, like a liquid flowing around his body. His brother stared at him hungrily, waiting for some barb or taunt in response. But there were no words for the way Hundr felt about his brother. Yaroslav had been a curse on Hundr's life from the day he was born, and the words he spat about Sigrid and his mother only added to the crucible of that hatred. Hundr flexed his hands around the hilts of his swords and took a deep breath to steady himself. There were six Valkyrie in the training square, and Yaroslav himself, all skilled warriors facing Hundr alone. His brother had undergone the same weapons training as Hundr throughout his childhood and so was a dangerous man to fight. Hundr kicked off his boots and splayed his toes in the small stones of the training square, their cool grip familiar under the soles of his feet. He set himself and raised his blades.

"Take him if you can, kill him if you have to," Yaroslav said, and the Valkyrie came on, armed with axes and knives. Only six here meant the rest of Sigdriffa's warriors hunted Sigrid and Ragnhild, and Hundr needed to get to them quickly.

Hundr strode towards them and, at the last minute, broke into a run. He flicked Fenristooth up faster than a shaven-headed woman could react to, and the tip of the sword laid her face open in a lurid line, ripping through lips, nose and eyes. He held Battle Fang in a reverse grip and slashed its edge across the thighs of a short, stocky woman and then down into the foot of the Valkyrie behind her. Hundr kept moving. An axe came for him, and Hundr swayed aside from it easily as though the blade moved underwater. He was alive with battle fury and empowered by vengeance, fast, lithe and deadly. His blades sang, and the Valkyrie fell. They tried to come as one, but Hundr was too fast. His bare feet gripped the stones, and he danced amongst them, his swords cutting and slashing in a blur of death and pain. He felt a thud on his back, but his brynjar held. A knife scraped across his skull, but Hundr did not stop. His own blood flowed down the back of his neck and into his brynjar, but he drank their souls with his twirling blades. Finally, Hundr came to a kneeling stop and let out a huge breath. Around him, four wounded Valkyrie warriors writhed and groaned. Two others backed away, glancing nervously at each other and then at Hundr's blood-soaked swords. Boots thundered in behind him, and Einar Rosti shoved past Hundr and charged at them, with Finn Ivarsson at the rear. They cut down the two remaining Valkyrie with brutal savagery so that their blood washed the small stones of the training square, turning them from shale grey to dark crimson.

The smirk had fled from Yaroslav's face. He backed away towards the rear of the training square, his spear levelled and moving cautiously between Einar and Finn. More boots tramped on the gravel behind Hundr, and the Norsemen who had sworn oaths to Finn strode past him and formed a line behind their young Lord, each man carrying a shield and a war axe. Bush came last, hirpling along on his bandy legs, and stood with Sigvarth, Thorgrim and Torsten, grim-faced warriors exhausted from battle but ready to fight again.

"What is the meaning of this?" screamed Yaroslav. He searched the square for understanding, and his top knot swung like the wagging tail of a dog.

"Leave him. Go to Ragnhild and Sigrid. This bastard is mine," said Hundr. Einar nodded. He and the others, including the Norsemen, flowed around Yaroslav like water around an eyot. "It's just you and I now, brother."

"You come to usurp me, bastard? You can never be Prince here."

"I don't want to be Prince. I came only for the Odin spear, and you impaled my friend and killed old Sveneld."

"You are a thief and a liar. I knew you would come to nothing," Yaroslav spat and brought his spear around into a fighting stance. His fish-scale armour twinkled in the sunlight, and his shaved head gleamed.

"I am the Man with the Dog's name. Men know my name wherever drengr sail the Whale Road. I am a Sea Jarl with five ships and men to crew them. I killed Ivar the Boneless and Eystein Longaxe and won the battle of Hafrsfjord to put King Harald on the throne of Norway. All of this I made for myself. You are not a man of reputation, and when I kill you, nobody will remember your name." Hundr spoke slowly and clearly, the words cleansing him of a lifetime of unfulfilled regret and ambition. Inside the Citadel of Novgorod, in a sea of blood, in his birthplace, Hundr realised he had become what he had always wanted to be. He was a drengr, a warrior of reputation and honour.

Yaroslav charged, his spear outstretched and his face twisted into a rictus of hate. Hundr moved around the spear point, batting it away with the flat of his sword but not fast enough to avoid its butt, which whipped around to clatter into his shins, sending Hundr sprawling. Yaroslav was skilled, and the speed of the attack surprised him. Hundr dropped Battle Fang and twisted just in time to parry a spear thrust destined for his throat. He scrambled on the gravel, and Yaroslav roared in triumph, stabbing and jabbing with the spear, but each time Hundr either dodged or parried the strike. He hooked his bare foot around one of Yaroslav's supple, deerskin boots and tripped him. As the Prince fell, Hundr leapt upon him, and the two brothers rolled in the gravel of the fighting pit, punching, kicking, clawing and snapping at each other. Hundr crashed his forehead into his brother's nose, crushing it to a pulp, and Yaroslav plunged his thumb into Hundr's eye. But it was his dead eye, and Yaroslav found only an empty socket surrounded by puckered flesh. Hundr drove a knee into the Prince's groin and leapt away from him. Before Yaroslav could recover, Hundr grabbed the ivory hilt of Fenristooth, the blade gifted to him by the dead Jarl Rurik of Vanylven and swung the sword in a high arc. It soared around, the sun glinting off the blade, and it came to a stop just above Yaroslav's face. The Prince flinched from the blow, which would surely have split his skull in two, but Hundr dragged the tip along his brother's face, cutting him from forehead to chin. Yaroslav clutched at the wound, and blood seeped through his fingers. Hundr stamped on his brother's belly, and as his legs curled up into a ball, Hundr sliced his hamstrings. The Prince of Novgorod rolled and howled in agony, and Hundr left him there, taking up his two swords and following the sound of battle towards Sigrid.

Hundr dashed from the training square across a grass-covered courtyard where the royal feasting hall reared above him. Its two enormous doors were open, and Hundr burst into them, where the fighting had ceased inside. Feasting benches had been tossed aside, and the light shone into the long, cavernous room from opened shutters and through the smoke hole in the centre of the high roof beams. The shafts of light illuminated dark pools of blood on a timber floor scattered with rushes, usually used to soak up ale and food spillages, but today they soaked the remnants of red war. Ragnhild was at the centre of the hall, prowling back and forth like a wolf, staring at the far side of the room where Sigdriffa and her Valkyrie gathered in a huddle. Four of their sisters lay still or sat propped against upturned benches, some dead and others injured. Finn, Bush, Thorgrim, Torsten, Sigvarth and the Norsemen stood by the east side of the hall, and one of Finn's new Norsemen writhed on the ground, his leg cut open to the bone and his face as white as milk. Einar held Sigrid in an embrace, her head bowed, nestled into Einar's chest.

"Is it over?" asked Hundr.

Einar turned to him, his slab of a face stern. "Ragnhild will fight Sigdriffa for the spear, then it's over," he said. "They will fight the Holmgang so that there's no more death."

"There has been enough of that over Odin's spear," said Bush, which was true. The thing had a cruel wyrd of its own, and it had brought nothing but suffering to those who had taken it and those who pursued it.

Sigrid lifted her head slowly, and Hundr gasped. She had taken a cut to her face, across her left cheek and ear, and she held a shaking hand to the wound, staring at Hundr from hooded eyes.

"Are you hurt anywhere else?" he asked. Sigrid shook her head. Hundr reached out for her, and she came to him, holding him tight.

"My face…" she whispered.

"Is not the reason I love you, my fierce, brave shieldmaiden," he murmured. Sigrid's blue eyes searched his one, and a smile played at the uninjured side of her face.

"Those bloody women are vicious," tutted Bush, shaking his head at the Valkyrie. "Thanks be to Odin that we don't have to fight them any longer. Where is the Prince?"

"Beaten and waiting for his fate," said Hundr, frowning and stretching his neck at the heavy, Odin weight of it all. The air in the hall was tense and heavy, and Hundr sensed something as if the wyrd of the spear and their destinies had all been guided to this place by the Norns themselves. A Norseman made King in East Anglia forsaking the Aesir, the death of a Rus Prince, the marching of a Rus army to conquer a city, Odin's own spear and Ragnarök itself in the balance.

"Behold Gungnir, spear of Odin," shouted Sigdriffa, striding into the hall's centre with the long spear held at arm's length above her head. Hundr recalled he had seen the weapon before, in England, where the Valkyrie High Priest Vattnar had carried it as a talisman alongside the Ragnarsson army years ago. Its head was oversized, and it shone where Sigdriffa held it into a ray of light. The blade was as wide as a man's head, and the shaft was smooth wood, engraved with runes, and chased up its length with silver thread. It was magnificent. "The weapon the All-Father will use to slay Fenris at the end of days. I brought it here to found a new temple, a place of worship worthy of the All-Father, a place of honour. Upsala has fallen under the control of cowards and nithings, the Valkyrie no longer fight, we sacrifice and pray, and grow fat and bored. So you and I will fight, Ragnhild, for the spear and the future of the Valkyrie. If I win, the spear stays here, and we found a new temple."

"When I win, Sigdriffa the Defiler," Ragnhild growled, "the spear returns to Upsala, and your warriors return with me."

"So be it." Sigdriffa handed the spear to one of her sisters and took up her axe and knife. She strode to the centre of the hall and clashed the weapons together, and Ragnhild did the same. Hundr held Sigrid close, relieved to find her alive. She turned in his arms to watch the two Valkyries fight.

"Can she win?" asked Sigrid. "Enough of us have died for this spear. I have killed for it. It must end today."

"Odin is a fickle god," said Hundr. "He is a

cunning betrayer; he could favour either of the two."

"Ragnhild will be victorious. Odin will not betray her. The spear must be returned, and I feel the gods in this thing," Gunnr intoned. She crouched on one knee beside Sigrid, out of breath from the fight and bloody from its brutality. It surprised Hundr to hear her belief in Ragnhild and to see that she understood Ragnhild's war prowess.

"So, Ragnhild is worthy of the spear again?" Hundr asked, recalling how forceful Gunnr had been upon leaving Upsala that it had to be a Valkyrie who handled the spear.

"She is more than worthy. She is the best of us."

Sigdriffa was young and lean, and she smiled at Ragnhild, moving around the open space of the hall with cat-like litheness. Ragnhild was all scars and power, she was older and shorter than Sigdriffa, and where Sigdriffa was golden-haired and attractive, Ragnhild was a grim beast. She moved with bunched shoulders, her axe and knife circling like a beast's talons.

"Finn," said Hundr, "Take your men and check the walls. Yaroslav will have sent for the rest of his druzhina from the town outside the Citadel. We don't know how many there are. If you see them approach, hold them at the wall and send us word."

Finn nodded and led his Norsemen out of the hall with a thunder of boots, shields, and axes.

Sigdriffa raised her axe to her sisters, and they roared her name in salute. She sprang at Ragnhild, lunging low with her axe, which Ragnhild stepped nimbly away from, and then whipped her knife up with astonishing speed. Ragnhild had to jump back to avoid it ripping open her guts. Sigdriffa smiled and beckoned Ragnhild on as though she were the master and Ragnhild was a mere pup. Ragnhild kept her temper and moved around in a circle towards Sigdriffa's left hand, her knife hand. Sigdriffa attacked again, knife first, this time followed by three vicious axe swings, which Ragnhild parried. Sigdriffa kicked out, connecting with Ragnhild's hip and forcing her back. She turned to her sisters and keened an undulating, high-pitched war cry which they echoed. Ragnhild came on again, circling to the left, breathing hard and licking her lips nervously.

"Is Ragnhild tired already?" asked Sigrid.

"No, but fighting isn't all about skill and strength," said Hundr.

Sigdriffa launched herself at Ragnhild, unleashing a dazzling flurry of high, low, axe and knife attacks. The steel slashed like a blur in the sunlight, illuminating the fighters beneath the roof's smoke hole as though the gods shone down on the two warriors who fought in their name. Ragnhild dodged or parried each blow, and when Sigdriffa leapt away from a wide, wild swing, she grinned. The swing was tired, and Ragnhild grunted as her arm came around. Ragnhild leaned over, resting the balls of her weapon-filled hands on her knees to suck in gulps of air. Sigdriffa laughed. She believed Ragnhild was old and finished and that her victory would be easy. She darted left, but it was a feint, and she came at Ragnhild with her axe sweeping overhand and her face set in a wide-eyed grimace of triumph. But Ragnhild let go of her axe and caught Sigdriffa's wrist with her free hand. All the feigned signs of fatigue fell away, and Ragnhild was suddenly all vicious speed and power. She twisted Sigdriffa's wrist, stabbing her knife into Sigdriffa's stomach, and with the strength built over a lifetime of fighting and the power required to draw her wickedly powerful bow, Ragnhild ripped the knife upwards. It sheared through the links of Sigdriffa's brynjar with an ear-piercing scorch of metal cutting metal, and she opened her enemy up like a gutted fish.

Sigdriffa dropped her knife, and her mouth fell open in surprise. Ragnhild twisted her knife to pull it free, and Sigdriffa staggered backwards, slopping her insides onto the floor rushes as she stumbled. Ragnhild left her there and marched to take Gungnir from the Valkyrie, fixing each of them with her fierce one eye. "The spear goes back to Upsala, and so do you," she growled. Each of them bowed their heads in solemn but devastated agreement. Finally, Sigdriffa fell to the hall floor, face first, and went to meet the Aesir she so revered.

"Ragnhild of the Valkyrie!" Hundr shouted, the sound of his voice echoing around the high, smoke-darkened roof beams.

"Ragnhild, Ragnhild, Ragnhild," roared Hundr's warriors in unison.

Ragnhild hefted the spear and raised it in salute at those who had sailed with her to recover the Odin spear. Then, she strode to Hundr and smiled sadly.

"It's done. The spear will return to Upsala. Thank you," she said.

"I told you already, there is no need for thanks. We are as brother and sister, you and I. I would sail the world for you, Ragnhild," Hundr smiled warmly.

"And I for you, my brother of the sword. Which is why I will return the spear to Upsala. But I will not remain there. I will go with you – if you will have me."

Hundr's head rocked back in surprise. "You

will always have a place beside me, but I thought your heart burned to return to the Valkyrie?"

"It burned because I had broken my oath to the All-Father. That oath is repaid, I think. I have done my part, but my place is not with the Valkyrie sisterhood. It is with you and Einar, Hildr, Sigrid and Bush. We are a family, which counts for more than a temple of sacrifice."

Hundr placed a hand on her shoulder, and their eyes met. She was right. Their bond was more than a temple of worship could offer. The Norns had wound the threads of their fates together, and Hundr was glad to see Ragnhild's heart restored and her oath repaired.

"It's over," sighed Sigrid, and she wept softly for those they had lost and would never see again in Midgard.

"Not yet," said Hundr. "I owe Odin a blót."

THIRTY

They found Prince Yaroslav of Novgorod at the end of a trail of glistening blood, where he had dragged himself like a snail across the fighting square. His cut hamstrings had prevented him from walking, and his wounds bled dark blood onto the tiny stones, which had borne the feet of young warriors learning the art of weapon skill for generations. The Prince flopped onto his back, gasping and whimpering, his face drawn and pale as though he were already dead.

"He will not live," said Einar, shaking his head. "Leave him here to die; let us begone from this place."

Hundr wanted to leave, to run away from the horror of Novgorod. To leave behind the unhappy place of his birth and where so many had died to recover Odin's spear. But there was a promise to be fulfilled before he could be free of Novgorod. Sigdriffa's Valkyrie marched with Ragnhild and Gunnr, heads bowed and crestfallen at the loss of their leader. Their dream of a new temple to Odin, a pure thing of honour and war in service of the All-Father was gone. Their charismatic zealot leader was dead, and they would return to Upsala in shame. But they were alive, where Valbrandr, Hekkr, Sveneld and others lay dead, victims of the warp and weft of Gungnir's wyrd.

"Thor's balls, I cannot wait to get back to sea. The stink of this place is in my nose. How does the wind ever get in here? Let us leave, as Einar says," said Bush.

"Go. I will meet you by the walls. Back the way we came," nodded Hundr, staring into his brother's trembling eyes. As a boy, Yaroslav had caused him so much pain, had taken away his dream of becoming a warrior of the druzhina and drove him away from the city. Those years had been cruel, cold, and hard. When he had left the city, Hundr had been but a boy. Forced to travel north alone, following the river, scavenging and stealing food to live until he reached the coast and found Einar. He had spent his life dreaming of returning to Novgorod as a hero, at the head of a fleet of warships and an army of warriors. To show his brothers and the city that had shunned him that he had become something. That he was not just a worthless half-Rus bastard. Now, Hundr realised he had become what he was because of his mother's love and Sveneld's training. He was a self-made warrior Jarl, a Viking sea master, and a leader of men. He was more than his brothers could ever be.

Hundr bade Sigrid go with Einar, and he took Gungnir from Ragnhild. He waited until the tramping of their boots had disappeared beyond the training ground, and they left him alone with the pained, panicked gasps of breath from his wounded brother. The spear was not a weapon; it was too heavy at the head, and the silver itself was weak and would surely bend and shift in the furnace of combat, never mind if Odin brought it to bear against the teeth and claws of mighty Fenris at the end of days. But the point was sharp enough for what must be done, and it was not Hundr's place to consider what would happen at Ragnarök or what weapons the father of the gods should wield.

"What I do now, I do in sacrifice to Odin. For the luck he cast upon me, for sending Sveneld to set me free and casting my enemies to ruin," Hundr said. He closed his eye and thought of Odin, grey-bearded and fierce. Hugin and Munin, his two ravens, thought and memory, sat one on each shoulder. In Hundr's mind's eye, Odin saw him, saw that Hundr brought his swords and his warriors to far Novgorod and made great slaughter amongst his enemies. The cunning god waited now for what was owed, for the blót that had been promised.

Yaroslav screamed when Hundr took out his eyes, turning Gungnir red with blood. Hundr took his brother's eyes and opened his veins, leaving him howling and bleeding like a savaged beast in his own palace. The same hunting hounds who had fed upon Sveneld's corpse came to lap their rough tongues in the Prince's blood, and Hundr hoped Odin accepted the sacrifice made with his sacred spear. Shouts of druzhina approaching pealed out from the high walls, and Hundr ran with the spear to meet Sigrid, Einar, Bush, Finn and their warriors to descend the long rope back into the riverboat. The druzhina appeared on the walls, helmets bobbing and spears wavering like a forest in the wind. But they were too late. The Citadel, emptied of warriors by Oleg for his war of conquest, had seen its Prince killed. Kvasir Randversson lay dead, as did Sigdriffa of the Valkyrie. The druzhina were too far away as Hundr and his warriors rowed along the Volkhov, heading north. Hundr doubted the druzhina could even mount a chase, so light were their numbers left to keep the city safe.

Hundr and his warriors made their way back to the Seaworm and the Fjord Bear. He left Novgorod a man far greater than he'd ever hoped to be when he'd escaped as a lad. Now a man of reputation, with crews, riches, a woman he loved, and friends at his side, the score was finally settled with his cruel half-brother, who had died with the knowledge of Hundr's hard-earned fate. That was more than enough for the Man with the Dog's Name. Ragnhild would remain with Hundr, and he would return with Einar to the peace and warmth of Vanylven. But, of course, Rollo still brooded in Frankia, becoming ever more powerful. He had unleashed the burned man in all his vengeful fury, and Rollo the Betrayer was an enemy who would need to be faced again, once and for all. But for now, Hundr had his beloved Sigrid. She was distraught at the wound taken to her face, so he held her tight, embracing her as they rowed towards the Whale Road and to his sleek drakkar warship.

THE VIKING BLOOD
AND BLADE SAGA

Viking Blood And Blade

865 AD. The fierce Vikings stormed onto Saxon soil hungry for spoils, conquest, and vengeance for the death of Ragnar Lothbrok.

Hundr, a Northman with a dog's name... a crew of battle hardened warriors... and Ivar the Boneless.

Amidst the invasion of Saxon England by the sons of Ragnar Lothbrok, Hundr joins a crew of Viking warriors under the command of Einar the Brawler. Hundr fights to forge a warriors reputation under the glare of Ivar and his equally fearsome brothers, but to do that he must battle the Saxons and treachery from within the Viking army itself...

Hundr must navigate the invasion, survive brutal attacks, and find his place in the vicious world of the Vikings in this fast paced adventure with memorable characters.

The Wrath Of Ivar

866 AD. Saxon England burns under attack from the Great Heathen Army. Vicious Viking adventurers land on the coast of Frankia hungry for spoils, conquest and glory.

Hundr and the crew of the warship Seaworm are hunted by Ivar the Boneless, a pitiless warrior of incomparable fury and weapon skill.

Amidst the invasion of Brittany and war with the Franks, Hundr allies with the armies of Haesten and Bjorn Ironside, two of the greatest warriors of the Viking Age. Ivar the Boneless hunts Hundr, desperate to avenge the death of his son at Hundr's hand. To survive, Hundr must battle against fearsome Lords of Frankia, navigate treachery within the Viking Army itself, and become a warrior of reputation in his own right.

Hundr must navigate the war, survive Ivar's brutal attacks, and find his place in the vicious world of the Vikings in this unputdownable, fast paced adventure with memorable characters.

Axes For Valhalla

873 AD. The Viking Age grips Northern Europe. Seven years have passed since the ferocious sea battle with Ivar the Boneless, and Hundr is now a Viking war leader of reputation and wealth. A voice from the past calls to Hundr for aid, and he must take his loyal crew and their feared warships across the Whale Road to Viking Dublin, in a vicious and brutal fight against Eystein Longaxe.

King Of War

874 AD, Norway. A brutal place, home of warriors where Odin holds sway. King Harald Fairhair fights to become king of the north.

Hundr, a Northman with a dog's name... a crew of battle hardened warriors... and a legendary war where the will of the gods will determine who is victorious.

After incurring the wrath of Ketil Flatnose, Jarl of the Orkney isles, Hundr and his crew become drawn into King Harald's fight for supremacy over all Norway. Hundr must retrieve the Yngling sword, a blade forged for the gods themselves, and find favor with an old friend, Bjorn Ironside, as he fights a vicious and deadly enemy, Black Gorm the Berserker.

Hundr must navigate the war, survive brutal

attacks, and make Harald the King of War in this fast paced adventure with striking characters and bloodthirsty action.

BOOKS BY THIS AUTHOR

The Curse Of Naram Sin

530 BC. The Persian Emperor Cyrus the Great is at war with Queen Tomyris of the Massagetae on the Scythian steppe. On either side of that epic conflict, are immortal forces locked in a battle between good and evil which stretches back to the dawn of time.

Xantho, slave to a Persian Satrap... bereft at the death of his wife and ashamed of his status... caught in the eye of a war between gods and magic wielding warriors.

The mysterious warrior Naram-Sin and Siduri, a powerful mage, guide Xantho through a rampaging war that will take him from the wild Scythian steppe, through time to the campaigns of Alexander the Great and Ancient Greece. They must stop the ruthlessly cruel and powerful Gula'an, servant of the underworld, before humanity is plunged into an eternity of darkness and suffering.

Xantho must navigate a war between immortals, survive brutal attacks, and find his place in the magically powerful world of mages and warriors in this fast paced adventure with unforgettable characters.

Warrior & Protector

989 AD. Alfred the Great's dream of a united England has been forged by his daughter Aethelfaed and grandson, King Aethelstan.

The Vikings have been expelled from York following the death of Erik Bloodaxe, and for two generations there has been peace between Saxon and Dane.

A new Viking warlord Olaf Tryggvason seeks revenge for Bloodaxe's death and the slaughter that followed, and has set his sights on a fresh assault on England's shores. With Skarde Wartooth they set sail for Saxon lands, hungry for glory, conquest and vengeance.

Beornoth, a brutal and battle-hardened Saxon Thegn, is called to arms to fight and protect the Saxon people from the savage Norse invaders. On a personal crusade, he joins the army of

Byrthnoth, Lord of the east Saxons in a desperate fight against the bloodthirsty Vikings.

Beornoth must lay his own demons to bed, survive vicious attacks and find redemption for his tragic past.

ABOUT THE AUTHOR

Peter Gibbons

Peter is an author from Warrington in the United Kingdom, now living in County Kildare, Ireland. Peter is a married father of three children, with a burning passion for history.

Peter grew up enjoying the novels of Bernard Cornwell and David Gemmell, and then the historical texts of Arrian, Xenophon, and Josephus. Peter was inspired by tales of knights, legends and heroes, and from reading the tales of Sharpe, Uhtred, Druss, Achilles, and Alexander, Peter developed a love for history and its heroes.

For news on upcoming releases visit Peter's website at www.petermgibbons.com

Made in the USA
Monee, IL
28 December 2023

50719286R00239